WICKED
LITTLE
SECRETS

Also by Kara Taylor

Prep School Confidential

WICKED
LITTLE
SECRETS

A PREP SCHOOL
CONFIDENTIAL
NOVEL

KARA TAYLOR

THOMAS DUNNE BOOKS
St. Martin's Griffin ❧ New York

This is a work of fiction. All of the characters, organizations, and events portrayed in this novel are either products of the author's imagination or are used fictitiously.

THOMAS DUNNE BOOKS.
An imprint of St. Martin's Press.

www.thomasdunnebooks.com
www.stmartins.com

Library of Congress Cataloging-in-Publication Data

Taylor, Kara.
  Wicked little secrets : a Prep school confidential novel / Kara Taylor. — 1st ed.
      p. cm.
  ISBN 978-1-250-03360-4 (trade paperback)
  ISBN 978-1-250-03361-1 (e-book)
  1. Boarding schools—Fiction.   2. Schools—Fiction.
3. Mystery and detective stories.   4. Youths' writings.   I. Title.

PZ7.T21479Wic 2014
[Fic]—dc23

                                                   2013032065

St. Martin's Griffin books may be purchased for educational, business, or promotional use. For information on bulk purchases, please contact Macmillan Corporate and Premium Sales Department at 1-800-221-7945, extension 5442, or write specialmarkets@macmillan.com.

First Edition: March 2014

10 9 8 7 6 5 4 3 2 1

For my parents, and for Ellen Hoffman,
who knew these books were in me before I did.

Revenge, at first though sweet,
Bitter ere long back on itself recoils

—Paradise Lost, Book IX

CHAPTER
ONE

They say only the good die young. At least, that's what they used to say about Isabella Fernandez.

Now no one talks about Isabella at all: even though she was murdered almost three months ago and our vice-principal is the one who killed her.

I guess that's the type of thing the Wheatley School—ranked number 2 on *U.S. News and World Report*'s list of best prep schools—would like to pretend never happened. Or maybe everyone sleeps a little better at night now that they know Isabella was sleeping with Dr. James Harrow before he cut her throat in the middle of the woods. Almost as if they believe she deserved what happened to her, or at least brought it on herself.

Here's a little-known fact: Almost 80 percent of people who get murdered know their killers. My dad used to remind me of this when I was ten and going through a phase where I couldn't sleep because I thought I'd get stolen from my bed in the middle of the night. He actually told me that, as if it would make me feel *better*. But then again, my dad also brushes his teeth in the shower to save time and explained the physical impossibility of Santa Claus to me when I was five.

Isabella was my roommate, so my parents are making me see a therapist in Boston every few weeks. His name is Dr. Rosenblum, and he always tries to get me to play Uno with him. He likes to use phrases like "Our goal here . . ." *Our goal here is to help you accept that the ordeal of Isabella's murder is over, and that James Harrow is no longer a danger to you.*

I need to make peace with Isabella's death, because although I only knew her for a week, we were friends. Isabella didn't care that even though before I got to the Wheatley School there were rumors going around that I was an arsonist. (Which is totally false, by the way. It's only arson if you set something on fire on purpose. I Googled it.)

The fire I set at St. Bernadette's Preparatory School on the Upper East Side of Manhattan was an accident. And, for the record, it wasn't my idea. It was Martin Payne's idea, and I was only hooking up with him because I was bored. I know having the nerve to be bored in the greatest city in the world makes me seem like a spoiled brat. I told Dr. Rosenblum I felt this way, and he suggested that maybe all of my acting out and getting into trouble back home was my way of trying to get my father to notice me. Like, from a young age I know I could never live up to his impossible expectations, so I tried to subvert them by mouthing off in class and filling up Jake Crane's gym locker with tampons. Or whatever.

Anyway, I don't know if Dr. R is right about all that, but he was right when he said that Isabella's murder turned my world upside down. I thought seeing her killer get arrested would flip it right side up again, but I'm learning that things are never that simple. The dead leave lots of things behind. Like messes you can't see. Or sometimes, actual things.

Like the photograph I found in an old library book Isabella checked out before her death—the one of Matthew Weaver, a student who disappeared over thirty years ago, standing with the Wheatley Crew team.

The one with *THEY KILLED HIM* written on the back.

For a while, I wondered if there was more to Isabella's death than Dr. Harrow blackmailing Steven Westbrook, a Massachusetts senator, over his affair with Elaine Redmond, the wife of the state attorney general. Did Isabella know about the photo? Did she figure out what happened to Matt Weaver before she died?

Dr. Rosenblum is the only person I've told about the photograph. He says the Matthew Weaver story is something of an urban legend burned into the collective consciousness of Wheatley. The appeal of his story is that people are drawn to the unknown. Dr. Rosenblum said a student was probably playing a prank when they wrote *THEY KILLED HIM* on the back of the photo.

He also asked me if I found myself bored in the weeks after Dr. Harrow's arrest. I'm not an idiot: He thinks I want there to be more to the mystery. Sort of like I'm having mystery withdrawals or whatever.

But part of me thinks he has a point.

Either way, I have too many questions and no ways to get answers. When I told Dr. R I felt this way, he agreed.

"Sometimes it's best for our sanity to let sleeping dogs lie," he said.

I hope he's right.

I sit on the steps outside the dining hall. Its proper name is the William J. Brown Refectory, because if it didn't have an unnecessarily pretentious name, this wouldn't be the Wheatley School. Brent said he would meet me here after crew practice.

A few minutes after I sit down, strong arms wrap around my middle, and a face covered in a thin layer of stubble grazes my neck. "You're warm."

"And you're wet." Still, I turn and run my hand through Brent's damp curls. He hasn't had time to get a haircut now that training for crew season has begun, and while I'm a clean-shaven-guy type of girl, Brent pulls off the extra scruff pretty damn well.

Brent leans in to me and closes his eyes, as if he'd be happy if I kept playing with his hair all day. A sharp cough sounds from behind us.

Murali Thakur is looking at us as if we might as well be hardcore making out all over the steps. He raises a thick black eyebrow. "Hello to you, too, Anne."

I shrug and grin at him, although an anxious feeling settles at the bottom of my stomach. If Murali is here, Cole Redmond must be nearby.

"Where's Cole?" Brent asks, his hand moving to my lower back, as if he can feel me tensing up.

"Showering." Murali squirts water into his mouth from his bottle.

Cole's mother, Elaine, was having an affair with Senator Westbrook when Dr. Harrow tried to blackmail him with incriminating photos. Since the district attorney put a gag order on anyone involved with the extortion until Dr. Harrow's trial is over, no one knows Cole's mother is the reason Senator Westbrook resigned. But his father moved out a couple of weeks ago, and even though Cole swears he doesn't hate me, every time I see him I wonder if we'll still be friends in a year or so when the media is allowed to talk about the affair and I ruin the Redmonds' lives all over again.

And here's the other awkward thing: Cole and Brent are best friends. Not typical teenage-guy "Yeah dude, wanna go to the gym?" best friends. Cole is the only guy at school who knows about Brent's diabetes. They actually argue about things like what nature noise they're going to use when they set their sleep-sounds machine before they go to bed every night. Brent likes the whale calls, while Cole prefers white noise.

They kind of have a bromance going on. And I'm totally interrupting it by dating Brent.

Brent and I say good-bye to Murali. When he turns the corner to the boys' dorm, Brent grabs my face and kisses me. "Hi." He leans his forehead against mine.

"Hi back. Where are we going today?"

I was confused when Brent told me he had a surprise for me today, since my seventeenth birthday was last weekend. We went out for my favorite food, sushi, and he snuck me into his dorm so we could stay up late watching a hidden-camera show where these two comedians play jokes on people. I didn't even remember telling Brent that I love the cookie crumble on ice cream cakes, but he'd hidden a small one in his freezer and we polished it off together.

"You'll see," Brent says. "But we have to leave now if we want to catch the train."

The walk to the station takes almost fifteen minutes. Even though it's only early April, I have to take off my cardigan. There are no clouds in the sky, and what seems like the entirety of the Wheatley School's population is crowded on the campus quad sunbathing.

Brent and I pass the time on the train by playing Would You Rather? I've just asked him if he'd rather get his nipples pierced or show up to class in his underwear every day for a month, when the automatic voice on the T announces we're at Fenway Park.

Brent motions for me to get up, and I barely stifle a groan.

"Oh, come on," he says, laughing as we step off the T. "They're playing the Yankees. I thought I'd bring a piece of New York to you."

"I'm not dressed for a baseball game." I gesture to my strapless Free People dress. Brent is in his signature weekend casual look: white T-shirt, khaki shorts, aviator Ray-Bans, and his compass watch. Not that having a guy who knows how to accessorize well is *important* to me, but it's a nice perk.

"Good thing I'm so prepared." Brent pulls two balled-up Red Sox caps out of his pocket and unrumples them. Unable to figure out the mechanics of fitting a baseball cap around my ponytail, he slides the elastic off and onto his wrist. My hair falls around my bare shoulders.

"Shouldn't this be a Yankees cap if you're bringing New York to me?"

Brent's eyes gleam. "Trust me: This is for your safety. Red Sox fans won't care how pretty you are. They'll throw beer on you."

I grab the neck of his T-shirt and pull him toward me. "You think I'm pretty."

He kisses my forehead, and the world seems to dissolve around us until he tugs my hand.

I was eleven the last time my father took me to a game at Yankee Stadium, but my memory is good enough that I realize Fenway Park is smaller and louder. I don't know, I've always found baseball in all its forms—major league, fantasy, et cetera—annoying. I follow Brent to the row of seats behind home plate.

A perky blonde in a Sox T-shirt holds up her hand, and I think she's waving at someone behind us, until Brent waves back. Her whole face lights up when she sees him, and I have to keep my crazy in check and not demand to know who this pretty chick is.

"Forgot to mention my sisters were coming," he says to me with a devious glint in his eyes.

"Oh. Sisters." I'm an only child, so despite having an imaginary sister named Samantha when I was six, the concept of siblings is alien to me.

My heartbeat picks up and we wriggle our way to the seats. It's not that I'm nervous or anything. It's just that usually I like to have advance warning about meeting a guy's family.

"Anne, this is Claire," Brent says. Claire smiles at me and my nerves dissolve. Her smile is perfect, unlike Brent's, but they have the same pointy nose and chocolate brown eyes. Claire tells me she's a senior at Brown and says she heard I was from New York. I nod, thankful she leaves it at that and there's no mention of me shooting the former vice principal.

"Where's Holly?" Brent says, nodding to the empty seat next to Claire. She gnaws her bottom lip.

"Don't be pissed. She's only home for a few days and wanted to see her friends." Claire's eyes move to the aisle, to a man talking into a cell phone and making his way toward us. Brent's cheery expression clouds over.

"You let *him* come?"

From the way Claire hisses, "They're his season tickets, Brent," I conclude that *him* is their father.

Things I know about Brent's father:

1. He owns the biggest newspaper in Boston.
2. Brent doesn't see him much.

"Sorry in advance." Brent squeezes my hand as his father makes his way toward us.

"Does he know who I am?" I blurt. "I mean, like, what I did? How I almost got you shot?"

"I don't know. But Steve Westbrook has sued his paper three times in the past year, so you're good."

I look over at Brent, unsure if he's serious. He gives me a lazy grin that makes my heart flip-flop.

Brent's father ends his phone call when he gets back to the seats. He's Brent's height—which is short for a guy—with wavy gray hair. He and Brent do an odd little standoff type thing before he extends a hand to his son. It's all really bizarre to me, seeing someone give their kid a handshake. My father always hugs me, even when he temporarily hates me.

Brent's father turns to me and takes me in. "Pierce Conroy," he says. "And you must be . . ."

"Anne Dowling," I say, even though it's obvious this is the first time he's hearing my name. His handshake is dismissive, as if he can't wait for this day to be over. I study his face. It seems very familiar to me. Probably because it's so much like Brent's: strong jaw, warm brown eyes.

We all shut up for the National Anthem. I sit between Claire and Brent, who gives clipped answers to his father's questions about the crew season. Claire says she loves my dress. We wind up talking about our favorite places on Newbury Street, and I don't even notice that Brent's seat is empty until he comes back holding a cardboard tray. He picks a fully loaded hotdog from the top and passes the tray down to Claire and me.

Claire tears a soft pretzel in half and hands a piece to me. Brent inhales the hot dog in two bites and takes a pull from his extra-large soda. Mr. Conroy watches from the corner of his eye the whole time. It doesn't take me long to figure out why: Brent is diabetic.

"Are you sure you should be—" Mr. Conroy starts, but Brent freezes him with a look and tears open a box of Cracker Jacks. Beside me, Claire sighs, as if this pissing contest is a frequent scene in the Conroy household.

Mr. Conroy's cell rings and he excuses himself. When he's gone, Claire mutters, "Real mature, Brent."

"I am the *epitome* of mature."

I snigger to myself. Just last night Brent donned a ski mask and mooned the security cam outside the boy's dorm because Murali dared him to.

Brent tosses a Cracker Jack at Claire and puts a hand on my knee. He doesn't move it for the rest of the game, except to stand up and shout whenever the Sox score a run. I feel like I should at least cheer my team on, but the Yankees wind up winning and I don't want to get followed and shanked on the way back to the train.

Claire hugs Brent good-bye, then me. "You're the first girl from school he's ever even talked about," she whispers in my ear. "Keep an eye on him, okay?"

"You enjoy the game, Dad?" Brent asks Mr. Conroy, whose mouth forms a line. He spent about six out of the nine innings on his phone. I can sort of see why Brent doesn't like his dad. The only thing Mr. Conroy seemed to care about was Brent's crew season. He barely acknowledged the "new girlfriend" thing.

Claire flicks Brent's ear and tells him to bring me home for dinner sometime.

"Where is home for you, anyway?" I ask around a yawn as we catch a train back to school.

"Bedford." We plop into two empty seats, and he plants a kiss on the top of my head. I grab his chin and pull his face to mine, making him kiss me on the lips, because even though there are people around, I don't care. I've waited long enough to be able to kiss Brent when I want to.

"Bedford," I repeat. "I have no idea where that is."

"I'll show you sometime."

"Good." And I mean it. I want to know everything there is to know about Brent Conroy. I know his favorite song is "Bohemian Rhapsody" by Queen and his favorite class is British literature, but I want to know the important stuff, too. That's why I can't help but say, "What's the deal with you and your dad?"

Brent stiffens. "It's stupid family stuff."

"You can tell me, you know," I say.

He hesitates. "My dad lived away from us for two-thirds of my life."

"Your parents were separated?" I wonder if anyone at school knows this.

"Not technically. But they may as well have been. We have a condo in Boston, near my dad's office. He stayed there more than he stayed at home with us."

I contemplate this. My mom has totally accused my dad of being a workaholic before, but when I was little he'd still come into my room no matter how late he got home to tuck me in and talk to me with my Baby Lamb Chop puppet.

"Anyway, every time he's home for long stretches of time, he acts like we're not practically strangers or anything," Brent goes on. "He tries to tell me what to do, when my mom and grandparents are the ones who raised me. And he's never afraid to tell me what a disappointment I am, as if I give a crap what he thinks."

I think of how Brent baited Mr. Conroy into saying something about eating all that crap at the baseball game. I picture the shell-shocked look on Mr. Conroy's face. A funny feeling comes over me. Brent has changed the subject, and I nod at what he's saying even though I can't really hear him over the ringing in my ears.

Because I know where I've seen Mr. Conroy before. He's the boy standing next to Matthew Weaver in the 1981 crew team photo.

CHAPTER TWO

The photograph is a 5×7, and the quality isn't great, but the shortest boy in the picture is definitely Pierce Conroy. Behind him is a broad-shouldered blond: Steven Westbrook. Next to him is Matthew Weaver, who left Aldridge Dormitory in the middle of the night and never came back.

I swallow and turn the photo over. I know what is written on the back, but for some reason my brain hopes the words have magically disappeared.

THEY KILLED HIM.

I remind myself to breathe. I run through all of the things I convinced myself of when I first found the picture.

Matthew Weaver has been *missing* for over thirty years, which means there's a tiny chance he's still alive.

And if he *is* dead, it doesn't mean he was murdered.

Whoever wrote on the back of the picture could have been playing a sick joke. Trying to mess with whatever unsuspecting Wheatley student checked the history book out of the library. During my first week of classes, Brent had told me people like to embellish the Matthew Weaver stories to scare the freshmen.

There is one thing I'm certain of, though: I can never, ever tell Brent about the photograph.

Poking into Isabella's murder was different. I knew someone at the school was involved, and I didn't care who I pissed off to get answers.

I think of Brent's hand on my knee at the baseball game. Now, I have too much to lose by chasing ghosts.

I never got a new roommate. The administration decided that would probably be as traumatic as my old one dying. Also, no one starts at the Wheatley School midyear. Except for me, but that's only because my father is sort of friends with Jacqueline Tierney, AKA Dean Snaggletooth.

I crawl into bed with a cup of chai and a book I haven't been able to read because I've been so swamped with homework. My mom and I used to do this together on Sunday nights, before I was banished to Boston. Thinking about all of the times I tuned her out because I had a hangover from Saturday night makes me feel guilty and homesick.

I never thought I'd be homesick. I wasn't the kid who cried and called her parents during her first sleepover: I was the kid who climbed into bed with her friends' parents the next morning, complimented them on their selection of processed-sugar-free snacks, and asked if I could watch the *Today* show.

Now my dorm is starting to feel like home, kind of. I picked up copies of my favorite books—*The Secret Garden* and *A Little Princess*—from a vintage bookstore on Newbury Street to fill the empty standard-issue shelf by my desk.

But it's not enough to cover up the fact that all of Isabella's stuff is gone now. Even worse, Isabella's not the person I think of every time I look at the wall where her *Star Trek* poster used to be.

I don't want to waste any more brain space on Anthony, her brother, ever again. I've had guys act like dicks to me before:

Tyler, the NYU junior I hooked up with who pretended not to recognize me when I ran into him at a party. Martin Payne, who cursed at me for calling the cops and ran away when St. Augustine's auditorium caught on fire.

But Anthony Fernandez is by far the worst.

I met Anthony at Isabella's wake and knew him for all of five minutes before I saw him punch his cousin in the face. Probably I should have figured I couldn't trust Anthony then. But I couldn't have found out as much as I did about Isabella without his help.

Then he was arrested for her murder.

After Dr. Harrow confessed, Anthony was cleared of all the charges—but it didn't change the fact he was caught on camera stealing over a thousand dollars from Isabella's bank account a few days before her death. I was pretty upset about it, because even though I've hooked up with some questionable specimens, I draw the line at potential felon.

Anthony didn't in the least think I deserved an explanation as to why he stole the money. That's probably what pisses me off more than anything: that I would have listened. I would have tried to understand, because I cared about Anthony. And not like in the way people say, "Oh, I care about the environment." More like the thought of Anthony going to jail and having unspeakable things done to him, made it feel like someone had shot a hole through my chest.

Anyway, it doesn't matter now: Anthony's parents didn't press charges for stealing the money, and he hasn't contacted me since.

It's after midnight, and I'm too wound up over everything to sleep. I fumble in the dark for my laptop. Obviously I'm not helping my insomnia by Googling Matt Weaver for the thousandth time since I found the photo, but I can't stop thinking about Brent's dad.

What I already know, thanks to Wikipedia: Matt Weaver had a full scholarship to Wheatley. He joined the crew team at the end of his freshman year. On March 13 of his junior year, he left his dorm in the middle of the night. He never came back.

A number of people were questioned in connection with Matt's disappearance, including his friends on the Wheatley crew team. The police backed off after a scathing news story surfaced about how the Weavers had pressured them into going after the boys despite the fact there was no evidence of foul play. The only witness mentioned by name was Paula McGuiness, a woman who said she saw a boy who fit Matt's description head into the woods—alone—the night he went missing.

Matt's disappearance is still considered an open case, but there hasn't been a real development in over twenty years. The most recent news mention of the case is from 2000, when police divers uncovered male remains in the Charles River. They were never identified, but the dental records didn't match Matt's.

I scroll down to the section labeled *Theories About Disappearance*, flagged by a huge banner that basically says everything I'm about to read probably isn't true.

Rumored Connection to Satanism

Renewed interest in the case was sparked in the early 1990s, after *Dateline* aired an episode speculating that Matthew Weaver disappeared in the midst of a satanic ritual. Several childhood friends who were interviewed claimed Weaver had been obsessed with paganism. A private investigator cited the presence of blood found on a trail in the Wheatley woods—once believed to be Weaver's, but which had turned out to be animal blood—as evidence some sort of sacrifice had taken place the night Weaver disappeared. Police and investigators have since dispelled these claims as part of a larger "satanic panic" that had gripped the nation during the time.

Okay, so I kind of wish I weren't alone right now. I'm not a wimp by any means—I've taken the E train by myself, at night—but certain things spook me. When everyone was obsessed with trying to summon Bloody Mary in the fifth grade, I chickened out and had a thing about bathroom mirrors for *years*.

I keep circling back to the same phrase: *some sort of sacrifice*.

But why would the crew team members sacrifice one of their own?

I must fall asleep at some point, because when I wake up, sunlight is leaking through the gaps in my blinds and Remy Adams is pounding on my door.

I know it's Remy because she's the only person here besides me who doesn't sleep until noon on Sundays. Also, the knocking gives her away: Remy only has one volume setting.

I stumble out of bed and unbolt my door. Remy beams at me from the other side with blue doe eyes. She's in a ratty T-shirt and striped cotton boxer shorts, but she still looks like Snow White with her flawless skin and elbow-length dark brown hair.

"Oh good," she says, "you're up."

Well, I am now. "What's up?"

Remy flops down face-first onto my bed. "Mrahhhhhhhhh," she says into a pillow.

I climb into bed next to her. "Oh, yeah," I say. "Totally hear what you're saying."

Remy rolls onto her back. "I just got bitched out by Bea."

I know who Beatrice Hartley, AKA Bea, is, because her face is plastered all over the Campus Life Council bulletin boards around the dorm. She's a senior and she looks like a Banana Republic model. Her name is pronounced "Bee," and lest anyone forget it, she has a bunch of bumblebee stickers on her door.

"What did you do?" I ask.

"Nothing. But it's too late to make a deposit at the Radisson for the spring formal, and apparently that's my fault because the SGA treasurer is responsible for that." The Wheatley Student Government Association is not some nerdy group of mouth-breathers who sell candy bars. The officers are actually in charge of things. If you're in the SGA, you're a B.F.D.

Remy's cheeks flood with color. "Meanwhile, Mr. President gets away with doing nothing because it's crew season."

"I'm sorry," I say. "But you lost me at 'spring formal' and 'Radisson.'"

So even the historic Wheatley School is not exempt from the obligatory dance in a hotel that probably smells like vomit from whatever sorority trashed it the night before. I want to laugh, but Remy is all worked up.

"I know it sounds lame, but it's always a good time," she says. "And everyone is going to blame me if we have to have the dance in the student-center ballroom."

"Do you want me to yell at Brent for you?" I ask. Brent is the president of SGA. It's no secret he only ran to piss off Alexis Westbrook, his archenemy and Senator Westbrook's daughter. Now that the senator has resigned and is being investigated for paying off Dr. Harrow, Alexis's family has relocated her to a new boarding school of bitchcraft and wizardry. Without Alexis to torment, Brent is kind of like a puppy that's finally caught its tail.

"Well, he would listen to you. . . ." Remy's voice trails off as she looks at me with hopeful eyes.

"Done," I say. "But just so we're clear, I'm doing it for you. I don't do dances."

"Anne!" Remy springs into sitting position. "It's the only thing to look forward to besides the end of the year."

I adjust my necklace so the silver heart pendant is facing forward. "I'll think about it." I mean it, too. I really don't want to disappoint Remy; she was my first friend here after Isabella. And if I'm being honest, I've been a pretty terrible friend. In the short time I've known Remy, I've ditched her dozens of times to do snooping instead, and I even stole her ID card to get into her room and steal back an incriminating video of Alexis that Isabella made.

I'm desperate to change the subject. "Have you started the French essay yet?"

Remy's forehead creases. "It's not due 'til Thursday."

I shake my head. "Tuesday."

"April said it's not due 'til Thursday." Panic creeps into Remy's voice.

I don't say it, but April Durand is not the brightest glow stick at the rave. It's not the first time she's unknowingly passed along false information.

"Omigod, I have to check Blackboard." Remy scrambles for my laptop, which is resting at the foot of my bed.

"Rem, chill. You still have two days to do the essay."

Remy is staring at the screen of my laptop, her lips pinched together. "Anne, what is all this?"

"What?"

"You have, like, four tabs open on Matthew Weaver."

I feel so blindsided I say the stupidest thing I'm capable of: "It's nothing."

"Seriously, Anne? This is straight up *weird*."

"I was just curious." My voice is so small and unconvincing. It used to be I could lie myself out of any situation. The thought that I might be losing my edge makes me straighten up and proclaim, "I was thinking it might be a good senior thesis topic."

This makes Remy pause. Any other person would look at me like I'm nuts, since senior year and starting thesis is five months away. But Remy has already taken the SAT and ACT four times and has her summer college-visits itinerary all mapped out.

"You think you could get an entire thesis on him, though?" Remy asks. "I mean, there's practically no information on that whole thing." I don't miss the way her voice has stiffened. "Plus, no one even knows what happened to him," she says.

I think of the photo and the slanted handwriting on the back.

Someone *does* know.

CHAPTER
THREE

I've been expelled from my beloved Manhattan school, questioned as a person of interest in a murder investigation, and nearly shot to death in the woods, but I'm convinced Monday morning is the worst thing that's ever happened to me.

I forgot to set my alarm last night, so I had to choose between going to breakfast and looking put-together for my first class. Under no circumstances would I ever forgo the second option, so I didn't eat. I tried sneaking a granola bar into British literature, but Fowler, the crusty old bastard, caught me and yelled at me in front of the whole class.

When I get to Latin and see that everyone has a sheet of paper on the desk in front of them, I almost turn and walk out the door.

We had a one-page translation due today that I totally forgot about. Shit. Just shit.

If Professor Upton still taught this class, I'd add forgetting my homework to the lengthy list of reasons she hated me. But Upton retired in the midst of the Isabella–Dr. Harrow scandal.

Our new teacher, Ms. Cross, is way more awesome than any teacher at this school has the right to be. She's young and always frazzled-looking in an adorable way, and she must be from the south because every now and then she lets a "y'all" slip out. The guys call her a TILF behind her back, and Lee Andersen, the hulking nerdy kid who sits across the aisle from me, now spends the class hunched over like he's constantly trying to hide a Woody Woodpecker.

And he probably is. Lee's a class-A creep, and I can say this without sounding like a judgmental bitch because I have proof he was stalking Isabella before she died. Professor Upton knew Lee was stalking Isabella, too, and when she went to Headmaster Goddard about it, he basically told her to keep her mouth shut.

Lee didn't kill Isabella, but he could have. Upton must realize that now, because why else would she "retire" in the middle of the year?

Anyway, Ms. C is actually pretty cool, and she likes me. That's why I'm so frustrated with myself for forgetting about the translation. I do the walk of shame to my table at the back of the room and don't look up when Ms. C stops in front of me.

She doesn't point out the obvious. Just smiles, tucks away a strand of hair that escaped from her bun, and says, "Anne, I was meaning to ask you to stop by my office sometime this week. After your last class."

"Okay," I say, but she's already moving to the next table.

I decide not to delay the inevitable, which is probably Ms. C giving me the "You can do better" smackdown. After calculus, I head back to the humanities building and meander through the halls until I see her messy red bun in front of a computer.

I stand in the doorway and clear my throat. Ms. C jerks her head up and beams. "Anne. Hey. Come in. I'm just finishing up an e-mail."

I sit across from her, noticing that the nameplate on the desk still reads PROFESSOR DIANA UPTON. Her office is mostly empty, save for a Boston Bruins pennant over her desk and a few unopened boxes.

Ms. C is in the middle of her lunch—cucumber salad—but

she covers her Tupperware and pushes it aside. "So I've been here for three weeks, and this parent of a freshman has e-mailed me four times." She shakes her head. "Your kid is at boarding school. Time to cut the cord."

I crack a smile. I can't believe she's talking to me like this. It's nice to know at least one teacher at the Wheatley School doesn't have a stick up her ass.

"So," Ms. C says. "I noticed on iCampus that you haven't had an academic advising session yet."

I vaguely remember my first day, and some woman at Student Support Services telling me I have two advisors: one academic and one for "resident life." She also said I should make appointments with both as soon as possible. "Oh. My bad."

"No worries," Ms. C says. "You do know I'm your advisor now, right?"

That means Upton was my old advisor. Dodged a bullet there. "Sure, sure."

"Basically I asked you here to remind you to start thinking about what classes you'd like to take next year. Registration starts at the end of the month."

A bizarre feeling settles over me. *Next year.* From day one, it had always been my mission to make it back to New York for my senior year. I nod.

"Also, it's time to put together a list of colleges for us to look into together." Ms. C pulls up my schedule and grades on iCampus. "With your SAT scores, I think you could shoot for a couple tier-ones. As long as you pull some of these grades up."

No doubt she's referring to the B in her class. "I haven't thought about college much. Except for maybe how to get around the expulsion on my transcript."

A smile plays at the corners of Ms. C's mouth. "Sometimes, it's best to own up and explain your mistakes instead of trying to hide them."

Somehow I doubt "that time I burned my school down" is going to win me any points with an admissions board.

"Where did you go to school?" I ask Ms. C.

She cocks her head at me, as if she's surprised I asked. "I went to UNC. Chapel Hill." She rolls her eyes. "Go Tar Heels."

I think that's when I decide I'm in love with her. She sends me off with a "Junior Year Checklist" of things I have not done, like *Schedule interview at first choice college* and *Take the ACT exam.*

"Anne," Ms. C says when I'm halfway out the door. "I'll give you 'til six tonight to get me that translation."

I could seriously hug her. "Thanks."

She beams at me again, and I think maybe I don't give this school enough credit. They had enough sense to hire someone like her, at least.

I swing by the library before dinner to type up my translation and e-mail it to Ms. C. When I finish, I find myself at the circulation desk asking where I can find old Wheatley School yearbooks.

"Second-floor stacks," the librarian tells me. "But if you want editions older than 1930, you'll have to go to the archives."

I thank her and head upstairs. The second floor of the library is only one of many places at the Wheatley School where I don't like to be alone. The first floor was renovated years ago to look like a replica of the Harvard Library, but the upstairs was left intact. Everything, especially the spiral staircase, creaks upon contact, and the ceiling is claustrophobically low. It stinks of old books and mold.

I find two rows of yearbooks on the shelf opposite the volumes of history books on the Wheatley School. I left the missing edition in my room. Since Isabella never returned it, I definitely don't want to get caught with it.

I run my fingers across dusty spines: 1979, 1980, 1981, 1982. Matt Weaver went missing in 1981. I take all four yearbooks and find an armchair in the corner.

The photograph in my bag feels like contraband. Which is

obviously silly, since I have real contraband in there. (Pepper spray. My dorm was broken into. I'm not screwing around.) I smooth down the peeling corners of the photo and flip through the 1980 yearbook until I find the student portraits. Matt Weaver would have been a sophomore that spring.

I scan the sophomore class for Pierce Conroy. For a split second, I fill up with hope that I was wrong about Brent's father being in the picture. But when I turn the page to the junior class, there he is, looking up at me with that familiar impish grin.

My mouth is dry. I flip back to the sophomore class. Right next to Matt Weaver is Steven Westbrook. I confirm that it's him in the crew team photo and see if I can attach any more faces to names.

It doesn't take me long to make my first match. Lawrence Tretter, a chubby boy with sand-colored hair in a crew cut. Then, Thom Ennis, the scrawny freckled guy on the other side of Matt Weaver. Travis Shepherd, who is good-looking in an odd way, despite having hair down to his shoulders and a small space between his front teeth.

I enter the names into a note on my phone. As I motion to check out the senior class, someone says my name.

I snap the yearbook shut, the photo tucked between its pages. Cole Redmond gives me a funny look, his laptop case slung over his shoulder.

"Hey. What are you doing up here?" I ask.

"Typing up my reflection on the Rembrandt slides." Cole and I have art history together. "Too many people downstairs."

What he really means is too many talk when they see Cole nowadays. In a school with only two hundred students, there are no secrets.

"What are you doing?" he asks, his eyebrows knit together. He nods to the yearbooks in my lap.

"You're going to think I'm a loser." I feign sheepishness. "I met Brent's dad this weekend, and I wanted to check out what he looked like in high school."

If Cole thinks it's bizarre I need four yearbooks to accomplish this task, he doesn't show it. A smile plays on his lips. Cole is ridiculously good-looking, but unlike Brent, he's unaware of it. Most of the time. "I'm sure Brent was thrilled about that."

"Elated." I play with the charm around my neck and meet Cole's eyes. "Hey. Are we okay?"

"What do you mean?" His hands go into his pockets.

"I mean, if you want to hate me, I understand."

"I could never hate you." Cole's hazel eyes are honest. And sad. "I hate what my mom did. And my dad for being a prick and driving her to do it."

"You can't blame yourself," I say. "There's no excuse for cheating."

"Yeah, that's what I used to say." Cole sighs. "Then someone you love does it. Hey, we're gonna be late for dinner."

Cole tries to help me put the yearbooks back, but I insist on doing it myself so I can sneak the photo back into my bag. I didn't realize Cole was an only child like me, so we commiserate together on the way to the dining hall. (Number-1 Only-Child Misconception: Everyone thinks our parents are indulgent and doting, when in reality we can't catch a break from their neuroses and nit-picking. As if they're afraid if we become screwups, their entire existences will have been wasted.)

Our friends are at our usual table. The girls—Remy, Kelsey, and April—are huddled together, looking at something on the screen of Remy's phone. Brent, Murali, and Phil have a total of about eight trays of food between them.

"Fat Tuesday passed, you know," I say, putting my bag down on the empty seat next to Brent.

"We have to bulk up. All protein." Murali bites into a hard-boiled egg. He's got a chicken fillet, no bread, and a bowl of peanut butter on the plate in front of him.

"*You* have to bulk up," Cole says. He's got three inches and fifteen pounds of muscle on all of them, easily. "I get to have some of that fatty-looking chocolate cream pie over there."

Brent grunts. Although muscular, he's the smallest guy at the table. "Wonder what Tretter would say to you having PIE the night before a piece."

I pause in the middle of searching through my bag for my anti-bacterial. "Tretter?"

Brent looks at me funny. "*Coach* Tretter."

"Oh. Right." I excuse myself and head for the salad bar.

What are the chances the crew coach isn't the same Tretter as the one in the photo? Lawrence Tretter.

Looks like I won't have to go too far to find the first person on my list.

CHAPTER
FOUR

A "piece," in rowing terms, is a simulated race that's just as exhausting as the real thing. The next morning, Brent slumps into British literature looking so defeated that Fowler doesn't even have the heart to ream him out for being five minutes late.

Brent slides into the seat next to me and squeezes my hand beneath the table. "You okay?" I mouth at him.

He squeezes my hand again.

I turn to the poem we're reading—Book II of *The Faerie Queene*—and sigh loud enough to get a laugh out of Brent and the girl sitting in front of me. I don't mean to be obnoxious, really, but I'm at my saturation point for boring poetry by British dudes who take themselves too seriously. And I love reading. I guess my poetry-appreciation mechanism is broken or something.

I rifle through the pages as Fowler drones on about allegory. It's the same garbage every day: *Blah, blah, Catholicism is evil, blah blah.* I really should focus, seeing as how we have a midterm in a few weeks, but I find myself turning to the inside cover of my anthology and tracing the name scrawled there in blue ink.

If it weren't for this textbook, I probably wouldn't even know the name Matt Weaver. He was one of a handful of people who had the anthology before me. He's also the only person who used felt-tip pen to make notes in the margins. I have firsthand experience with said notes, because a couple of months ago, I (unsuccessfully) tried to pass off his commentary on *Paradise Lost* as my own.

Something *pings* in my brain. I didn't notice any of Matt's notes in *The Faerie Queene*. Assuming Fowler has been following the same exact syllabus for the past thirty years—not a stretch at all—Matt never got to read *The Faerie Queene*.

Which means he was reading *Paradise Lost* around the time he went missing.

Probably it means nothing. I'm making connections where there are none, just like the people who thought Matt disappearing on the thirteenth meant he was a satanist. But I can't shake the feeling that something, anything, he was thinking at the time might be revealed in one of his notes.

As I flip through the book in search of Matt's trademark blue ink, I stop somewhere in Book VIII of *Paradise Lost*. There's an explosion of writing on the page. I look over at Brent. He's mastered a half-interested expression, his face resting on his palm. I know he's actually semi–passed out. I study the markings on the page more closely.

I have to stifle a gasp. They aren't markings but an incredible drawing of Adam and Eve. It must have taken Matt hours to draw this: Every vein in the leaves, every strand of Eve's hair is sketched out with painstaking detail.

Eve's hair falls in front of her face like a curtain, ending at her naked hip. There's something familiar about the way Adam's hair reaches his ears, curling up at the ends. I look closely at his face.

Holy *crap*.

Matt Weaver drew himself as Adam. I've looked at the photo in my bag enough times that I've memorized his face. His attention to detail is almost frightening, down to the freckle on his upper lip.

Adam/Matt is frowning, a tear pooling at the corner of his eye. In his hand is a half-eaten apple. A serpent with hollow black eyes is coiled around his arm.

I flip back to *The Faerie Queene*, doing a quick glance around the room to make sure no one saw what I saw. It's just a drawing, yet I feel like I've looked into someone's most private thoughts.

Matt Weaver saw himself as Adam. So what did he do to get kicked out of Paradise?

Brent and I are quiet as we leave class. We haven't gotten to spend any time alone together since the baseball game on Saturday. It must frustrate him as much as it frustrates me, because when we're alone on the path leading to the quad, he pulls me behind Harriman Hall.

He places one hand behind my neck and one on my hip, finding a sliver of skin between my skirt and sweater and tracing it with his thumb. I close my eyes as his lips find mine. My hands hang at my sides.

Brent pulls away. "Is everything okay?"

I look down and pluck an imaginary piece of lint from my skirt. "Yeah, of course. Why?"

"Don't know. Just seems like there's something you're not telling me."

For the first time, I wish Brent were an unperceptive idiot like every other seventeen-year-old guy I've met. I want to be honest with him. Whatever this thing is we're doing together, I want to do it right. But I can't show him the photo. There's no way around the implications that his father could have been involved in a murder.

"I'm fine." I lean forward on the balls of my feet and plant a kiss on his forehead. "Just stressed."

Brent seems satisfied with this. And it's the truth: Ever since I realized his father is in the photo, I can't stop thinking about Matt Weaver. About the person who knows what happened to him—the coward who wrote on the back of a picture instead of coming forward with the truth.

And what bothers me most of all is this pressing weight I feel now. Almost like if I don't try to uncover the truth, no one will. Matt Weaver's parents will die never knowing what happened to their only son. If they haven't already.

I lace my fingers through Brent's as we head to lunch. How could I even begin to tell anyone about this? They'd say the joke is on me this time. That my brain wants to believe Matt Weaver was murdered because I'm still not over what happened to Isabella. That if I don't cut the crap, I'm going to wind up like one of those lunatics who spends all day on conspiracy-theory forums and keeps an arsenal of guns in the basement.

There's only one person who would believe me. And I'm definitely not calling him.

It's a quarter to the ass crack of dawn on next Saturday, and I'm on line at a coffee shop by the Wheatley T station with Remy. She has to be at the Boston College Athletics box office at 8:00 A.M. to pick up tickets for her brother's lacrosse game. At some point in the week I guess I agreed to go with her. I yawn—a little too loudly, with a dramatic arm movement—and Remy elbows me in the ribs.

"To your right," she whispers.

I rub my eyes and glance over at the area where you pick up your drinks. I curse under my breath and angle my body so I'm facing Remy and not him.

Headmaster Goddard. He accepts a mug of coffee from the barista with a nod. His white hair is combed neatly to the side, and he's wearing a beige fisherman's cable sweater. A copy of *The Boston Globe* is tucked under his arm.

"I've never seen him off campus." The way she says it, the headmaster may as well be a unicorn.

We watch Goddard choose a table by the door. He unfolds his

newspaper and takes a sip from his coffee, black. Like his soul, I imagine.

Professor Upton's voice fills my head. *I'm wondering if we should have done more about his . . . obsessive behaviors.* She meant Lee.

And then Goddard's: *If he never touched that girl, this isn't even a conversation.*

He couldn't even use Isabella's name.

"I hate him," I say.

Remy is quiet as we approach the counter. I order a cinnamon dolce latte, extra foam. She pretends to think about what she wants for a moment before ordering the same thing. It's our pattern.

When our drinks are ready, Remy practically hides behind me. We have to pass Goddard on our way out, and her eyes are on the floor as if we're doing something wrong by daring to be in his presence. I want him to see me, though. I want him to know I haven't forgotten anything.

I don't even have to feign a cough or a sneeze to get him to look up. "Ladies. Good morning." Goddard's lips spread into a patronizing smile.

"Morningheadmaster." Remy is practically twitching next to me.

"Ms. Dowling." Goddard nods to me.

I can't think around the buzzing in my ears. All I can think of is the missing tape—the one that proves Goddard knew Lee was stalking Isabella and did nothing. Dr. Harrow is the last person that had it, but the police couldn't find it in his house. Could Goddard have gotten to it first?

My temperature rises at the thought. At the memory of how casual Goddard sounded on the tape, as if Professor Upton were coming to him about a leak in her classroom ceiling, and not about a student stalking another.

Ah. Diana. Come in. I've just brewed a lovely Ethiopian roast.

Harrow may be in jail and Upton may have retired, but it's

done nothing to stem the corruption that's happened on Goddard's watch.

I finally find my voice. "Good morning, Headmaster."

Goddard nods to us. "Enjoy the lovely spring day, ladies."

My voice quavers as I say, "Enjoy your lovely Ethiopian roast."

Remy drags me out the door before I can see the expression on his face.

I'm an only child. So naturally, I take issue with the concept of doing a pain-in-the-ass favor solely because a sibling says you have to.

"Why can't your brother go to the box office himself?" The train car is crowded, so we have to stand and hold on to the rails. Every time we stop at a station, I make sure to squeeze some antibacterial onto my and Remy's palms.

"He says he's busy." Remy chews the inside of her cheek. "Also, he said if I don't do it, he'll tell our parents we went to a party at his frat house a few months ago and April threw up in the bathtub."

The T lurches to a stop. The doors open as a voice overhead announces the stop. Next is Boston College. A tall blond girl wades through the crowd to the doors, not bothering to say excuse me. Her horsey face is pinched as if she's annoyed the crowd hasn't automatically parted for her.

"Holy Cow," Remy says, wobbling as the train begins moving again. "Was that—"

"Alexis." I let my fingers curl around the pole more tightly. "Yes."

At school, there's some sort of unspoken agreement not to discuss Alexis Westbrook. She's as embarrassing a subject as an ingrown butt hair. Before everything went down with Alexis's dad and he was forced to resign, Isabella had exposed Alexis for being a racist lunatic, and most of her longtime friends, including Remy, abandoned her.

Personally, I don't understand the element of surprise. I knew Alexis was a lunatic after being around her for five minutes.

"She's probably visiting her mom's and brother's graves." Remy's voice is small. "Her mom was born in Chestnut Hill; Alexis goes every month to see them."

Alexis's mother and younger brother were killed in a car accident when Alexis was pretty young. I try to imagine what growing up without my mom would be like. Not hearing her tap on my door every morning before school to make sure I was awake. I mean, I miss having that now, with my mom in New York. I don't want to think about never having it again.

My experiences with death are pretty limited. I've been lucky that way. Grandpa Harold died when I was six, and I didn't even know Isabella that well. How different would I be now if I hadn't been so lucky?

It's hard for me to feel sorry for Alexis Westbrook after she tried to frame me for Isabella's murder and made my life a living hell for months. But it's also hard not to.

Alexis haunts my thoughts until Remy and I get back to the dorms. After lunch, I Google Steven Westbrook's wife.

I skip over all the recent news articles about the senator's resignation and go straight to the Personal Life section of his Wikipedia page.

Steven Westbrook married Cynthia Durham in 1989. The two met at the Wheatley School while Westbrook was a sophomore and Durham a freshman. They later reconnected while pursuing MBAs at Harvard's Business School. The Westbrooks had two children together: Alexis and Bryce.

Death of Durham-Westbrook

Sometime after midnight on July 7, 1995, Cynthia Durham-Westbrook and her son left their vacation home on Martha's Vineyard. Senator Westbrook said his wife regularly took the

infant Bryce on car rides when he would not go to sleep. When
Durham-Westbrook had not returned two hours later, Westbrook
called the police. The Westbrooks' family car was found over-
turned on the side of Blue Star Highway. Durham-Westbrook and
her son both sustained fatal injuries.

   While there were no witnesses, an investigation into the deadly
crash suggested Durham-Westbrook fell asleep and drove off the
highway. Senator Westbrook filed a lawsuit against the makers of
the family's car, citing brake failure as the cause of the crash. The
lawsuit was eventually dropped; due to extensive fire damage to
the Westbrooks' vehicle, investigators were unable to conclude
what caused the crash with 100 percent certainty.

Remarriage to Mary Ellen Cormier

Steven Westbrook married Mary Ellen Cormier, daughter of Wall
Street executive Jonathan Cormier, in 1997. The couple had their
first child, a son, one year later.

I close my laptop and brew a cup of chai. I sit it in front of me
on the desk, unable to touch it.

My best friend, Chelsea, is really superstitious. Not, like,
won't-walk-under-a-ladder or freaks-if-she-breaks-a-mirror superstitious. I'm talking about wastes-a-shitload-of-money-on-
psychics-and-palm-readers superstitious.

I think of all the Wheatley School students who have wound
up dead (or presumably, at least): Isabella Fernandez. Matthew
Weaver. Cynthia Durham. I've never believed in curses or any of
that garbage. But I will admit it: I'm starting to worry that if I
stay at the Wheatley School, I might be next.

CHAPTER FIVE

The last time I went to a party in Aldridge, the boys' dorm, my roommate was brutally murdered. So naturally I'm a little hesitant when, later that night, Brent calls while Remy and I are hanging out in Kelsey and April's room and tells us to come over.

"I'm too tired. Can't we stay in tonight?" Kelsey is lying on her back on her bed, her strawberry blond hair fanning out on the pillow behind her. I could jump on the bed and hug her. As much as I want to see Brent, I'd really rather hang here and watch movies than get dressed up and sneak out to the boys' dorm.

I don't even recognize myself anymore. All it took was three months at boarding school to accomplish what my parents couldn't in sixteen years.

"Come on," April says. "We haven't gone over there since . . ."

I'm the only one who's listening to her. She doesn't finish her sentence and goes back to browsing the formal dress section on Lord & Taylor's Web site. Remy is already straightening her hair with the flat iron on April's desk.

"I am done staying in every weekend," she announces. "DONE."

And that's how we wind up going.

Sneaking out requires a little more finesse post-murder on campus. The stairwell door, which the girls used to use to leave the dorms after 10:00 P.M. curfew, is now booby-trapped with an alarm. The alternative system we've come up with is this: Pick the lock on the first-floor kitchen window. Close it and leave it unlocked. Climb out and press ourselves against the side of the building where the security camera outside Amherst doesn't reach. Then James-Bond it over to Aldridge.

Of course, all of this could be avoided if I just tell the girls what I know: that the underground tunnel system the Wheatley School used for navigating campus in bad weather never really closed in 1960. That there are accessible entrances all over campus. One is even in the basement of Amherst.

But I'm not dumb enough to tell anyone about the tunnels. People would start using them to sneak out, and if they got caught by the security guards who occasionally patrol down there, the school would probably seal the tunnels for good.

We get to Aldridge without any major incident, although Kelsey fell out of the window and ripped her tights. Murali lets us in through the first-floor lounge window.

As some crew-team perk or whatever, the guys live in a four-person suite with their own living room/kitchenette and bathroom. Cole and Phil are sitting on the floor around the coffee table, fooling around with a deck of cards. Phil raises a plastic blue cup and grins at us.

"We're playing Kings. Beers are in the fridge."

It appears we're the only guests this evening. Absent, thankfully, is Sebastian Girard, who exaggerates his French accent to hit on me, and Jill Wexler, who is tall and thin and blond and in love with Brent. Which isn't grounds to hate her. I'm not like that.

But the last time Jill and I were at the same party, she almost got me expelled-and-or-jailed afterward. So I'm happy no one invited her tonight.

I make my way to the iPod dock on the kitchen counter as the girls rummage through the fridge. Whoever left his iPod here forgot to make a playlist. I scroll through the library, which includes a lot of The Who, Neil Young, and Tom Petty. I choose my favorite Billy Joel song—"Vienna"—and turn the volume up.

"Good taste." A clean-shaven chin nuzzles into my neck from behind. "Wouldn't have pegged you for a Billy Joel fan."

I turn into Brent so we're stomach-to-stomach. "He was my first concert. Madison Square Garden."

"There's an old soul somewhere in this wild child." Brent leans in to kiss me but instead brushes his nose against mine. I lean in to meet his lips. He turns his head, teasing me.

"Do you always have to play hard to get?" I ask.

"Says the girl who wouldn't go out with me until I almost got knifed," he says.

I smooth my hand down from the collar of Brent's T-shirt to his navel. "Hey, at least I still wanted you after I got you."

I don't realize how messed up that sounds until Brent smiles and it never makes it to his eyes. He holds my gaze. "Just go easy on me, okay?"

I want to tell him I didn't mean it like that, that he really is different from all the Martin Paynes in my life. But I don't get the chance, because Remy yells from the hallway, interrupting me.

"Brent. Why do you guys have twenty bottles of Sprite in your bathroom?"

"Why *don't* you have twenty bottles of Sprite in your bathroom?" Brent's voice is playful, but I sense him stiffen in my arms.

"Oh, no," April says over the sound of Murali, Phil, and Cole's laughter. "There are tons of bananas in the fridge. You're not doing the Sprite-banana challenge, are you?"

"What's the Sprite-banana challenge?" Kelsey asks over the rim of her beer.

"You don't want to know." April shakes her head. "I saw it on

YouTube. You eat a bunch of bananas then drink Sprite. And then you puke a lot."

Remy squeals. "Why would you *do* that?"

"Relax," Murali says. "We're not. The new recruits are."

"What, like hazing?" As soon as the words leave my mouth I want to take them back. Brent's mouth forms a thin line, and Phil lets out an awkward laugh. Cole shuffles the deck of cards, his eyes on his hands.

"We don't haze," Murali says brightly. "We initiate. Hazing violates the Wheatley Code of Conduct."

This gets real laughter out of everyone. But my head is swimming. One of the articles I found online about Matthew Weaver's disappearance mentioned that the crew team had been punished the year before for hazing new members. Projectile vomiting bananas and Sprite sounds innocent enough, but what if the team in the photo went too far and something happened to Matt in the process?

"Come on. Relax a little." Brent takes my hand and guides me to the table. I don't want him thinking my mind is elsewhere tonight—and truthfully, I don't want my mind to be elsewhere—so I grab a beer and join the game at the coffee table.

For the next two and a half hours, we play President. The first person to get rid of all of her cards is the "President." The last is the "Asshole." The President gets to boss everyone around, and everyone else basically gets to verbally abuse the Asshole. Also, the Asshole has to do what everyone says. Phil is the Asshole for most of the game. Kelsey makes him distribute his best cards evenly among all of us, which prompts a drunken conversation about socialism. Remy has him strip down to his boxers, and we're all on our fourth beer, at least, by the time Brent strips down to his boxers and demands Phil kiss his bare ass.

"On that note," Phil says, standing up, "I think I'll go to bed."

We play for all of five minutes after he's gone before Remy gets up to go to the bathroom. When she doesn't come back, April and Kelsey snicker between themselves.

"They're so hooking up," April says.

Cole throws his cards down and gets up. "I'm done, too."

We're all quiet as he storms down the hall. Cole and Remy dated for a few months last year.

"Oops," April says.

"Seriously, Apes, you've got to cut that shit out," Brent says.

Kelsey hiccups and says she wants to go back to Amherst. Clearly, the party's over now, but I'm really having fun and want to stay here with Brent. Murali agrees to walk April and Kelsey home, and then it's just Brent and me on the couch.

We listen to his iPod for a little while. There's a lot of making out and some wandering hands, but Brent is too drunk to fully appreciate the beauty of a lacy front-clasp bra. I don't know who falls asleep first, but when I open my eyes it's 3:00 A.M. Brent's arm is draped over me. He twitches lightly in his sleep.

I have to pee something fierce. I don't want to wake him up, so I plant a kiss on his cheek and slip out from beneath him. I'm still a little buzzed, so I wind up on my knees on the carpet between the couch and the coffee table. As I crawl away from the couch, my foot brushes a stack of magazines beneath the coffee table. They all spill over.

"Damn it." I try to push them into some semblance of order but wind up making it worse. A bunch of photos slide out of a yearbook tucked among the magazines. I spot one of Cole, asleep, with *BALLS* written on his forehead in Sharpie. Brent, Murali, and Phil playing beer pong in another. Phil's California-sun-streaked hair is long, and Murali's face has a little extra baby fat. These were probably taken last year, or earlier.

I can't help but give them a quick browse, especially after spotting a picture of Remy and Cole at what I assume is last year's formal. They're sitting at a round table, their heads tilted in to each other. Brent is behind them, sticking his tongue out in photo-bomb fashion.

So sue me for wanting to know who *his* date was.

I paw through the pictures as Brent snores lightly. A dark,

poor-quality photo—probably from a cell phone— catches my attention. Maybe it's the beer, but the picture makes me want to throw up.

Eight guys stand shoulder to shoulder, their wrists bound in front of them with rope. I don't recognize anyone in it. Probably because they all have potato sacks over their heads.

Whatever this is, it's sick and I don't like it. I scuttle off to the bathroom and lock myself in. Then I do the stupidest thing I've done all week.

I call Anthony.

The thing is that deep down I know it's a terrible idea. But drinking makes me feel like I'm incapable of having bad ideas.

I know he's not going to pick up after the fourth ring. Something in me deflates when I reach his voice mail.

"Hey, leave a message, and I'll call you back."

"Hi. Um. It's me. Anne. Look, I know we haven't talked in a while. But I really need to talk. To you. It's important."

Then I hang up.

CHAPTER
SIX

Approximately an entire day after I call him, I still don't have an answer from Anthony.

I shouldn't have called him at all. It's as if I'm only capable of forgetting about Anthony Fernandez long enough to forget why I even want to forget about him.

Everyone is in self-imposed isolation today: We all got drunker than we meant to last night, and there's lots of shit due in class tomorrow. When I finish my biology lab report, I trudge to the kitchen downstairs because I need more coffee and I'm out of pods for the brewer in my room. Darlene, my RA, is at the microwave with her back to me. She turns around when she hears me shuffle in.

"Hey, Anne." With two fingers, she removes a bag of popcorn from the microwave. If she suspects I didn't spend the night in my own dorm, she doesn't let on. Mercifully, I was able to take my Walk of Shame through the side entrance, which you can get into with your school ID starting at 6:00 A.M.

I wave to Darlene and rub my eyes. Things you need to get over at boarding school: people seeing you without makeup;

everyone knowing your secret to supersoft hair is using baby shampoo. I even had to amend my "Never Wear Yoga Pants in Public" rule.

Darlene leaves me, and Remy wanders in. We wordlessly sit at a table and watch the coffee brew.

"So," I say. "You and Phil."

Remy groans a little. "It's nothing serious."

But Cole doesn't seem to think so. He and Remy are usually very chatty, but at dinner that night he positions himself between Murali and Kelsey and barely says a word to anyone.

I follow Brent to the stir-fry line so he can get his second dinner. "What the hell is that about?"

"Cole being Cole. Remy being Remy." He dumps some broccoli into his bowl, chooses a sesame ginger sauce, and tells the chef he'd like chicken.

Brent looks to see if anyone's watching, then kisses my temple. It's sweet, but it's also his way of saying *I don't want to talk about our friends and their bullshit.* "Last night was fun."

"Yeah." I ignore the nagging sensation in my brain. The voice screaming that something isn't right. I want to ask Brent what the hell that photo was—the one of the guys with their hands bound—but it'll look like I was snooping around his dorm while he was passed out.

"We hanging out tonight?" he asks as we make our way back to the table.

"Why?" I tease. "Can't get enough of me?"

Brent laughs. "How could I possibly, when you're so charming and *modest*?"

I elbow him. He hooks a finger through the loop in my skirt and pulls me to him. "No, but really. Just you and me."

I try to focus on how amazing his fingers brushing through my ponytail feels, but I keep circling back to the photo. And to the thought that maybe whatever freaky thing the guys were doing in it is related to Matt Weaver's disappearance.

"Tempting, but I want to get a head start on Fowler's paper," I say. "I'm going to head to the library after dinner."

"Okay." He leans in but passes over my mouth and kisses my upper cheek, almost next to my eye. It would make sense for him to ask to come with me to the library since we both have to do that paper, but I know he's too proud to risk the rejection.

And I feel as relieved as I do guilty. Because even though I *am* going to the library, I don't plan on starting Fowler's paper.

Someone's checked out the edition of *A History of the Wheatley School* that has the first news story I read about Matt Weaver tucked inside. I should have taken the article when I had the chance.

I hate to do it, but I have to go to the microfilm section. At least one of the old newspapers there has to have a mention of what the 1980 crew team did to get slapped with hazing charges.

The librarian gives me the mandatory speech about how to use the projector.

"What are you looking for in particular?" she asks.

"Oh, just some history on sports at Wheatley," I say.

She suggests I look at old editions of *The Wheatley Register*, the school newspaper. I thank her and she returns to her desk. I doubt any mention of disciplinary action would be in *The Wheatley Register*. It's more of a "Look at how smart our students are; they can write about foreign policy and hydrofracking" type of paper.

I opt instead for the local paper. Once I find the bin labeled 1981, a sense of dread corners me. I don't have time to go through hundreds of newspapers. For all I know, the hazing charges weren't even newsworthy.

I close the drawer of microfilm. Anne, defeated. I really am searching for a needle in a haystack. What am I thinking, wasting my time like this? Even if I do find evidence that the crew team killed Matt Weaver, there's no way the police will touch a thirty-year-old murder without a body.

I check out a book of criticism on Edmund Spenser before I trek back to the dorm, partly because I feel bad about lying to Brent. A clap of thunder sounds in the distance. I quicken my pace so I don't get caught in the downpour that's sure to come. The tunnels underground would be pretty useful right now.

The tunnels. Of course. How had I not remembered sooner the rooms in the tunnels? At one point, part of the tunnels was the basement of the administration building. When Anthony and I were searching for info on Isabella, we came across a room of old files. And there were lots others.

I bet the answers I'm looking for are down there.

By midnight, all of the lights in my hall are off. My pepper spray, phone, and backup flashlight are in my bag. I crawl out of bed and take the stairs down to the first floor.

Darlene is at the desk, her head down. A textbook is open in front of her. I slip past her and head down the laundry-room stairs.

The rain *plink*s against the gutters by the basement windows. I apply some rosebud salve to my lips and start to push the book-case against the far wall. It's heavier than I remember, and I've broken a little sweat by the time I'm done.

There's a damp chill in the tunnels. I keep a path of light in front of me and one hand on the stone wall to steady myself. A drop of water lands on the back of my neck.

I follow the signs pointing to Lexington Hall, an old class-room building. I figure anything of importance to me will be in one of the basement rooms there, where all of the hard-copy rec-ords are from before the system was computerized. The room that used to be Lexington Hall 180N is basic student records; I'll have to do some poking around to find out where they keep discipline records. And since discipline isn't really a "thing" at the Wheatley School, there can't be many.

I shine my light through the glass pane on the door marked 182. I have to get on my toes to see inside. It looks like a storage room, packed with those old-fashioned desks that have places to hold your inkwell. I'll come back to this room if I have to, but I'm pretty sure it's not what I'm looking for. I move on to 184.

Pointing my light inside reveals some sort of office. I can't see much except for a large framed black-and-white portrait on the far wall. I stretch up as far as I can on the balls of my feet to get a better look. There are about twenty people in the photo wearing striped shirts with WHEATLEY printed on the front.

The door lock is as old as the building and easy to pick. When I step inside, I have to cover my nose and mouth to block out the smell of mildew and lime. I load the flashlight app on my phone and place it face-first on the desk as a crappy makeshift lamp and shine my flashlight on the photo.

Charles River Regatta, 1953

There are a bunch of vintage-looking photos of action shots hanging on the walls. Also, there are three saggy, mismatched couches arranged in a semicircle. I sit at the desk, noticing something strange in the trash can beside it.

Protein-bar wrappers.

I shine my light on them to get a better look. A chill passes over me. I know the wrappers well: They're the protein bars Brent eats before Brit lit every day.

I may have found the crew team's secret lair, and there's no telling when they'll be back. I sit up with urgency and shine my light over the floor, searching for some indication that the guys have been down here recently. There's a discarded chip bag, a copy of the school paper, and . . . an enormous coil of rope.

I swallow away the bitter taste on my tongue as I follow my

light up the wall by the rope. There's a six-foot-wide filing cabinet pressed against it.

Bingo.

After a bit of a struggle, I pry the first drawer open. A quick
browse through faded folders tells me the drawers ascend by date.
I thumb to the section labeled 1981.

Most of the papers inside are records of physical examinations
for individual athletes. There're also a bunch of letters from colleges congratulating the athletic department on having their student recruited.

The master folder breaks off into sections labeled by sport. I
flip through them until I find ROWING. It's a thin file; two seniors
received full scholarships to row at Harvard and Yale. I pause
when I find a typewritten letter titled NOTICE.

March 14, 1981
As consistent with clause 23 of the Wheatley School Code of
Personal and Academic Conduct, all members of the crew
team shall be suspended for one (1) race pending charges of
inappropriate conduct, including (a) leaving campus after
proscribed curfew hours and (b) endangering the welfare of a
fellow student.

Let it be known that the student in question was treated for
moderate hypothermia at St. Andrew's Memorial Hospital in
Wheatley at approximately two thirty in the morning on
March 11, 1980. When questioned, the disoriented student
alleged he succumbed to hypothermia while performing a
task ordered on him by his older teammates. Wheatley
Athletics prohibits any manner of hazing by or upon its
athletes. As punishment, all team members will not compete
in their race against Ellison Prep on Saturday, March 21, 1980.

This is the "hazing incident" the newspaper article on Matt
Weaver's disappearance mentioned. I read through the notice

again, trying to pick up on any clues about the younger student's identity. Matt would have been a sophomore in 1980. If it were his first year on the crew team, he would have known the student who got hypothermia. And if the school did a really good job keeping the student's identity away from the police and the news, it may have even been Matt.

I freeze at a sound on the opposite end of the tunnels. No . . . it's coming from above, in the garage.

A car alarm.

I curse the idiot teacher who decided to hang around until one in the morning. Security will be here in a manner of minutes if the alarm doesn't shut up. After two failed attempts to get a clear photo of the hazing notice on my phone, I pocket the paper and shut the filing cabinet drawer. It sticks a bit, so I have to shove it.

I wind up slamming the whole cabinet into the wall. The photo of the 1953 crew team hanging adjacent to the cabinet shivers.

"No, no—!"

I lunge for it, but it's already falling to the ground. The glass shatters everywhere. Above me, the car alarm continues to wail.

"*Damn* it." I bend down to see if there's anywhere I can hide the broken frame so no one knows I was here. But it's dark, and there's a lot of glass. I pick up the frame and photo, which are still intact, and prop it against the wall.

The car alarm wails on. There's the sound of a door slamming— the same garage door that leads down into the tunnel entrance.

I turn and don't stop running until I'm back in the basement of Amherst.

CHAPTER
SEVEN

My own alarm goes off at what feels like the exact moment I finally fall asleep. I manage to make it to breakfast, but when I get there, everyone is quiet and facing the far side of the dining room.

I grab an orange juice and creep to our table. That's when I see him at the front of the room. The headmaster.

His watery eyes almost seem to twinkle with amusement as he watches me. As if he's purposely waiting for me to sit down before he starts talking. He nods to me as I settle into my seat.

"Ladies and gentleman. I'd like to introduce you to our new physics instructor, Dr. Rowan Muller."

There's tepid applause. No one except Brent and I knows the real reason Professor Andreev took "a leave of absence": He was using Isabella and Sebastian to decode information he stole from a military lab. For the past few weeks, an old guy named Mr. Mc-Shane was his temporary replacement. Brent and Cole loved him: Instead of teaching physics, he told stories about serving in World War II and regularly fell asleep in class.

"Hallo." A clean-shaven man in a V-neck sweater with a dress shirt and tie underneath stands where Goddard was standing moments before. "Um, well then. Morning, everyone."

Everything else he says dissolves just short of my ears, because Dr. Muller is cute. He's young—not as young as Ms. C, but probably thirty at the most—and he's from South Africa. I'm not the only one practically drooling into my juice over his accent. He's what Chelsea would call "a perfect specimen." He almost makes me want to take physics next year. Almost.

Apparently I'm not the only one charmed by Dr. Muller. Ms. C never grabs breakfast in the dining hall on her way to class like some of the other teachers, but today, she's hanging around the group of people waiting to introduce themselves. And there's a dare I say *girlish* flush to her cheeks.

Not everyone shares our enthusiasm for the newest addition to the staff.

"Why do you look bent out of shape?" I ask Brent as we leave the hall.

"Now we'll have to do stuff in class again."

"Imagine that." I poke him in the side. "Having your parents pay thirty grand a year for you to actually do stuff."

"Hey, my dad's the one who told me to bring up that time Robinson met Andy Warhol right before he's about to assign homework," Brent says.

I'm about to ask Brent why he never told me this valuable nugget of info about my art-history teacher, when wind chimes sound from my bag. My text message alert.

My fingers feel like they don't work when I see the message is from Anthony's number:
so what do u want from me anyway?

"Who's that?" Brent says it casually, but guilt ignites in me nonetheless.

"Just a friend from back home."

Brent nods, thoughtful and unsuspicious, which totally makes me feel worse. "Does it seem weird to you that Goddard showed up this morning?"

"Well, he did have a reason."

"Yeah, but Goddard never used to talk to us. He would always send Harrow or one of the deans."

"Maybe it's because Harrow is gone, so Goddard has to help Dean Snaggletooth out?"

"I guess." Brent looks unsettled. "I don't know. I just feel like he's trying to send a message or something. That he's watching."

We're quiet on the rest of the walk to class, but I can tell we're thinking the same thing. If Goddard is trying to let someone know he's watching, it's me.

I hang back at the end of art-history class next morning, waiting for a sophomore boy to stop kissing Robinson's ass so I can talk to him. While I'm waiting, I get another response from Anthony:

Drunk dialing me now?

I ignore it, swallowing away annoyance.

Robinson squints at his projector remote when the sophomore is gone, trying to find the power-down button.

"Here, let me help."

Robinson looks surprised to see that I'm still here. I smile and slide the remote out of his long thin fingers. "It's the red button."

He watches me with amused eyes. Robinson is about a hundred and a half years old, six feet tall, and ninety-five pounds. "Did you know that I'm color-blind, Miss Dowling?"

"You're . . . a color-blind art teacher?" I stare into his milky blue eyes. "Huh. Doesn't that make your job harder?"

"Who says?" Robinson is British, so he pronounces it funny. Like "say-z," not "sez." I shrug.

"One doesn't need to view a piece of art in color to appreciate its beauty." He smiles at me. "How are you faring with this week's assignment?"

"Fine." And by fine, I mean that at least now I know an assignment, in fact, exists. "I actually wanted to show you some-thing."

"Oh?"

I open my Brit-lit anthology to the page with Matt Weaver's drawing.

"Adam and Eve," Robinson says automatically. He putters over to his bookshelf, mumbling to himself. I'm about to explode with impatience by the time he selects a book that probably weighs more than he does and drags it over to the desk.

"Henrick Goltzius. *The Fall of Man.*" He licks his fingers and flips to a busy colored painting. "Many artists have been inspired by the story of Genesis. If the subject holds interest for you, I'd be happy to lend you this book for your final paper."

"Thanks," I say. "But it's not me who drew this. I was hoping you might recognize the drawing as a former student's."

Robinson chuckles. "I've had *many* students over the years, Miss Dowling. I can't say I can be of much help."

"Oh . . ." I trace Eve's hair. "Well, Matt Weaver was one of the students who had this book before me."

"Well, then. Isn't that interesting." Robinson rubs his chin. "Matthew was very talented."

"Could he have drawn this?"

Robinson's face falls. "It's possible. May I escort you to fourth hour? We don't want to be late."

Robinson extends an arm to me. I study his face as we leave the classroom.

He couldn't be more full of crap if he were constipated. He knows exactly who drew that picture.

Reason number 1 Ms. C is awesome: She hates Mondays as much as we do. Every week, she lets us quietly work on exercises from the textbook. Once we're done, we can chill and work on what-ever we want as long as we're not obnoxious about it.

I finish my work faster than everyone except Lee Andersen, who is browsing Stanford's Web site. If that's where he wants to go to college, I'm totally on board with that, because California is nice and far away from me.

When Ms. C's back is turned, I send a response to Anthony: *what do you know about Matthew Weaver?*

I tuck my phone in my lap, beneath the folds of my skirt, even though I know it'll probably be another whole day before Anthony bothers to respond, if he responds at all. I have to wonder if he's making me wait for his responses on purpose.

If this is a game, I'm tired of it. But a part of me hopes it is, because the alternative is that he really doesn't care that I reached out to him after all.

I let my laptop whir to life and set out to do what I meant to do over a week ago.

I type the first name on my list into Google: *Lawrence Tretter.* The results are as I expected. Larry Tretter is still beefy, sour looking, and living in Wheatley. He's been the Wheatley crew coach for the past seventeen years. Under his leadership, the team has won six high school championships and various college invitational events.

Thom Ennis is trickier. There are tons of people with the same name in Massachusetts alone. I refine my search terms to include Wheatley School. I get a hit for Thom W. Ennis, attorney at law. He lives and practices in New York City. My brain races, wondering if my father knows of him.

I copy the number for Ennis's office into my phone before I move on to Travis Shepherd.

Travis Shepherd is important enough to have his own Google bio. I know it's the same Travis Shepherd as the guy in the photo because the bio has a recent picture of him. He's striking: brown hair streaked with gray and thick dark eyebrows above brown eyes. And he's apparently the CEO of Shepherd and McLoughlin Associates.

I almost miss that some of the most popular hits for Shepherd are news stories dated 2008. I peruse some of the headlines:

FORTUNE 500 CEO DENIES ACCOUNTING FRAUD
CHARGES AGAINST COMPANY

INSURANCE BROKERAGE FIRM SETTLES $100M LAWSUIT

ACCOUNTANTS AT SHEPHERD
AND MCLOUGHLIN FIRED IN WAKE OF STATE
DEPARTMENT INVESTIGATION

Looks like Steven Westbrook isn't the only Wheatley alum having trouble keeping his nose clean. From what I can tell, Shepherd didn't know about the alleged accounting fraud until the lawsuit was filed. But something about his smile strikes me as sketchy. Sketchy enough to murder a classmate?—I don't know.

When I hear Ms. C's voice behind me, I close my laptop.

"Anne. I have something for you." She hands me three brochures for colleges: Brown, Wesleyan, Barnard.

I stare at them. "I can't get into any of these."

Ms. C just smiles and tucks a strand of penny-colored hair back into her bun. "We'll see."

I run my hands over the glossy finish on the Barnard brochure. Last year, a rep from the admissions office came to speak at St. Augustine's. I was texting back and forth with Chelsea during the presentation. We have special text-notification sounds for each other, and mine is a cow. Anyway, her phone mooed right in the middle of the admission rep's speech, and I laughed so hard I snorted. Ms. Cavanaugh kicked me out and made me see Headmaster Bailey.

I thought Bailey would find a mooing phone as hilarious as I did, but she wasn't laughing when I got to her office. Instead, the first thing she said to me was, "Anne, at some point you're going to realize that the only person standing in your way is you."

I think I understand what she meant, now.

Cole, Brent, and Murali are hanging outside the athletic building when I get out of my last class. They all have final-period athletics together, during which they get special access to the rowing equipment. The rest of us have to take a sport that's not really a sport, like squash or dance.

Phil isn't with them. The looks on their faces tell me I don't want to go there, though. When they see me, Brent smiles, but I get the feeling it's only for my benefit.

"What's wrong?" I ask.

"Nothing," Brent says, ignoring the way Cole's eyes are probing him. "Coach was just a little rough on us today."

I can't help but look through the doors of the athletic facility. It's a newer building, with clean locker rooms and a pool we're allowed to use when the swimming team isn't using it. I've only ever been on the girls' side, where the dance studio is.

It's possible Larry Tretter is still in the building.

"Hey, I left my bag in there after dance today," I say. "I'll meet you guys in the Amherst lounge to study for Matthews's history exam in fifteen?"

Cole grunts in approval, and Murali blathers on about how it's not fair we're being tested on the Israeli-Palestinian conflict since we wrote an essay on it two weeks ago. They start heading for the dorms, but Brent hangs behind.

"You have dance class on Tuesdays," he says.

Fricking frick.

"I left it there Thursday. I just remembered now 'cause I have class tomorrow."

"Oh." Brent's eyes are focused on a point beyond me as he leans in and kisses my cheek. "I'll see you in a few, I guess."

I'm completely stunned that he *I-guessed* me. I mean, *I guess* isn't that bad in itself, but it's a sign that next time I'm going to get a *Do what you want.* Or even worse: *Whatever.*

For a split second, I consider forgetting the whole thing and going with Brent. I hate keeping things from him. But I can't let the Matt Weaver thing go until I know his dad wasn't involved. And telling Brent about the photo is *not* an option.

There are a couple of stragglers leaving the boys' locker room. A few of them wave to me on their way out, even though I can't remember or don't know their names. The girls' locker room is at the end of the hall. I study the plaques and pennants on the walls as I amble down there.

I stop in front of a trophy case with two bronze oars crossed over the top. There are lots of championship trophies inside, but the one on the center shelf catches my eye. There's a photo beneath it of the crew team gathered around the trophy.

In minuscule letters, the words IN LOVING MEMORY OF MATTHEW WEAVER are etched into the frame.

I turn my head to the office next to the trophy case. ROWING, the inscription on the door says. It's cracked open just enough for me to see inside.

Larry Tretter is a carbon copy of his photo on the athletics Web site, down to his maroon Wheatley crew T-shirt. A tall blond guy with ridiculously good hair sits across his desk, his back to me.

"Heyward looks pretty good so far," the guy says. "The freshman."

Tretter grunts in response. "Lazy. They all are. It'll be a goddamn miracle if we make it to the semifinals after you all graduate."

"They just need to be scared, that's all." The blond guy leans back in his chair and lowers his voice. "That's what The Drop's for."

Tretter's enormous cheeks flood with color. "You know you can't talk to me about that shit, kid."

The guy snorts. "Fine. If someone were trying to scare the shit out of them, there's The Drop. Hypothetically."

"It's not a joke." Tretter's hand comes down on his desk so hard it rattles whatever is in his drawers. I jump a little, but the guy seems unfazed. "People have gotten hurt. What's your father told you about it?"

"Nothing." It's just one word, but he says it so snottily, I can tell there are a million Daddy Issues hidden underneath.

Tretter pushes himself away from his desk and stands up. The guy follows suit.

"I can't know about what you guys are doing. I don't want to see it, smell it, or hear about it. Got it?"

The guy smirks and gives Tretter a two-finger salute. I can see his face now. I don't know his name, but I've seen him hanging around Justin Wyckoff, Kelsey's ex-boyfriend. Justin is a senior who carries himself with the smugness of a guy who is content with being a Hollister model and living off his trust fund for the rest of his life.

"Shep," Tretter says. "Don't be stupid."

I don't catch the expression on Shep's face, because I'm trying to get the hell out of there before they realize I was listening. I'm halfway down the hall when the guy calls, "Hey."

I stop and let him catch up to me, furiously applying rosebud salve to my lips.

"I don't think we've officially met." He extends his hand to me. It's nonthreatening enough, but I don't trust him. "You're Anne Dowling."

"In the flesh." I shake his hand. "Nice to meet you . . ."

"Casey Shepherd," he says. "But everyone calls me Shep."

CHAPTER
EIGHT

I see Casey Shepherd again that evening in the dining hall at a table of seniors. The only ones I know by name are Justin, Bea Hartley, and Vera Cassidy. Bea Hartley is Casey's stuck-up girlfriend. She and Vera live on the floor above me. They're the type of girls who never sneak out or party—at least on campus—because they're so involved with saving orphans and polar bears so the Ivies will be impressed.

Casey catches me watching him and waves with two fingers. I can't help the tiny bit of flush that creeps into my cheeks. I mean, I can tell Casey Shepherd is a yuppie brat, but he's a really good-looking yuppie brat.

I decide to track down Kelsey. She dated Justin, so she can probably tell me more about Casey.

I find her on the all-day omelet-station line, examining her split ends. In her black velvet headband with the bow on the side, she looks so innocent that I'm overcome with jealousy. I remember when the hardest decision in my daily life was whether or not to get a haircut.

"Hey." She scoots over so I can stand next to her on the line.

"So I think I made a new friend today," I tell her.

"Really? Who?"

"Casey Shepherd."

We inch up the line. "Oh. Shep."

I can't tell if it's a bad *Oh. Shep* or a good *Oh. Shep*. "He seems nice."

Kelsey gives a half nod. "He's from, like, the richest family in Massachusetts. His dad owns a huge brokerage firm."

So Casey is Travis Shepherd's son, like I suspected. "Wow."

"I mean, he's nice," Kelsey says. "But he dates Bea Hartley, who's totally stuck up. But in like a sneaky way, you know? Whenever I hung out with Justin, she and Vera were always around, saying stuff like 'Oh, Kelsey, you're from Berkshire County? That's so *cute*.'"

I glance over at Bea Hartley. She's wearing the unofficial Wheatley casual uniform: a J.Crew cardigan, jeans, and pearl earrings. Her long brown hair falls across her profile as she leans in to Vera, a tall girl with deep skin and curly black hair. They laugh together in a way that makes you feel like you're not smart enough to be in on the joke.

"So Cole asked me to the formal," Kelsey blurts.

I swing my head back to her. "What?"

"He said he was thinking we should go together." Kelsey shrugs.

"And you said . . ."

"I said yes." There's a silent *but* at the end of her words.

"You don't want to go with him?" I ask.

"No, of course I do." Kelsey's cheeks flush. "I just feel like . . . maybe he asked me to get Remy pissed. They usually go together."

"Why do you always think like that, Kels? You're gorgeous and funny. He probably just wants to go with you."

A smile quivers on Kelsey's lips, and I hope for her sake I'm right.

———

The next morning, I call Thom Ennis's office.

"Ennis and Cameron Associates."

"Hi. I'm looking for Mr. Ennis."

"This is his assistant," the clipped voice says. "Is there something I can help you with?"

"I'm a student at the Wheatley School," I say. "I'm writing an article for the newspaper on notable alumni, and I wanted to see if Mr. Ennis would be interested in being interviewed."

"I'll leave him a message. What did you say your name was?"

"Chelsea," I say. "Chelsea Brady."

The assistant takes my number and hangs up.

I find myself flipping through Matt Weaver's Brit-lit textbook—*my* Brit-lit textbook—during art history this morning. If Matt's drawing of himself as Adam is a clue about the events leading up to his disappearance, maybe there's something else hidden in the pages.

It turns out there's not much else in his handwriting. A few of the other owners of the book highlighted some passages here and there. (By the way, huge pet peeve of mine=highlighters. They stain your hands, and they're neon. I hate neon.)

I turn back to the Adam drawing. If Matt screwed up like Adam did, according to what is, in my opinion, a quite sexist story for why humanity is so screwed up, then Eve convinced Adam to eat an apple. Who is Matt Weaver's Eve, and what did she convince him to do?

A number with a New York area code calls me as I'm leaving my last class. I answer and turn the opposite direction of the crowds of students heading back to the dorms.

"Ms. Brady? I have Thom Ennis on the line for you."

"Oh, okay. Cool."

I want to smack myself for sounding so stupid as the line

clicks. I inhale deeply as a man's voice says, "Thom Ennis. What can I do for you?"

I give my bullshit interview story again.

"I wrote for *The Wheatley Register* back in the day," he says. "Cargill still running that thing or did she retire?"

"Um, she retired." I hope I'm right. "Thank you for calling me back, Mr. Ennis. I know you're busy."

"I always have time for Wheatley alumni."

"So, um. I have a few questions about Wheatley rowing."

"Sure. Shoot. I was on the team all four years."

I swallow and tighten my grip on my phone. "What can you tell me about The Drop?"

Thom Ennis is silent for a beat. "Is this a joke? Who are you?"

"I know about The Drop." It's taking everything I have not to let my voice shake so he can call my bluff. "I know all about Matt Weaver, too."

"What did they tell you?" He growls.

I don't even have the chance to come up with something, because Thom Ennis hangs up on me.

CHAPTER
NINE

A bad idea is like a virus. Once you've got one, it multiplies into a million other bad ideas.

Calling Thom Ennis was definitely a bad idea. If he contacts the other guys in the photo and tells them some girl from the Wheatley School is asking questions about Matt Weaver, I'm in deep shit. I need to be more careful planning out my next move.

Brent comes over Thursday night, since we have off for something called Founder's Day on Friday. We lay on my bed, watching *The Fellowship of the Ring*, because I've never seen it and according to Brent this means I have some sort of severe cultural deficiency.

"Did you know Cole asked Kelsey to the formal?" I ask Brent.

Brent keeps running his fingers through my hair, turning all of the nerve endings on my scalp into live wires. "I'm guessing to piss Rem off."

"I was hoping you wouldn't say that."

Brent shrugs. My cheek moves with his shoulder. "It's not like Cole. But Remy has that effect on him."

"I'd imagine she has that effect on lots of guys."

"Yeah, maybe. I just feel bad for Kels. She's had a thing for Cole for ages."

We turn back to the movie for a few minutes before Brent says, "Do you want to go to the formal?"

I trace the outline of his ear. "I don't know. No one's asked me."

He rolls his eyes. "Do you want to go with *me* to the formal?"

"I don't want to go to the formal," I say. "But if you need a date, I can tough it out."

"You're so generous." He laughs with his whole body. He's wearing a plain navy V-neck T. As good as he looks in his Wheatley blazer, I love seeing him like this. Relaxed, on my bed. I kiss his exposed collarbone. A shudder ripples through his body and he leans in to me.

The knock on the door feels like it comes moments later, but when we sit up, my alarm clock says it's 9:53 and the movie's credits are rolling. Through the door, Darlene informs us it's almost weeknight curfew. Translation: Brent needs to get the hell out.

He groans and touches his forehead to mine. "It feels like I just got here."

"We've got all weekend." I brush my lips against his without fully kissing them, because I know it drives him crazy.

When he's gone, I change into pajamas and climb into bed, accidentally kicking my phone on the floor. I bend to pick it up and realize it's not even my phone. Brent's must have fallen out of his pocket and onto my bed.

I bite the inside of my cheek. Ever since Isabella's murder, there are absolutely no exceptions to curfew: 10:00 P.M. on weeknights, 11:00 on weekends. Darlene will probably tell me to hang on to the phone and give it to Brent in the morning.

I place the phone on my nightstand and shut the lamp off. I've resolved to forget about it and fall asleep, when the screen lights up. Thinking it's one of the guys texting to make sure Brent's phone is here, I lean over and check who the message is from.

Casey Shepherd.

Some people argue there's not a fine line between right and wrong: It's more of a fifty-foot impenetrable wall with barbed wire across the top. I'm more of a gray-area type person. That's why I tell myself that since Brent chose to make the settings on his phone such that you don't need to open a message to read it, it's not *totally* wrong for me to glance at it:

Meet in basement of Aldridge after practice tom. Need to move TD from next fri to sat 10:30.

TD. The Drop? The two words mean virtually nothing to me, but they still inspire a sense of dread.

Tretter told Casey that people have been hurt during The Drop. It's possible he was talking about the boy who got hypothermia. It fits, since Tretter and his friends would have been sophomores the year the crew team was suspended for hazing.

THEY KILLED HIM.

What if The Drop had turned deadly?

CHAPTER
TEN

I'm woken up earlier than I'd like to be by the sound of my phone ringing. When I see it's Anthony calling, I'm simultaneously more annoyed and less annoyed. If that's even possible.

"'Lo?"

"Sorry I woke you." His voice says *I don't give a rat's ass I woke you.*

"What's up?" I roll on my side, my heart hammering in my throat. I have no real reason to be nervous about talking to Anthony, except for the fact I'd forgotten what his voice sounds like.

"Figured we should talk for real," he says. "At the rate we're going, we won't have a whole conversation 'til next Christmas."

"Okay. Let's talk."

"Not over the phone. What are you doing today?"

I was going to catch up on homework and maybe go out for sushi with Remy and the girls in the afternoon. "Nothing."

"Come to my shop around noon. I'll be outside."

By his shop, Anthony means Alex's Auto Body in Somerville. I get on the T at 11:30. For the entire ride, I can't stop putting on lip salve and curling my toes in my boots. It would have been nice to have more time to prepare myself for seeing Anthony. Mentally, of course.

In any case, I didn't want to look like I put any degree of thought into my Seeing Anthony Outfit, so I opted for my usual weekend fare: a denim chambray shirt and a beige wool skirt. Hair in a messy French braid. One stop away from his shop, I realize I'm wearing my hair the same way I did the day I met Anthony and I have mini panic attack. What if he notices and reads too much into it?

Of course he won't notice. He has two X chromosomes. I need to get ahold of myself, stat.

Anthony doesn't see me as I turn the corner. He leans against the brick wall of the body shop, cracking his knuckles. I hope it means he's as nervous about seeing me as I am about seeing him.

"Hey." I keep a good five feet of space between us. Anthony takes me in, his face expressionless. His hair is shorter, cleaner. "How have you been?" I ask.

"Holdin' up." He shrugs. "You?"

"I don't know. Trying to stay out of trouble, I guess."

There's a hint of a smile on his mouth. "I'd ask how that's working out for you, but you texted *me*, so . . ."

"Shouldn't you be in school?" I ask him. I don't know why it didn't occur to me earlier, when he said to meet at noon.

"Could ask you the same thing," he says.

"It's Founder's Day. I have off. Why aren't you in school, Anthony?"

"I don't go anymore."

The nonchalant way he says it makes my blood pressure rise unexpectedly. "You dropped out?"

"You sound surprised. I missed enough classes between my sister dying and me being under house arrest."

"But you're going back next year, right?"

Anthony's eyes are on the ground. "Can't. My dad got a lot worse after Iz died. I picked up some extra shifts at the shop for when my mom's home, to help out."

I don't know why, but I'm angry with everyone. At Dr. Harrow, for killing Isabella. At Anthony's mother, for not trying harder to keep Anthony in school. At Anthony, who doesn't even sound like he cares about his future. "But you have to go to school. Can't your mom get someone else to take care of your dad?"

"Okay." Anthony lets out a sharp laugh. "I'll tell her to hire a butler, too, while she's at it."

I hate myself for letting a tear slip down my cheek, because it's not the first time he's said something awful like that to me as if it's my fault that I have it easy and he doesn't. "You're throwing your future away."

"Why do you give a shit, Anne?" There's anger in his voice, but the look in his eyes says he actually wants to hear my answer. "You got your fifteen minutes. What else could you want from me?"

I want to scream at him. I want to call him names classy girls from the Upper East Side would never call a boy. Because *Anthony's* the one who wanted to help me find who killed Isabella. *He's* the one who ditched me when the whole ordeal was over and didn't even have the balls to face me when he dropped off her books.

He takes a step toward me. "That's what you wanted, right? To prove yourself to all those yuppies and be one of them?"

That's it. *No one* calls me a social climber and gets away with it.

"Fuck you," I yell. A man walking his dog at the curb pauses and stares at us.

Anthony puts his arm around me and leads me across the street. I'm crying so hard I'm choking on my own snot and tears. I hate him, and I can't even pull myself together for long enough to tell him that this is never what I wanted. I never wanted to come to Massachusetts at all.

Anthony guides me under a green awning and down a set of stairs. We're in a dimly lit pub that smells like French fries and motor oil. He walks me past a hostess and sits down at the bar.

I sniffle and lift myself onto the stool next to Anthony's. The bearded man behind the counter nods to him and places silverware in front of us, as if Anthony bringing hysterical girls in here is commonplace.

"I was a jerk before," Anthony says when the guy disappears into the kitchen. I know this is the closest thing to an apology I'm going to get from him.

Anthony's eyes are on the mirror behind the bar. I can't tell if he's looking at his reflection or mine. My cheeks are splotchy and my mascara is smeared. "I thought I was never gonna see you again," he says. "This is just . . . I dunno. I can't process."

Sums up my feelings exactly. "I'm sorry. I shouldn't have called when I knew you didn't want to see me anymore."

"It's not that." Anthony unwraps the napkin holding his silverware together. He turns the fork over in his hand. "I was pissed you found out I took that money from Iz. I wanted to explain, but then I saw that Wheatley guy with you there."

So that's what this is about.

"Seeing that one of *them* was in on what we were doing . . . I felt like a dumbass." Anthony cracks his knuckles. "It messed me up. You and I were supposed to be the good guys."

"Brent *is* a good guy," I say. "I knew I could trust him."

I ignore the voice in the back of my head that's wondering if things are different now. If I can't trust Brent.

The older man comes back with two waters for us. Anthony orders a burger and I order a plate of fries.

"So I guess you're seeing him now," Anthony says. "Brent or whatever his name is."

"Kind of."

I wait for some sort of reaction from Anthony, but he sips his water as if he couldn't care less who I'm dating or not dating. I should feel relieved that things won't be weird between us, but it feels like a kick to the stomach that he's forgotten so easily everything that happened between us.

I don't want to think about the possibility it all meant more to me than it did to him.

"So Matt Weaver, huh?" Anthony says. "What's that about?"

I don't even know where to start. So I pull the photograph out of my bag and hand it to Anthony.

"That's him." Anthony points to Matt. I nod.

"Turn it over."

He does. I study his expression as he reads what's there and sets it down on the table.

"Whoa," he says. "That's gotta be a joke, right?"

I put the photo back in my bag. "I thought so at first. But I've found out some stuff that suggests otherwise."

I brief Anthony on what I've uncovered so far: the crew team's suspension, The Drop, Matt's drawing, Thom Ennis's freakout when I mentioned Matt's name.

"You found all that out on your own?"

I nod.

"I can't . . . I mean, this is just crazy." A low whistle escapes him. "Don't you have other things to do? I don't know, maybe homework or something?"

"Obviously it's been a while since you've done homework if you think *that's* more interesting than a cold case."

Anthony flicks his straw wrapper at me. He's smiling, I notice, for the first time since we met up today.

We're both quiet when the food arrives. I shake some salt and pepper on my fries and let him chew a bite of his burger.

"There're *tons* of stories about what happened to him," Anthony says after he swallows. "The one I heard the most was that his parents borrowed money from the Winter Hill Gang to save their diner and couldn't pay it back."

"Winter Hill Gang?"

Anthony lowers his voice. "Irish Mob."

"Oh."

"Another one," Anthony says after a swig of water, "is that he was on LSD or 'shrooms or something and got kidnapped by someone who thought he was a typical Wheatley kid with a ton of money. When they realized his parents couldn't ransom him out, they killed him and dumped him."

I haven't heard the kidnapping theory before. According to most of the Internet articles I read, everyone said Matt's disappearance was probably drug related. But then again, it was the early eighties, so I guess people blamed drugs for everything.

"There's a weird theory I came across," I say slowly, "that he died conducting some satanic ritual."

Anthony laughs.

"What?"

"That theory probably came from the same people who thought listening to Metallica would turn kids into devil worshippers."

I point to Anthony's untouched pickle. "Can I have that?"

He nods, his lips bent as if he's deep in thought. "You said you've only talked to one person so far. The guy in New York."

"Thom," I correct him. "Yeah. Why?"

"I think I know who we could try next," Anthony says. The corner of his mouth quivers, like he knows something I don't.

"Okay. Who?"

"A little birdie told me Matt Weaver's parents still live in town."

I snap my head up. "I've been Googling them like crazy and couldn't find anything."

Anthony's upper lip lifts into a smirk as he steals a fry from my plate. *I kissed those lips.* I have to look away from him.

We split the check even though Anthony gets annoyed I try to pay for his burger. After an awkward wave good-bye thing outside the pub, Anthony turns and calls back to me.

"Nice hair, Anne."

CHAPTER
ELEVEN

The night Harrow was arrested, Brent said he'd give me time to figure out how I felt about Anthony. My parents flew up to Boston the next morning, so I didn't really see Brent in the days after that. Everything was a whirlwind of police interviews, visits to Dean Snaggletooth's office, and my parents going total Black Ops on me.

I thought things might start to go back to normal when they finally left for New York. Then, on my way to the refectory, I got stuck behind Jill, Brooke, and Lizzie, Alexis's best friend. I didn't catch everything Lizzie said about me, but it sounded a lot like *life-ruining bitch*.

I turned around. I didn't know where I was going until I was knocking on Brent's door. I didn't even think he'd be there, since most of the building had left for dinner, but he opened the door in a white T-shirt, the collar wet from his dripping hair. Before he could ask what was wrong I grabbed him and kissed him.

He kissed me back like I've never been kissed before, his hands moving to my lower back, pressing me into the wall. At that moment it felt like everything in my universe had been realigned.

Now Anthony has totally screwed with the order of my universe again.

I know there's technically nothing wrong with spending time with Anthony. But there's also something wrong with not telling Brent I'm spending time with Anthony, and I definitely can't do that without telling Brent *everything*. I mean, Brent knows Anthony and I made out a couple of times. I didn't want to tell him, but I didn't want the question hanging over us, either. Full disclosure. Whatever this is that Brent and I are doing, I want to do it right.

Which is why I haven't figured out the *right* way to tell him why I need to see Anthony again.

Anthony texts me Saturday morning to tell me he has an address for the Weavers. I meet him on Main Street, about a ten-minute walk from campus. He's waiting outside the Wheatley post office, leaning against a black car.

I balk. "You got rid of your motorcycle?"

"Hell, no. This is my mom's car. Didn't want the Weavers looking outside and thinking we were Hell's Angels." He nods to the passenger seat. "This is more comfortable, anyway."

*Un*comfortable doesn't even begin to cover the first few minutes of the ride. Apparently we have no idea what to talk about when we're not pissed at each other. I fill the awkward silence by fiddling with the radio. I settle on a station that's playing "Hot Blooded," one of my dad's favorite songs.

"You like Foreigner?" Anthony asks, surprised.

"If that's who sings this, then yes."

I think I catch him smile as he turns the volume up. I smile in spite of myself, but it only lasts long enough for Brent to text me.

Just got out of practice. Can't find you ☺

I quickly type out a reply. *Had to run off campus. Back soon.*

Anthony raises an eyebrow as I drop my phone into my bag.

"What?" I demand.

"Nothin'." He changes the station, even though the song isn't over.

The Weavers live on Knoll Street. All of the houses are tall and uncomfortably close together, as if whoever designed the neighborhood wanted to stuff as many people and postage-stamp lawns into it as possible.

"How did you find their address?" I ask as Anthony parks at the curb.

"Dennis."

Dennis is an old friend of Anthony's who works at the Wheatley Police Department.

"He just *gave* you their address?"

Anthony stiffens. "Why would I lie about that?"

"That's what I'm trying to figure out." I stop in my tracks. "You seem pretty defensive."

"It's nothing. Just forget it."

I hesitate then follow Anthony up the driveway. He's probably just paranoid about getting Dennis into trouble.

The Weavers' porch is a lawsuit waiting to happen. In contrast, a row of neatly groomed potted plants stands off to the side.

"What should I say?" My toes curl as Anthony rings the doorbell.

"Just say you're from the school."

A female voice explodes inside the house. "Don! There's someone at the door." After a beat: "The DOOR."

There's the sound of the door being unbolted, then it swings open. A tall thin old man with a pointed chin scrunches his eyes at us. He takes in my skirt and says, "I can't buy any cookies today. My wife's making 'em."

The man has a hearing aid, so I raise my voice. "Mr. Weaver?"

"Yep. Who's asking?"

"My name is Anne. This is Anthony. We were wondering if we could talk to you about your son."

A woman with white curls cropped closely to her head appears behind Mr. Weaver. "Is someone asking about Matty?"

Mr. Weaver shrugs as if he didn't hear a damn word I said.

Mrs. Weaver nudges him out of the way and gestures for us to come in.

I'll be the first to admit that the elderly and their ways seriously freak me out. Like my dad's Aunt Marjorie, who has couches in her living room covered in plastic dolls with freaky faces.

The Weavers' house mostly strikes me as empty—and sad. It smells faintly of lavender and cigarette smoke.

I sit stiffly on the couch. Anthony follows. The Weavers sit on the couch opposite us.

"I'm Joan, and this is Donald," Mrs. Weaver says. "What did you say your names were again?"

"Anne, and this is Anthony. We wanted to interview you for the Wheatley student newspaper," I say. "Sort of as a tribute to your son."

Joan's noses twitches, almost as if she smells bullshit. "It's been a long time since we heard from anyone at the school."

"I hope we're not intruding," I say.

"Oh, no, not at all." Joan looks at her husband. "We don't get lots of visitors, that's all. Matty was the only family we had."

I study Mrs. Weaver's face. Her cheeks are sunken, but she still went through the effort to put blush on them this morning. She must be in her seventies.

"I'm very sorry for your loss," I say.

Don Weaver surprises me by grunting. "We ain't buried him yet."

A timer goes off in the kitchen, punctuating the painful silence. Mrs. Weaver motions to get up.

"I'll get it." Her husband hoists himself off the couch and hobbles down the hall.

"I have to apologize if my husband seems abrasive," Mrs. Weavers tells us. "I don't think he ever let Matty go. Won't let me touch anything in his room. He's taken everything so hard, from the years of not getting answers, to losing our diner."

"What do I do with this tray?" Mr. Weaver bellows from the kitchen.

"The cooling rack!" Mrs. Weaver yells.

"What?"

"THE COOLING RACK!" Mrs. Weaver stands up. "Can I get you anything from the kitchen? What good timing that you picked today to visit! You can help us with the oatmeal raisin cookies."

"Actually, do you have a bathroom I could use? My stomach hurts," I add.

Mrs. Weaver points to the stairs. Foolproof tactic: Say you have a stomachache and head for the bathroom, and no one will ask questions. When Anthony and I are alone in the living room, he whispers, "Are you going to check his room out?"

"Yup."

He glances down the hall, where Joan disappeared. "Be quick."

I pad up the narrow carpeted stairs. The house is small; there are only two rooms and a bathroom on the upper level. One door is open, revealing a typical old-person bedroom with a black cat curled up on the quilted comforter. It blinks at me and rolls on its opposite side.

I make my way to the bedroom at the end of the hall. It's a little sad that there are no photographs of grandchildren on the walls. I push open the door to the second bedroom.

I feel as if I've stepped into the seventies, from the shag carpet to the wood paneling. I do a quick survey of the walls and suck in my breath.

The devil is watching me.

It's an enormous poster on the far wall, next to the closet. The creature's eyes are sunken, as if the sockets carved out of the metal skull. Its horns protrude from his mouth, curling up into the lake of flames that serves as the background.

motörhead

is spelled out in intricate black lettering.

It doesn't mean anything. Matt Weaver was into death metal, probably like every other teenage boy in 1981. I'm not here to search for animal guts or pentagrams or any of that nonsense. I don't know what exactly I'm looking for, but I know it has to be something the police may not have thought of.

The drawings. There are lots of them, mostly in charcoal pencil, tacked to the paneling. They all have the intensity of the sketch in my Brit-lit anthology, almost as if the drawings poured out of Matt on their own.

One in particular catches my attention. It's by the bedroom window. I walk toward it, struck by how, with only a pencil, he was able to capture the way light reflects off of snow.

"Mountains," A gruff voice says behind me.

Crap. Lie. Cry. Run. I turn around slowly. "I—I'm sorry, Mr. Weaver. I was looking for the bathroom and couldn't help but notice the drawings—"

"The mountains," Mr. Weaver repeats, as if I'm not even here. "Promised him we'd go skiing one day. Close the diner, take a real vacation."

His voice is far off in a way that tells me he was never able to take Matt skiing. I feel inexplicably sad and guilty all of a sudden.

"I'm so sorry for intruding," I begin, but Mr. Weaver holds up a hand.

"Look all you want." His tone has softer edges now. "Someone oughta." Before he turns to go back downstairs, he adds, "The one above the dresser is my favorite."

I almost can't bring myself to move once Mr. Weaver is gone. My hands are shaking at my sides. *Get it together, Anne.* I turn to the drawing above Matt Weaver's dresser and do a double take. I've seen it before.

Eve is even more beautiful in this drawing: Her hair is pulled away from her face, exposing round, sad eyes framed with thick lashes. Her mouth is heart shaped and her cheekbones high. I can't shake the feeling as if there's something familiar about her face, which is silly, because there's no way my mental version of Eve could match the one Matt had.

I run my fingers across her face, dying to understand Matt's fixation with *Paradise Lost*—or specifically, this scene. My fingers slide over an imperfection in the wall behind the picture.

I pause and feel the bump again. The shape has jagged edges.

There's something behind the drawing.

Downstairs, I hear the low murmur of voices. It's possible Mr. Weaver has already told his wife that I'm looking at the drawings, and even so, she might come up here to check for herself. I don't have a ton of time.

The drawing is held to the wall by thumbtacks. I wedge my fingernail underneath the one on the top corner and peel the drawing down far enough to see what's behind Eve's face.

Whatever it is, it's concealed by yellowed layers of tape. I peel them away until a key falls into my hand.

It's tarnished with a wire ring through the top. It's too small to fit in a door. My guess is it goes into a padlock. I slip the key into my pocket. How long have I been up here? I don't know if I have time to look for the matching lock without making the Weavers suspicious.

I open Matt's closet doors, wincing at the horrible squeaking sound as it slides along the tracks. There's not much inside: some clothes, board games, a record player, and some vinyl records and cassettes. Nothing with a lock.

There's nothing but carpet under his bed. If there isn't something with a padlock in Matt's nightstand, the police probably got to it first.

Sketchbooks abound inside the drawer. I flip through them quickly, but the most interesting thing I find is a hidden copy of *Playboy*. Nasty. I push the sketchbooks aside, estimating that I have about two more minutes before Mrs. Weaver decides to check on me. A glossy card sits at the bottom of the drawer.

I've only been to one funeral that I remember clearly, but I know this is a prayer card.

Sonia Rae Russo
1966–1981

Psalm 23 is printed underneath. I do a quick calculation in my head: Sonia Russo was fifteen when she died. I take a photo of the prayer card and hurry back downstairs.

Anthony is still on the couch, nibbling the edges of one of Mrs. Weaver's cookies. I can see from where I'm standing that the bottom is totally charred.

"Sorry about that." My voice wavers with nerves as I sit next to Anthony. From my spot on the couch, I see that he's hidden half-chewed cookies inside the napkin on his lap.

"Did you have any other questions about Matty?" Mrs. Weaver asks. "I was just telling your friend here about the lovely Charles River memorial his friends at Wheatley created for him."

I look over at Anthony, who uses a subtle nod to say he'll tell me about that later.

"It seems like Matt had a lot of friends on the crew team," I said. "Did he also have a girlfriend?"

"Oh, of course there was a girl." Joan's eyes twinkle. "He was a teenage boy, after all. Matty was nuts about her, but I don't think she ever returned his feelings."

Sonia Russo? "Do you remember her name? I'd love to talk to her."

Anthony nudges me.

"For the article," I add.

Joan gives me a wry smile. "I'm afraid she's passed away. I just thank the Lord Matty never had to see what happened to her."

I lean forward, resting my elbows on my knees. "What do you mean?"

"She was that senator's wife," Mrs. Weaver says. "The one who was in that awful car wreck."

Cynthia Westbrook. Without looking, I feel Anthony react to this piece of information next to me.

"We'd better get going," he says, pulling me out of my vortex of disbelief. *Cynthia Westbrook. Alexis's mother.*

"Thank you for everything," I say to Mrs. Weaver on the way out.

"Of course, dear." She actually hugs me, which makes me feel a million different types of awful. Her bony fingers grasp my shoulders. "When you're done with that article, send me a copy, if you don't mind. I'd like to read it."

"Why do you look like you just saw a ghost?" Anthony asks once we're back in the car.

"Because I think Steven Westbrook's dead wife is Matt Weaver's Eve."

CHAPTER
TWELVE

Anthony idles by the post office curb while I Google *Cynthia Westbrook* on my phone.

There are two popular images of her that come up: a wedding portrait of her and Steven Westbrook, and the picture of Cynthia with Alexis and her younger brother.

Cynthia Westbrook was good-looking. Not good-looking in the polite way you'd describe Alexis, who actually looks like a horse, but pretty. She has the same defined cheekbones and fair, freckle-free complexion as Matthew Weaver's Eve.

Another picture captures my attention, even though Cynthia isn't in it. A man in a suit with his back to the camera holds the hand of a little blond girl. She can't be more than five, and she's wearing a black velvet dress. A stuffed dog with floppy ears is tucked under her arm.

Steven Westbrook attends funeral of wife and son
with daughter, Alexis

I have to look away. It's a picture capable of making an emotionally castrated person cry. Anger ignites in me, despite the fact that the little girl in the photo is nothing like the wench I know. How could Steven Westbrook hurt Alexis by having an affair with her friend's mother? The man in the photo is holding his daughter's hand as if she's all he has in the world and he would do anything to protect her. I want to know what happened to that man—and if he's capable of murdering a classmate.

"What's the matter?" Anthony asks.

I close the tab with the photo. "Nothing."

"Is it her?"

"I think so."

"This sort of complicates things," Anthony says. "Matt Weaver had the hots for the senator's future wife. Could be the crew-team angle is completely off."

"You're thinking maybe this was a jealousy thing?" Disbelief creeps into my voice.

"Don't you watch *48 Hours*? Love triangles end in murder all the time."

"But we don't even know if there *was* a Matt Weaver–Cynthia–Steve Westbrook love triangle," I say.

Anthony shrugs. "Guess we'll have to find out. Who's up next out of the guys in the photo?"

"Coach Tretter is right under my nose. And I can probably get to Travis Shepherd through his son, Casey."

"Anyone else?"

I notice the hardness to the way he says it first. Then I move my gaze to his hands, tapping out an annoyed beat on the steering wheel. I straighten in my seat. "Did I do something?"

Anthony's jawline hardens. "Depends. Did you not tell me your boyfriend's dad is in the picture on purpose?"

"How did you—"

"Joan Weaver. Said some guy named Conroy was one of the people who donated money for Matt's memorial. Said he has a son at Wheatley who's probably our age."

Crap. Anthony must have seen the name BRENT CONROY

pop up on my phone when he texted me earlier. "I was going to tell you."

Anthony finally looks at me. I search his expression frantically for a sign he's not mad. "Is that what this is all about? You want to make sure you can bring this guy home to daddy?"

"That's not what this is about." It's a lie, of course. As much as I want to know the truth because I'm convinced the crew team had something to do with it, I *need* to know Brent's dad didn't.

"Don't lie to me," Anthony says. "The Weaver case—this case—it *means* something to me. I grew up watching and reading everything I could on it, thinkin' that someday maybe I'd be an FBI agent and maybe reopen the case. I know it sounds stupid coming from me, since I couldn't even get hired as a traffic cop now. But I used to want to be something."

I don't know what to say. I'm surprised he's sharing something so personal with me, in spite of all the weirdness between us. Brent has never told me anything like that. I have no idea what his dreams are or what he really wants, besides being able to eat an entire sleeve of Oreos without going into diabetic shock.

It's perilous territory—comparing Brent and Anthony like this. Especially since I can't picture a version of my life without Brent in it. Anthony has been missing for long enough that I know I can be happy without him. Better off, even.

But he's the only person who understands why I can't let the Matt Weaver thing go. Why I can't let anything go, really.

If this is going to work—us seeing each other again, poking around into the case—I have to let Anthony go. Or at least the version of him—feverish, kissing me, wanting me—that I've been hanging on to all this time.

Brent and the guys are hiking when I get back to the dorms, so I spend the rest of the afternoon doing homework. I want to find out if Sonia Russo was a student at Wheatley, but Student Records and Registration isn't open until Monday anyway. After dinner, I agree to watch TV with Remy, Kelsey, and April in the Amherst common room. I guess the only mystery I'll be attempting to solve tonight is why otherwise intelligent girls are obsessed with re-runs of *The Bachelor*.

When April brings up the subject of spring formal after-parties, Kelsey mumbles something about being cold and going to get a sweatshirt from their room.

"She thinks I'm mad at her." Remy pulls her knees up to her chest, as if she wants her corner of the couch to swallow her whole.

"You weren't exactly enthusiastic when she told you Cole asked her to the formal," April says.

"I said *'Great!'*" Remy's voice slides up an octave. "What did you guys want, balloons and a dance?"

"She obviously wants you to tell her that it's okay, Rem." April rolls her eyes.

They bicker some more, with me sitting between them, cracking open pistachio nuts. Occasionally, they try to get me involved, but I keep my mouth shut, because I can't keep listening to this shit and giving my opinions without charging eighty dollars an hour.

"Hey," I cut in. "Where are we going for the after-party, anyway?"

Remy's lips told together. "We have a few options."

She says it in a way that makes me think we're going to wind up in the boys' dorm, sipping wine coolers Sebastian smuggled in.

"Usually Cole has a party at his family's condo on Beacon Hill," April says. "But his dad is living there now, so . . ."

"Sebastian said we can use his family's boat," Remy says.

"Ugh." April makes a face. "It'll be too cold for that."

I'm fairly certain Sebastian's boat is heated, because when rich people say *boat* they really mean *big-ass yacht*. "What are our other options?"

April shrugs. "Casey Shepherd is having a party."

This gets my attention: Being inside Casey's house could mean collecting valuable intel on Travis Shepherd. "Why don't we go to that?"

"We never really hang out with Casey. The guys think he's a tool," April says.

I catch Kelsey look over at Remy, who is silent as she twirls a lock of hair around her finger.

"Come on," I plead. "We always hang out with just us and the guys. It's like we're hobbits or something."

"You've been spending *way* too much time with Brent," Remy grumbles.

"Also," April says, "I don't know if we're invited."

"That won't be a problem," I say. Because I'm going to *get* us invited.

They should really know how I operate by now.

The guy at Student Records and Registration doesn't seem happy to see me. He barely looks up from his computer as he says, "What can I help you with?"

"I was wondering if you could tell me the year a former student graduated," I say. "But she would have gone here thirty years ago."

"She should still be in the system." The guy's eyebrows knit together. He looks as if he wants to ask me what the hell I need this information for at eight on a Monday morning.

"Great. Her name is Sonia Russo," I say.

I apply some lip salve as he types the name into his computer. "Are you sure she was a student here?" He asks. "I can't find her."

"Thanks. That's all I needed to know."

I'm out of there before he can ask any more questions. I text Anthony on my way to class:

Sonia Russo never went to Wheatley. . . . Think you can pull a few strings?

I have to do deep breathing exercises before British literature. It's the first time Brent and I will be alone since Thursday night. We won't really be able to talk or anything, but still. I need to make things right with him, even though he doesn't know something is wrong.

When Fowler isn't looking, Brent puts his hand my knee. He traces up my leg, far enough to make me blush and nearly choke when I'm called on to read a verse from the anthology.

"I miss you," I say when class is over. He pulls me in so our hips are touching.

"Now you see why I hate boarding school so much. No time to be alone."

"Guess we'll have to get creative. What are you doing Saturday night?"

Brent's eyes move to my hands, which are playing with his tie. "We have this thing for crew. But I'm all yours after that."

"What type of thing?" I try to keep my voice innocent.

Brent shrugs. "Just a bonding thing we do every year."

Frustration pulls at me. Why can't he tell me? "Brent. You guys aren't doing anything dangerous, right?"

"Of course not. What makes you think that?"

That awful photo. The way Tretter talked about The Drop. Everything. "You guys are always so secretive."

Brent traces the space between my thumb and forefinger. It would feel amazing if he wasn't avoiding my eyes. "It's just this tradition. The secrecy is part of it."

"I just don't want you to get in trouble. Or worse."

Brent looks at me as if he finally hears what I've been dancing around. "Worse? It's all harmless."

I wish I could tell him why I can't believe him, and that I'm not being a paranoid girlfriend. That his team is hiding something. His father could be hiding something.

And worse, I have to consider that Brent could be hiding something, too.

It's not hard to find Casey Shepherd after classes: Practically the whole school is on the quad, soaking up as much afternoon sun as possible before club meetings and sports practices begin. Casey is sitting under the giant oak tree—prime hanging-out real estate— with Bea, Vera, and a dark-skinned guy with a closely shaved head.

They're immersed in conversation as I pass them. I hang by a bike rack off the main path, pretending I'm waiting for someone. From the corner of my eye, I see Casey look up and notice me. Across the quad, I spot Ms. C leaving the humanities building. She's not alone—Dr. Muller walks with her, carrying a stack of textbooks. Ms. C leans in and says something in his ear. They laugh, and he touches her arm. Good for Ms. C—I appreciate a girl who moves fast when she sees something she wants.

I look back over at the group under the oak tree. I casually head for the dorms, but I make sure to lock eyes with Casey.

He smiles and waves me over. "Hey. How's it going?"

Casey makes room for me to sit. I kneel on the grass next to him.

"Guys, you know Anne, right?"

Bea gives me a stiff smile. "You live on the third floor."

Vera waves to me. The guy nods. "I'm Erik."

"So you're from New York," Casey says.

"Yup. Manhattan."

"That's pretty sweet," Casey says. "Columbia tried to recruit me to row, but I'm still holding out for the naval academy."

I have to press my fingers to my mouth as I nod politely, because I'm not sure what's funnier: the thought of Casey trying to find his way around Harlem, or picturing him being forced to shave his Calvin Klein locks.

"The naval academy is watching him row next week," Bea informs me. "There's no way he's not getting in."

Casey gives Bea an *Oh, stop it* nudge with his shoulder, and I have to swallow the urge to vomit everywhere. I force a smile instead. "Do you know where you're going to college, Bea?"

She lights up. Clearly I've touched on her favorite topic. "Well, Princeton is my first choice, but Wellesley offered me a full scholarship—"

"Wellesley is a lesbian school," Casey cuts in. "You're not going there."

Bea's lips fold into a line, but she doesn't argue. I stare at Casey, suppressing the urge to blurt *Controlling douche says what?*

His misinterprets my blank stare as me checking him out. Casey smiles and nods to the Brit-lit textbook by my knees. "Do you have Fowler?"

"Yep. Does he ever . . . lighten up?"

Erik shakes his head as Casey says, "Not really."

Bea stares us down. "Actually, he's a really great teacher if you pay attention to his lectures."

And if Bea paid attention to anything, she'd know that it's impossible to start a sentence with the word *actually* and not sound like an obnoxious bitch. I return her frosty smile. "Guess I should quit snorting coke and running Ponzi schemes from my laptop during class."

I think I've sufficiently horrified her and Vera, but Casey is laughing beside me. "Trust me, the only thing that matters is his final. Half of it's on *Paradise Lost*."

"Wonderful."

"Little secret: Get *The Satanic Epic* by Neil Forsyth. I read it and I *slew* his final."

As strong as his jerk vibes are, I have to respect a guy who uses the proper past tense for the word *slay*. "Thanks for the tip," I say.

As I say I have to meet my friends and I get up, I think I hear Casey whisper to Erik something disgusting about giving me a tip anytime I want.

Great. At least I know what I'm dealing with now.

In the mailroom that afternoon, there's a slip of paper waiting for me. I have a package. I already got a few for my birthday a couple of weeks ago: a tea infuser from Chelsea, boots from my mother, and an SAT-prep book from my dad. So I wonder who would be sending me something now.

There's no return address on the small brown parcel. Somehow, I don't think there's a birthday gift inside. I wait until I get to my room to open it.

I slide my finger beneath the wrapping and feel plastic ridges. A cassette tape? I peel the rest of the paper away, revealing an unlabeled VHS tape. I turn it over in my hands, looking for some sort of note.

I find myself wandering to Remy's room. Her door is open and she's standing in front of her mirror, fixing her hair for the SGA meeting.

"Where can I find a VCR?" I say from the doorway.

Remy blinks at me. "Um, the nineties?"

"No, really."

"I think the first-floor common room has one," she says around the bobby pin between her lips.

I take two steps down the hall before convincing myself to turn back. The first-floor common room is practically Amherst Command Central: There are always meetings in there, or stupid "social events" where underclassmen can make their own ice cream sundaes while listening to people like Bea Hartley convince them to volunteer for her senior service project.

The only way I can watch this video is after everyone goes to bed. But that's okay, because I'm no stranger to the night.

I'm lying on my stomach, Spark-Notes-ing *The Faerie Queene* when Darlene starts knocking on doors down the hall. "Lights out," she says each time. Technically, we're allowed to stay up as late as we want, as long as we turn our room lights and music off by eleven on weeknights.

Finally, there's a soft knock on my door. "Anne. Light's out."

"'Night, Darlene." I turn my lamp off and listen to her footsteps fade down the hall. I watch the minutes tick by on my phone until Darlene's door closes. I can barely keep my eyes open, but at the same time, I can't stop thinking about the video.

I finish up my homework and wait until twelve-thirty before slipping the video in the front of my NYU sweatshirt and heading downstairs. The only light in the hall is coming from the bathroom. It's quiet enough that I can hear a toilet flush. I use the stairwell to go directly down to the lounge so I won't get caught roaming the halls in the middle of the night.

The only sound in the first-floor lounge is the whir of the refrigerator. The full moon outside creates a small circle of light in the middle of the room. I use it to find my way to the television.

There are a million different devices plugged into the TV. With one hand, I hold my phone up for light, and with the other, I switch around a few wires to get the VCR to work. It swallows my cassette, the clicking sounds inside matching my heartbeat as the tape settles into place.

White lines flick across the screen. I quickly turn the volume down so Emma can't hear anything from the RA desk down the hall in the lobby. I kneel on the carpet, tucking my feet under my legs, as the image on the screen loads mid-shot, as if the first few moments of the program got cut off.

A man walks toward the camera. The woods behind him could be the woods anywhere.

"Join us tonight, as Dateline investigates a decades-old mystery."

On the bottom of the screen, a title flashes: INTO THIN AIR: THE MATTHEW WEAVER STORY.

The muscles in the small of my back constrict. Who sent me this?

The shot on the screen cuts to a view of downtown Wheatley.

The camera quality isn't very good, and there's no Dunkin' Donuts on Main Street, so I figure this episode has to be at least five or ten years old.

The camera zooms in on a dumpy-looking diner on the corner of Main Street. In the window, there's a newspaper article with Matt Weaver's picture next to it. The headline says VIGIL HELD FOR MISSING WHEATLEY STUDENT. The still image fades into a shot of a river, as the host explains Matt's background: the only son of local business owners, the first in his family to attend high school, crew-team champion. I curl onto the lounge couch.

"On March eighteenth, 1981, Weaver attended his classes at the Wheatley School. He skipped dinner, telling his friends he had a headache. Weaver went back to his dormitory and slept until eleven, when he woke up his roommate, Blaine Goldsmith."

The recording of a man's voice plays. *"He told me he'd be right back, so I went to sleep. Sure, it was a little weird that he was dressed and everything, but Matty was always coming and going like that."*

The screen fills up with a still of the forest behind the school as the host speaks again.

"That's the last anyone saw Matthew Weaver alive."

I fast-forward through a commercial break. The next scene opens with the host sitting across from an older man. The caption on the screen reads OFFICER PATRICK CARROLL, FORMER DETECTIVE.

"Mr. Carroll, what do you think happened to Matt Weaver?"

"I think he was murdered."

The sound of voices pulls me away from the TV. I jump up and shut the VCR off and wait for footsteps in the hall. *Just say you were sleepwalking.*

The hall and lounge are quiet, though. That's when I see them— the shadowy figures outside the window.

I drop to my knees and clutch my arms over my chest. Remind myself no one can see *in* the lounge windows. Only out. It's impossible someone was watching me.

I wait for the voices to fade away, but they get louder. Someone is yelling. I grasp the windowsill and look out onto the steps between Aldridge and Amherst.

There are three guys standing out there by the basement door to Aldridge. In the light of the moon, I get a glimpse of Casey Shepherd's face. He looks like he could kill someone.

I crank the window open the inch it will allow, praying the guys outside won't notice. I peer out in time to see Casey shove a short guy with a bowl haircut. Zach Walton.

"You show this to anyone, Walton, and we're all done. You hear that? Done." Casey shoves Zach again, who doubles over, arms wrapped around his stomach.

"Dude, this is serious." I can't see his face, but I recognize Cole's voice. He motions for Zach to bend over and pull up his shirt. Cole uses the light from his phone to show Casey what's on Zach's back: an oozing burn that's turning a color no burn should be. I cover my mouth to hold in a gag.

"He has to go to the infirmary," Cole says. Casey curses and grabs Zach by the collar of his flannel shirt.

"I'm coming with you," Casey says in his face. "That way there's no confusion over who did this to you. Who did this to you, Walton?" Casey gives him a shake.

"I did this to myself." Zach's voice is weak. Casey drops him. Before they disappear around the corner, Cole yells something at Casey. I only catch a piece of it: "Told you this would happen again".

CHAPTER
THIRTEEN

Zach Walton looks like he's going to cry all throughout calculus, so I feel lousy for cornering him after class. When I smile at him, his face scrunches up like a kid who knows he's going to be spanked. Our last conversation—and *only* conversation—was not very pleasant for Zach, since Alexis Westbrook had manipulated him into sending me a threatening rose-gram on Valentine's Day.

"What do you want?" He pushes his Buddy Holly glasses up his face. Zach is a classic postpubescent disaster: greasy mushroom cut, forehead speckled with acne. I feel a motherly urge to clean him up a bit.

"Looks like you're in a bit of pain there, Zach."

He tenses up. "I'm fine."

I come at him with a finger, like I'm going to poke him in the back. He jumps. "What the *hell*?"

"Why would you let them do that to you?" I hiss.

Zach ignores me as he picks up his messenger bag, letting it droop pathetically across the crook of his arm. I help him pull it up over his shoulder, careful not to touch his back.

"Thanks," he mumbles, trying to wiggle past me.

"Hey. How did they do that to you?"

Zach doesn't stop. I catch up with him in the hallway, even though my next class is in the opposite direction. "I saw! Last night, from the Amherst lounge."

"What? Were you spying or something?" he mutters.

"Look. I know we got off on the wrong foot," I say. "I think what you did was stupid, and you probably think I'm a bit of a psycho."

Zach doesn't disagree. His eyebrows knit together. "What did you see?"

"Enough to know you're insane if you think being on the crew team is worth *that*." I point to Zach's back. He flinches, as if he's still not sure I'm going to hurt him.

"It was an accident," he deadpans.

I grab Zach's shoulder and readjust him so he's facing me. "Really? You think I, of all people, am going to believe that?"

Zach's eyes flick to the right, then to mine. "Why do you care? It was just a dumb . . . thing. It's my fault I got hurt."

"What did they do?" I demand.

"There's no *they*." He breaks from me and hobbles away. I clench my fists and follow, even though I know he's not going to give me anything else.

"Okay, no *they*. So was it Shep?"

Zach freezes, as if the name were an arrow in his spine.

"He's the ringleader, right?" I say.

"Just leave me alone," Zach says over his shoulder before he starts to walk away from me again.

"You might not be as lucky next time."

Zach slows and turns his head to me.

"The Drop." I say it just quietly enough that we could be talking about tomorrow's calc test. "That's the last part of initiation, right?"

Zach meets my gaze for the first time. There's a new emotion on his face. Surprise. It hits me: He doesn't know about The Drop. Isn't that the point?

"Whatever they have planned for you guys," I whisper, "I think it's going to be really bad."

He looks over his shoulder at the group gathering outside his classroom. Despite the fact no one seems to be paying attention to us, he lowers his voice. "I don't know what you're talking about."

He ducks into his next classroom before I can tell him I know he's lying.

CHAPTER
FOURTEEN

During breakfast the next morning, Kelsey is trying to convert us all to vegetarianism, when Shep comes over to our table.

He has the type of presence that automatically shuts people up. Everyone is silent as he stands behind Cole. Shep smiles at me—at least I'm pretty sure it's me—and sticks out his hand for Cole to slap. Cole does so without smiling. In fact, none of the guys look happy to see Casey Shepherd.

"Got something for you," Casey says to me. I sense Brent stiffen as Casey pulls a book from his messenger bag.

"*The Satanic Epic*," I read off the cover. "Hey, thanks."

"No problem." He slaps Brent on the shoulder before winking at me and heading back to his table.

Everyone immediately snaps their heads toward me. I shrug.

"I talked to him about Fowler's class the other day. He said this would help with the final." *Play dumb.* "Do you guys not like him or something?"

When no one answers, April pipes up, "He's nice."

Brent snorts. "Yeah. He's perfectly nice. Until there aren't girls around, and he acts like the dickweasel he really is."

"He seems pretty interested in you," Brent says after a beat. He's not looking at me.

"Lots of guys are interested in Anne," Murali laughs. "We hear things."

I roll my eyes. "It's just because I'm new. It'll wear off. Plus, it's not like that. Casey's got a girlfriend."

"That's never stopped him before," Cole says.

The table goes quiet, and I look up from my breakfast. Cole is staring at Remy, and the look on her face says he was staring at her when he made the comment about Casey.

Remy's face falls as she waits for someone to defend her. I have no idea what's going on, and before I can jump in, she throws her napkin down on her tray and gets up. Within seconds of her storming off, Kelsey and April follow.

"So," Brent says. "How about that bacon shortage?"

Cole mumbles something about needing to turn something into Robinson and gets up. Murali sighs and heads for the juice machine with his empty glass.

It's just me, Brent, and Phil left at the table. "What the hell was that about?" I ask.

"They're always like this." Brent looks to Phil for affirmation. "They're just usually better at hiding it."

"I don't know, man," Phil says in his drowsy, California-esque drawl. "I'm just gonna sit here with my peanuts and hope it's all a phase."

When I was six, I wouldn't leave the house or do anything without wearing my Cinderella costume. *That* was a phase. This is . . . I don't know what it is.

But I know I don't like it.

When my last class is over, I have a text from Anthony dated almost an hour ago.

Call me when u get out

I head back to my room without stopping, hoping Anthony

isn't at work or something by now. I'm relieved when I hear his voice after the fourth ring.

"You like my package?" he asks.

I choke. On nothing. Just air. Anthony waits for me to stop coughing. "Anne . . . the video I sent you."

"*I know.*" Thank God he's not here to see how red my face is. "I just had a tickle in my throat."

"Anyway, I got something on Sonia Russo," he says.

I collapse onto my bed and kick off my flats. "Already?"

"I have friends in important places. Sonia Russo died thirty years ago, probably."

"Probably?"

"They never found her body. She had a heart condition, though, so she would have been dead in a few months without treatment." Anthony pauses. "She went missing in January the same year Matt Weaver did."

I take a couple of seconds to process this. "But . . . if it's an open case, why was it so hard to find anything on her?"

"No father, drug-addict mother. She was living with a foster family when she went missing. They didn't even report her gone until three days later."

"So no one cared about her," I say. "I wonder how Matt Weaver knew her."

"She spent almost two years with the foster family in Wheatley. If she went to school, she would have gone to Thomas Hutch Junior High with him. They might have been friends."

He's quiet in a way that lets me know he's thinking the same thing I am. "It can't be a coincidence they went missing the same year."

"I don't know," Anthony says. "Something feels different about her case."

I prop up my pillow behind my back so I can lean against the wall. "What do you mean?"

"They're pretty sure her foster parents had something to do with it, even if they couldn't prove anything. The foster father,

Dwight Miller, has been in and out of prison for years. Bunch of different domestic-assault charges."

He says it *"chaages,"* as if there were no *r.* I used to think his accent was funny, but now it's one of those sounds that makes me feel like I'm home. Like my dog scratching at my bedroom door, or the oven timer in my kitchen going off.

"So what have you got?" Anthony asks.

"I'm working on Shepherd. His son goes to school here." My gaze lands on the book on my desk. *The Satanic Epic.* "I think I'm making progress."

My stomach folds into itself as I think of Brent. Anthony will think I should try to get more information on the Conroys, and I don't want to believe that Brent's dad was involved. Not yet.

"I'll ask around town about Sonia," Anthony says as there's a knock at my door.

"Hey. I've got to go." I nearly drop my phone as I scramble to look through the peephole. Remy is on the other side of my door. "Let me know if you find anything."

I hang up. I have to take a deep breath before I let Remy, even though there's totally nothing wrong with talking to Anthony. Remy tries to smile, but her eyes and nose are red.

"Are you okay?" I ask, shutting the door behind her.

She starts to nod, then shakes her head. When she lets the tears out, I put my arms around her. Remy squeezes me, her body shaking with sobs. I give her an awkward pat on the back. I'm the world's worst hugger. Maybe it's an only-child thing, because Cole gives pretty awful hugs, too.

Cole. This is what this is about.

"Talk to me." I sit on the bed and pat the spot next to me. Remy sits and wipes her face with both hands.

"Casey Shepherd is the only guy I've been with besides Cole," she sniffles. "It was freshman year, and he said he and Bea were broken up. They're always on and off. . . . He was my first, and I hate myself for it. Cole was the only person I trusted enough to tell."

I know this is supposed to be about Remy, but I feel guilty she's telling me now. Almost as if I don't deserve her trust. "Don't ever say you hate yourself for that. You know what I hate? The idea that we're supposed to hate ourselves for having sex."

"No one's going to see it that way. Bea already hates me, and if this gets out . . ." Remy chokes back a sob. "How could Cole humiliate me in front of everyone like that?"

"It's because he's being a huge man-baby over the Phil thing," I say.

"He has no freaking right." Remy is moving from depressed to pissed off. "He's been with other girls since we broke up. I'll *kill* him if Bea finds out and tells everyone I'm a home wrecker."

"You won't have to. I'll kill him for you."

Remy smiles at me and blinks tears away. "I don't know what I'd do without you."

I meet her gaze just as her face turns serious. "Anne, just promise me you won't hate me. If they start saying stuff about me."

"You definitely don't have to worry about that," I say. 'Let them talk'—that's my motto. "Let's make some tea."

Remy is quiet as she gets up and looks through my mug collection. She picks up my favorite one with a Henry VIII picture that disappears on the outside when you put hot liquid inside. There's something else she's not telling me—I know it by the way her nose is twitching like a rabbit's. She always does that when she's uncomfortable.

I want to probe her, to find out what she's not telling me. She's stubborn, but with a little dedication, I'm also capable of getting people to spill just about anything.

But she's not the one I should be using that skill on. When Remy's not looking, I open the copy of *The Satanic Epic* sitting on my bed. Once I get close enough to Casey to figure out if his father was involved with Matt Weaver's disappearance, I'll have to teach Casey that it's not nice to treat girls like garbage.

CHAPTER
FIFTEEN

The next day is especially painful. Remy isn't talking to Cole, Cole is still pissed at Phil, Kelsey thinks Remy is mad at her for going to the formal with Cole, and everyone else does everything they can to avoid the awkwardness of it all, even if that means getting their meals to go.

On the plus side, I get to spend more time with Brent when he's not at crew practice. We study for Fowler's exam Thursday night until around nine, when he has to get back to the dorm and give himself an insulin injection. After he leaves, I sneak down to the laundry room with my basket. It's just for show, though.

I double-check all of the machines to make sure they're empty and no one will be back to collect their clothes. I push the bookcase away and slip through the tunnel entrance.

When Anthony and I first discovered the room full of student archives, I looked for Matt Weaver's file out of curiosity. Someone moved it. Or destroyed it.

But the other men in the photo should still have active files. I know that because I looked through Steven Westbrook's a couple of months ago.

I bypass the crew team office/hangout and head for the student archives. The door is still unlocked from the last time I picked it.

The filing cabinets toward the end of the alphabet are the closest to the door, so I start by pulling Lawrence Tretter's and Travis Shepherd's files. It's all pretty boring stuff: transcripts, letters of recommendation from professors, alumni donation records. Apparently Larry Tretter was on academic probation for most of his time at Wheatley, and he only got into two colleges: the University of Massachusetts at Lowell, and Fairfield University in Connecticut. He chose Lowell.

There's a copy of Tretter's acceptance letter and a copy of a newspaper article at the back of the file. I resist the urge to crumble it and throw it against the wall. I could be swaddled in my microfiber sheets, asleep right now, instead of in a dank basement rifling through useless information. I stifle a yawn and read the newspaper article. It's dated 1980:

TRETTER, SHEPHERD, CONROY, AND WESTBROOK LEAD
MEN'S 4 TEAM TO VICTORY

The men's 4 team . . . The first article I read about Matt Weaver said *he* was on the men's 4 team. I replace Tretter's file and flip through Shepherd's. The same news article is tucked at the back of the file, after Shepherd's acceptance letters (he got into Yale, Dartmouth, Harvard, UPenn, and Georgetown). But there's another article after that. This one is dated 1981.

I ignore the cold biting at my fingers and hold it up to the light from my phone.

WHEATLEY MEN'S 4 ROWS TO CHAMPIONSHIPS

The headline is followed by a picture of Pierce Conroy, Steven Westbrook, Travis Shepherd, and Matt Weaver.

According to the caption, Matt Weaver replaced Larry Tretter on the men's 4 team.

I tuck the clipping in the pocket, my thoughts swirling. Losing your spot on the men's 4 relay team sounds like a good enough reason to hate the new kid. What if Tretter was angry enough to murder Matt over it? Like that crazy mom in Texas who killed a high school cheerleader because she became captain instead of her daughter.

I close the archives door behind me and head down the tunnel. The sound of voices freezes me to where I'm standing.

They're male voices. *Security guards?* They don't come down here often. But of course they chose tonight.

The voices come closer, cornering me. Crap. I squeeze my eyes shut and flatten my back against the wall, praying they don't sweep their lights over the pitch-dark curve where I'm hiding.

"Cole, get your ass out of my face." The voice is unfamiliar. But not old enough to be a security guard's.

"Get your face out of my ass. Who has the flashlight?"

"Only use it if you have to." Brent's voice makes my heartbeat accelerate. "We can't risk being seen down here."

"By who?" This time it's Casey Shepherd's voice. "We're the only ones who know about the tunnels, and Coach said the guards wouldn't be down here tonight."

I freeze, waiting for Brent to tell him he's wrong, that I've been down here many times before. He doesn't, and I swallow away guilt for doubting him.

If they say anything else, it's drowned out by the sound of something scraping against concrete. Something heavy. I peer around the corner.

It's dark; I can only make out the outlines of four bodies because one of them is using his iPhone for a small radius of light. The fourth figure is larger than the others, even Cole. There's only one guy I know of at Wheatley that's his size: Casey's friend Erik.

I strain my eyes to see them disappearing into a room across the hall. At their feet, I can see large blocks of some sort. Their voices are almost indiscernible. But I know what room they slipped into.

The crew team lair where I broke the picture frame. I break a sweat as I wait for them to notice the glass on the floor, get angry that someone trespassed into their hangout. A minute or so passes before they emerge from the room.

"Well, this was fun," Casey snaps, closing the door behind him. "Let's do it again real soon."

"I'm sorry. Did you have a better idea?" Brent asks. "Besides trying to sneak six cinder blocks in our rooms while Kyle is on duty."

"He wouldn't say anything to me," Casey retorts. "Not after I saw him at a movie with another dude."

"That doesn't mean anything," Cole says.

Casey laughs. "Sure it doesn't, Mr. I-Like-When-Girls-Put-Their-Finger—"

"Can you just shut the hell up so we can get out of here?" Brent says.

"What's your problem, Conroy?" Casey's voice again. "Think you'd be getting plenty of your own, dating the hottest girl in the junior class."

My face heats up. *Really, I'm flattered, Casey, but you're a swine.*

"Don't talk to me about Anne," Brent snaps.

"Why? Haven't fucked her yet?" Casey sounds gleeful, like a sadistic little boy standing over a bunch of ants with a magnifying glass. "Or do you prefer to sit back and watch? I heard your dad was into some freaky shit like that in his day—"

Casey is cut off by the sound of scuffling. One of the guys yells, and I break out into a cold sweat, picturing Brent's hands around Casey's neck.

"Knock it off, Shep." I'm relieved to hear Cole's voice. "Save the asshole routine for when we face Ellison Prep, all right?"

My heartbeat reaches my ears as the footsteps come closer to me. It's dumb luck I didn't wear perfume tonight, or else they would for sure be able to tell I'm hiding. Their voices disappear around the corner leading back to Aldridge, and I allow myself to breathe again.

I should run to Amherst and never look back, but I can't help it—I stop at the crew team room. The door is locked. Either the guys have a key or someone on the team is as skilled as I am. I don't appreciate the thought.

Once I'm inside, I shine my light on the wall where I'd left the photo I'd knocked down. In its place is a stack of cinder blocks.

The glass from the broken frame is gone. Swept up.

Someone definitely knows I was here.

No-no-no. I yank open the filing cabinet where I found the letter about the 1980 hazing. *Please still be here.*

"Crap." I resist the urge to kick the filing cabinet. Someone has erased all evidence of Wheatley Rowing. The drawer is empty except for a manila envelope that wasn't there the other night.

My brain screams at me not to touch it.

Leave. Get the hell out!

I've never believed in out-of-body experiences. But I can't remember picking up the envelope and opening it. It's as if someone else took over my hands and made me do it, while I looked on, trying not to scream at the photo inside.

It's of Isabella's face, white as snow. Her lips are an ashy gray. The rest of the photo is red. So, so much red.

The wound in her neck is so deep that it's a miracle Dr. Harrow didn't take her head clean off.

CHAPTER
SIXTEEN

Occam's razor: It's a theory of logic stating that the simplest explanation to a problem is usually the best one. It's my father's worst nightmare in the courtroom. Example: His client's wife is killed, and the guy doesn't have an alibi. Occam's razor says the best explanation is the husband did it. It's *always* the husband.

What I know: Someone is trying to stop me from digging into the crew team's past.

What I wish I didn't know: Brent and the other guys were in the tunnels earlier tonight.

The simplest explanation is that they were the ones who left me the photo.

I left the photo in the drawer. How could I bring that into this room, the room she and I shared together before Dr. Harrow did that to her? What kind of sick son of a bitch could do that to a person and claim it was an accident?

I hug my pillow to my stomach, hoping it will block out my nausea. The picture was obviously a crime-scene photo—one that the public wasn't supposed to see. The only people who should have access to it are the police, the prosecutors and attorneys, and maybe the media, if someone from the first two leaked it.

Cole's father is the attorney general of Massachusetts. Brent's owns the biggest newspaper in Boston.

Have I completely underestimated what the guys are capable of? I close my eyes and picture the burns on Zach Walton's back. The cinder blocks the guys were dragging through the tunnel, to do God knows what with during The Drop.

If that's how they treat their own recruits, I doubt they'd think twice about using a photo of Isabella's corpse to scare an outsider.

It's the simplest explanation: Someone on the team left that photo for me to find.

I wake up in a pool of blood. In a panic, I search my body for the source. The pain never comes. Just fear.

I'm staring down the barrel of Dr. Harrow's gun. I look up, but a black mask covers his face. He says nothing as he pulls the trigger this time.

When I sit up, my body is wracked with chills and a cold sweat. I have to get out of bed and turn on the light to make sure I'm awake for real this time. Still shaking, I look out my door's peephole into the hallway. Everything is quiet.

But I never fall back asleep.

My terror eventually evolves into anger. Whoever left me the photo wanted to scare me, but I've been nightmare-free for so long that now I'm just pissed off and determined to figure who could have gotten their hands on the photo.

By breakfast time, I have a plan. Which absolutely does not involve telling Anthony what happened last night. I don't know if he knows about the crime-scene photo, but I'm not going to be the one to tell him.

Regardless, the photo qualifies for responsible adult involvement, and since I can't exactly go to Dean Snaggletooth or anyone who works at school, there's really one person left.

Anthony gave me Dennis's cell phone number a couple of months ago, for emergencies. Like my personal line to the cops, without having to call 911. I walk to breakfast with the girls and tell them to save me a seat; I have to call my mom quickly.

Dennis picks up on the fourth ring with a gravelly voice that suggests I woke him up. "Dennis. Who's this?"

"Hi. It's Anne. Dowling," I add. "I'm, um . . ."

"Yeah, I remember you," he says. "What's up? Everything okay?"

The question lands on me like a thousand-pound weight. *Don't think about what you saw. Just describe it.* "It's not an emergency or anything, but I found something at school. Something . . . I don't know how someone could have been able to get."

Dennis is quiet. "You mean like a gun?"

"No, nothing like that." I sigh. "A picture. A really, really bad picture. Of Isabella."

"Shiiiit," Dennis says. "Where'd you see it?"

"That's the thing. I think someone left it for me?" My voice slides up an octave. "Like as a cruel joke."

"Man," Dennis sighs. He doesn't offer anything else, so I press on.

"Were the crime-scene photos leaked anywhere? Like somewhere a student might be able to get them?"

A few clicks sound on Dennis's end. Keyboard keys. "Someone hacked into our database and leaked the pic you saw to a few news outlets. Offered the rest for cash. No one published it, though."

"So how would someone still have the picture?"

"Someone who saw it must have leaked it again," Dennis says. "I'll run a search online."

"Thanks," I say, nauseous. There's no doubt someone in Brent's dad's office would have received the picture.

"Anne." Dennis's voice is gentle. "Sorry you had to see that."

I am, too. "Thanks. Also for what you did for Anthony the other day."

I don't bring up the Weavers by name, so I'm not surprised when Dennis says, "What did I do for him again?"

"You know." I lower my voice as the line to get inside the refectory gets thicker and closer to where I'm standing off to the side. "The address."

"Address? I don't know what you're talking about," Dennis says. "I haven't heard from Anthony in over a month."

"Oh. Thanks anyway." I hang up, unable to process the fact that Anthony lied about where he got the Weavers' address. Brent and the guys have arrived, and he's heading right for me.

"Everything okay?" Brent wraps his arm around my waist. "You looked upset on the phone."

"It's nothing. Just my mom." My mouth doesn't respond when Brent leans and presses his lips to mine. He pulls away, hurt flitting across his eyes before he tugs my hand toward the line. I can't hear what he, Cole, and Murali are talking about over the sound of my own thoughts.

Brent may have left that photo for me.

Anthony *definitely* lied to me about how he got the Weavers' address.

The Drop is tomorrow night, and unless I figure out who I can trust before then, it looks like I'll be flying solo.

CHAPTER
SEVENTEEN

It's almost nine o'clock. There are little more than twenty-four hours until The Drop. To distract myself from going sick with worry, I'm making brownies with Remy, April, and Kelsey in the common-room kitchen. That's when Brent calls.

"Come over," he says.

I lick a stripe of batter off my finger and glance at the girls. They're arguing over how to deal with the oven, which refuses to heat above three hundred degrees.

"That might be a tough sell," I say. I don't know if I'm talking about just the girls. The image of Isabella's throat, cut and bloodied, is still fresh in my mind.

"Not them. Just you."

I decide I can't be neurotic about this. I haven't doubted Brent's intentions since we started dating, and I'm not going to make that mistake based on a coincidence. Thousands of people working in the media could have been able to access that leaked photo. "Okay."

We hang up. "I'm going to hang out with Brent for a little while."

None of them ask to come, since two-thirds of them hate our

guy friends at the moment anyway. I sign out at the front desk since I'll be back before eleven, the weekend curfew.

Brent is waiting for me in the lobby of Aldridge. A smile spreads across his face as he sees me through the window. I hold up my fingers and wiggle them at him.

Cole, Phil, and Murali barely look up from the TV when Brent and I get up to the suite. I thought Cole was still pissed at Phil, but I guess in guy world all arguments can be put on hold for the sake of Mario Kart.

They grunt hi as Brent and I go to his room. While Cole's side of the room is all New England Patriots and Wheatley crew paraphernalia, Brent's walls are mostly bare, as if he's a guest in a hotel room. There's a Led Zeppelin poster and a frame with pressed flowers inside. When I look more closely, I see that they're four-leaf clovers.

"I used to collect them," he says from behind me. I turn and kiss his cheek, shamelessly scoping out the rest of his room. We always hang out in mine, since I don't have a roommate anymore. His bookshelf is what really catches my eye: It's not the small school-issued one above the desk, but a real, proper bookshelf. I do a quick scan and spot *Persepolis*, *The Hobbit*, *As I Lay Dying*, and a Spanish dictionary.

"Quite an eclectic taste you've got," I say.

He shrugs. "I try."

I trace his freshly shaven face, my body warming at the realization he did it for me. Brent can't be the one who left me that picture of Isabella. He's the guy who gets embarrassed when I tease him about the time he and Cole watched *Love Actually* together. He's the guy who will be a complete jackass in public if it means getting a laugh out of me.

I don't know how he could go along with all of the messed-up things Casey Shepherd and the other guys are doing to the new recruits, but I know he's not the mastermind. And even if he suspected all of the hazing rituals played a part in Matt Weaver's death, he would tell me, right?

I don't know who kisses who first, but we're moving to his bed; his is made, Cole's isn't. Brent sits up, his back against his pillow, and I sit on his lap facing him. He kisses my neck, and when I kiss his earlobe his whole body contracts into mine.

"GODDAMNED SPIKED SHELL!" Murali screams from the living room.

Brent rolls his eyes and turns to the iPod dock on his night-stand. He chooses a U2 album and raises the volume.

"I always wanted to kiss a girl to this song," he murmurs. "Even if it's reversed and I'm the brown-eyed boy and you're the blue-eyed girl."

"Stop talking," I say into his mouth.

His kiss is more urgent after that; his tongue finds mine, and I slide my hands up his shirt. He breaks away from me and takes his shirt off, holding my gaze the whole time. I trace his bare chest, letting the heat from his body linger on my fingertips.

I know where this is going the second his hands move up my back and rest on my bra clasp. "Is this okay?" he asks.

I lean into him again, this time gently tugging on his lower lip with my teeth until a shudder escapes his throat. "Seriously," I say. "Stop talking."

"Okay. I do that when I'm nervous."

I laugh and let my hand move down his stomach, feeling the smooth skin and trail of hair below his bellybutton. "You? Ner-vous?"

He nods. "I mean, not that I haven't thought about this. Be-cause I have. A lot. It's just, maybe your room is quieter."

Is he saying he doesn't *really* want to do this? I freeze. He's never acted this nervous when we've hooked up before. Is this about what Casey Shepherd said in the tunnels? Does Brent feel pressured or something?

The frantic knock at the door makes us both jump. Brent curses at the sound of Cole's voice.

"Let me in!"

"Busy!" Brent yells, his cheeks flooding with color.

"MAYDAY! Surprise room check!"

"Shit." Brent scrambles into his jeans as I fumble for my shirt. "Shit shit shit."

When I'm dressed, I follow Brent into the living room. Murali is pouring can after can of beer down the kitchen sink, and Phil is tearing down the photo of Kyle the guys use as a dartboard. On the other side of the room, Cole is turning around the giant tapestry with all of their beer-pong scores for the year written on it. The other side bears a giant Wheatley School crest.

The whole thing is very methodical, as if ridding the dorm of contraband is a science the guys have perfected.

"Should I go?" I ask Brent.

Brent swears underneath his breath. "I mean, you're allowed to be here until eleven. . . ."

We both know there won't be time to pick up where we left off, though.

"It's okay." I kiss him. He hooks a finger in the collar of my sweater when I try to pull away, kissing me deeper.

"Text me later."

I don't feel like waiting for the elevator, or worse, running into Sebastian in there. So I take the steps two at a time to the first floor. I have to sign out, or Brent will get in trouble for having a female visitor after curfew.

I freeze when I see a beefy man talking to the RA at the front desk.

Larry Tretter.

"Just make sure he picks it up in the morning," he says to the RA.

I can't just stand here, watching them, so I wait behind Tretter as he signs himself out. Since Isabella's murder, protocol for entering and leaving the dorms has gotten stricter. Even teachers aren't off the hook—especially since Isabella was sleeping with one of them.

Tretter finishes signing his name and turns around. He locks eyes with me.

"Hi," he says.

It's a totally uncomfortable *hi*—the type superawkward people use when they don't recognize someone but don't want to be rude about it.

I give Tretter a polite smile. Then he's heading for the door.

I rush to sign myself out, scrawling "10:30" in the OUT box next to my name. I have no idea if it's actually ten thirty, but weekend curfew is eleven, so I assume I'm close.

I follow Tretter out of Aldridge, keeping a safe distance behind him. There are a couple of people hanging outside the dorms, killing time until curfew. A group of guys is huddled off to the side of Aldridge: Dan Crowley, Peter Wu, and Zach Walton. And the thin trails of white coming out their noses is probably not frost.

My plan to sneak after Tretter undetected implodes as a male voice calls my name.

A French male voice.

I squeeze my eyes shut as Sebastian Girard practically gallops toward me. "Anne. Hello there, *belle*."

"Hi, Sebastian." I force a smile. Sebastian doesn't mean to be such a relentless pain in the ass. It's just in his DNA or something.

"What are you up to?" he asks.

"Just headed back to my room." I punctuate the last few words, in case he'll get the hint, but he starts to prattle on about how he just got back from a Bruins game in the city.

I strain to get a look at Tretter, who has paused by the bike rack outside of Aldridge, cell phone pressed to his ear. He's staring at the group of guys hanging to the side of the dorm. When Zach Walton notices Tretter, he throws down his joint and crushes it with his heel.

"Thom, can I call you back in a few?" Tretter hangs up and stalks over to the group of guys. "Better be a cigarette you were smoking there, Walton."

Zach looks as if he's going to need a new pair of underwear soon. "Y-yes it was, Coach."

Tretter glares at all of the guys and heads down the path that cuts across the quad. The one that leads to the parking garage.

"Hey, Sebastian, I've gotta go." Just for shits and giggles, I give him a good old European send-off. I kiss both his cheeks and say "*Au revoir.*"

Sebastian is so shell-shocked he doesn't say anything when I head in the opposite direction of Amherst. I can't follow Tretter through the quad; he'll know I'm behind him—and the security guards usually patrol the main path this close to curfew so they can herd everyone back to the dorms.

Shit. Curfew. I glance at the screen of my phone. There're twenty minutes until I need to sign back into Amherst and check in with Darlene. The parking garage, where I assume Tretter is headed, is a seven-minute walk from here, at least. But I have a strong feeling he was on the phone with Thom Ennis before, and he could be calling him back any minute.

I cut through the path between the humanities building and Harriman Hall. There's not a lot of light behind the buildings, but I'm parallel to Tretter and out of his sight. Something scurries through the leaves in the wooded area on the other side of me. Probably just a squirrel.

I peek through the space between the administration building and the campus coffee shop. Tretter moves quickly down the path, slowing when a security guard nods to him. He stops to talk to him, and I press myself against the side of the administration building. My foot jiggles as I watch the minutes pass by on my phone. *Hurry up, Tretter.*

I hear a muffled "*Good night*" and see Tretter make a right toward the parking garage. I make sure I'm hidden away from the streetlamps as I cut across the path, following him.

My phone chimes in my hands. Shit.

Tretter stops in his tracks and does a 360 turn. I power my phone off and freeze where I'm standing.

Tretter's enormous jaw sets. It's too dark for him to see me. He pulls out a set of keys from his back pocket and enters the ground level of the parking garage. I creep around the side, keeping him in my line of sight as he walks to a huge black SUV and leans against it.

He's talking on his phone within seconds, but I'm too far away to hear him. I get on my knees and crawl under the cables separating the ground level from the outside, as quietly as I can. I flatten myself against the back of a silver BMW a few cars down from Tretter's.

"You're sure it was a girl?" he asks.

The expression on Tretter's face hardens at Ennis's response. He obviously doesn't like it.

"Who said I'm calling you a fool? You got a lot of nerve, Thom, calling me after all these years because some kid pranked you—"

Thom's response is almost loud enough for me to hear. I make out the words . . . *said she knows about Matty.*

The color drains from Tretter's face as my blood runs cold. Thom Ennis is talking about me—about the phone call.

"Don't you ever mention his name to me again," Tretter hisses. "So help me God, I will hunt you and your family down and *you'll* be the one—"

A chorus of laughter from the opposite side of the parking garage nearly sends me toppling over. Tretter snaps his phone closed as a familiar voice comes toward us: Professor Robinson.

I peek around the BMW. Robinson is flanked by Matthews—my history professor—and the new physics teacher. They both appear to be holding Robinson up.

"Lawrence!" Robinson booms. He stumbles toward him and clasps Tretter's enormous hands. "What are you doing here so late?"

"Long evening at the office," Tretter mumbles, unable to make eye contact with Robinson, whose nose is bright red. His hair, which is always parted down the middle, is sticking up in all different directions. He looks more like the Mayor of Who-ville than my art-history teacher.

"I'm afraid I had a little too much champagne at Professor

Matthews's symposium on the crisis in the Middle East." Robinson slaps Matthews on the back. "Can you believe this lad was sitting in my classroom not too long ago? How long has it been since you were in my class, Lawrence?"

Tretter mutters something that sounds like *"thirty years."*

"All right then." Robinson shakes Tretter's hands again. "Rowan here has kindly agreed to drive me home."

Tretter grunts a good-bye to everyone and slips into his SUV. Matthews tells Rowan—Dr. Muller—and Robinson he'll see them on Monday and heads for the staircase to the second level of the garage.

Dr. Muller turns and walks straight for the BMW.

Of all the freaking cars for me to hide behind.

"There you go, chap," Muller says as he helps Robinson into the passenger seat. I crouch down lower, praying that Muller doesn't turn around before he gets in the car.

My pulse is working so fast my ears are ringing. As Muller makes his way to the driver's side, he looks right at me. Confusion registers in his eyes as he opens his mouth slightly.

And gets into the car without a word.

When the lights on his BMW disappear out the parking garage entrance, I fumble my way to my feet and bolt out the back. I don't have time to worry about why Muller pretended not to see me hiding behind his car: I'm too busy replaying Tretter's conversation with Thom in my head.

It sounded like Tretter knows where Matt's body is.

And I am *so* not making curfew.

I blow through the front entrance of Amherst at ten after eleven. Darlene looks up at me from the front desk and sighs.

"Please," I say. "Just this once."

"I really can't. You know why we have to be so strict." Darlene frowns at me. "Where were you? Actually, I don't want to know."

She's looking at my sweater. It's gray with little black birds embroidered on it. But you can't tell, because it's inside out.

My cheeks are hot enough to speed global warming up about a thousand years. "It'll never happen again—"

"It can't," Darlene says. "Because if you're written up again after this, you have to see Dean Tierney. Sorry, Anne."

Damn it, damn it, damn it. I trudge upstairs, not stopping by the common room when I see Remy and the girls watching a movie. When I get to my room, I flop on to my bed and flip to the last page of the first notebook I see on my desk.

I write their names in a circle: Larry Tretter, Thom Ennis, Steven Westbrook, and Travis Shepherd. I put Matt Weaver's name in the middle, and next to his, Cynthia Durham. I chew the inside of my cheek and add Pierce Conroy to the outer circle, even though I don't want to.

I draw a line from Cynthia Durham to Steven Westbrook and Travis Shepherd. She dated Travis but married Steve. Matt was in love with her. Could that have been what got him killed?

I tap my pen against Tretter's name. Maybe he and Thom weren't involved at all. . . . It could be that they're covering for either Steven or Travis.

Or maybe I just want to believe that because it would mean Brent's father wasn't involved.

I roll onto my side and turn on my phone so I can read Brent's message.

It's a picture of the elf from latest *The Lord of the Rings* movie we watched. The one with really long hair. Someone's added the caption BITCH I'M FABULOUS.

It completely cracks me up, considering what a fail this night has been. Brent's not big on sending me texts, but when he does, they're worth the wait.

I lay flat on my back. I got really mad at my dad once, for telling me I couldn't have coffee with Sal anymore. Sal was my favorite homeless guy in New York. He used to hang outside the coffee shop I stopped at on my way to school in the morning, so

I'd buy him a cup and sometimes we'd chat. Turned out Sal hadn't always been homeless. He lost his house after September 11, and then the FBI kidnapped him and implanted tracking devices in his brain. Or so he says.

My dad said Sal is a paranoid schizophrenic and I need to stay away from people like him. I got really upset at the way my dad talked about Sal. The poor guy has no family or anyone who cares about him. I got into a huge argument with my dad about why he couldn't do more—he's a lawyer, after all. Why couldn't he help Sal?

Daddy put on his *You'll never understand this, Anne* voice and said that you can't change the way things are by saving one person. He said the best we can do in life is surround ourselves with people who make us happy, because the rest of the world is too big to find meaning in.

And that's what hit me when I read Brent's text message: Maybe he could be that person. The one who makes it okay that horrible things are going to happen and I'm going to be too powerless to stop them. That there are questions out there I will never be able to answer.

But if everyone just forgets about terrible things they can't understand—like what happened to Isabella and Matt Weaver—who will be left to remember?

CHAPTER
EIGHTEEN

News travels fast in a school with a student body smaller than the average church congregation. When I get to breakfast the next morning, the whole table apparently knows I got written up for missing curfew.

"I saw you sneak in last night," Remy says, before my butt is even in my chair. She wiggles her eyebrows at me. "Were you and Brent a little—"

"A little what?" Brent slides into the chair next to me, a bowl of granola in his hands.

"Oh nothing." Remy grins. "Just wondering what you and Anne were up to last night that made her miss curfew."

Brent's eyebrows knit together as he looks at me. I can see him calculating: I left his room with half an hour until curfew. The confusion on his face turns to hurt, and I think he's going to call me out on it. But he mumbles something about forgetting coffee and gets up from the table.

I follow him. "You're upset."

"No. Just curious . . . What *were* you up to that made you miss curfew?"

My defenses fly up. "I got held up."

His expression is strained. "For over half an hour?"

I shut my eyes and breathe in, because I can't bear to look at the disappointment on his face anymore. "It was nothing. I promise."

"Okay. It was nothing."

Sometimes I can't figure Brent out at all. But right now, he's crystal clear: He doesn't believe me.

"Be honest with me," I say. "Do you trust me?"

He swallows and meets my eyes. "I want to."

I almost wish he *hadn't* been honest with me.

I don't get the chance to gauge how bad things between Brent and me really are, because he has an SGA meeting after breakfast. Sometime around eleven, I decide I'm pissed. That he doesn't trust me, and that he had the audacity to tell me to my face.

I'll be the first to admit that I don't make the best decisions when I'm mad. But it doesn't stop me from tracking Casey Shepherd down that afternoon. None of my friends have brought up his after-party again, so like I thought, I'll have to secure the invite myself.

On the way inside, my phone *ping*s. I have a text from Anthony.

is something wrong‽‽‽

I delete it, like I've done with his last few messages, and put my phone on silent. I know if I accuse him of lying about how he got the Weavers' address, I can say goodbye to the new, calm Anthony. First, I need to figure out *why* he lied.

And why he wouldn't want me to find out he knows more about the Weavers than he let on.

I find Casey Shepherd alone in the library, cloistered behind a study carrel with headphones in. I come up behind him and tap him on the shoulder. He jerks in surprise but smiles and takes his earbuds out when he sees me. "Hey, you."

"Hi. Got a sec? I need a guy of your stature to get a book down for me."

"Your boyfriend can't reach it?" Shep smiles and leans back in his chair. The front two legs come off the ground a little bit, and I sort of hope he falls back and cracks his skull open. But that would defeat my purpose.

"Nope. You gonna help me or what?"

Casey stands. "Lead the way."

I direct him to the European literature section. "See that book on Spenser criticism? On the top shelf?"

Casey reaches it without exercising the balls of his feet. "Here you go. Reading *The Faerie Queene*?"

"Yep. Fowler's giving us an exam on Thursday."

Casey props his elbow up on the shelf and leans into it. "I just might have a copy of that exam from last year."

"Might you now?" I raise an eyebrow at him.

He smirks. "I bet Conroy can't give you that."

I give Shep a shy smile. "You know, I'm sure he can't."

Casey's blue eyes flash with satisfaction. "I'd watch out for Brent, if I were you."

I try to keep my tone teasing. "Are you trying to tell me he's the big player around here?"

"Heard you met his dad." Casey closes the space between us. He smells like Axe and a touch of weed. I try to stay expressionless and not show him I'm a little freaked out that he seems to be keeping tabs on me.

"Rumor has it Conroy Senior was into some freaky stuff back in the day." Casey's eyes move down my body in a way that makes me want to climb out of my skin. "Between you and me, I think you can do better than Junior."

I tighten my grip on the Spenser criticism book. "Thanks for the *tip*."

He smirks and runs a hand through his hair. "What are you doing after spring formal?" He says it as if it's not a question. My stomach flutters.

"I don't know."

"I do. You're coming to my house on the Cape."

I return his knowing smile. "Can't ditch my friends."

"Bring them. Just make sure Conroy can hold his liquor."

A laugh bubbles in my throat, because Brent told me the last time he had vodka he woke up without eyebrows. My chest muscles clench. I suddenly want to be wherever he is, even if it means apologizing for this morning and pretending I never heard what Shep said about his father.

Someone clears his throat behind us. Cole waves at us, his eyes trained on me as if to say *What the hell are you doing?*

" 'Sup C?" Shep says. Cole grunts in response, clearly not appreciating being called C.

"Shep and I were just talking about spring formal," I say quickly.

"Yeah," he cuts in. "You guys are coming to my place afterward"

"Are we now?" Cole is still looking at me.

"Yup. Catch you guys later." Casey nods to me and pushes past Cole, purposely knocking shoulders with him.

"So," Cole says to me.

"So *what?*" I can't keep the annoyance from seeping into my voice. Cole has a lot of nerve, judging me for talking to Casey Shepherd. Because last time I checked, I'm not the one who helped him burn Zach Walton's skin until it turned purple.

"I've gotta go," I mutter, brushing past Cole. He calls my name.

"He's not a good guy, Anne," Cole says. "Be careful."

"I know." I level with Cole. "I wouldn't want to get burned, right?"

He doesn't say anything as I turn and leave him in the stacks.

When I leave the library, I have two missed calls from Anthony. As I'm turning my volume back on, he calls back, and I accidentally answer it. *Damn it.*

"Um. Hey."

"What the hell is going on?" He asks. "I've been trying to get you for three days."

"I've been busy."

"That's crap. I told you I had something important on Sonia Russo. What happened?"

"Maybe I should be asking you that," I say calmly. "I talked to Dennis yesterday."

"Dennis?" Anthony sounds confused.

"Yes. Funny how he has no recollection of giving you the Weavers' address."

"You called him to *check up on me*?"

I wince. I can't tell him the real reason I called Dennis. "Don't deflect, Anthony. I need to know I can trust you."

"This has nothing to do with you. Drop it, okay?"

"You agreed to help me," I say. "It has everything to do with me."

"Well, here's your help," Anthony snaps. "Someone went to the police after Sonia went missing and said they saw her on the Wheatley campus the day before. Her name is Vanessa Reardon."

Reardon. Reardon. I chant it in my head, since I'm walking and have nowhere to write it down. "I have to find this woman."

"Don't bother. She took back her statement and said it may not have been Sonia she saw after all. Then Reardon transferred schools. Last known record of her is from 1993, when she got married. She's moved three times since, all unlisted phone num bers. Phones, cars, everything registered under her husband's name."

Sounds like Vanessa Reardon is running from something—or someone.

"Anyway, Dennis was able to pull her phone records," Anthony says. "To see if she's keeping in touch with anyone in Massachusetts. Only two numbers came up, and one is registered to Steve Westbrook."

"She's keeping in touch with *him*?"

"No. His daughter."

Well, I was not expecting *that.*

"Now if you want to call Dennis to make sure I'm not lying, go ahead," Anthony says. Then he hangs up.

My stomach dips. But it's not Anthony's attitude that's bothering me.

If what Dennis found out is true, I have a *much* bigger beast to slay.

A beast named Alexis.

CHAPTER
NINETEEN

The first thing I do when I get back to Amherst is text Brent: *Are we okay?*

The message is barely done sending when I get a text from Remy: *Where are u? In the CR* ☺

I head up the stairs and find the girls on the common-room couch, pawing through Kelsey's epic bucket of nail polish.

"Hey." I plop down on the couch next to Remy.

"Oh, good, you got my message," she says. "We were thinking about grabbing dinner in the city after dress shopping. Indian or sushi sound good?"

Crap. I figured when I'd told Remy we could go dress shopping "whenever," she wouldn't pick the night of The Drop.

"Actually, I don't know if I'm up to it tonight," I say. "I don't feel good."

"Aww, come on," Remy says at the same time Kelsey asks what's wrong.

"Cramps," I say automatically. "I'm really sorry guys."

"I have extra-strength Tylenol!" Remy says. "Take some and we'll wait for you to feel better."

All three of them watch me with such hope in their eyes that it kills me to lie to them. And I really would rather hang out with them than following the guys around, waiting for them to do who knows what.

"These aren't normal cramps," I say. "I get them *really* bad. Like my ovaries are exploding." I mime fireworks with my hands, adding a few *pew-pew*s here and there for effect.

The girls blink at me. "Ew." Remy looks disappointed, but she doesn't push the issue.

"Speaking of the formal, I saw Cole earlier," April says. She looks at me. "He said Shep invited us to his after party?"

Kelsey looks at me expectantly, while Remy's eyes are on the bottle of Essie Russian Red in her hand.

I shrug. "Yeah. It's no big deal."

"It's perfect," Kelsey says. "We were just talking about not knowing what to do this year . . . right Rem?"

Remy looks up from the nail polish. The corners of her mouth turn up, but her eyes are unsmiling. "Yeah, sure."

A voice in the back of my head screams *You are a horrible person!* Remy trusted me enough to tell me what happened between her and Shep, and now I'm going to ruin her spring formal by subjecting her to being around him all night.

"We really don't have to go," I blurt. "If you guys don't want to."

Remy finds my eyes. There's a hint of a real smile on her lips now. "No, we should. I couldn't turn down a party on the Cape even if it were at Creepy Lee's house."

The girls laugh, but I'm quiet. If only they knew how creepy he really is.

I hang out in the common room until the girls have to leave for the city. They try to bribe me into coming one more time before giving up and going to the bathroom across the hall, leaving their purses and Kelsey's nail polish on the couch.

I eye Remy's peach saddlebag. Her phone is sticking halfway out the side pocket.

The nagging voice in my head is back. I hate myself for even *thinking* about using Remy to get to Alexis again, but this is the best chance I'll have.

I glance at the door to make sure the girls are gone; my pulse is in my ears. I reach for Remy's phone. Alexis is the first person in Remy's contacts. I copy her number into my phone and make sure to arrange Remy's bag exactly as she left it.

Moments later, the girls come back to collect their stuff.

"Bye, Anne!" Remy grins at me on her way out. "Feel better!"

It takes everything I have to return her smile. On my way back to my room, I get a text message. My heart sinks when I see it's not from Brent.

But strangely, it's from Anthony.

What's the plan for tonight?

The Drop. He thinks he's coming with me.

I ignore it and turn my phone off.

It's a quarter past ten. Casey had said The Drop was to be at ten thirty. I stand by my dorm window, looking out onto Aldridge through a pair of binoculars. I count up to the third floor, to the corner suite. The lights flick off.

Brent and the guys are on the move.

I lower the binoculars to the side door. I know the guys still use it to sneak out, because I heard Dan Crowley, AKA Bill Gates, Jr., brag about how he found a way to disconnect the fancy new alarm system.

After what feels like an eternity, no one emerges from the door. As I suspected, they're using the tunnels.

I double-check myself in the mirror. I'm in all black, with my hair tucked into a knit cap. In the dark, no one should be able to tell it's me. But hopefully it won't come to that.

I sneak down to the laundry room and enter the tunnel beneath Amherst. I wait there pressed against the wall, straining my ears for voices.

The sound of walkie-talkie feedback from down the tunnel nearly gives me a heart attack. I can't make out what the voice on the other end says, but I recognize Cole's voice.

"Shep says the tunnels are clear. Let's go."

I hide in the dark as footsteps sound. I don't know how many of them there are. When the beam of their flashlight disappears around the corner, I tiptoe down the tunnel after them, feeling the walls to find my way.

The guys made a right toward the basement of Lexington Hall, where the parking garage is now. I follow, making sure to stay several feet out of the range of their light.

When their footsteps stop, I press myself against the wall again. A door creaks open, followed by muffled voices.

"We have to carry these the whole way?"

"Quit complaining, or I'll make you carry his, too." Brent. His voice makes my inside coil up with unease.

The guys shuffle off, making a right down the hall instead of heading for the stairs that lead to the parking garage. What are they doing? The garage exit is the only way out of the tunnels from here.

When their voices fade away, I creep down the hall. I have to move an inch at a time so I don't fall flat on my face: This is unfamiliar territory to me, and I can't risk using my flashlight.

My heart shoots into my throat when I see a light at the end of the hall. I exhale when I realize it's just the guy's lantern: They left it behind, propped against the wall. The guys are nowhere in sight.

I inch toward the wall. As it comes into focus, I feel my lips form the words: *Holy crap.*

The wall is turned at a 45-degree angle. I lift the lantern up to reveal a soft-looking brown stone. There are words carved into the front:

The harder the conflict, the more glorious the triumph.

—Thomas Paine December 19, 1776

I move the lantern to illuminate what the wall is hiding.
It's another tunnel.

CHAPTER
TWENTY

I know I'm no longer under the school the second I see the dirt floor and walls. The ceiling is so low that I'd probably have to crouch to fit if I were a foot taller. It can't be a comfortable walk for the guys—especially Cole, who is over six feet tall.

A chill creeps up my spine. Something tells me the school doesn't know this part of the tunnels exists.

I follow the makeshift tunnel, crinkling my nose at the smell of wet earth. If my internal GPS is right, they're headed for the forest. I have to suck in a breath and remind myself that the walls aren't actually closing in on me, even though it feels that way.

I can't hear the guys anymore, probably because they're so far ahead of me and their voices won't echo off the dirt walls.

I lose track of time eventually. Cold and exhaustion take over my muscles so bad I have to talk myself out of turning around. It's been an hour, minimum, since we left the dorms. I have no idea where they're going, and the thought of getting there just to repeat this walk back to the dorms later makes me want to cry.

The sound of voices makes me stop in my tracks. Have they reached the end?

"How are we supposed to get them up there?" I recognize Zach Walton's voice.

"One person climbs up at a time, and the person at the bottom passes it to them," Cole says.

There's some grunting and cursing, but eventually it's quiet. I wait for what feels like an eternity to follow them. My phone says it's only been ten minutes.

Moonlight peeks in from a hole in the ceiling. I look to my right: There's a makeshift ladder leading up to it. Thankful I wore boots, I make sure my phone is tucked safely in my back pocket and climb up the ladder.

I poke my head out of the hole in the ceiling. We're somewhere in the forest, and I'm in a crudely constructed shack of some sort. It takes some finesse to lift myself out of the tunnel and onto the dirt floor, but I manage to get one leg out and shift myself onto my stomach.

I stand up and brush myself off quickly before going to hide behind a tree next to the shack. By the light of the full moon, I see the guys more clearly. They're heading down a dirt path that cuts through the woods. I can make out Brent, Cole, Murali, Erik, and a couple of other upperclassmen I don't know. Trailing behind them are six younger kids carrying cinder blocks. Zach Walton is among them, trailing behind.

What the hell are they doing? I tiptoe behind another tree, trying to get closer. As quiet as I try to be, my boots still crunch the leaves underneath them. The sound blends into the cacophony of creepy noises out here—owls hooting, animals darting from tree to tree, knocking acorns and other debris to the ground.

I have to steady myself as the forest clears, and where the guys are headed comes into focus. A lake stretches ahead of us, the moon reflected on its surface. An enormous cliff overlooks it; it slants away from the lake, like something you'd go rock climbing on.

I hear one of the guys say something that sounds like *quarry*.

"All right, listen up, ladies," Casey Shepherd's voice rings out from a ledge halfway up the cliff. "Tonight we separate the real men from the pussies."

My throat tightens with horror as Erik and the other seniors thrust potato sacks over the heads of the new recruits. Brent, Cole, Murali, and Phil spin the guys around and bind their hands behind their backs before leading them up the side of the cliff. Erik and the remaining guys trail behind them, carrying the cinder blocks.

Bile churns in my stomach as they disappear from my view.

Casey cackles as the guys join him on the ledge of the cliff. They're easily a hundred feet from the lake and the ground. I'm getting sick just looking at them. There aren't many things I'm afraid of. In fact, there are only three things: My father. Public bathroom soap. And heights.

The upperclassmen guys disappear around the side of the ledge as Casey addresses the recruits.

"You're about to be tied to the cinder block you carried up here. On the count of three, you're all going to do a little cliff diving. Last one to jump and the last one to untie himself will face the jury. They'll pick a loser to be publicly humiliated at next week's race.

"Meet your jury," Casey cackles.

He motions for the three guys to step forward. Erik, Cole . . . and Brent.

"Wait, you're gonna tie us to those blocks?" One of the guys squeaks. "We'll die!"

"The water's only eight feet deep," Casey barks. "But if I were you, I'd start thinking about how you're going to untie yourselves."

I swallow down a gag. They can't do this—the guys could get seriously hurt—

"You've got to be kidding," one of the other guys says. His voice is tiny, as if he hasn't even hit puberty yet. "You guys are nuts. I'm not doing this."

Casey gets in his face. I don't want to imagine the kid's expression behind the potato sack. "You sure about that, Halpern?"

Halpern's voice shakes. "I'm pretty sure I don't want to die, yeah."

Casey nods to Erik, who yanks the potato sack off Halpern's head. "Don't bother showing up to practice Monday, then."

"But—"

"You think I'm messing around?" Casey grabs Halpern by the neck. I swallow away a whimper. *Please stop him, Brent.* "You think being on a nationally ranked team is a joke? You think everything we do is a fucking joke?"

"No," Halpern stammers.

"Then get out of my sight, dipshit. And don't. Show up. For practice Monday."

Halpern shakes himself free of the rope around his wrists and hurries down the side of the cliff. He runs back toward the forest without a glance at the rock I'm hiding behind.

"Anyone else have a problem?" Casey asks. The guys are silent, unmoving. Except for Zach Walton: His legs look as if they're going to collapse. I picture his face beneath the potato sack, pale and sweating. *Leave,* I want to scream at him. *Being on the stupid team isn't worth it.*

I can barely watch as the upperclassmen rest the cinder blocks behind the recruits. Each block has rope tied around the middle; the guys loop the other end of the rope around each recruit's bound hands.

I'm shivering and sweating at the same time. *Please don't do this, you guys. Please don't get hurt.*

"Ready?" Casey asks.

When no one replies, he counts down from three. The recruits jump off the cliff.

And a scream rips from my throat.

CHAPTER
TWENTY-ONE

I take off running as soon as I realize what I've done. In the split second it takes me to get on my feet, I look at the lake.

All of the recruits are . . . floating?

That can't be right.

Casey's voice booms across the night. "What the fuck was that?"

I keep running until my chest feels as if it's going to explode. With a surge of panic, I realize that I don't know how to get back to the tunnel that leads to school. *Find the shack.* Footsteps sound in the leaves several yards behind me.

"Who's there?" It's Casey's voice. He's pissed off.

"Go cover the entrance," Brent says. "I'll get them."

One set of footsteps takes off in the other direction. I can't breathe. And the other set is closing in on me—

My foot snags on a log sticking out of the ground. I stick out my hands to break my fall and cry out in pain. I'm trying to drag myself to my feet when Brent jumps over the log and lands on the ground next to me.

"Anne?" His eyes are wild, his knit cap pulled down over his ears.

"I—" I can't get the words out. I lean over, giving into dry heaves.

Brent pushes me down until we're hidden by the log. "Did you follow us here?"

I nod. "The recruits—"

"We replaced the cinder blocks with foam ones," Brent whispers. "It was all a prank. Anne, what the hell are you doing here?"

"I thought . . . I thought The Drop was how . . . how he died."

Brent's eyes are worried, like he's watching someone who has gone completely batshit out of their mind. "How *who* died?"

My eyes sting. My chest stings. Everything hurts. "Matt Weaver."

Brent's mouth hangs open.

Casey's voice makes us jump. "Conroy, what's going on?"

Brent turns to me. "Stay here. I'll distract him. When I yell something about a bird, run for the tunnels."

I nod as he launches himself off the ground and runs toward Casey. "Got away."

"It sounded like a girl," Casey says. "You got outrun by a *girl.*"

"It was kids. Two of them." Brent sounds out of breath. "They were just messing around."

I can't hear the rest of what Casey says, but it sounds like an angry rant against whoever screwed up The Drop.

I squeeze my eyes shut, willing my heart to calm down. When Brent yells, "Dude, was that a hawk?" I force myself to get up and make a break for the tunnel entrance.

Over an hour later I get a text from Brent.

Meet me in the basement of Amherst

I'm shaking as I get out of bed. I'm still in my black jeans and sweater, and my hair is an eagle's nest.

I want to shrivel up and disappear and never have to face Brent. This could be the end of us, and it's all my fault.

And worse, I don't want this to be the end.

I slip my room key into the pocket of my sweater. As an after-thought, I stick the crew team photo in there, too. It's the only thing I've got other than an insanity plea.

Brent's sitting against the wall near the tunnel entrance when I get to the basement. He's not smiling, but his voice isn't angry when he speaks. "I never used this entrance before. The bookcase is a nice touch."

I sit next to him so our shoulders are touching. "You never responded to my text. The one asking if we were okay."

A sigh escapes his nose.

"Well, are we?" I ask.

"Anne, what is going on with you?" He turns to me. From the light of the moon leaking into the basement, I can see all of the freckles on his nose.

I draw in a breath and pull the photo out of my pocket. Brent takes it, his eyebrows knitting together. "Where did you get this?"

"It was between the pages of a history book from the library," I say. "Brent . . . turn it over."

He does. I watch his eyes move across the words. He sets it down on his knee, the back facing up. "You think this is about Matt Weaver?"

I nod. "I know it sounds crazy—"

"It does." Brent considers the photo. "Anne, someone wrote this to mess with people like you."

"People like me? What is that supposed to mean?"

"I didn't mean it like that." He tilts his head back into the wall behind us. "It's just . . . you're new here. And Matt Weaver is this ridiculous urban legend meant to scare new people."

"Brent, he was *real*. I met his parents," I say. "Someone knows what happened to him."

He surprises me by finding my hand in the dark. He laces his fingers through mine. "And you think that someone might be my dad."

"I didn't say that. But something's going on with the others . . . Westbrook, Tretter—"

"Wait, you think Coach is involved?" Brent stares at me. "The only thing he's guilty of is being a dumbass."

"I heard him and Casey talking about The Drop. Tretter sounded like he didn't want you guys to do it . . . almost as if someone had gotten hurt before. Or worse."

Brent is quiet. "Trust me. The Drop is harmless. It's not how Matt Weaver died."

"How do you know?"

Silence envelops us. Suddenly it feels ten degrees colder down here. With the arm that's not tangled with Brent's, I hug myself.

He finally says something. "Because my dad is the one who came up with The Drop. He knew Matt Weaver, and he says all of the rumors about him being murdered aren't true. He was just a messed-up kid who couldn't handle the pressure of going to school here."

I kind of wish he hadn't said anything at all. How can he accept everything he's been told so easily? That Matt Weaver simply went for a walk, never came back, and that's all there is to it?

He squeezes my knee. "Talk to me."

"What you guys did—The Drop—it's really messed up." My voice is almost a whisper. "You could give them a heart attack or something. I almost had one watching them."

"I know. But it's a tradition." Brent's eyes are on the wall opposite us. "Anne . . . you can't tell anyone what you saw. We'd be in deep shit. Goddard could end us."

"I doubt that. Goddard is really good at not telling anyone what *he* sees."

"I'm serious. This isn't a joke. Rowing has won more awards for Wheatley than any other team or club." He looks at me, pleading with me. "And the *team* didn't *kill* Matt Weaver. That's insane."

"Okay." What else can I say? That I don't believe him? That his own father might know who killed Matt Weaver?

He squeezes my hand, but I don't think it's enough to close this new distance between us.

CHAPTER
TWENTY-TWO

My dad took a high-profile murder case in New Jersey when I was really young. Some eighteen-year-old girl was on trial for killing her parents. The prosecution said she was a manipulative teenager who hated her mother for not letting her date an older guy. She'd stabbed them both to death during an argument gone wrong. That was the theory, at least.

The evidence against the girl was pretty bad. Neighbors had heard her screaming at her mother in the morning, and she was found at the crime scene covered in both her parents' blood. My dad tells me he took the case after the girls' aunt pleaded with him: *Just keep her off death row.*

My dad doesn't half-ass anything, though, and he noticed something off about the crime scene. The lights were off in the house when the police arrived: Either the girl had turned off the lights after killing her parents or she had really come home to find them that way, like she said she did. Why would anyone kill their parents, call 911, and turn off the lights while they waited for the police?

If the lights were off when the couple was killed, my dad

argued, it couldn't have been a crime of passion. An intruder could have broken into the house and been waiting for the girls' parents.

After a hugely drawn-out trial, the girl was found not guilty. Reasonable doubt. Five years later, the real intruder was caught murdering someone else and confessed he'd killed the couple in a robbery gone wrong.

My dad calls the case his "white rabbit." He couldn't ignore the lights being off in the couples' home. No matter how nasty or publicized the trial got, and despite getting death threats, the lights were my dad's white rabbit, and he couldn't stop pursuing it. He knew the real story was out there, waiting for him to bring it to the surface.

The photograph—the THEY KILLED HIM one—is my white rabbit. I know now that I'll never be able to let Matt Weaver go unless I get the answers I'm looking for.

"Anne. Wake up."

A soft elbow connects with my shoulder. I rub my eyes and sit up. Kelsey is peering at me through her red-framed Ray-Bans. She only wears her glasses in dire situations.

It's midterm week. And apparently I fell asleep facedown in my biology notes.

Kelsey points to my face. "Hey, I was working on the genetic-dominance problem set, too."

I retrieve my compact mirror from my purse and examine myself. In addition to the gray bags under my eyes there is a perfect imprint of $AaBbCc$ on my cheek.

"I give up," I say around a yawn, as Remy returns from one of the library printing stations, weighed down by a stack of papers. She doesn't talk to us as she sits at the table and begins highlighting. The look on her face is scary. I'd hate to see her right before the SATs.

Less than a minute later, Brent tracks us down, wearing his crew sweatshirt and gym shorts. His hair is wet.

"This is cute." He traces the letters imprinted on my cheek and goes off to find a free chair. He may as well be shopping at Walmart on Black Friday.

"I don't see how their coach can make them have practice during midterms," Kelsey whispers to me. "That's *inhumane*."

I don't miss the irony in her statement. Brent returns from the circulation desk, chair in hand and smile on his face. I don't know who is better at convincing people to do things for them—me or Brent.

"I don't see how your coach can make you practice this week," Kelsey repeats as Brent sits between us.

He shrugs, but Remy looks up for just long enough to say, "Their first race of the season is on Saturday."

I eye Brent. "I didn't know that."

"It's not a big deal," he says.

"Don't say that in front of your dad," Remy mutters.

Brent suddenly looks uncomfortable. "Your dad is going?" I ask.

"Says he is. We'll see about that, though."

"I want to go," I say. "Especially if your family will be there."

Brent is quiet. Is this about the other night, and me messing up The Drop? Is he mad he had to lie to the team about the kids in the woods?

"You really don't have to." Brent isn't looking at me. "It'll be boring."

I feel kind of like I've been kicked in the stomach. He doesn't want me there. Is it because his family will be there? That doesn't make sense, though: I already met his sister and dad.

Something else occurs to me. If Brent's parents will be there, so will the other guys'. My blood rushes to my head. Travis Shepherd will probably be there, and Tretter definitely will be. . . .

That's almost half the people in the photo in one place.

I watch Brent, who is playing with the strap on his watch. Is he thinking the same thing—that if I show up to the race, it will only be to stick my nose where he asked me not to?

"I'm hungry," Kelsey moans. She takes off her glasses and rubs her eyes. "Can we take a dinner break?"

"I guess." Remy sighs. "But we might lose the table. . . ."

"I'll stay," I offer. "I'm really not hungry." It's the truth.

"Are you sure? You need to eat." Remy looks at me, obviously torn between her motherly instincts and her neurosis over losing the perfect study table. "We could bring you something back."

"It's fine." I wave them on. "I'll grab something on the way back to Amherst tonight."

The girls collect their bags, leaving their books behind. Brent kisses me on the cheek before he stands up. "Everything okay?"

"Of course," I say. "I'll see you later, maybe."

And I'll definitely see you at the race on Saturday.

I'm not the only one skipping dinner in favor of studying. Lee Andersen's roommate, Arthur Colgate III—AKA Peepers, due to the lenses that magnify his eyes to twice their size—is at the table next to me. He's created somewhat of a fortress around himself with textbooks.

I turn to my page of biology notes, tapping my pen against it. There's no way I'll be able to focus now. Not when Brent is being so weird about me going to his race.

"Hey," I say to Peepers. He looks at me. Or not. I can't really tell, with the way his eyes move behind his glasses.

"Would you mind watching this table for a couple minutes?" I ask him. He nods.

I head for the second floor, bringing my purse with me. I'm not really sure what I'm doing until I find myself standing in front of the old-yearbook shelf again.

If a picture tells a thousand words, maybe there are enough in these to tell the whole story about what happened to Matt Weaver.

I find the 1981 yearbook and find my usual armchair. It's occupied by a sleeping freshman boy. I return to the stacks where the yearbooks are and sit on the floor.

Vanessa Reardon's photo is in the 1981 sophomore class section, on the same page as Lawrence Tretter. She's cute, in a tomboyish way: Her hair is in a pixie cut, and there are freckles on her nose.

I look through the rest of the yearbook, even though if there were any mentions of Matt Weaver in it, the school would have sanitized the yearbook. I'll bet Isabella's photo won't even appear in this year's edition.

I stop at a page titled "Spotted Around Campus." Below the title is a collage of candid photos. Steven Westbrook is in a third of them, flashing his stupid horsey smile and putting his arm around whomever he's with. As if he were already campaigning for senator.

The image quality is different for each picture, and some are Polaroids. I'm guessing students volunteered their personal photos, so my chances at finding something incriminating are pretty slim.

I turn to the next page of photos. A picture at the center catches my eye. It doesn't look like it was taken anywhere on campus—the furniture is too nice, too expensive. The crew team guys are in it, except for Pierce Conroy.

Travis Shepherd sits at the center of the couch, his arm around Cynthia Durham. Matt Weaver is next to Travis, and Larry Tretter sits on the arm of the couch, sulking. Steven Westbrook is on the other side of Matt Weaver.

None of them looks happy to be having the picture taken—probably because of the plastic cups in their hands. I'd bet anything it's not apple juice in there. But what really grabs my attention are the two girls off to the side. Their expressions say they don't think they're in the photo at all.

I recognize one: Vanessa Reardon. The other is unfamiliar. She's rail thin and wearing a paisley dress that's too big for her. Her hair is supercurly and black.

I flip back to the student portraits. My eyes are drooping by the time I've been through all of them, but I don't find the mystery girl. I'm not surprised, because she doesn't look like a Wheatley student, anyway.

I turn back to the photo. Even though the picture isn't the best quality, it's obvious the girl is beautiful. Her eyes are almond shaped, and she wears her sadness in her expression.

I consider the yearbook in my hands. All the books on this floor are considered reference materials—meaning nobody is allowed to check them out. There's no visible security device on the yearbook, so I'm willing to bet there's one of those invisible stamps inside that will set off the door alarms.

I glance down the aisle to make sure I'm alone. Very carefully, I tear the page with the collage out of the yearbook, almost positive I've found Sonia Russo.

I need to find Dan Crowley. It's a Friday night, so it doesn't take a private investigator to figure out he's probably in his dorm playing *Call of Duty* with Peter Wu.

I coax a freshman into signing me in and I head to the fourth floor of Aldridge. I have to bang on Dan's door a few times before it swings open. He gapes at me and says, "Give me five minutes," into his headset.

Dan Crowley was useful when I needed to hack into the school's record system a few months ago. He has a lisp, which I'm not sure is natural or from his tongue ring. His hair isn't gelled into a Mohawk tonight.

"Hey," I say, at the same time the person on the other end of his headset asks, "Is that a *girl*?"

Dan yanks it off. "Wassup?"

"Got a second? I need your help."

"Step into my office."

Dan Crowley's side of the dorm room is a geek's wet dream. His desktop computer is hooked up to two thirty-inch monitors, and he's converted his closet into a nook with a television, mini fridge, and Xbox.

"I need some e-mail addresses," I say.

Dan's brow furrows. "They're all on the student directory."

"No," I say. "Like . . . alumni e-mail addresses. Important alumni."

Dan scratches his goatee with his thumbnail. "So you need master list access."

"Master list?"

"It's how mass e-mails go out without everyone seeing all the recipients. If the people you're looking for are subscribed to the alumni master list, you'd just need the address and you could e-mail all of them."

My head is swimming. "But I don't want to e-mail all of them."

Dan sighs. "I could *probably* get you individual addresses if you tell me their names."

Ten minutes later, I'm sitting on Dan's beanbag chair, splitting a bag of Starbursts with him as he bends over his desk, typing things I can't see into his computer. Coach Tretter was easy, since he's on the Wheatley faculty web site, and I already have Thom Ennis's e-mail.

"Shepherd and Conroy are on the alumni master list," Dan finally announces. He scribbles their e-mail addresses on the Post-it and hands it to me. "You absolutely cannot tell anyone I hacked it."

I cross my heart. "Snitches get stitches."

I get up from the beanbag and realize I'm looking at Zach Walton's bed. At least, that's his jacket lying on it. The windbreaker he had on the other night.

"Zach is your roommate?" I ask.

Dan nods. "Since freshman year."

I sit back down on the beanbag. "Have you noticed anything weird about him lately?"

Dan fiddles with his tongue ring. "Maybe. Depends."

"On what?"

Dan glances at the door. "Those e-mail addresses you asked me for—do they have anything to do with Zach?"

I level with him. "Maybe."

Dan swivels his chair so he's facing his computer. He logs on to a Web site and turns one of his monitors on. "C'mere."

I stand and watch over his shoulder as he pulls up a video feed of the Aldridge common room. It's empty except for a senior in pajamas who's making Ramen.

"There's a *camera* in the common rooms?" I ask.

"Only 'cause I put one there."

I stare at Dan. He sighs. "I wanted to catch who was eating all of my mom's baked mac and cheese."

I look at him. *Really?*

"You don't understand. She puts bacon in it," he says.

I watch Dan enter a date and time into a drop-down box on the site. As the recording loads, I realize he's going back to a few nights ago.

I feel my jaw drop. Brent and Murali are on the screen. He and Cole barricade the common-room door with a couch. Casey Shepherd, Erik, and Justin stand over a bunch of guys lying on their stomachs, wearing nothing but their boxers.

"What are they *doing*?" Cole, Erik, and another senior are holding boxes of table salt. They pour it over the backs of the recruits.

"The salt-and-ice challenge," Dan says. On screen, the older team members are placing huge chunks of ice on the guys' backs, on top of the salt. I watch in silence as the minutes tick by. The guys begin to wriggle in pain.

"It burns their skin," Dan explains. "Whoever gives in to the pain first loses and gets punished. Whoever can put up with it for the longest gets a reward of some sort."

After a while, the half-naked recruits succumb, like toy soldiers. One boy stands up and runs to the garbage can. He pukes his brains out. Before long, Zach and one other guy are the only ones left lying on their stomachs. There's no sound on the tape, but Brent and the other guys stand off to the side, clearly cheering them on.

The recruit who isn't Zach finally gets up and runs to the sink. Cole rushes over to Zach, but his eyes are closed. He passed out. Casey Shepherd runs over and smacks him in the face. While Zach regains consciousness, Erik and Brent argue as Casey and Cole drag Zach outside.

"You okay?" Dan asks me. "You look like you're gonna faint."

"I'm fine." My voice is far off. I can't stop seeing the recruits jumping off the cliff at the quarry. Any one of them could have broken his neck on the way down, easily. "Dan, you have to show this to someone."

"Hell no, I don't." Dan shakes his head. "I'm not messing with those guys. If that's what they do to their own teammates, can you imagine what they'd do to me?"

CHAPTER
TWENTY-THREE

I meet Remy in her room Saturday morning so we can go to the race together. While she curls her hair, I sit on her bed, trying not to be weirded out by the empty side of the room that used to be Alexis's.

"Rem, why didn't Brent tell me about the race?"

She doesn't look away from the mirror. "He probably forgot. You know him."

"I'm not dumb. He doesn't want me there. Why?"

Remy turns to me, her face guilty. "Brent didn't say anything to me, but I'm guessing it's because Cole's mother will probably be there."

"Oh."

"It's nothing to worry about," she says. "I mean, no one *blames* you for what Dr. Harrow tried to do, but things could get awkward since the Westbrooks are friends with a lot of the parents that will be there. And people talk. . . ."

"It's okay. I get it. What about the Shepherds?"

Remy looks surprised. "What about them?"

"Are they friends with the Westbrooks?" I ask.

"Oh, my God, no." Remy wraps a cranberry-colored scarf around her neck. "Casey's dad donated a million dollars to Mr. Westbrook's opponent last election."

Ouch. "Pretty harsh way to treat a former rowing buddy."

"Mm-hmm." Remy surveys herself in the mirror. She's wearing a Wheatley School sweatshirt, which is, of course, cranberry. She turns to me. "You're not wearing any Wheatley gear! How will people know who you're cheering for?"

I don't want to hurt her feelings, but I'm not exactly oozing Wheatley pride. "I dunno."

Remy takes her scarf off and wraps it around my neck. The Wheatley crest is sewn onto the tail ends. "Here."

"Thanks." I humor her while she adjusts it; I'm desperate to get the conversation back to the senator. "So did they have a falling out or something?"

"Who?"

"Travis Shepherd. And Mr. Westbrook."

"Oh. No, I don't think so." Remy spritzes some perfume on— Philosophy Amazing Grace—and we head downstairs. "When Alexis's dad ran for Senate last term, some people accused him of doing whatever he could to get elected, even if it meant flip-flopping on important stuff. Mr. Shepherd stopped supporting him when he changed his policy on tax breaks for corporations."

I say silent thanks that Remy is well versed in Massachusetts's politics, as we wait for the Wheatley sports shuttle bus that will take us to the harbor. I consider everything she said about Shepherd and Westbrook, wondering if there's another reason they had a falling out.

When Remy isn't looking, I pull up the draft of the e-mail I wrote this morning, addressed to the members of the 1972 crew team.

I just hope they remembered to bring their BlackBerries to today's race.

There's already a lot of other Wheatley students camped out on the sides of the Charles River. Most are sitting on blankets, which I wish I'd thought of, since the grass is damp in that early May way. Luckily, I'm with Remy, who not only remembered a blanket but trail mix, bottled water, and a copy of *Marie Claire*.

"In case we get bored," she explains. "The men's eight is after the lightweight race."

I have no idea what a lightweight race is, but I know that the men's 8 is Brent's race. I help Remy lay the blanket down, eyeing the white tent set up to our right. Jill, Lizzie, and Brooke, Alexis's former peons, stand outside of it, putting the finishing touches on a homemade "GO WHEATLEY!" banner. They've painted brown oars all over it, and now they're writing the names of the guys on the oars with glitter pens.

I'm not surprised to see Jill filling in Brent's name. When she senses me staring, she nudges Brooke and whispers something to her.

Sometimes I worry that Jill and Brent have more in common than he and I do. She's taller than him, but that's okay. Her hair is the color of corn silk, and she plays every sport Wheatley has to offer. She's editor in chief of the newspaper, and she'll probably go to Dartmouth or UPenn or Northwestern.

And she's probably not the type of girl to lie to her boyfriend.

A few teachers emerge from the tent with Styrofoam cups of coffee, along with people in Wheatley sweatshirts whom I assume are parents. Inside the tent is a banner reading "WHEAT LEY SCHOOL ALUMNI ASSOCIATION."

I think I know where the members of the 1981 team will be when they get here. I glance at the screen of my phone: We're twenty minutes early.

I shield my eyes from the sun as I look across the river to the boathouse. About thirty guys are milling around the area where I suppose the boats launch from. I can pick out the Wheatley guys by their black and red Under Armour. The sun catches all of the gold strands in Cole's hair. He looks up and waves at us. We wave back while Cole nudges Brent.

At first he smiles, as Remy hollers across the river at him. Then confusion registers on his face. He lifts a hand and locks eyes with me.

I return his wave, unsmiling, before Brent turns back to the boathouse. Coach Tretter comes out and gathers the guys. He looks pissed, but then again he always looks pissed. The guys stand, bored, while Tretter gives them what looks like a thorough tongue lashing. Probably his version of a pep talk.

I do a 180-degree scan of Wheatley's area. It looks like Brent's dad is a no show. Our tent is packed now, making it impossible for me to tell if anyone else from the photo is actually here or not.

If none of them came, my plan won't work.

A bullhorn sounds across the river, and someone announces the lightweight race. There's cheering from the sides as the smaller guys load into the boats. Remy prattles on as they take off. The Wheatley lightweights—mostly lowerclassmen and Zach Walton—are getting killed by Ellison Prep.

Across the river, Tretter is having a full-on hissy fit: red face, stamping his feet. He disappears behind the boathouse.

The sides of the river are packed with spectators now, so I have to crane my neck to get a good look at the Alumni Association tent. It's also crowded, with more people crammed around the edges than inside.

"Should I do my hair like this for the formal?" Remy points to a model in *Marie Claire* with a soft braided chignon.

"Sure," I say. "Hey, I'm gonna take a walk."

I leave Remy and make my way toward the tent. That's when I lock eyes with an older man, briefly, before he passes me without recognition. His hair is streaked with gray, but he has the same pointed chin and strong jaw as his son.

I pull up his Google bio on my phone to make sure it's him: Travis Shepherd.

Shepherd rests his hand on a rail-thin blonde's lower back his wife—as his fellow alumni kiss his ass. His smile is barely detectable, and he never quite makes eye contact with the people speaking to him.

I find a tree to lean against so I can keep an eye on him. On the other side of the tree, a bunch of kids in Ellison Prep sweat-shirts are setting up a lemonade dispenser. I watch Travis Shepherd schmooze with the other Massholes and refill his coffee. Whenever he thinks no one is looking, he checks his BlackBerry.

I don't know if this is going to work, now that Pierce Conroy isn't here and Tretter is distracted by the race. *Do it, Anne. Smoke them out.*

I pull up the e-mail on my phone and send the message before I can talk myself out of it.

To: ltretter@wheatleyschool.edu, travishepherd@shepherd
mcloughlin.com, steve.westbrook@gmail.com, thomennis@
ecassociates.com, conroy@mediasense.net
From: someone_knows@gmail.com
Subject: I know

Attached to my message is a scanned copy of the THEY KILLED HIM photo.

CHAPTER
TWENTY-FOUR

I let myself watch the blood drain from Travis Shepherd's face as he reads my e-mail. Then I hide behind the tree. Seconds later, he storms past me and over the bridge leading to where the bus dropped us off earlier.

Remy texts me: *Where are you?!* I delete the message and follow Shepherd with my eyes. He disappears behind the boathouse and reemerges moments later, followed by Coach Tretter.

They're definitely trying to get away from the crowd. I follow them up the riverbank to the parking lot. There's a yacht-club building at the center of the lot.

I blend in with the bored spectators heading toward the yacht club. I spot Tretter and Shepherd off to the side, overlooking the harbor. I circle around the back of the yacht club and duck behind a dumpster.

Coach Tretter is sweating beneath his Wheatley sweatshirt. "I didn't send it."

"Then who the hell did?" Travis Shepherd growls.

"Steve?" Tretter says.

Shepherd runs a hand over his face and points to his Black-
Berry, letting out a sharp laugh. "Does this look like something
Steve would do? Someone with *balls* did this, Larry."

I decide to take that as a compliment.

Larry Tretter mumbles something I can't make out. But whatever it is, it angers Shepherd.

"I have worked too hard all of my life to let Weaver fuck up
things for me again," he growls. "And before you finally grow
that conscience the apes forgot to pass down to you, remember
that I *own you*, dumbass."

Shepherd starts to stalk away from Tretter, who calls after
him: "Wait."

Shepherd turns around. Tretter catches up with him. I can't
hear what they whisper to each other, but Tretter's ruddy cheeks
get even redder, as if he wants to take a swing at Shepherd.

"None of this would have happened if you had minded your
own business," Shepherd snaps at him. "Couldn't stand him
being better than you, huh, Lawrence? Or were you afraid that
piece of townie trash would tell everyone your daddy had to buy
his little simpleton's way into Wheatley?"

I wince, expecting Tretter to smash Shepherd's face in. Instead, Tretter mutters something that sounds a lot like *"e-mail"*
and *"she."* Shepherd grabs Tretter by the collar of his sweatshirt.
Well, at least I know where Casey gets that particular habit from.

"She's *dead*," Shepherd seethes in Tretter's face. "Or did you
forget?"

Shepherd lets go of Tretter, who looks rattled despite being
twice Shepherd's size. Shepherd cracks his neck and looks out to
the river. "Now if you'll excuse me, *Lawrence*, I have to watch
that pack of lazy brats you call a crew team lose a race."

"Your son is one of them," Tretter calls to Shepherd's back.

They're both gone, but I can't bring myself to get up from behind the dumpster.

She's dead.

Who did he mean—Cynthia Westbrook or Sonia Russo? I think of Isabella and the photo tucked into the library book. *She* could be anyone.

All I know is that a lot of bodies are turning up where the 1981 crew team is concerned.

CHAPTER
TWENTY-FIVE

My sparkly tights that I want to wear to the formal are a little snug around the butt area, so I get up early on Sunday morning to go for a jog. There's only one problem: I refuse to go anywhere near the woods or the athletic track, because someone will see me and realize I've never been jogging a day in my life.

I have to run toward town, which almost ends in disaster, since the Wheatley School is on a hill. Trying to run downhill turns into a bizarre little forward hop. The sun is up, I'm sweating my ass off, and the only thing that could possibly make this worse is running into the last person I want to see right now.

Anthony pulls up next to me on his motorcycle. "Hop on."

"Were you *following* me?"

"No. I was coming to see you." He hands me his helmet. The motion makes his hoodie ride up, exposing a tanned sliver of skin above his belt.

I swallow. "As you can see, I'm busy exercising."

"That's what that was?"

"What do you want, Anthony?"

His faint smile falls. "I need to show you something. It'll explain why I lied to you."

I throw a glance over my shoulder. "Let me go back to my room and change."

"No," he says. "We have to go now."

I could not be any crankier that Anthony has dragged me into town wearing nothing but my workout pants and a tank top. Then he stops in front of the Main Street Diner.

"This is what's so important?" I hop off his bike. "The Weavers don't own this place anymore."

Anthony is quiet as he nudges his kickstand with his foot. He gestures for me to follow him up the steps, but we don't go inside. He points to something through the window. It takes me a couple of seconds to realize he means the old man sitting at the counter, reading a newspaper.

"Every morning at nine he comes here," Anthony says. "Orders two eggs over easy with toast, a black coffee, and buys a paper. Every day, for the past twenty years."

I turn my head to him, waiting for the punch line. We're standing closer to each other than I'd noticed. So close I can see the ghost of a scar on his upper lip and the beginnings of stubble on his jaw.

"My mom's Uncle Pat," Anthony finally says. "Raised her since she was twelve, when her parents died. Closest thing to a grandpa I've ever had. He's the detective in the *Dateline* special I sent you. Pat Carroll."

Whoa. "Why didn't you tell me before?"

"I haven't spoken to him since my sister died," he says. "He and my mom hadn't been getting along since my dad got sick. Pat never wanted her to marry him."

"Why not?"

"My mom's family was supertraditional. Pat never married. Wanted my aunts and my mom to marry nice Irish-American boys. Imagine how he felt when she chose a nice Mexican-American boy."

Anthony and I watch his great-uncle tap his coffee cup for a refill. The waitress doesn't stop to chat with him.

"He never let my mom forget it," Anthony says. "They fought all the time, until me and Iz were like three or four. Pat *loved* her. Every Sunday he'd come pick us up and take us somewhere different. Museums and stuff."

He clears his throat. "Anyway, none of that's important. But Pat's the reason I was so into the Weaver story as a kid. Pat was always talking about the case. About how it was the biggest thing he regretted about his career."

"Why?" I ask.

"I'm hoping he'll tell you that himself."

I wait outside and let Anthony approach his great-uncle alone. I expect to see a touching sort of reunion, but Pat simply clamps Anthony on the back and says nothing when he sits down. Almost as if he's been waiting for him.

I'm starting to get a little cold without a jacket, so I move into the foyer of the diner. Anthony spots me and waves me inside. Reluctantly, I join him and his uncle at the counter.

Pat Carroll is a brick shithouse of an old man. He's at least six feet tall, two hundred pounds. His long mouth is partially obscured by a thick white mustache.

"It's nice to meet you, Mr. Carroll." I hold out my hand to him. He ignores it.

"Heard you been askin' around about Matty Weaver." His voice is gruff, with a thick Boston accent.

I look at Anthony, who nods to me. "Tell him what you found,."

I describe the photo to Pat, whose beady eyes grow with interest. He doesn't respond but dips his toast into the puddle of yolk on his plate. I don't realize I'm staring until he says, "What is it?"

"You must have terrible cholesterol," I say.

Pat Carroll lets out a belly laugh. "Wouldn't know. Haven't been to the doctor since Reagan was in office."

He smiles at me, something transpiring in his expression. Maybe deciding he can trust me. "S'pose you already know we checked out the crew team when Matt went missing," Pat says. "Couldn't'a been clearer they were covering for one another."

Pat dumps some sugar into his mug. "Matty worked here weekends when his parents owned the place. Girl he worked with told me a story. His first year at the school, couple of those guys came in. Purposely made a mess for Matty on the table. The kid was nearly in tears. She remembers that rat bastard senator calling him 'townie trash.'"

"What about Westbrook's girlfriend?" I ask. "Cynthia."

Pat looks confused. "Cynthia Durham? Wasn't Westbrook's girlfriend back then. She was dating the other weasel. Shepherd."

"Travis Shepherd?"

"Yep. Real slimy kid. One of the first to pull the 'Call my lawyer' card." Pat drains his coffee. "I always thought he was the ringleader. All the students I questioned said he took Weaver under his wing. Accepted him into the group. They said Weaver followed him around like a puppy. If you ask me, it was more like Shepherd was pulling Matty's strings."

Is that why Larry Tretter hated Matt? Because he replaced him not only on the men's 4 team but as Travis Shepherd's puppet?

Or was Shepherd right, about Matt knowing Larry Tretter wasn't smart enough to get into Wheatley without his father's money? I couldn't imagine being angry enough with someone for knowing my secrets that I'd want to *kill* him or her. But then again, I'm not a 230-pound teenage boy with the strength of a gorilla. All it would take for Larry Tretter to put someone in a coma is a punch to the head. He easily could have gotten carried away and killed Matt in anger.

And how does Cynthia Durham fit into all of this? Did Travis Shepherd figure out how Matt felt about her, and go to extremes to make sure he didn't lose what was his?

"There were lots of things about their story that didn't add up," Pat says. "Like what the security guard said."

"You mean the basement thing?" Anthony says.

Pat nods. "Around ten thirty, a security guard heard something from the basement in the boys' dormitory. Voices."

"The guys?" I ask.

"Coincided with their alibi," Pat says. "Westbrook, Tretter, Ennis, and Shepherd said they were all together. Playing poker. But we questioned the security guard, and he says he heard a conversation between three people."

"So they lied?"

"I thought so," Pat says. "But the consensus was there still could have been four guys down there."

I drum my fingers on the counter, considering this. Or one of the guys could have left to meet Matt in the woods.

"I was convinced they were lying, that one of them knew something." Pat's voice is far off. "I should have put more heat on them. But the school pressured us into backing off. They owned the town back then. Even worse than they do now."

Anthony and Pat avoid each other's eyes. I know they must be thinking of Isabella.

"So that was it?" I ask after a moment. "Case closed?"

Pat clears his throat. "We were understaffed and overworked back then. Too many other active cases, and the Weaver one had no real leads or suspects. I never stopped working on it, but the more involved I got, the more I magically found new cases popping up on my desk."

Pat sets his fork down on his plate with a clatter, his expression clouding over. "In the early nineties, people started losing their heads over rumors that satanism was involved. Same time as the witch hunts for teachers abusing kids. I used it as a guise to look at the guys again. That's when the captain offered me two options: Take a generous retirement incentive or get transferred to Roxbury."

"They wanted you to back off," I whisper.

It takes him a minute or two to respond. "Thirty years on the force, and that's how they chose to get rid of me. By paying me off. I shouldn't have gone down without a fight."

So that's what Anthony meant about his uncle regretting how he handled the Weaver case. The security guard's statement was his white rabbit, and it wound up becoming his downfall.

With a chill, I wonder if the photograph will be mine.

"Hey," Pat says, as Anthony and I are about to leave. He's talking to me. "Whatever it is you're looking for with this case, I hope it's not a happy ending."

Anthony is quiet until we're out of the diner. "So do you think any of what he said is connected to The Drop?"

I shake off memories of the other night. The betrayal in Brent's eyes. The sound of the recruits hitting the water. I describe what I saw to Anthony.

"He couldn't have been killed that way, though," I say. "It's dangerous, but it's only for new recruits. If Matt's first year on the team was his sophomore year, then he would have done The Drop before he disappeared."

When I'm finished, Anthony looks angry.

"What?" I cross my bare arms in front of my chest.

"They caught you? How could you be so careless? You should have let me come with you."

"Because it would have been *so* much better if they caught both of us," I say.

"Why?" Anthony snaps. "Afraid of what your boyfriend will do if he catches you with me?"

I'm stunned. Anthony shakes his head. "Don't think I don't know why you've been avoiding my calls."

"That's not it," I hiss. "You *lied* to me. I didn't know if I could trust you."

"Then prove it." Anthony thrusts his helmet at me. "Let me drive you back to campus. And drop you off right in front of your dorm."

I feel the blood drain from my face.

"Exactly," he says. "I'm tired of being your dirty secret, babe."

"*Babe?* You should know why I can't parade you in front of him," I explode.

"No, I don't. Enlighten me." Anthony takes a step toward me, and I'm terrified by the look on his face, because it's the same one he had the first time he kissed me. Even worse, I can't convince myself to back away from him.

But he stops short, inches from me. "I'm over *this*. Maybe you should wait to call me until you are, too."

Before I can respond, he's on his bike, tearing away from me. Pressure builds behind my eyes, and a phantom sensation comes over my lips. Almost as if I still feel his on mine from so long ago. I want to kick myself for not being quicker, smarter with him and letting him have the last word. Again.

The worst part is he's right: I'm not over what happened between us.

CHAPTER
TWENTY-SIX

Brent, Cole, and Casey Shepherd leading the men's 8 team to victory Saturday morning only lasts a day or two as a water-cooler topic: The spring formal is on Friday night, and everyone is buzzing about that. Apparently some freshman's parents own the Park Plaza Hotel in Boston, and they agreed to let Wheatley have the dance there as long as no one disturbs the wedding going on in the ballroom next door.

Anyway, what everyone is really freaking out about is Goddard's new decree that anyone planning not to return to campus after the formal needs written permission from their parents. Also, we have to sign a form saying we promise not to get drunk, high, naked, or some combination thereof and wreak havoc on the city of Boston.

Most of my friends convince their parents that Casey Shepherd is having a small, G-rated get-together on the Cape. My mom even agrees to write me a note allowing me to go, as long as I don't tell my dad. But it's Kelsey's parents who take issue with April driving us to the Cape in her mom's SUV.

"Does she think I'm a bad driver or something?" April asks,

stabbing her potatoes a little too manically at dinner Monday night.

Everyone looks at one another.

"Whatever." April slams her fork down. "I only failed the road test the first time because the lady hated me for no reason."

"What were your excuses the other two times?" Murali mutters into his soda.

"Hey," Brent says, as April growls at him to shut up, "we can't all fit in Apes's car anyway. I'll borrow my sister's car for the weekend and drive half of us. Kelsey can come with me."

And that's how that gets settled.

I am not buzzing with excitement, however. Everything that happened with Anthony has left me in a permanently foul mood, and Brent's intense practice schedule has left little time for us to get past the weirdness of The Drop debacle. As a distraction, I throw myself into full-on Weaver mode.

In my downtime Wednesday night, I pull out the notebook in which I have the crew team picture and Matt Weaver's key hidden. I think about Pat's story about the security guard's version of the night Matt disappeared.

Three voices. But four guys in the basement, allegedly. What if Matt were the phantom fourth guy? The woman said she saw him go into the woods around the same time. He could have met up with the guys who were playing poker, then left to meet his doom. The only question is Which of the guys was waiting for Matt in the woods? And why would the others lie to cover for him?

I wish I had access to the official statements Matt's friends gave about that night, but I have a feeling they were "lost" when the police department switched to digital records. How else could Steven Westbrook run for senator twice without any of his opponents digging up the connection between the hazing charges and Matt Weaver's disappearance? Unless he's paying people to be quiet—which isn't exactly a stretch, considering his record.

But even if Westbrook paid someone to make sure his adventures at Wheatley never came out, it doesn't necessarily mean he's capable of murder. In fact, I don't think I've ever believed the senator had it in him to kill someone. He certainly would have had the motive to kill both Dr. Harrow and Isabella, who were trying to blackmail his family.

I pull up a picture of Steven Westbrook on Google, trying not look at one of the most popular hits: the picture of him and Alexis at Cynthia's funeral. In his latest campaign photo, he looks exactly as he does in person. Bleached teeth, overstretched smile. Milky brown eyes and blond hair. Golden tan that probably came out of a hose.

As fake as he looks, there's also a wimpiness to the way he carries himself. As if he's someone else's puppet—which I guess is the same for all politicians, if you think about it. I bet he never imagined he was involving himself in a murder investigation when he paid James Harrow not to go public about his affair.

Travis Shepherd was right. Westbrook doesn't have the balls.

My brain is about to shut down from information overload. None of these theories accounts for Sonia Russo's disappearance or the mysterious Vanessa Reardon.

And my only link to Vanessa Reardon is *not* going to be a willing participant in this investigation.

I reach for my phone. My throat is suddenly dry. Calling Alexis can end one of two ways: with her telling me to eff-off and hanging up, or with her not answering at all.

With trembling hands, I scroll to find her number. I almost drop my phone when it starts to vibrate with an incoming call.

"Hey," I say to Brent, over the sound of my heart thumping.

"What does your dress look like?" he asks.

"Why? You don't want to get the same one?"

"Ha-ha. I'd like to match my tie, so we don't look stupid."

I glance over at the dress draped across my bed. It's silver, with long sleeves and a low back. I ordered it online because I'm basically a shell of my former self. "Go with black."

"I'm intrigued," he says. "Okay, gotta finish this physics lab. Love you."

He hangs up before I can process the last two words. Or re-spond. I sit back in my chair, using my feet to spin myself in lit-tle half circles. I can't help the smile blooming on my face. As if I didn't have a million other things to obsess over, now I'll be overanalyzing the last sixty seconds for the rest of the night. Did he hang up because he was afraid I wouldn't say it back? Or does the fact he said "Love you" and not "*I* love you" make it not that big of a deal?

But most importantly, does it mean we're okay now?

Suddenly, I wish he hadn't hung up. I wish I had the chance to say it back. To cling to this good thing, which sometimes feels like the only good thing I haven't screwed up completely yet.

I've spent too much time obsessing about Anthony. Wonder-ing what could have been. Holding on to something that never existed, when I have the real thing right in front of me. Brent, a boy who cares what color dress I'm wearing and loves when I tease him and pushes all of my buttons in the best possible way.

I can't let our relationship be the thing my white rabbit de-stroys.

I breathe in through my nose and try to distract myself by starting my reading for Matthews's class. Halfway down the page, my eyes go to my phone again.

Instead of calling Brent back, I dial Alexis's number.

It rings once, twice, then two more times before I sigh with relief.

"Hi, you've reached Alexis. I'm unavailable at the moment. Please leave a message, and I will be happy to call you back."

I wonder if her father's speechwriter scripted that little bit for her. In any case, I doubt Alexis will be happy to call me back, so I hang up before the voice mail beeps.

CHAPTER
TWENTY-SEVEN

Remy opens her bedroom door and squeals when she sees me. "Get out! I love it!"

She lets me in and makes me do a twirl for April and Kelsey, who are sitting on Remy's bed. I catch a look at myself in the closet mirror. The dress *does* fit great. The material is shimmery without being tacky, and the back is just low enough to prevent me from getting kicked out for indecency. I did my own hair—a high bun—and chose a pair of dangly rhinestone earrings I borrowed from my mom.

April and Kelsey get up and coo over my dress. They're both in black: April's dress is short and one-sleeved, and Kelsey's is strapless and long. Remy's is blush-colored and down to her feet. The sweetheart neck is made of lace, and her hair is in the braided chignon she wanted. She looks like a woodland fairy.

We all do the last-minute primping thing and make sure our bags are packed for the Cape. A shuttle will take us from school to the formal, where April's parents and Brent's sister will have dropped the cars off. We'll leave our stuff in there and head straight to Casey's house from the dance.

I wiggle my toes in my pewter heels. I made a promise to myself to have fun at the dance and not obsess over what I might find at the Shepherds' house until later.

The DJ sucks, the hotel ballroom is about a hundred degrees, and Remy's Enchanted Forest theme is more like Central Park Crack Den, but I'm having an amazing time. Brent actually likes to dance, and my friends seemed to have forgotten the petty drama of who was going to the dance with whom, now that we're here and that doesn't even matter anymore.

I take my shoes off and step on Brent's feet. He spins us around a few times before we collapse in laughter over the awful techno. "This is serious fist-pumping music."

He pulls me to him and kisses me, despite the fact everyone can see us. I shiver as his gaze travels down the front of my dress and he traces the small of my back with his thumb.

"What are you thinking?" I ask.

"Things. I'll tell you about them later." Brent grins at me, showing off his slightly uneven two front teeth. During pictures earlier, he told me how he chipped his tooth—falling off a bike when he was little. He got it fixed, then broke the bond again on a beer bottle when he was drunk last year.

"Be right back," he says.

Cole and Murali come over and start doing some awful dance, like they're in a *Saturday Night Live* skit. I laugh, because at least they realize how lame this all is. From the corner of my eye, I see Brent approach the DJ. The DJ looks skeptical as Brent gestures with his hands, clearly trying to make his argument more convincing.

Brent heads back toward us, looking pleased with himself. I figure out why when the DJ fades the techno song out and starts Billy Joel's "Uptown Girl." Everyone on the floor stops dancing. They look around, confused, before shrugging and finding someone to spin around to the music.

"This is for you," Brent shouts over the music. His smile is so big it looks like it's going to split his face in half. I laugh and grab him. Next to us, Murali and April are trying to show Cole and Kelsey how to swing dance.

As Brent spins me around, it hits me. This is the happiest I've ever been. Not happy as if I haven't known happiness before, but as if I never knew it could be like this. That I could feel like this with another person. I'm searching for the words to tell Brent this when my clutch purse begins to vibrate.

It has to be after ten. Who would call me this late? I ignore it and keep dancing with Brent. When the song is over, I break away.

"I have to run to the bathroom," I tell him. "Dance with Remy. She looks bummed."

We glance over at Rem, who is halfheartedly swaying with Phil. She's watching Cole and Kelsey, like a puppy who didn't want her toy until another dog ran off with it in its mouth.

Brent rolls his eyes and heads over to them while I search for a bathroom. On the way, I check my missed call.

It's from Alexis.

I hurry into the bathroom, past a freshman who is vomiting into one of the sinks. Her friend pats her back.

I pause and watch them. "Really?"

The girl's friend shrugs at me. "We snuck vodka in. . . . Do you think she'll be okay?"

"Get her water," I say. "There's a vending machine in the lobby."

The girl nods and leaves. I lock myself in one of the stalls, hoping Pukey out there is too wasted to eavesdrop.

Please pick up, Alexis, please pick up.

She does, after the second ring. "Who is this?"

"Alexis?"

There's silence on her end. Does she recognize my voice?

"Yes. . . . Who is *this*?"

"Don't get mad," I say. "Or hang up. I really have to talk to you. It's important."

More silence, but I can practically hear her putting the pieces together. "Anne?"

"Yes." I squeeze my eyes shut as she hisses, "Are you freaking kidding me? How did you get this number?"

"That's not important. Please, just listen to me!"

"About *what*? How you ran me out of my school and ruined my father's life?"

I decide it won't help me to point out that her father ruined his own life. "I know you hate me. And you have every reason to. But I think your dad might be in trouble. Do you know someone named Vanessa Reardon?"

Alexis is silent. "What does my dad have to do with my god-mother?"

"Don't flip out at me . . . but I think your dad knows what happened to Matt Weaver. Your godmother, too."

"Matt Weaver?" Alexis lets out a sharp laugh. "You're really something else, aren't you?"

"Alexis. Come on. I'm trying to explain." My hands are sweating. "Someone might try to frame your dad for Matt Weaver's death. Possibly the same person that scared your godmother into leaving Massachusetts."

Alexis is silent. She knows, then, that Vanessa is running from something. Or someone.

"It's true, then, right? Vanessa is afraid of them? The crew team."

"I don't know what you're talking about," Alexis snaps. "If you call or come anywhere near me again I'm calling a lawyer."

Crap. I'm losing her. "Alexis, I never meant for you to—"

"Spare me," she seethes. "Have fun with your new friends. I can only hope they stab you in the back just like they did to me."

I swallow. My throat is dry. "I—"

"I'm hanging up now, Anne. And one more thing: How does it feel to be screwing Remy's sloppy seconds?"

The call ends just as the phone is about to fall out of my hand.

I tear off a sheet of toilet paper and dry my palms. There's a horrible taste in my mouth. I'm suddenly aware of how small the stall is, how bad the bathroom smells. . . .

I stumble out of there, managing not to throw up everywhere. My head is spinning in circles.

Remy. Brent. What? That's impossible.

They would have told me.

I hang in the hallway outside the ballroom and apply more rosebud salve. I think of happy things, like my dachshund, Abby, licking my nose, in the hopes it will lower my blood pressure. I can't fall for what is probably one of Alexis's bitchcraft tactics. She's lied about Brent before, and she probably lied about Brent and Remy to mess with my head and screw up my night.

I march back into the ballroom, committed to acting like nothing is wrong. But then I see them dancing.

Remy whispering something in his ear.

Brent laughing.

I'm not going to let myself cry. I worked too damn hard on my eye makeup.

There's a lump at the back of my throat the whole drive to Cape Cod. I'm in the front seat of Brent's sister's Jeep Wrangler. Cole, Kelsey, and Murali are in the back, laughing and recapping the night's events as if they happened a week ago. I stare out the window onto Route 6, counting the lights passing us.

I look down as Brent's hand moves to my knee. "You okay?" He asks.

"I'm fine." I don't even have the energy to force a smile. Should I be mad, that Brent and Remy hooked up? Technically, it's none of my business who he'd been with before me, but Remy is my friend. One of them should have at least been honest with me so it didn't come out like this and become a big deal.

Unless it was a big deal.

I don't want to think about it.

The Shepherds' Cape Cod home looks like a dollhouse I used to have. It's a two-story white colonial with a blue door and shutters. I can hear the ocean from the backyard.

Brent offers to carry my overnight bag, but I hug it to myself and follow Cole and the others up the driveway, past a Range Rover with a Wheatley sticker on the back window. There's a three-car garage at the head. April and the others are still behind us.

Casey is waiting for us in the doorway. He's taken his suit jacket and tie off. "Everyone's in the kitchen. My mom's cool with whatever as long as we stay on the first floor."

Cole and Murali brush past Casey wordlessly. I pause in the foyer.

"Great house," I tell him.

"It's all right," he says. "We only spend half the year here, anyway."

I consider the chandelier hanging over the two-story foyer. The marble floor and spiral staircase. I follow Casey down the hall to the kitchen. Everything is sparkling and granite like it's recently been renovated. Bea Hartley, Vera Cassidy, and a handful of senior girls I don't know by name are gathered at the island counter. Bea is opening a bottle of wine as Vera arranges cheese and crackers on a platter.

"Hi, girls," Bea says. I realize Kelsey is behind me, clawing at the top of her strapless dress. She's been paranoid about it falling down all night. The girls offer polite smiles. Thankfully, the guys break the awkward silence by parading into the kitchen carrying beer kegs.

"Bea, get the cups out," Casey barks.

Bea's expression hardens but she goes to the pantry anyway. I motion to help her.

"I love your dress," I tell her. She blushes and looks down at her simple cream-colored cocktail dress. I want to like Bea Hartley, I really do. She's not a psychotic bitch like Alexis Westbrook.

Bea just needs to lighten up and realize she's not a First Lady yet. And ditch the controlling assface of a boyfriend.

Nausea swirls in my gut as I make eye contact with Brent. His eyebrows knit together, trying to figure out what my problem is. I look away and accept a glass of wine from Vera. I'm going to need plenty of them to get through the night, especially once Remy gets here.

We move to the living room off the kitchen. I make small talk with the senior girls as the guys set up music and beer pong. I only absorb half of what they're saying. When Remy arrives, I feel like I've been punched in the throat. I drain two more glasses of wine as I pretend to be immersed in conversation with the girl next to me. Her name is Brianne, and she just got into Cornell. Everything else falls short of my ears, which are starting to buzz.

The wine is making me feel as if I've been sitting in the sun all day. Brent is watching me from the beer-pong table across the room. Someone touches my shoulder, and I sway a little as I turn to face Remy.

"You're being weird," she says. Her eyes are glassy and her breath smells like mint schnapps. There's no way I see this conversation ending well.

"I'm just tired." I shrug her off and head for the kitchen, wobbling on my heels. I find Cole leaning against the counter, staring into a glass of beer. His tie is off and the top of his shirt is unbuttoned. His hair is askew.

He smiles as I join him at the counter. "Not feeling it tonight, either?"

I shake my head, biting back tears. I want to ask him if knows about Remy and Brent, but these aren't the answers I came here for tonight. Everything is so fucked up.

"Why did you and Remy break up?" I blurt.

Cole drains the rest of his beer as if he can't get it down fast enough. "Really?"

"Sorry."

He sighs. "She didn't feel the same way about me. I'm always going to be the fat little kid Alexis bossed around."

Cole turns to the counter and cracks open another beer. He hands it to me then opens one for himself. I shouldn't mix it with the wine, but I'm past caring. We do a pathetic clink of our rims and drink in silence.

"Brent and Remy," I finally choke out. "Is it true?"

His face falls, and I immediately wish I hadn't asked. Cole puts his arm around me, and I rest my head on his shoulder, vowing not to cry. A cacophony of cheers and frustrated yells sounds over the bass emanating from the living room.

I look up at Cole, breathing in his Abercrombie & Fitch cologne. He looks back at me, his eyes sad. Or maybe it's just my double vision that's making it seem that way. I touch the beauty mark beneath his right eye. He laughs and flicks my bun.

He pulls me in closer to him, and we stand like that for a little while. It's completely innocent—just two friends who've realized that maybe they've fallen for the wrong person. Or people. I think of Brent, then Anthony, and all of the things they've kept from me. The things I've kept from them. It could be so much simpler if I let myself fall for a safe guy like Cole, but that's not how it works.

We break apart at the sound of giggling in the kitchen archway. Remy stumbles across the threshold, her arm on April for support. April dances over to the kitchen, singing along with the song playing in the living room, but Remy pauses, watching us with hurt in her eyes.

"I have to pee," I announce. I stumble out of the kitchen, past the pockets of people clogging up the hallway. I was too busy drowning my sorrows in alcohol to notice how many people showed up. I spot Jill Wexler, which only makes me want to throw up even more than I already do.

The line in the hall suggests there's a bathroom downstairs, but I don't want to run into Brent. I sneak up the spiral staircase despite Casey's warning that his mom said it was off-limits.

The upstairs smells like cinnamon and pine needles. It's dark. I lean against the wainscoted wall. *Pull yourself together, Anne. It's not like you didn't hook up with other guys before Brent. You even hooked up with* Anthony.

But Remy . . . Remy is the closest thing I have to a best friend here. How could she not tell me? How could *Brent* not tell me? He had the perfect opening when I told him what happened between Anthony and me.

I stumble down the hall in search of a bathroom. There's a light on and jazz playing in one of the bedrooms, so I head in the opposite direction.

I stop outside one of the doors. Even in my drunken state, I can tell there's something different about it. It's closed. Locked.

I pull a bobby pin out of my bun and force the lock open. I slip into the room and close the door behind me, feeling the wall for a switch. When the light flickers overhead, a weird sensation settles over me.

I just broke into Travis Shepherd's office.

I have to take off my heels so they don't make noise on the cherrywood floors. An executive desk takes up most of the room, and that's about the only detail I can absorb in my current state.

Damn it. I really should have planned this better. I've found Travis Shepherd's office, but I'm too drunk to accomplish anything. What am I looking for? What's the freaking point, anyway?

I lean on the wall for support. There are framed degrees and photos on the walls. Travis and Casey fishing. Travis and a rail-thin blonde on their wedding day.

I stumble over to a framed collage behind the desk. There are a bunch of older photos inside, including a duplicate of the crew team photo that has slowly been ruining my life.

My pulse races. I haven't seen the photo that's below it, though.

The picture is of Travis and Pierce Conroy. Probably, when it was being taken, they didn't even realize the person behind the camera was accidentally in the frame.

I squint at the background of the photo. There is a long mirror on the wall behind Travis and Pierce. Someone sits at a desk, snapping the photo. Most of the face is visible around the Polaroid camera.

I blink a few times to make sure I'm really looking at Matt Weaver.

A woman's voice sounds down the hallway.

I don't hesitate: I take the frame off the wall, slip the photo out, and replace the frame. I shove the photo in the side of my dress and stumble out of the office, nearly colliding with a woman in a silk sheath dress.

Her blond hair is swept away from her face, which bears an uncanny resemblance to Casey Shepherd's. "What're you doing up here?" she demands. Her words are slurred, as if I've interrupted her own private party.

"I thought this was the bathroom," I blurt.

Mrs. Shepherd gets in my face, her eyes gleaming with an emotion that scares me. "I know who you are," she says. "You're that little bitch."

"Excuse me?" I don't know who this drunken yuppie is calling a bitch, but I am in *no* mood to let that comment slide.

"Did you know Elaine Redmond has been getting death threats?" Mrs. Shepherd's face is inches from mine. "Apparently some people think she and the senator are responsible for that little whore getting herself killed—"

"Shut up!" I yell. "You didn't even know her—"

"Anne?" The voice makes my blood run cold. I turn to see Brent at the top of the stairs. Mrs. Shepherd smirks at me and stumbles off to her bedroom, and I swear I don't even know which one of us is drunker.

Brent's hand is on my arm before I can go after her. "What the fuck was that about?"

"Leave me alone," I snipe at him. I'm totally being unfair, but the floor is spinning out from under me and I'm just so *mad*.

"Anne." His voice and his eyes are hard, and when I look at

him I don't see the Brent I fell for. I see who I'm afraid the Wheatley School will turn him into. I see his father.

"I can't deal with this anymore," he says. "I can't trust you when you're acting like this."

I reach in my dress and pull out the photo I stole from Travis Shepherd's office. "You can't trust *me*? I thought your dad wasn't friends with Matt Weaver, Brent."

He motions to take the photo in my hand, but I yank it away. His face is furious. "You've got to be kidding. I told you to drop this."

"Since when do you tell me what to do? I am not Bea-freaking-Hartley," I yell. He looks over his shoulder and motions to shush me. I take a step back from him. "No! I'm not going to be quiet. Do you have any idea of who your father is, Brent? Because I'm starting to get a picture, and I don't like it."

Brent is speechless. Color floods his face. "I can't believe you."

"What's so hard to believe? You thought I'd just let this go after what happened with Isabella?"

"That's *exactly* the problem," Brent hisses. "I don't *get* you, Anne. I don't get this freakish OCD you have about Matt Weaver. You're out for blood. Goddard's, my dad's—I don't know. It's like *you* don't even know anymore."

"Fuck you," I say. And I mean it ten times more than I did when I said it to Anthony a few weeks ago. I never thought I could be this mad. I stalk past Brent, heading for the stairs.

"Anne—"

"No. You can't take that back. And just because you said no more lies, I know about you and Remy."

"What? What does that have to do with anything? That was before we were together—"

"You didn't tell me. Just like you didn't tell me about your diabetes until you freaking almost died." I can't stop myself. "When are you going to let me in, Brent? You tell me you love me, then hang up on me? God, at least if I'm crazy and obsessive about things, I *let you* see that side of me."

I expect him to follow me down the stairs, to say something, anything, except what comes out of his mouth next.

"So this is it?"

I can't fight around the pounding in my head and come up with a good reason this shouldn't be the end. I know it's wrong because I'm angry—and drunk—but all I want to do is hurt him as much as he hurt me.

"Yeah, I guess it is it," I say, and take off down the stairs.

He doesn't follow me. When I get back to the living room, I expect something to have changed. But no one has a clue Brent and I broke up. If anything, everyone's having a better time than before.

Some genius—definitely a guy—figured out the only way to get girls interested in beer pong is by turning it into a strip game. Two senior guys are down to their boxers, and Remy and Jill Wexler are in their bras and underwear.

Kelsey and April see me from across the room and start waving. Beer flies out of April's cup and onto the floor. They're too drunk to care they're making a mess. They have the right idea: I join them, because it seems like oblivion is the only thing I'm going to find here tonight.

CHAPTER
TWENTY-EIGHT

I wake up with my cheek pressed to what I hope is not vomit. I blink a few times. I'm on a couch, and the wetness on the arm is just spilled beer. The pain behind my eyes is unlike anything I've ever felt before.

Something is sticking to my side. I reach down into my dress and pull out the photo I took from Shepherd's office. I quickly turn it facedown, in case Casey is nearby. Although I'm willing to bet he fell asleep somewhere a little more comfortable.

"Anne?" An arm brushes against the couch cushion. I look down at the floor. Kelsey waves to me. "What are you doing down there?" I ask.

"We both fell asleep on the couch," she croaks. "Kind of like . . . snuggling. I guess I fell."

I massage my temples. I need a scalding hot shower and a coffee.

"*Damn,*" Kelsey says from the floor.

I don't know why that's what finally sets me off. I lock myself in the bathroom while everyone else wakes up. I pull out the photo I stole from Travis Shepherd's office and clutch it to my chest as I sit on the edge of the Jacuzzi tub.

And I let myself cry.

I'm silent as everyone loads their stuff into the cars, ready to head back to school. Brent doesn't look at me as he opens the back door for Kelsey, who crawls in, moaning, "I'm never drinking again."

I turn to April. "Can I ride back to school with you?"

She looks from me to Brent's car, confused. "Sure."

I climb into the backseat. Murali calls shotgun, so Remy gets in next to me. Phil opens the door and yawns. "I guess I'll ride with Brent."

I watch him head over to the jeep and say something to Brent that I can't hear. Brent's face is emotionless as he climbs into the driver's seat.

As we pull away from the Shepherds' house, Murali and April rehash Brooke Dempsey's meltdown after someone spilled wine on the back of her white dress. I close my eyes and lean back in the seat, avoiding Remy's probing gaze.

"All right, what is going on?" she cries out when we pull onto the highway.

"What? What happened?" April nearly slams on the brakes in the merging lane.

"Jesus, Apes, pay attention," Murali yells. "Remy, you can't just yell things when she's driving, or we're all going to die."

"Sorry. I'm just confused. But Anne is avoiding me. What did I do?"

"Nothing," I lie. "Brent and I broke up. I don't want to talk about it."

A hush falls over the car. April murmurs *Oh, no,* and Murali stares out the window.

"Can we not act like someone died?" I snap. My brain is pounding against the walls of my skull. "It's not a big deal."

Remy pats my knee. "It happens, when you're dating someone you have to see every day. . . ."

I shut my eyes again. If she keeps using her *This is why we can't have nice things* voice on me, I'm going to puke. Or maybe it's April's constant slamming on the brakes whenever a car passes in front of us. In their defense, she's going thirty in a sixty-mile-an-hour zone.

"You guys will be okay," Remy says. "Maybe you just need space from each other—"

I grab the back of April's headrest. "Pull over."

Murali turns and looks at me. "Oh, crap—"

"PULL OVER!"

"I can't get over!" April cries. "No one will fucking let me over!"

Her response is to stop in the middle of the highway. The driver behind us leans on his horn, and Murali yells at April to keep driving and put on her signal.

And that's how I wind up vomiting all over the backseat of her mother's SUV.

We have to stop at a car wash, so we don't get back to campus until after four. When I go to power my phone on and see if Brent left me any messages, nothing happens. There is a layer of sugary film on the screen.

"Shit." I try to piece together the events of last night, but everything after doing shots of cake-flavored vodka with April and Kelsey is a blur. I sniff my phone and gag. Yup, that's cake vodka all right.

I flop on my bed and entertain a series of angry thoughts. One: If alcohol companies don't want teenagers to drink, why make vodka taste like my favorite dessert? Two: My favorite dessert is ruined for me, because every time I smell cake now, I'm going to think of that cake vodka and want to puke. Three: Now I need a new damn phone.

I'm not going to sit around all day feeling hung over and sorry for myself. I spend a good forty minutes in the shower, scrubbing all evidence of last night off my body. The tears and crusted mascara under my eyes. The kisses Brent traced along the back of my neck while we waited to go inside the dance.

I'm toweling off in my room when there's a knock at the door. I freeze. Even though I have no desire to forgive him for what he said last night, part of me hopes Brent got someone to let him into Amherst so he could see me.

I'm willing to accept full responsibility for picking a fight with him. I was pissed he didn't tell me he hooked up with Remy, and maybe if I'd stayed sober, we could have talked it out. And I probably shouldn't have insulted his dad like that.

But still, I never would have stooped as low as Brent did when he said I wasn't over Isabella. He was one of the ones who helped me solve her murder—and now he's just like everyone else who thinks I ruined his school's precious legacy?

"Anne, I know you're in there." Remy knocks again.

I swallow. "I'm naked."

"Oh, come on. Let me in."

I slip into my bathrobe and open the door for her. I didn't think it was possible to look worse than I did earlier, but Remy looks terrible. Her eye makeup has downgraded to raccoon-mask status, and she smells like booze.

"You need to shower," I say, as politely as I can.

"I wanted to talk to you first." She motions to sit on my bed. I lay my towel down first.

"Are you mad at me?" Remy asks, her doe eyes not completely hidden behind last night's mess of mascara. "When we got to the party, you were weird all of a sudden."

I can't look at her, because all I see is her and Brent together. Doing things we did. Doing things we never got to do. "Remy, I know you and Brent hooked up earlier this year."

Remy's mouth opens a little. "Is that why—?"

"No, it's not. We were about to break up anyway." Tears build in my eyes as I realize how true that is. "But I'm upset neither of you told me."

"Anne, I swear, it was nothing; we were both just drunk at a Halloween party—"

I hold up a hand. "I don't want the details, Rem."

"I wanted you to like me so badly." Remy has tears in her eyes, making me want to believe her. "It was so obvious you were into him, and I thought you wouldn't want to be my friend if I told you."

"I'm not like that," I say.

"I know that now, but the more time went on, the less sense it made to tell you. You guys are like *meant* for each other. Everyone knows it. I didn't want to screw that up over a stupid hookup."

I let her hug me. Some of the coldness in my chest begins to thaw. I can't be mad at her for not wanting to hurt me. I didn't tell Remy I broke into her room to find the video Alexis stole from Isabella, because I didn't want to hurt her. Most of the time when we say we don't want to hurt someone, we don't want to screw ourselves in the process, but I guess you have to do whatever you can to get by.

Remy wiggles her bare toes and tucks her feet beneath her. "Who . . . did tell you?"

"It doesn't matter."

"You should talk to Brent." Remy drags out each word as if she's still afraid I'm pissed and will tell her to stay out of it. "Maybe you can work through whatever happened."

I think of Brent's face when I accused him of being like his father. "I doubt that, Rem."

I sleep through the afternoon and until nine Sunday morning. The throbbing in my head is gone, but my body still feels wrecked. I make a cup of coffee—food is still too ambitious—put on my sunglasses, and walk to the pharmacy on Main Street. The photo I took from Shepherd's office is in my bag. After I buy a bottle of Extra Strength Tylenol, I sit at the do-it-yourself photo kiosk.

I choose "enlarge" from the machine's photo-editing options. I put the picture facedown on the scanner and watch it load on the screen in front of me.

Tears sting my eyes as the faces come into focus. If I didn't know any better, I'd think it was Brent in the photo, not Mr. Conroy. The only thing that's different is their hair. Brent has soft brown waves, while his father's hair is dirty blond and cut close to his head.

But I'm not here to cry over Brent. I do not cry over guys. I get over them. Even ones like Brent. No, especially ones like Brent.

When the picture is done loading, I choose my new size: 10×12. I want to get a better look at the box on Matt Weaver's desk. I swipe my credit card through the kiosk and wait for the picture to print.

I keep checking my phone, forgetting that it's not operational. And by not operational, I mean not even Gandalf the White could bring it back to life. I'll have to wait until I feel better tomorrow to take the T into wherever the nearest Verizon store is.

The kiosk announces my photo is ready. I don't have to hold it close to my face to see the details now. The quality is still far from perfect, but I can determine two important things from the picture:

The room is Matt Weaver's dorm at Wheatley.

The box on his desk has a padlock on it and the stamped initials M.L.W.

There are about a million places Matt Weaver's lockbox could be, but at least now I know with a reasonable level of certainty what the key from his room opens. I don't know if there's anything inside the box that could be a clue to why he was killed. If the box didn't have something important inside it, though, Matt wouldn't have gone through the trouble of hiding the key so well. At least that's what I have to believe.

It's dinnertime when I get back to campus, but I'm not ready to face Brent yet. Or Remy. I could sneak in and sit by myself, but it'll be hard to go unnoticed with so many people still away from campus, milking the term *after-party* for all it's worth.

I notice him waiting on the bench outside of Amherst when I look up from getting my ID out of my wallet. He jumps up when he notices me, and I nearly drop my bag. My whole body warms when I see his face. *He's here. For me.*

Not Brent. Anthony.

"What are you doing here?" I ask. I can't let him see how I happy I am to see him. Not after the way we left things off.

"I've been trying to call you since Friday night. I was worried . . . , but I also have to talk to you."

"Anthony—"

"No, hear me out." He brushes his hair out of his eyes and motions as if he's going to put his hands on my shoulders, but he catches himself and puts them in the pocket of his hoodie. "I was a dick to you. Not just the other day, after the diner. Way before that. I should never have just left that night without explaining why I had to do what I did to my sister." He runs his hands down his face. "I—I'm not good at this stuff. But I've been thinking, and I think I treated you like that because I wanted you to be pissed at me. Like making you mad would have been easier than letting you down."

"Anthony—"

"No, there's more. I don't want to pretend I don't give a shit what you think of me. Because I do. I don't want to be the waste product you think I am. It's all I think about lately." His eyes are pleading, begging me to understand what he's really saying. "You're all I think about, and I can't stop."

I can't breathe. It's not that I haven't imagined him coming back and saying that to me. Part of me even wanted him to. Desperately.

I step toward him, taking his face in my hands. "Then don't."

He stares at me, stunned. "What . . ."

"It's over." I'm choked up, as if saying it finally makes it true. "And before you ask, it's not because of you. But *you* left me there that night, with Brent. You made the choice for me. I'm still pissed about it. And I'm probably stupid for forgiving you . . . so please just kiss me before I change my mind."

So he does. His lips are even better than I remember: smooth and full of heat. I keep holding his face, tracing the side of his jaw up to his sideburns. I run my fingers through his hair and pull as his tongue finds mine. His hands move to my lower back, pressing me into him.

His lips move to my ear. "Are you sure you want this? Because I don't know any other way to be around you."

Losing Brent is still raw, but this is definitely what I want. I've wanted it for longer than I admitted to myself. But the thrill of kissing Anthony again dulls the guilt flooding me. Seriously, not even an Adele album can cover the range of emotions in me right now.

And I can't help but feel that this was supposed to happen. That the picture was supposed to lead me back to Anthony so we could finish what we started. So we could solve the case his great-uncle couldn't. So we could help Mr. Weaver bury his son.

Brent was wrong: It's not that I can't let Matt Weaver go. I just don't want to.

CHAPTER
TWENTY-NINE

Anthony and I lie facing each other on my bed. For the record, we're fully clothed and have been since I brought him up here an hour ago. For once, he's doing most of the talking. He wants me to know the truth about Isabella, he says. Not because he wants to speak ill of the dead, but because he thinks I should understand how different they really were and why he had to do some of the things he did.

I trace the tattoo on his neck as he tells me things were different before his father got sick. Mr. Fernandez worked for a construction company in Boston. Their family used to drive to Hyannis every summer and rent a cabin. Anthony's father liked to hunt, and he took Anthony all the time. Isabella would get jealous, so eventually they brought her along. Iz was the center of her father's world, Anthony said.

Isabella never had a lot of friends at public school: She was smarter than the other kids and didn't have anything in common with them. The school wouldn't let her skip ahead a grade, so her parents pulled extra shifts to send her to precollege programs at

MIT. Isabella worked her ass off to get into the Wheatley School. That was the year her father was diagnosed with MS.

That's when she changed, Anthony said. He dealt with his father's illness by getting angry and fighting anyone who looked at him the wrong way. Isabella went off to boarding school and rarely came home. Anthony thinks it was too difficult to see her father's deteriorating condition.

"I was in denial about her and the vice-principal." Anthony's eyes are on my ceiling. "My sister was too smart for that. But she needed someone. And we weren't there for her."

"Why did you steal from her?" I whisper.

Anthony faces me. "You're going to think I'm an idiot."

I shake my head and take his hand. It's warm, and he relaxes into me. I missed the way he smells up close—like hair gel, Eclipse spearmint gum, and a hint of motor oil.

"Okay." He sighs through his nose. "I've always been kind of good at poker . . . ; my cousin taught me. I play every week with these guys at the firehouse. It's how I met Dennis. Before he became a cop."

I nod. I never actually believed the first version—that Dennis is the older brother of one of Anthony's friends from school.

"So I started winning almost every week," Anthony continues.

"Sounds like you're more than 'kind of good,'" I say. "Were you counting cards?"

"Jeez, can I finish my story? It's almost impossible to count cards in poker."

"Okay, so maybe I don't even know how to play poker."

A smile twitches at the corner of Anthony's mouth. "So, a couple of the guys got pissed I was winning every week. But this guy Tank came up to me one night. Asked if I wanted in on a higher-stakes game."

"Sounds sketchy."

Anthony gives me a look. "Sorry," I say. "Go on."

"The buy-in was a grand. Fifteen people. The winner would

get ten grand," Anthony explains. "I *knew* I had a shot at it. Or at least second place. Do you know how much that kind of money could have helped my family? I could have helped my mom with mortgage payments, or gotten someone to come take care of my dad. . . ."

I run my thumb over his palm, feeling all of the ridges and hardened skin. I still can't believe he's here. "You asked Isabella for the money?"

He nods. "I didn't have the cash. Most of my paychecks went toward groceries, gas, and stuff. My mom was too caught up in her own shit to realize how much I was paying for. She'd kill me if she knew. Isabella didn't even know. When I asked her for the money, she laughed in my face. So I took it. I lost it all in the tournament . . . the same night she was killed."

Anthony's face is stony. All of the anger I'm used to seeing in his eyes isn't there, though. He's not the same person I met after his sister's death. Or maybe he's always been this person and I never looked closely enough.

I don't know what to say. I can never understand what Anthony's been through—the responsibility of keeping his family afloat, the pain of losing his sister, and the crushing knowledge that his father is next.

I've been so lucky by comparison. I've always had it all—popularity, friends, parents that would forgive me for just about anything—and I threw it all away by almost burning my old school down. I press my lips to Anthony's cheek and whisper in his ear, "I'm never going to be good enough for you."

"Stop." He takes my face in his hands and kisses me, slowly, deeply. I let him.

Being sent to Wheatley was my fault, but it was also my chance to do something right for once in my life. I thought that was getting justice for Isabella, but now I see that was just the beginning.

CHAPTER
THIRTY

Sunday morning, Anthony comes by to drive me to the Verizon store, but since I'm not the account holder, I have to wait for them to call my dad and get permission to give me a new phone. Apparently, being a dumbass and spilling Smirnoff on one's phone is not covered by insurance.

We decide to walk around on Boylston Street after, because I can't stomach the thought of going back to campus. I update him on my weekend—leaving out the epically ugly breakup.

"I can't believe you were in Shepherd's house." Anthony shakes his head. "He's the richest guy in Boston."

"Believe it, because I got a souvenir." I hand him the photo I took from the office. Anthony peers at it. "Is that—"

"Yeah, that's Matt. But look closely at what's on the desk."

Anthony and I stop at a crosswalk while he studies the picture. "M.L.W. . . . What's Matt Weaver's middle name?"

I snatch the photo away from him. "Don't you see? There's a padlock on the box."

I watch Anthony's face change as the gears turn in his head. "Oh . . ."

"We've got to go back to the Weavers and see if they have that box."

The light changes. Anthony is parked across the street, and I start there with a new sense of purpose. He trails after me. "Anne, that box is more than thirty years old. Don Weaver looks like he has trouble finding his dentures every night. And if they've found it already, wouldn't they have thought it might help the police? They left no stone unturned, remember?"

"The stones they were allowed to touch, at least," I murmur.

Anthony studies my face. "You think the box could be somewhere on campus?"

"Could be," I say. "It was in his dorm room in that photo. In any case, we should find out if his parents have seen it before."

I go to check the screen of my phone, forgetting that it's dead. Anthony smirks. "Time to get a watch."

I sigh. "What time is it?"

Anthony glances at his wrist. "Early enough to make a detour."

Joan Weaver is sitting in an Adirondack chair, facing her house. She looks up at the sound of a motorcycle approaching her curb. She's wearing a wide-brimmed hat and garden gloves. There's a stack of weeds next to her chair.

Unlike last time, she doesn't smile when she sees us. In fact, she looks like she's been expecting us. I almost lose my nerve as Anthony presses a hand to my back, guiding me toward her.

"Hi, Mrs. Weaver," he says, as if sensing my hesitation. "I hope we're not intruding."

Joan gives me a look that cuts right through me. "Did you need more for that newspaper article on Matty?"

Anthony's hand moves down my back reassuringly. *Lie.*

"Mrs. Weaver . . . , I was hoping we could ask you a few questions," I say, "not for the paper."

Anthony stiffens beside me as Joan takes off her gloves. "You never were writing an article on him, were you?"

"I'm so sorry I lied to you." Pressure builds behind my eyes. "But I think I can help you and your husband find out what really happened—"

"Do you know how many times I've heard that over the years?" She doesn't sound angry. Just tired, which makes me feel worse.

Anthony slips his hand in mine as Joan turns toward her house.

"Wait." I step away from Anthony, searching my bag. "I need to show you something."

Joan faces me, her mouth settling into a line. Before she can decide it's not worth it to humor me, I show her the photograph I enlarged yesterday morning.

"Have you seen this box before?"

Joan peers at the photo, silent. The look of sadness on her face tells me she couldn't care less about the box. Her wrinkled thumb moves over her son's face. She swallows and hands the photo back to me.

"Please, Mrs. Weaver. Do you have this box?"

She shakes her head. "He kept his important things in there. Baseball cards, his coin collection. We never found it in his room. Figured he brought it to school and it got lost in the shuffle."

Or someone stole it.

Joan Weaver retreats into her house without saying good-bye to us. I want to kick something.

"Excuse me."

Anthony looks to our right, and I realize the voice is coming from next door. The woman there has a hose at her side, trickling water onto the driveway. She waves us over.

I look at Anthony, who shrugs. We walk to the street, then up the woman's driveway. She's in jean shorts and a sweatshirt, her hair tied back with a bandana. She looks like she's in her late thirties.

"Couldn't help but listen to you guys," she says. "You know, Joan and Don don't really like people coming around about Matty."

"We gathered that," Anthony grunts. I jab him in the ribs.

"We're just trying to help," I say.

"Yeah, I heard you found a box. What does it look like?" Her forehead creases.

I pull the photo out of my bag and hand it to the woman. She wipes her hands on her sweatshirt before taking it.

The woman's forehead creases. Then she laughs. "*That* box? No, he definitely didn't have anything important in there." She looks up from the photo. "If this is the same box I'm thinking of, there's nothing in there but Jingles."

"Jingles?"

The woman hands me the photo back. "My hamster. He died when my parents weren't home, and Matt helped me bury him in the garden. I wanted to use a shoebox, but Matt went home and put him in that box. He said the cats wouldn't be able to dig him up that way."

I blink. "Oh."

"Sorry you came out here for nothing," the woman says. "Good luck with whatever you're doing."

She doesn't say it unkindly. More like we're a couple of kids playing Sherlock Holmes and she wants to humor us. We thank her for her time and head back to Anthony's motorcycle. "I can't believe we came out here for a dead hamster," he says.

I put my hands on his shoulders. It's weird how much taller than me he is. Brent was my height. I push the thought out of my mind. "We have to come back and dig up that box."

"Are you crazy? You heard her."

"Yeah, but did that woman say she *saw* Matt put the hamster in the box?"

Anthony rubs his eyebrow. "You really think he buried evidence along with a dead pet?"

"I don't think he buried the hamster at all. But yeah, I think there's something important in the box. Why else would he hide the key as well as he did?"

Anthony doesn't have an answer for that. "I just . . ."

"What?" I ask, as we climb on his motorcycle. He looks over his shoulder and smiles at me.

"I really don't want to know what he did with the hamster, then."

Anthony and I stop at a place called Tia's Taqueria for lunch. I hang back and let him order, my mind racing around everything Joan Weaver told us.

He accepts a paper bag from the cashier, and we sit at the counter by the window. "I got tacos and burritos. Which do you want?"

I shrug. "Whichever."

He raises an eyebrow at me. "You want me to pick for you, don't you? I'm half Mexican, so that makes me real qualified, right?"

"Actually, I'm just not hungry and didn't want to be rude," I mutter. "Ass."

A ghost of a smile plays on Anthony's mouth. "I like when you curse at me."

"Trust me. That's not cursing." I break off a piece of the shell from the taco Anthony placed in front of me. I can't bring myself to eat it.

"What are you thinking?" He asks me around a bite of burrito.

"That we'd better come up with a plan fast if we want to get to that box before someone else does."

CHAPTER
THIRTY-ONE

I get an anxious feeling in my stomach as Anthony gets off at the exit for the Wheatley School. I haven't felt this sick about going there since my mom dropped me off over three months ago. At least then I didn't know what I was facing. Now I know I'll eventually have to see Brent, finish my homework, and go to sleep in the room I should be sharing with Isabella.

I tighten my grip on Anthony. As if he can sense what's wrong, he stops at Dunkin' Donuts. He lets me rest his head on his shoulder for a while. I like the way his chin falls right at my hairline, his stubble grazing my forehead.

"How are we going to pull off sneaking into that woman's yard and digging up her garden?" I ask.

Anthony shifts in his seat. "I'll drive by her house this week and figure out her schedule, see when she's not home. Did you notice the sticker on her car window?"

I shake my head.

"UMass Nursing School," he says. "Maybe we'll get lucky and find out she works nights."

I don't want to go back to school. I'm fine with staying in this smelly Dunkin' Donuts with Anthony forever, but he has to get home to watch his dad before his mom leaves for work at seven.

When he drops me off, we share a kiss good-bye that would probably get a couple thrown out of a church on their wedding day.

Anthony's eyes are closed when I pull away.

"What?" I ask.

He shakes his head with a little laugh. "I just can't believe we're back here."

I wait for him to say more, to ask what exactly *we* are, or if I'm using him to get over Brent. But we both know those kinds of questions aren't Anthony's style. I close my eyes and wait for the wave of guilt at kissing him, but it never comes. Instead, I feel free. Brazen. Like myself, only amplified. It's how I've always felt around Anthony.

"I'll e-mail you until they ship my new phone," I tell him.

He nods, his eyes tracing a line from my face down to the hips of my jeans. I flush.

"Be careful," he says. Then he rides away.

Maybe it's because she still feels like she's the reason Brent and I broke up, but Remy follows me around like a sad basset hound until dinner. Kelsey and April are quiet in a way that makes me seriously curious about what went down at the party after I passed out. When we get to the dining hall, Remy leads us to a table for four.

"Thanks," I say, as we settle in. "I'm not ready to face him yet . . . or any of them really."

The way April and Kelsey stiffen across the table from me says that the guys have just walked in.

"They look confused," April narrates. "Wait, now Brent is telling them to find another table. Okay, they're moving away from us."

"Apes," Remy hisses. "Really?"

"It's fine," I say. "Everything will be fine in a few days."

"Do you think you'll get back together?" Kelsey asks, pushing her glasses up and down like she does when she's nervous.

I bring myself to look over at Brent. I'll admit, I half expected him to show up outside my door after our fight, professing apologies and undying love. But he looks unfazed as he cuts Cole on the soda-fountain line. They exchange jabs. Cole looks over at us and offers me a meek smile. I return it, but Brent keeps his eyes on his cup as he fills it with half root beer, half Diet Coke.

I ignore the pang in my chest. I guess this is what a real breakup is supposed to feel like—getting crushed just seeing the other person going on with his or her life, doing the little things you used to do together, like experimenting with different soda combinations. I've never known this feeling before. I'd always considered guys disposable, and I've dumped my fair share. A breakup is new territory for me.

I realize the girls are still waiting for my answer.

"No, I don't want to get back together. He's just . . . not the person I thought he was."

Remy rubs my back, holding in her usual advice and judgment. I hear her voice in my head, the things she said after she told me she slept with Casey Shepherd.

Anne, just promise me you won't hate me. If they start saying stuff about me.

How many other people know about her and Brent? How many people are going around thinking my best friend here is the reason Brent and I broke up?

Kelsey's voice pulls me back to the table. "I don't think anyone knows what kind of person Brent is. He doesn't let us."

I don't know what to say, even though I know she's right. The only times I felt like I truly got to see the real Brent were in moments of desperation—three months ago, when he got sick and had to tell me he had diabetes and was scared of telling people, and then three days ago, when he got so angry at me he snapped.

"Let's eat," I announce. "I'm not feeling sorry for myself, so you guys definitely are not going to sit around feeling sorry for me."

We split up to go to our usual dinner stations—mine is the salad bar. I'm scooping grilled chicken onto my lettuce when I notice him down by the dressings. Our eyes connect. He turns away as I set my plate down and call his name.

"Brent."

He doesn't look at me. Real mature. But he doesn't run away or anything, so that's progress.

We meet each other halfway, at the middle of the salad bar. He runs a hand through his hair, and I get this weird, hopeless feeling, knowing I can't do that to him anymore. I half expect him to hug me or something, even though that's stupid.

"Hi," I say.

"Hi." Brent scratches the back of his neck and eyes me. "Is this really how we're going to do this?"

"I'm not sure what you want me to do. Pretend I don't care that you don't trust me? Promise you didn't say those awful things?"

Brent takes a step toward me. "You can*not* put this all on me, Anne. You spied on me and my friends. That's psychotic." He lowers his voice to a whisper. "Now you want me to believe my father killed Matt Weaver? What's next, I'm leading a double life as a Craigslist killer or something?"

I can barely look at him I'm so angry. "You think I'm crazy."

He sighs. "No, I don't."

"Really? 'Cause I'm pretty sure like five seconds ago you called me *psychotic*."

"I said what you *did* was psychotic." Brent tugs at the roots of his curls. "God, Anne. Would you listen to me?"

"No." I lean in closer to him, so I don't have to raise my voice to make my point and therefore make a scene. "You listen to me. One: What you guys to do the new recruits is psychotic. Two: No, I'm not going to stop until I get the truth about what happened to

Matt Weaver. And three: I didn't ruin Cole's mother's or Sleaze-bag Westbrook's lives. They did, when they screwed each other."

Brent's face contorts and my stomach dips. Oh no. I turn over my shoulder to see Cole watching us from the soda machine, his cheeks pink. He looks away from us. I want to rush over and apologize to him, but I know he'll just pretend he didn't hear.

"Nice." Brent shakes his head.

I don't know how I got here, from falling headfirst for Brent to wanting to shove his face into a wall. But I never wanted to hurt Cole. Brent calls my name as I grab my salad and head back to my table.

"Why can't we talk about this?" His voice is pleading. It cuts right through me and makes me think maybe I do want him back. I search his face, trying to see the Brent I fell for: the guy who doesn't really care about being crew team cocaptain or SGA president—the guy who always believed me when no one else did.

"My dad is an asshole," he says. "But he's not a criminal. Think about my family and what this could do to them."

One of the guys at his table calls him over, and Brent looks from him to me. I can see him calculating: Does he keep talking to me, or does he go back to his dinner as if nothing is wrong?

He lets out a little sigh of frustration. "Can we talk later—?"

"Whatever, Brent." I turn away from him, blinking away the pressure building behind my eyes. If he wants to choose his stupid crew team over me, that's fine. I've already made my choice.

CHAPTER
THIRTY-TWO

I'm one of the first people to get to art history the next morning. I sit at my desk in the back corner of the room; Cole and Murali sit to the front and left of me. They're later than usual today, so I open my notebook while I wait for them.

My leg jiggles when I see there's only a minute to the start of class. I can't help it: The thought of being late (and watching other people being late) gives me hives. I inherited my compulsive need to be early everywhere from my anal father. I may not always be a model student, but at least I'm always on time.

Anyway, Cole and Murali are usually here early, too. So when Robinson hobbles into the room, sloshing coffee onto the floor and tittering about an upcoming exhibit at the Museum of Fine Arts in Boston, I get a little worried.

The classroom door bangs behind me, and Cole and Murali trail in. I raise my hand to wave them over, but they slip into the empty seats in the opposite corner, by the door. Murali's eyes meet mine, his mouth unsmiling. Cole doesn't look at me as he sets his laptop case down. His hair, which is usually neatly combed to the side, falls in front of his eyes.

I'm still watching them unpack as if there's no circle of empty seats around me. As if they haven't sat next to me every morning since I started this class. Robinson is passing out glossy cards with the MFA exhibition information on them.

"Friday night is the opening." Robinson beams. "As curator of paintings of the Americas, I'll be hosting the event. Free admittance for Wheatley students. The free champagne, on the other hand . . ."

I tuck the card in my bag, my gaze still on Cole. *Please look at me.* He does, for half a second, as if he's checking to see if I'm watching him. The hurt in his eyes cuts me to a million pieces, and I wish, for the hundred-thousandth time in my life, that I had the ability to keep my mouth shut.

What I said about Cole's mom and the senator was awful, but I was only trying to get to Brent, to make him show some sort of indication he gives a crap we broke up. I don't know if he just doesn't care or if he's really that emotionally challenged. Or maybe it's my fault because he finally felt comfortable enough to tell me he loved me and then found out I lied to him about the Matt Weaver thing.

I watch Cole, thinking about how he wears his hurt for everyone to see. Then Anthony, who wears his anger like a badge. For the first time, I feel the weight of how much I miss Brent. Not because of his adorable, not-perfect smile or the way he hugs me from behind or even the way he'll stay on the phone with me until midnight because I'm bored or need him to explain the complicated sci-fi movie we watched earlier. I miss the way that with Brent, things felt simple. Even when they weren't.

Even if they'll never be, and that's why we're not together anymore.

I remind myself that I'm not going to pull my grade up from a B+ in this class by thinking about boys, and I turn my laptop on. Every Sunday night, Robinson e-mails us links to the paintings we're going to discuss during the week so we can look at them on our computers while he lectures (read: play Bubble Breaker and read the online edition of *Entertainment Weekly*).

Today, I actually want to pay attention.
Until I see the e-mail from the unknown recipient in my inbox.

To: dowlinga@Wheatleyschool.edu
From: luvspugs95@gmail.com

Subject: I have what you need

I open the e-mail, expecting a message from a Nigerian prince requesting a business partnership with me. I definitely *don't* expect what the first line says:

I can tell you what happened to Matt Weaver.

I look around to make sure everyone is watching his or her own computer. I scroll down to see how long the e-mail is before I read the rest. It's only a couple of lines.

Meet me by the Massacre Monument in Boston Common, today at 5. E-mail me back to let me know you'll be there. And I would be, if I were you. I have proof.

I bang out a response so fast I retype it three times to get it right, no typos.

Who are you??

I sit back as the e-mail floats into cyberspace. Robinson starts walking down the aisle, noticing people are starting to doze off. I minimize my e-mail window and pull up the painting we're looking at today: Thomas Sully's *The Passage of the Delaware*.

I keep my eye on the e-mail tab for the rest of class, waiting for it to change to "Inbox: (1)." It never does.

I can't tell Anthony about the e-mail. He'll tell me not to go and insist it's probably a trap. He'd say it might even be one of the men in the photo, in which case it would be totally stupid to go alone. He'd be right, too—but that's what pepper spray purchased off the Internet is for.

Also, I figure my chances of being kidnapped or killed in a place as crowded as the Boston Common are significantly lower than being killed by my vice-principal in the forest. And that didn't happen, so there you go.

I don't have to make excuses to Remy about why I'm missing dinner, since everyone assumes I just don't want to see Brent. Good. I hope they all sit together like the big dysfunctional-yet-happy family they were before I came and messed everything up.

The map I printed tells me to get off at the T station called Downtown Crossing. I have to switch train lines fifteen minutes out of Wheatley. The one I get onto is packed with commuters.

I spend the train ride trying to figure out who sent me the e-mail. He or she said to meet at "5," and it looks like I'll be at Downtown Crossing by 4:40. I do some calculating in my head: The person must have known how long it would take me to get to the Common at the end of the day, which could mean they know what time the last class at Wheatley ends.

The train car lurches, taking my stomach with it. I have a horrible feeling I'm walking into a trap set by a Wheatley alum. What are the chances of someone who could actually help me waiting by the Boston Massacre Monument? Someone like Vanessa Reardon?

I'm sweating a little beneath my sweater. There's only one person who could have told Vanessa Reardon I was searching for answers about Matt Weaver, and the thought of seeing her again makes my insides shrink.

An automated voice overhead announces we're at Downtown Crossing. I head northwest on the street above the T station.

Boston Common is not the tiny-ass little park I pictured in

my head. My map says that Beacon Hill, where most of my friends' parents live in multimillion-dollar brownstones, is nearby. The minutes tick by as I wander through the Common, past couples lying on blankets and kids flying kites. Stupid, archaic map. I desperately need a working phone again. It's already 4:58. I don't know how much time whoever is waiting for me will give me to show up.

A cool wind sweeps through the trees, and I wish I'd grabbed my jacket before I left. A statue that sort of looks like a giant white crayon emerges in my line of sight, and I pick up my pace. I'm happy to note that there are plenty of people around to witness what could very quickly turn into an ugly situation.

She's sitting on a nearby bench, her back to me. By now, I'd recognize that three-tone blond hair anywhere. I talk myself out of turning around, and suck in a breath before sitting next to her.

"Hi, Alexis."

She doesn't look at me. "You showed up."

"Please drop the CIA movie script. I hope you're not wasting my time." I can't help my escalating level of annoyance now that I know I came all the way out here for Alexis Westbrook. I don't believe that *she* has proof of what happened to Matt Weaver, and I'm nervous about what sort of payback she's plotting.

"I'll leave, if you want." Alexis's voice is calm. "I can also make a call to the Wheatley School and let them know you've been *harassing* me about a thirty-year-old case my father had nothing to do with."

I'm silent. She has me where she wants me, and I hate her for it. But what does she want from me? To screw up my life as bad as I've screwed up hers? "One phone call isn't harassing, Alexis."

"Trust me, Goddard won't agree. He's dying to expel you, but he's waiting until Dr. Harrow's trial is over so he can do it quietly," Alexis says.

I'm not surprised at this, but it still brings an acrid taste to my mouth. "Yeah, well, I bet you're all sorry Harrow didn't kill me, too, then."

"Shut *up*."

I don't know what I expected her to say, but it wasn't that.

"My father had nothing to do with Isabella," Alexis hisses. "Dr. Harrow manipulated him and destroyed our lives. None of us knew he killed Isabella, so if you're going to keep flinging accusations around, at least get your story straight."

"Is that why you're here?" I ask. "You think I want to accuse your dad of killing Matt Weaver?"

Alexis opens her mouth slightly, sticking her jaw out and making her *I can't believe I have to deal with you* face. "Matt Weaver's been gone for over thirty years. Why are you interested in him all of a sudden?"

"Why do you think I'll tell *you* that?"

An annoyed sigh escapes Alexis's nose. Her eyes are angry slits. All she needs is a ring through her nose to look like a bull. She motions, and I think she's getting up to leave. Instead, she pulls a manila envelope from the Vera Bradley bag next to her.

"My dad and his friends . . . they were all cleared. They were never even *suspects*," she says. "But if you're going to cause problems, you should know the truth, at least."

I raise an eyebrow, but I have to admit I'm curious now. "And what's that?"

Alexis hands me the manila folder. "No one killed Matt Weaver. He killed himself."

CHAPTER
THIRTY-THREE

I don't trust people easily. It's yet another trait I can blame on my dad, who listens to criminals and their bullshit all day. But Alexis Westbrook also tried to frame me for Isabella's murder and succeeded in breaking up Brent and me, so I trust her as much as I'd trust a pit bull if I'd just rolled around on top of raw meat.

The manila folder in my hands is clean, with a string tied tidily around the circle fastener. It reminds me of Alexis, actually. Neat and perfect on the outside. Probably vile and dirty inside. "What's in here?" I ask.

"When you called me, I started looking for proof my dad was even friends with the dead townie."

That's Alexis for you. Such a beautiful way with words.

"I found these in the attic of my old house. They were in a box of my mom's things." Alexis's sapphire eyes are actually glassy. I didn't know she had working tear ducts. She looks away from me.

Carefully, I untie the fastener and look inside the envelope. It's like one of those little Russian dolls: There are about twenty more envelopes inside. I look over at Alexis, who nods.

I take one of the yellowed envelopes out and peek inside. There's a folded letter on loose-leaf paper torn from a spiral notebook. The handwriting is dark and slanted. On the outside of the envelope, someone has scrawled *Cyn*.

"Your mom."

Alexis nods. I scan the letter quickly, noticing words like *I hate myself* and *I don't deserve to live.* At the bottom, he signed his name: *Matt.*

I'm scanning back up to the line *I never meant to hurt Vanessa like I did,* when Alexis snatches the letters out of my hand.

"Hey. That's evidence," I say.

"Of what? There's no crime if he killed himself. And no body." Alexis puts the envelopes back in the folder, delicately.

"You can't prove it was suicide if you don't turn the letters over," I say.

"Relax. I made you copies." Alexis hands me a stack of letters.

"This is manipulating evidence," I say. "How do I know you're not holding back ones that mention your dad?"

"Stop with the lawyer garbage." Alexis rolls her eyes. "None of them mention my dad. He didn't even date my mom in high school."

Alexis interrupts me before I can begin reading the letters. "You're so convinced my dad is the bad guy here. Why don't you ask your boyfriend where his dad was when Matt Weaver groped my godmother while she was passed out drunk?"

I feel as if she's punched me. Casey Shepherd's words to Brent come back to me:

Or do you prefer to sit back and watch? I heard your dad was into some freaky shit like that in his day.

Oh my God.

"Face it," Alexis continues. "Just like your roommate, your darling little friends aren't who they think they are."

"Because you're so perfect yourself," I mutter.

"I've spent my entire life acting like some trained pony for my father to show off. Why shouldn't I be allowed to be a normal human being and vent a little bit?" She spits. "I didn't even mean the things I said."

"It sounded like you did. Or else you should be up for an Oscar."

"Don't act so high and mighty, Anne. Like you've never said something you wish you could take back?"

Her accusation isn't pointed—there's no way she could know what I said about Cole's mother earlier—but it still cuts right through me.

"What do you expect me to do with these letters?" I ask.

Alexis gives a small shrug. "Be convinced. If you're not, things are going to get really difficult for you."

Her warning is clear: Leave her family alone. Again. This time, something tells me to heed the warning. Alexis picks up her bag and gives me a look that says she hopes she never has to see me again.

All I want to do is read the letters when I get back to campus, but I'm starving, so I swing by the refectory and make a salad to go. I check my phone for any updates from Anthony, even though I know it'll be a few days before he can figure out the best time for us to dig up Matt Weaver's box.

I dodge all of the usual suspects on the way back to my room, sharing an elevator with two chatty underclassmen who freeze up when they see me. I wonder what their problem is, until I see the heart-shaped birthmark on the shorter girl's chin. These are the two sophomores I bitched out when I heard one complaining about not getting a day off after Isabella's murder.

I don't look back at them when I get off at my floor, despite the angry memories the shorter girl's face brings back. When I get back to my room, I suddenly feel so exhausted I could puke. I lie on my back and let myself imagine what my life would be like if I hadn't gone to the party the night Isabella was killed. If I'd caught her sneaking out to meet Harrow, maybe she would have told me what was going on and I could have convinced her to stay. She could be lying on her stomach on her bed right now, reading the book she never got to finish.

I would never have met Anthony. I would never have found the picture of Matt Weaver, and maybe my life would have some shade of normality to it right now. I would still be the Trust Fund Fuckup from Manhattan whose daddy got her out of trouble and into the best prep school on the East Coast.

But because my roommate was murdered and I shot her killer in the leg, I'm the hero.

So why don't I feel like one?

I curl on my side with the letters Alexis gave me.

"He killed himself." I whisper it, trying the idea out. Why would he do it? Over his guilt that he assaulted Vanessa? Over the pressure of being on the team?

Matt Weaver committing suicide doesn't seem to fit. Or maybe I just don't want it to, because it means I broke up with Brent and alienated most of my friends for nothing. For an awful boy who molested a girl while she was drunk.

I read the first letter.

Cyn,

I wanted to talk to you about the other night but it seems like he's always watching you. I don't like it. I don't think he's good enough for you, and I know he's hurt you before. I want you to know I'm not like him. You know I'm not and I would never hurt you. Please believe me about what happened with Vanessa. I never wanted things to be like this. I wish I'd never even met any of them and you and I could still be friends like we used to.

Matt

PS: Please don't tell him about this.

I trace the words *I don't think he's good enough for you*. Travis Shepherd, no doubt. From the paranoid postscript, it sounds as if Matt was afraid of him. It doesn't exactly fit Pat Carroll's story that Matt followed Travis around like a puppy . . . but then again, maybe something changed and Matt saw the real Travis.

I read through the rest of the letters, searching for an answer as to why Matt hated himself. He doesn't give one. He begs Cynthia to forgive him in a way that makes me think he's apologizing for more than whatever he did to Vanessa.

The last letter is the one Alexis showed me. The one she thinks proves Matt killed himself.

Cyn,
This can't be the only way you'll talk to me now. I watched you the whole time in class today hoping you'd look at me, but you never did. You hate me and I don't blame you. I hate me. I hate who they've turned me into. I hate myself so much sometimes I feel like I don't deserve to live. I need you to see all of them for who they really are. They made me like this. Pierce was the one who got Vanessa wasted and let her into Aldridge. He told me she *wanted* me to do all that stuff. You've heard the rumors about him, and Travis is even worse. There's so much I need to tell you.
    Matt

I get up from my bed and walk to the window. I have to lean against the ledge, hang my head to stop the blood from rushing to it. Pierce Conroy was there. Brent's dad was there, and *watched* as Matt hurt Vanessa.

THEY KILLED HIM.

I've never been surer of it. Matt Weaver didn't kill himself: Someone killed him to shut him up. To stop him from telling Cynthia whatever he wanted to tell her in his last letter. *There's so much I need to tell you.* Did he ever get the chance, or did they get to him first?

CHAPTER
THIRTY-FOUR

I haven't started my Latin project due tomorrow, my life is going down the crapper, but I really start to cry when my hair straightener breaks on Monday morning.

Sometimes it's the little things that set you off. In any case, I'm about two seconds away from completely losing my shit, which only sucks more, considering I'm five hours away from everyone I love and trust.

I crawl into fetal position on my bed. *Breathe, Anne.* Probably, the wise thing to do would be to go to Student Support Services and say, "Hi, I'm losing my shit." But I know what Student Support Services does to people acting like I am. People like Molly, Isabella's friend. I think *danger to herself* is the phrase Dr. Harrow used to describe her. Anyway, Molly doesn't go to the Wheatley School anymore, and the last I heard, she was in a psychiatric rehabilitation facility in Rhode Island.

I can't trust anyone at this school.

Except for maybe one person.

Classes don't start for another forty minutes, but Ms. C is in her office, like I expected. I peek in and see her eating a bowl of cereal at her desk, and for half a second I entertain the notion that maybe she lives here.

Ms. C looks wiped, her chin propped up on the hand she's not using to eat with. I almost decide to leave her alone and turn around, but she sees me and smiles a little. "Hey. You're up early."

I enter her office and sit across from her. Her hair is loose, falling over her shoulder, and she has no makeup on. Tired lines crease her eyelids.

I'm dedicated to telling her in a calm and mature manner that I need an extension on the project, but what comes out of my mouth is a serious of sobs and honks punctuated by "I. Can't. Do. This."

Ms. C says my name a couple of times and picks up her chair. She plants it next to me and rubs my back. "Is this about the project?"

I nod, wiping my eyes. "Yes. No. Kind of."

"Are you stressed out?" Ms. C asks. "This is a rough time of year, with your class workload plus the SATs and everything."

"Yeah." My normal voice is returning. "I guess that's it."

"Take until next week for the project." Ms. C pats my knee. She's wearing one of those Irish rings with the heart and the crown that's supposed to tell whether you're single or not, depending on which way you wear it. Chelsea and I have matching ones, which we bought together from the market at Union Square. My stomach ties itself into a knot.

"Thanks. I really appreciate it."

Ms. C cocks her head and watches me, as if she's curious why I don't sound more relieved. "Anne, is there something else going on?"

I stare at my lap, watching the plaid on my skirt blur into zigzag through my tears. It's easier than looking at her face and sensing whether or not she sees right through me.

"Anne, you can tell me."

I look up at Ms. C. "Have you ever thought you knew someone . . . like *really* knew them in a way no one else did . . . and
then they turned out to be not who you thought they were?"

Maybe I'm imagining it, but Ms. C tenses up. Her eyes probe
mine with suspicion, almost as if she knows what I've been up
to. But there's something else behind them: fear. As if I've totally
scared the crap out of her. I sometimes have that effect on people.

"I'm not sure what you mean," she says. "Is this about you
and Brent Conroy?"

His name still makes me feel destroyed inside, but I'm also
surprised Ms. C sounds like she knows we broke up. "You know
about that?"

"We know everything around here." Ms. C says it with a smile,
like she's trying to be funny, but it totally creeps me out. Even
though I'm really counting on the fact that Goddard doesn't
know *everything*.

I hesitate. "It's just . . . I'm hearing all this stuff. Rumors about
things Brent's dad did when he went to school here."

"What kind of stuff?"

I shoot a glance at the door and lower my voice. "Do you
think . . . back then . . . if a girl—a student—was raped, she
wouldn't say anything about it?"

Ms. C gets up and closes her office door. She's quiet for a minute before she says, "Anne, that happens now, everywhere, and
girls still don't say anything."

I think of Isabella and how she did say something when Lee
was stalking her. A lot of good that did. I guess my face gives
away what I'm thinking, because Ms. C puts a hand on the arm-
rest of my chair.

"Dou you need to tell me something? Because I can help you.
I'll keep it between us until—"

"No, it's not like that," I say. "There was a girl named Vanessa
Reardon. This guy . . . did stuff to her when she was drunk, and
the school didn't do anything about it. It just reminds me of what
happened to my roommate."

Ms. C's mouth forms a line. I don't need to tell her who my roommate was. "You mean . . . your roommate's relationship with Dr. Harrow?"

I swallow away the sick feeling in my throat. For the first time, I need to tell someone Isabella's story. Not the one everyone thinks they know. The one that Goddard doesn't want anyone to know.

Ms. C hands me a room-temperature water bottle, and I tell her about Lee Andersen. I tell her everything, from his painting and the obsessive notes to the way Isabella had to switch her schedule around to avoid him. I tell her that Harrow knew Lee was stalking Isabella, because she told him—she trusted him—and instead of protecting her, Harrow bugged Goddard's office and got him on tape telling Professor Upton to deal with Lee discreetly.

"I had the tape, but Harrow stole it back and got rid of it before he was arrested," I say. "Now no one will ever know that Lee is a creep and may be dangerous. I mean, what if he finds a new Isabella and hurts her this time?"

Something blazes in Ms. C's eyes. If she's anything like me, she's angry thinking about how Lee will never have to take the consequences for making a girl's life a living hell. All because of who his father is. "Did you tell this to the police?" Ms. C asks.

"Of course. They never found the tape. I just don't know why Harrow wouldn't go public with it. He could have taken Goddard down with him."

Ms. C squeezes the pencil in her hand so hard her knuckles turn white.

"This other girl . . . Vanessa . . ."

"Reardon," I say.

"Reardon. Do you know for sure she was assaulted by another student?"

"I think so." I shut my eyes. "It's just that . . . if someone you lo—, *cared* about, if their dad was maybe involved in something horrible, you'd want to know it wasn't true, right?"

I don't know if Ms. C knows I'm talking about Brent, but her face softens. "I'd hope it wasn't true," she says gently.

The area behind my eyes tightens. "I need it not to be true."

"I'm glad you came to me, Anne," Ms. C finally says. "I don't know how I can help you, but I promise I'll try."

"Thanks," I say for what feels like the millionth time. I don't know if I'll ever stop owing her for everything she's done for me. Guilt claws at me as I get up to leave. It's not fair of me, leaving out that this whole thing is about Matt Weaver. If she knew, would she be so quick to help?

"Ms. C . . . be careful. People here don't like to talk."

A small smile spreads across her lips. "That depends on who they think is listening."

I have a pink note waiting in my mailbox Thursday afternoon that says there is a package waiting for me at Student Support Services.

My phone is here!

I feel whole again.

I peruse the obscene amount of voice mails I managed to collect over the past few days. One from my father, saying he hopes my phone arrived safely and that I'll be less irresponsible in the future. A few from Chelsea, from before I e-mailed her to tell her my phone was broken. One from a very angry man with a Brooklyn area code who says if I don't get rid of all the birds in my apartment, he's calling the county board of health. I'm pretty sure that was a wrong number.

There's only one message left, and I hate the part of me that wishes it was from Brent. But when I hear Anthony's voice, I have to sit down on one of the student center lounge couches.

"Hey. I know you won't get this for a few days, but call me. If I don't hear from you by Friday, I'll swing by."

I replay the message twice, loving how the throaty bass of his voice warms me from the inside. Part of me wants to ignore the message, just so he'll show up tomorrow and I can hold on to that time when Anthony was this mysterious bad boy who came in and out of my life without warning.

But things are different now. Anthony is different now—at least to me. He's just a boy who works too hard. A boy with a messed-up family and a sister he'll never get to reconcile with. A boy who's good at poker and likes Pearl Jam and eats too fast and makes me feel like he wants more than any guy ever has when he kisses me.

I can't play games anymore. Not with Anthony.

I call him back.

"You have a phone again," he answers. "I'm sure it was a very difficult week for you."

"For your information, it was."

Anthony laughs over the sound of a vacuum. "Are you at work?" I ask.

"Yeah. Are you alone?"

I stick my feet up on the couch I have all to myself. He doesn't know the half of it. "Yep."

There's a beat of silence on his end. "The neighbor . . . she's gone every week night from seven to eleven."

"It sounds like there's a *but* involved."

Anthony sighs. "Her father lives with her. Doesn't go anywhere, from what I can tell."

"Damn." I pull at a thread hanging off the hem of my skirt. "So what are we going to do?"

"I have some ideas." Anthony's tone tells me he's not going to tell me these ideas over the phone. "What are you doing tomorrow night?"

"I don't know," I say.

"Want to grab dinner and dig up a dead hamster with me?"

"Are you asking me out on a date, Anthony?"

He's quiet, but not in an awkward way. "Give me a little credit. I can do a lot better than that. Take you somewhere real classy, like you're used to."

I blush all the way to my toes. "So you do want to take me on a date."

"You're not gonna stop 'til you get me to answer that, are you?"

I can't stop smiling. "Yeah, pretty much."

Anthony breathes into the phone. I can't tell if he's frustrated or nervous. "I'll pick you up tomorrow at seven thirty."

My day turns out to be pretty damn great. Matthews hands back my paper on Ireland and Bloody Sunday with a big 98 circled in blue pen, and Dawson tells me I have good pirouette technique.

When I get to Latin and Ms. C isn't smiling, though, I know something is wrong. Ms. C is *always* smiling. She silently hooks up the class projection machine to her laptop. As a BBC documentary about the fall of Rome loads on the screen, the class is split between relieved sighs and annoyed grunts about how our parents aren't spending upward of thirty grand a year for us to watch movies.

"I want you guys to take notes on this," Ms. C says. "We'll finish up the documentary on Monday and discuss on Tuesday."

I watch her hand back our latest homework assignments, entertaining the paranoid notion that she's avoiding me. When she comes around to my table, she locks eyes with me. She nods to the paper she places on my desk. I got an A–.

"Thanks," I say, but she's already on to the next row. What the hell is going on?

That's when I notice she's watching me. She nods to the paper again.

Confused, I pick it up. On the table beneath it is a glossy card. The same one I have in my bag, announcing Professor Robinson's art opening tonight at the MFA.

A small "Oh" escapes me. Ms. C turns and heads to the front of the room and raises the volume on the documentary, as if the whole exchange never happened.

Something goes off in my brain. Not exactly a lightbulb, but a brief flash, like from a camera. I remember standing outside Robinson's office, listening to his memories about Matt Weaver.

Is this hint Ms. C's way of telling me Robinson is the way to find Matt?

CHAPTER
THIRTY-FIVE

The only time I wore my black lace BCBG dress was to Isabella's wake. I didn't think I'd ever want to wear it again for that reason, but it's the classiest thing I have for the art exhibit. There was a time when I didn't have to think about being classy. Back when I collected vintage earrings instead of misdemeanors.

I show up at the tail end of the opening at the MFA, partly because I figure Robinson will be a couple of flutes of free champagne deep, and also, art bores me. Apparently it bores everyone else in Boston as well: There are only a handful of people checking out the early American paintings, and half of them look obligated to be here. Thankfully, no one from my class showed up.

"Anne!"

Robinson finds me first. He looks absolutely tickled to see me, which makes me feel a little guilty. He takes me by the shoulders and steers me to his fellow curators.

"Another one of my students!" He booms. I smile and shake a bunch of wrinkled old yuppie hands like the good little Wheatley puppet I'm pretending to be. I tune out most of the conversation, waiting to get Robinson alone for a minute.

When the curators move on to the next Very Important Person, Robinson pops a chunk of cheese from the reception table into his mouth. *Full mouth. Now!*

"Professor," I say, "can I talk to you about something?"

Robinson's smile wilts a little, but he swallows his cheese and says, "Of course, my dear."

"Remember a few weeks ago, when I asked you about Matthew Weaver?"

Robinson runs his tongue over his teeth in that way old people do to make sure they're not falling out of their mouths. "I believe you mentioned him, yes."

"I've been thinking. About his fixation with *Paradise Lost*." I almost lose my nerve. "Do you think whatever happened to him had anything to do with Vanessa Reardon?"

I don't know what I expect Robinson to do. Deny it? I definitely don't expect him to meet my gaze, sigh, and say, "Let's take a walk, shall we?"

It's in between dark and light outside, and it smells like lilacs and rain. A man leaving the museum takes off his suit jacket and drapes it over his wife's bare shoulders. She doesn't thank him.

Professor Robinson stands beside me, rubbing his hands together as if to warm them. "Anne, every teacher feels defined by their best and worst moments. Our best moments keep us going from day to day. Our worst . . ."

His voice trails off. He sighs. "We replay them in our head, wishing we had done something differently."

"I don't think it's just teachers who feel that way." My body is here, with Robinson, but my mind is back in New York City. In the auditorium with Martin Payne, reaching for his lighter.

Robinson nods. Afraid he's not going to give me more, I say, "What do you wish you had done differently?"

He turns his head toward me. "Anne, I don't think I can share the memory I regret the most with you."

"I know what Matt Weaver did to Vanessa Reardon," I say quietly. "I just . . . want to understand why no one helped her. Like no one helped Isabella Fernandez."

Robinson sighs—a heavy sigh, like someone who knows too much and is too tired to do anything about it. "Vanessa came to me several days after the incident. She was somewhat of a favorite of mine. A very talented girl. In any case, she trusted me." Robinson looks at a point in the distance. "She said she didn't know who else to tell, but that she had had a little too much to drink at a party over the weekend and woke up in Matthew's bed. She couldn't remember what happened the night before, and she was afraid to tell the dean. The poor thing was scared, but she didn't want to get in trouble for drinking. And Matthew was a friend.

"I told her I would speak with him. When I asked him what happened, he broke down. He hadn't realized Vanessa wasn't in her right mind. He said that his friend pressured him into . . . doing what he did. He'd even brought Vanessa to his room."

"And that friend was Pierce Conroy."

Robinson doesn't confirm or deny this. "I sat Matthew and his friend down and told them that if they didn't confess to the dean, I would do it for them. They seemed very ashamed. Contrite, even. But the next morning, Vanessa came to me crying, begging not to tell on the boys. She said she had remembered the events of the night wrong."

Robinson looks at me, the skin beneath his eyes drooping as if weighed down with sadness. "I told the police all of this when Matthew went missing, of course, but Vanessa was sticking to her changed story. That Matthew hadn't pressured her into anything."

"Is that what you regret?" I ask. "Not doing more when Matt disappeared?"

"Matthew was lost long before he went missing," Robinson says. "I only regret listening to Vanessa when she asked me not to tell."

My phone vibrates in my coat pocket. If Robinson hears it, he doesn't react. "I've been teaching at Wheatley for over forty years, Anne. It should be something I'm proud of, but recent events have reminded me exactly how little has changed since I first started there."

"Do you think Vanessa Reardon knows what happened to Matt?" I ask.

Robinson looks at me. "I can't say, Anne. I would assume she would have said something by now if that were the case."

I'm not so sure I agree. Dr. Rosenblum's voice fills my head. *Sometimes it's best . . . to let sleeping dogs lie.*

My phone buzzes impatiently. I sneak a glance at the message. It's from Anthony.

Ready soon?

"Professor, I promise I won't tell anyone about this. I just really needed to know."

Robinson's eyes twinkle. "I'm an old man. They're all biding their time until they can force me to retire, anyway."

We smile at each other. Robinson reminds me it's getting dark, and I promise to be careful getting back to school. My phone says it's 8:15.

"Anne," Robinson says, when I reach the bottom of the museum steps, "they're not all bad, you know."

I nod to him and retrace my steps to the T station, thinking of Matt Weaver's weird obsession with *Paradise Lost*. Maybe we *are* all bad, and getting by on the moments where we try not to be.

CHAPTER
THIRTY-SIX

The platform for my train is packed. Frat boys, couples dressed up in date clothes, high school kids listening to iPods.

But he stands out. The tall man in grease-stained jeans and a hooded sweatshirt. Hollow cheeks, thick blond beard. On his cell phone.

His eyes flick away when I return his stare. Something clicks in my brain. He was behind me on the stairs leading down to the platform. Could he have been behind me for longer and I wasn't paying attention?

My thoughts twist together until they form a single word: *Move.*

When the train pulls in, I push my way through the crowd. A couple of people snipe some choice insults at me, but I'm the first person on the train. I look through the window and see the man's head towering over the crowd. He tries to push his way past a woman with a stroller, who promptly begins to scream at him.

Now I run. As the crowd fills up the train car, I make my way through the doors on the opposite side so I'm on the other side of the platform. The train pulls away, leaving behind a few pissed-looking guys in BU sweatshirts who couldn't fit.

Hooded-sweatshirt guy is on the train. My hands tremble as I call Anthony.

It took fifteen minutes for another train to come. Nearly forty-five minutes after I called Anthony, I'm emerging from the tunnel entrance in the administration parking garage. I hop over the cables and run until I spot the outline of a white car in the distance. Anthony flashes the headlights twice.

If the guy at the T station was following me, he would have headed back to campus to wait and see when I show up. Assuming he found a way to get past the guard at the gates (and believe me, there are ways), he's probably staking out my dorm right now.

In case that's true, I make sure to be spotted going back into the dorm at exactly 9:30 P.M. As far as anyone knows, I never left after that. I even left the sound of my thunderstorm sleep machine on loop so everyone will believe I'm sleeping.

If hooded-sweatshirt guy has his eye on my comings and goings, he's going to be very bored tonight. At least I hope so.

Anthony scratches the space behind his ear as I tell him all of this. "We have to circle campus. See if we can spot him."

Anthony turns the key in the ignition, and I shudder along with the engine. "Absolutely not."

"Anne, if he's following you, then *tall with a beard* isn't going to help us figure out who he is."

"I don't even know if he was following me!" I say. "I'm probably being paranoid. Besides, if he did follow me back to Wheatley, he won't be able to get into the dorms."

Anthony makes a *That's what you think* snort. "I'm calling Dennis."

"Please." I grab his bicep. It's so warm I almost draw my hand back. He relaxes a bit at my touch. "Anthony, I probably imagined the guy. Let's not get freaked out. We only have two hours to find the box before the neighbor gets home."

Anthony turns the radio on and signals to turn right. Away from the school. I sigh with relief.

"Nice dress," he says, after a beat.

"Is it going to be a problem?" I ask.

Anthony takes his eyes off the road for a second, taking me in. One side of his upper lip quivers. The side with the thin scar.

"Yeah. For me maybe."

I look down at the hem of my dress. When I'm sitting, it rides almost all the way up my thighs. I desperately want Anthony to put his hand there, to feel his skin on a part of me he hasn't touched before.

Anthony keeps his hands to himself, but I notice he's running them through his hair more than he usually does. Rubbing his chin. Adjusting the radio station and volume.

I smile to myself and lean back in the seat. I've still got it.

Anthony parks in an unfamiliar neighborhood, all the way down a dead-end street. There are no streetlamps. I look out the window. The dead end leads into a small wooded area littered with beer cans, cigarette butts, and Styrofoam coffee cups.

"This isn't the house," I say.

"I know. But the Weavers' street is well lit. These woods lead to the neighbor's backyard."

My eyes are on the woods. A dirt path cuts through the trees and bramble. "So we're going the back way."

"Yes," Anthony says, humoring me. "It's the best chance we have at not getting caught."

"Getting caught," I repeat. I don't know why this possibility hadn't occurred to me earlier.

One of Anthony's knees bounces up and down. "Anne, if you want to wait here, it's okay. You have a lot more to lose than I do—"

"No." I swallow. "I dragged you into this. If we go down, I'll take the fall."

He reaches and touches my jaw, as if to pull me in for a kiss. But he only runs his thumb over my bottom lip and turns to get out of the car.

I follow him to the trunk, hopping from foot to foot. Anthony pulls out a shovel—not like a little one you plant daisies with; it's a *big ass* shovel, with a square head. The kind Mel Gibson defended his house with in that awful movie about aliens.

My breathing becomes shallow as I follow Anthony through the woods. I stare up at the back of his head, wondering if he's also trying to tune out the noises: the crunching of leaves under our feet, the snapping of branches overhead—all of the sounds I'll forever associate with the moments before Dr. Harrow almost shot me.

There's a light on over the Weavers' back porch. An eight-foot fence surrounds their backyard.

The neighbor's house is dark, save for a small lamp in the second-floor window. Their chain-link fence is considerably shorter. It's too dark for me to make out much in the backyard except for a rotting picnic table and brick patio.

Anthony sticks the toe of his boot into one of the chain links and hoists himself over the fence. He lands on the other side without a sound. Panicked, I point to the window with the light in it.

"What if he gets up?" I whisper.

"We won't give him a reason to." Anthony reaches for me over the top of the fence. "C'mon."

I look down at my sequined black ballet flats.

"Dear God. Just take them off if you don't want to ruin them," Anthony hisses.

"That's *not* what I was thinking. I was just happy I didn't wear heels." I grab Anthony's hand. He's so strong that I feel my feet coming off the ground. I feel around with the ball of my foot for one of the links.

"Swing a leg over the top now," Anthony says.

"But I'm wearing a dress."

"Anne. Seeing what kind of underwear you're wearing is the *last* thing on my mind right now."

I don't point this out, but he kind of implied it's *one* of the things on his mind, at least. I swing a leg over and let myself do a little roll-fall into Anthony's arms. He sets me down and picks up the shovel.

We survey the backyard together, although it seems as if Anthony has already scoped it out from this angle. He points to the garden extending from the patio to the far corner of the fence.

I inch closer to it, examining the plants. The fence is lined with bushes covered in delicate yellow flowers shaped like four-pointed stars. "Forsythia," I whisper. "Perennial. Not a good place to bury something."

Anthony raises an eyebrow at me.

"My mom is the editor of a garden magazine," I explain.

Anthony's eyes sweep across the garden. He kneels down and cups a handful of dark brown wood chips in his hands. I kneel down beside him, examining the pansies planted in a row. I run my hand over the wood chips, exposing a few rocks arranged in a circle.

"Check this out." Anthony reaches for one of the rocks. Someone has painted the name JINGLES on its smooth, tan surface.

Anthony and I look at each other. He stands up and plants the head of the shovel in the garden. A whimper catches in my throat. I can't believe we're doing this.

"It's okay." Anthony steps on the base of the shovel and tosses a pile of dirt and wood chips aside. "Why don't you keep watch, make sure no one pulls into the driveway?"

I know he's just trying to get me out of his hair so he can focus on digging, but I nod and walk the perimeter of the backyard. I try to peek over the fence and into the yard of the house on the other side—at the same moment a screen door slams on the porch.

I press myself against the fence. Anthony looks over at me, frozen.

I don't breathe as the sound of jingling metal comes toward me. A dog collar.

Anthony presses a finger to his lips and keeps digging. I nod and stay still against the fence. I look down at my feet to see a black nose peeking out from the space between the fence and the ground.

The dog sniffs my feet. And barks.

I look over at Anthony, who mouths, *Don't move.* He drops the shovel and gets on his knees, clawing at the ground. He found something.

The dog barks at me again. "Nice puppy," I whisper. "Nice, nice puppy."

The nose disappears from under the fence, followed by a howl. I run over to Anthony.

"Now might be a good time to wrap up over here."

"Look." Anthony wedges his foot in the hole he's dug. More dirt falls away, exposing the corner of a metal box. I drop to my knees and help him dig. The wall of soggy earth surrounding the box collapses.

Bark. Bark. Bark. Bark.

Someone opens the screen door over at the Weavers' old house. A male voice calls out, "Chiefy! Get inside."

Anthony puts his hand on my back. *Don't move.* By the light of the half moon, I can make out the letters stamped on the metal box: M.L.W.

The dog next door scratches at the wooden fence and whines. The man on the porch is quiet. I can almost hear him think: *Is someone out there?*

I yank on the sleeve of Anthony's flannel shirt. He hands me the box while he grabs the shovel and kicks some dirt back into the hole. Chiefy barks his head off as Anthony mouths, *Go!.*

We run for the chain-link fence, making Chiefy go berserk. A light flickers on in the house. Anthony throws the shovel over the fence and climbs over in two fluid movements. I hand the box off to him, but for some reason, I can't get a good grip on the fence this time.

"Come on," he urges me. "You did it before."

I lift one leg over the top of the fence at the same time I lose my footing with the other. I fall sideways, my dress getting caught on a gnarled piece of chain link. Pain slices through my side, but I don't stop to look down. Anthony holds his hand out to me and we run.

"Do you think anyone's coming?" I can barely get the words out as Anthony starts the car and peels away

"Depends on if he saw us." Anthony tugs at his ear, leaving a streak of dirt behind on the lobe. I examine my own shaking hands. The spaces under my fingernails are filled with dirt, my thumbnail almost torn clean off.

The metal box on my lap isn't heavy. When Anthony makes a wide turn, something slides around inside.

"Did you bring the key?" Anthony asks.

"No. I hid it in my room." I run my finger across the initials, feeling the grooves in the metal they form. M.L.W.

"Guess that's where we're headed, then."

Normally, the thought of Anthony coming to my room would invoke a different reaction in me, but all I can think about is the pain in my side. "We have to sneak in through the tunnels," I say. "I never signed out of the dorm earlier. Don't want to make anyone suspicious."

"How are we going to get in?" Anthony asks.

"Parking garage entrance. I wedged a bobby pin in the lock when I snuck out of it earlier." As an afterthought, I add, "My friend Remy taught me that."

Anthony smiles a little. "At least you learned something at school."

There is someone in the laundry room when Anthony and I reach the Amherst tunnel entrance. The pain in my side is so bad and I want to open Matt Weaver's box so badly that I find myself on an angry rant as Anthony and I wait in the dark basement, listening to the sound of someone turning the ancient dryer dials on the other side of the wall.

"Who the hell does laundry this late on a Friday night anyway?" I hiss. "I swear to—"

Anthony presses a finger to my lips. His irises are a brilliant gray in the dark. He stares at me. I kiss the tip of his finger, not caring that it's caked with dirt. He drags it down my chin and neck, tracing down to my belly button, pulling me to him.

I set down Matt Weaver's box so my hands are free. Anthony grabs them and wraps my arms around his lower back. He lifts me by my thighs so I'm back against the wall, legs wrapped around his waist.

Our tongues meet, and I slide my hand up the back of his flannel shirt. The smoothness and warmth of his skin shocks me. I want to feel every part of him, and he presses his waist into mine, letting me know he feels the same.

He doesn't pull away at the sound of a dryer door slamming and footsteps barreling up the laundry-room stairs. "Let's go," I say into his mouth.

"No." He kisses me, his teeth pulling gently at my lower lip. I sigh and tilt my head back as he pushes the hem of my dress up my thigh, his hand moving from my hip to my rib cage. His touch feels so good I don't even care about the dull throb in my side from where I scraped the fence.

Anthony freezes.

"What?" I say breathlessly.

He shows me his hand. It's covered in blood.

I'm lying on my bed, eyes closed. Sneaking Anthony up to the third floor through the stairwell and into my room took a lot of out me. Also, it feels like someone may have taken a cheese grater to my body.

Anthony unzips my dress slowly. I suddenly feel warm in places I'm not comfortable feeling warm at this very moment.

"How bad is it?" I ask, eyes still closed.

His lack of a response makes my heart skip a beat. "Anthony!"

"Shh." He helps me out of the dress, and I should be mortified, but all I can think of is the blood on his hand and the throbbing in my side.

I look down, taking in the bloodied mess on my side: a five-inch scrape from my rib cage to my hip.

"It doesn't look deep." Anthony examines the cut, his fingers on my hip. "But we need to clean it now."

I sit up, wincing, thinking of the old rusted links in the fence. I really need some sort of ointment to stop it from getting infected, but if I ask the RA on duty to use the first-aid kit, that'll invite a lot of unwanted questions.

The campus convenience store—they're open until midnight on the weekends. I'll run there and buy some bandages and disinfectant.

Anthony watches me pull on a V-neck and pajama pants. "I'll be right back." I nod to Matt Weaver's box, which is on the floor by Anthony's feet. "The key is under my desk drawer, but wait for me to open it."

I hurry downstairs, wishing I'd brought a jacket. I break into a run, hoping I can make it in and out of the convenience store without running into any of my friends buying late-night snacks.

I don't make it past the quad. I see a van idled at the curb outside of Amherst. There are no plates on it.

I turn and look at my dorm building. Through the lobby window, I see the driver of the van flash some sort of ID at Emma and scribble something in the sign-in book as she smiles at him. The back of his uniform says JR'S ELECTRIC.

He turns and heads for the elevator, giving me a full view of his bearded profile.

The man from the train platform.

CHAPTER
THIRTY-SEVEN

"Who was that guy?" I yell at Emma.

She actually backs away from me. Looks at me as if she's trying to figure out what sort of drugs I took tonight. "The guy who's supposed to fix the light that's out in the elevator."

I grab the sign-in binder. The guy signed in as *Thomas Petrocelli*. I make a quick slash across the next free space in the log and take off for the elevator, but it's already ascending. *Please don't stop at 3. Please don't stop at 3.*

Bile rises up my throat as the light overhead blinks *1, 2, 3.* I run for the stairwell and take the steps two at a time. It feels as if there is a knife lodged in my lungs.

I burst through the stairwell door to see him at the end of the hall. Outside my door, jiggling the handle and pulling a metal tool out of his back pocket. He swings his head toward me as I force my on-fire lungs to form the word: "Stop!"

The guy curses and looks at the elevator. Looks at me, blocking the stairwell entrance. The door to my room swings open and Anthony steps out, exclaiming "What the—?"

As if in slow motion, the guy grabs Anthony by his collar and throws him to the ground like he weighs as much as a rag doll. I cry out as he uses his foot to stop my door from swinging shut and shoulders his way into my room.

Anthony is on his feet before I make it halfway down the hall. The fake electrician flips the light in my room on, and seconds later I hear a grunt.

I freeze in the doorway, watching Anthony swing at the guy's stomach. He absorbs the punch and comes back with an uppercut that nearly sends Anthony sprawling. In the half a second it takes Anthony to rebound, the guy's gaze lands on me.

"What did you dig up from the yard?" he demands, lunging for me.

Anthony sidesteps him, throwing another punch at his throat. As if in slow motion, the guy winds up and charges at Anthony, throwing him up against the wall. He presses his arm to Anthony's throat.

"Where is it?" The man's voice surprises me. Anthony lets out a choking noise, which only makes the intruder jam his arm into his throat harder.

It takes every ounce of self-control I have not to look at the box on the floor by my bed. "It's a key. I'll get it," I stammer. Anthony wriggles in protest. "Just don't hurt him."

"Now!" The guy barks with a glance at the door. There's a line of sweat at his forehead. *Please don't notice the box.* I scramble to my purse, willing my hands to stop trembling long enough for me to find the battery-sized can at the bottom. I pull the tab out of the top and lunge at the guy, unloading a steady stream of pepper spray into his face.

"You fucking. Little. Bitch." He breaks away from Anthony, who swiftly kicks him in the stomach, knocking the wind out of him. The guy calls me a few more names I've never been called before in my life and bolts from the room, his hands pressed to his face.

Gasping for air, Anthony and I take off after him. The stairwell door slams at the exact moment the elevator door opens.

Remy lets out an "Oh!" when she sees Anthony standing in the middle of the hall.

At the opposite end of the hallway, someone shuts off the music. I spin to face Anthony. "Get back in my room" I say. "Now."

Darlene pokes her head out into the hall, staring back and forth from me to Remy. "Did I hear yelling?"

"Yes," I blurt. "I was sleepwalking, and Remy tried to wake me up, so I kind of freaked out."

Darlene looks to Remy for affirmation, but she just stares at me blankly. "Yeah," she finally says. "That's what happened."

Darlene glances at me skeptically. "Are you okay now?"

"Yup." I wrap my arms around my middle, hoping Darlene didn't notice the bit of blood on my T-shirt. "Sorry."

Remy blinks at me as Darlene disappears into her room. "Anne, what the *fuck* is going on with you?"

I'm pretty sure it's the first time I've ever heard Remy curse, so I'm dumbstruck. "What?"

She jerks her head toward my door. "What is he doing here? Did he hurt you?"

"No, of course not."

"I heard, like, a commotion before. Doors slamming."

"We had a little argument." Even I don't sound like I believe what I'm saying.

"Anne, he's trouble." Remy's voice is barely above a whisper, as if Anthony will hear and come out of my room and do unspeakable things to her.

"Jesus, Remy, judgmental much?"

Remy recoils as if I've slapped her, but I'm too exhausted and too scared of what that guy could have done to me and Anthony to feel guilty. Frustration at Remy I never knew I had boils to my surface: I need someone to blame for the past few weeks, and she makes it so easy with her doe-eyed *I didn't know every guy here is in love with me!* expression.

I can't stop the words from tumbling out of my mouth. "You

didn't know Isabella, and you don't know Anthony. He's not trouble just because he doesn't summer on Nantucket or play tennis at the country club, so just *leave us alone*."

I can hear her crying as she runs off to her room, but I can't make myself care. Just like I couldn't stop the Old Anne from slipping away from me—the girl who didn't care about anything but whose party she was going to go to over the weekend, because she never had to. She never had real problems or even knew people with real problems. People like Anthony.

He's sitting on my bed massaging his neck when I storm back into my bedroom. "That was harsh," he says. "But thanks to her, that dickhead is long gone by now."

I didn't expect him to thank me for sticking up for him. I sit on the bed and run my fingers over his collarbone. "Are you okay?"

"Fine," he mutters. "Was he—"

"The guy from the T platform? Yeah."

"You never lost him. He must have followed us to the Weavers'." Anthony rubs his eyebrow, where a bruise is blossoming. "Do you think the chick at the desk downstairs suspects anything?"

I shake my head. "But it's only a matter of time before she realizes that there was never a broken light and reports him. We've got to find him before they do if we want to figure out who sent him."

"You definitely don't know who he is?"

"I've never seen him before tonight."

Anthony considers this. "I don't know if Dennis will help us with something like this, Anne. Not if we don't tell him what it's really about."

I don't realize I'm shaking until Anthony puts an arm around me. All I can see is the bearded man throwing Anthony against the wall . . . the look in his eyes that said he would have killed him. "Do we have any choice now?" I ask.

"I'll call him in the morning," Anthony says. "I'll sneak out early, before anyone is up. I just don't want to leave you here alone in . . . after that."

"You were about to say 'in case he comes back,' weren't you?"

Anthony touches my jaw, pulling my face to his. "He won't. He thought no one was here before. We caught him off guard."

I close my eyes and try not to feel anything but Anthony's warm breath on my face. But my mind keeps circling back to ten minutes ago.

Someone knows I have Matt Weaver's box. He, she, or—even worse—they sent that fake JR's Electric guy to get it. He could have seriously hurt either of us. I've put Anthony in danger—*myself* in danger—for a person who has been presumed dead for over thirty years. A person I never knew.

Brent was right. I'm *not* over Isabella.

I push the thought away and move over to my desk. The key is right where I left it: taped to the underside of my bottom drawer. I hold it up for Anthony to see.

"Time to open Pandora's box?" He smiles.

The handle on Matt Weaver's box is rusted into place. I run a finger over the initials again. "We'll see if what's in here is really worth killing over."

I get the key stuck in the lock; Anthony has to take over and work his mechanic magic. I'm worried we have the wrong key until there's a popping sound. The lid is also rusty, and warped with age, so Anthony has to pry the top open.

I forget to breathe as I re-position myself to see inside the box.

"Oh my God." Five gold letters spell out a name:

SONIA.

I reach for the necklace but Anthony grabs my wrist.

"Fingerprints. We don't want the cops to trace anything back to us. Do you have gloves?"

"You're killing me, Anthony," I mutter as I rummage through my top drawer. I purposely pick a magenta pair for Anthony. He gives me a dirty look.

I hold up the necklace to my lamp.

I look over at Anthony. He's wearing an expression that says he sees something I don't. He takes the necklace from me and holds the nameplate part of it closer to the lamp. The ridged edges of the letters are caked with brown.

Anthony points to the bottom of Matt's box. It's hard to see them, but they're there. Small, rust-brown flakes barely larger than dust particles. It doesn't match the almost-black dirt on the outside of the box.

"Is that blood?" I say. Suddenly, I'm dizzy.

Anthony is quiet as he removes the second item from the box. A yellowed piece of paper, folded in half. He reads the note to me.

> If you're reading this, something happened to me and I couldn't come back. I need you to do something very important. Please call the police and tell them there's a body at 207 South Lake Drive, Brody. Behind the lake house. If her mother is still alive, please show her this note. I need her to know why I had to wait to tell where Sonia is. I had to get away from this place first, so I wouldn't wind up just like her.

"Brody is almost an hour from here." Anthony's voice is low. "Really remote. Right on Lake Brighton."

"Perfect place to hide a body." My stomach is sick as I try to keep my eyes off of Sonia's necklace, lying at the bottom of the box.

Anthony drags his hands down his face, leaving a streak of dirt beneath his eye. "We need to get as far away from this as possible. Let the cops find her body."

I nod mechanically, not even realizing a tear has slipped down my cheek until Anthony wipes it away. "Hey. You okay?"

"I'm fine," I lie. "It's just . . . she really is dead. And it's stupid, because I don't even know her, but I really didn't want her to be. Why can't these stories end differently for once?"

"Yeah, well, it's not over yet," Anthony says darkly. "But you really need to sleep first. Before you get so overtired you can't."

I'm about to tell Anthony that I know the feeling well, and I've already reached that point—then I remember the pills in my nightstand. The "emergency" supply of Ativan Dr. Rosenblum gave me when I admitted I was having trouble sleeping. Nightmares of Dr. Harrow. Dr. Rosenblum pretty much grilled me with questions designed to make sure I wasn't planning on starting an underground prescription-drug ring at the Wheatley School before giving me a grand total of ten pills.

There are two left. I take them both and climb into bed. Anthony lies behind me, curling his body around mine protectively. The last thing I feel is his chin resting on the top of my head, before I give in to a sleep guaranteed free from dreams of Matt Weaver dressed as Adam, soundlessly mouthing the words *Find me*.

CHAPTER
THIRTY-EIGHT

Anthony is gone when I wake up. It's still dark out, which makes me question how early he left. I should be worried about whether or not he remembered to pull the bookcase back over the tunnel entrance after he slipped through, but I'm too exhausted to get up and check.

The screen of my phone says it's 5:15 A.M. I turn on my lamp and sit up, lifting up my shirt. When I brush the dried blood away from my cut, it doesn't look nearly as bad as it did last night. But something else isn't right.

Matt Weaver's box. It's not on the floor of my closet, where we left it.

I throw my comforter off of me. *Panic, panic, panic.* There's a note on my desk, written on a piece of my computer paper.

Left around 2 so no one would see me dropping the box off at
the Brody Police Dept. Going home after that. Call me when
you wake up.

I'm going to. But first, I check the news app on my phone, even though I know nothing will be there. Yet.

Anthony answers his phone by yawning. "The box is safe."

"No one saw you, right?" I ask.

"Nope. Had to resist driving by Two-oh-seven South Lake Drive, though."

"That's the last place you need to be seen," I hiss. "God, Anthony."

"Relax. You know I'd never put us in danger like that." His voice is a step above a whisper now. "We need to lay low when word about Sonia's body gets out. Our friend from last night probably works for whoever killed her and Matt."

"Assuming we're dealing with the same person."

I think of what Matt did to Vanessa Reardon, with a sick feeling in my stomach. Had he done the same thing to Sonia? If so, had she fought back?

"Either way, whoever's behind this is going to get spooked," Anthony said. "It might be a couple days before the cops follow up on the tip about the body. Doesn't give us much time to figure out who the fake electrician is, but I'll call Dennis in a few hours."

I remember something. "Thomas Petrocelli. That's the name the guy used to sign in. And for him to get past the security gate, he had to have shown a legit ID."

"I'll have Dennis check it out," Anthony says. "I'm going to try to sleep a bit until my dad wakes up. I had kind of a wild night."

I blush. "Did you get *any* sleep?"

"Nah. You're a cover hog. And you mumble a lot."

"Sorry."

"Don't be. I'll call you in a few hours." His voice becomes serious. "Try to stay out of trouble until then, okay?"

"Aye, aye, captain," I say around a yawn of my own. We hang up, and I settle in to try to sleep for a few more hours. But not before making sure my door is bolted and my pepper spray is next to my pillow.

I'm starving when I wake up for real; I haven't eaten since lunch yesterday. The only problem is that I might see my friends in the dining hall, and two-thirds if not more of them hate me at the moment.

I need to apologize to Remy. I circle the dining hall searching for her and scarfing down a banana as I go. I spot Kelsey and April sitting alone at a small table by the window. They don't smile when they see me. At least they're not with the guys.

"Hey." I tread carefully, trying to gauge how much Remy told them about last night. To my surprise, Kelsey actually pulls out a chair for me. Neither of them looks pissed, which they would definitely be if they knew the awful things I'd said. They just seem . . . worried.

"Where is Rem?" I peel the top off my coffee cup, letting some steam out. April and Kelsey look at each other.

"In the bathroom," April says.

"Is she okay?" I ask.

"It's Casey," Kelsey whispers. "He and Bea broke up."

"What does that have to do with Remy?"

Kelsey looks like she's going to be sick. "Casey didn't realize we were behind him on the omelet line. He said something horrible to Justin and Erik."

"What did he say?" I demand.

"I don't want to repeat it," Kelsey whispers, like a little kid who heard her parents curse for the first time. April is staring at me in a way that makes it totally obvious whatever Casey said is *really* going to make me angry.

"Kelsey." I set my coffee cup down. "Come on." *I don't have time for this bullshit*, I want to scream in her face.

"Casey said, 'Bea still thinks I'm fucking Remy Adams. I'm not, but how much you want to bet by the end of the year I'll have nailed her and her new best friend, Anne, now that she dumped Conroy?'" Kelsey hunches over her own coffee cup, as if she's done something wrong. "Sorry."

I don't blink. "Where is he?"

"Casey?"

"Yes."

April chimes in. "I think he's in the atrium. . . ."

I look out the pane of glass separating the main dining hall from the atrium. It's warm today, so there aren't any free tables out there. Casey is sitting at the biggest table, spinning the umbrella stuck through its center and telling a story to his friends. Bea, Vera, and the other girls are not with them.

"Anne, wait!" Kelsey calls, but I'm already at the atrium door. I don't stop until I'm standing in front of Casey Shepherd, who gives me a smile as if he can't believe his luck.

"Anne." He stands up to give me his chair. How chivalrous. "We were just talking about you."

"I'll bet you were." I return his smile. Then I punch him in the nose.

Dean Snaggletooth pulls a bottle of Tylenol from her desk and pops two before she says a word to me. I almost ask if her I can have some, but I don't want to give her more inappropriate behavior to put in my file.

"In two sentences or fewer, please explain to me why you attacked Casey Shepherd," she finally says.

"I didn't 'attack' him." Crap. There's one sentence. I gnaw my bottom lip. "He made an extremely lewd comment about me and one of my friends."

Dean Snaggletooth stares at me. The morning light trickling in through her office window exposes the stray gray hairs in her red bun. "And you think that is an acceptable reason to resort to violence?"

Anger at her needles me. "Look, Casey isn't the sweet little boy he pretends to be. I could tell you things. *Lots* of things."

Dean Tierney's mouth pinches into an *Oh really?* smile. I think she's about to put the nail in my coffin, tell me I'm expelled, when her desk phone rings. She sighs and answers with, "I'm dealing with something."

Tierney is quiet for a moment. "Tell him he'll have to take a seat until I'm finished here."

She stares right at me as she listens to the voice on the other end of the phone. I break her gaze and glance around her office, finding mundane objects to focus on. The framed photo of a horse on Tierney's bookshelf. Her degree from Smith College.

I squint to get a better look at it. When I read the name on the degree, it feels as if the room is collapsing around me.

Jacqueline Annette Reardon

"Reardon," I say.

Tierney's eyes snap to me. "Excuse me?"

"Your maiden name is Reardon. Are you related to Vanessa?"

Tierney's hand quivers just enough so I can hear the voice at the other end of the phone: "Hello? What should I tell him?"

"I said tell him to wait, damn it." Tierney's face is red as she hangs up. I squirm in my chair. I've never seen her like this before. Even when the FBI agent monitoring Professor Andreev showed up at school looking for me, Tierney maintained her ridiculously punishing composure.

"Is there a reason you're so interested in my sister, Anne? Because my patience with you is wearing dangerously thin."

The look on Tierney's face is dangerous in itself. I'm too floored to be scared. *Sister. Vanessa Reardon is Tierney's sister.*

"I know what they did to her," I blurt. "Matt Weaver and Pierce Conroy. They hurt her and no one did anything about it. You know that, right? It's why you didn't go to school here?"

Tierney looks as if she wants to leap across her desk and choke me. "I don't know where you're getting your information, Miss Dowling, but those are some serious accusations you're making."

"How could you?" The words tumble out of my mouth. "How could you let Lee Andersen off with a slap on the wrist for stalking Isabella? He could have hurt her, just like Matt Weaver and Pierce Conroy hurt Vanessa—"

"Get out of my office." Tierney's voice is calm. So calm I feel like I've been punched in the chest.

"What?" I say.

"Get. Out. Of my office. *Now.*"

I stand up and back toward her door. I don't know what the hell just happened. Tierney's secretary is arguing with a man in the waiting area. I almost trip over the carpet when I see that it's Travis Shepherd.

He does not look amused to see me, but he smiles and extends a hand. "You must be Miss Dowling. Tell me, did Casey deserve it?"

I stare at his hand. His nails are rounded, his palms callous-free. I don't accept the handshake. Never trust an older man who gets manicures.

"I apologize, Mr. Shepherd." I put on my best sheepish smile. "I got carried away at something Casey said, but boys will be boys, I guess."

Travis Shepherd smiles again. He never smiles with his teeth, I notice. "Well, hopefully we can clear this up and put it behind us."

I don't know what to say, so I settle for a polite "Thank you" as Tierney's office door opens. When she sees Travis Shepherd, anger flashes across her stiff poker face. In that moment I realize that however much Dean Snaggletooth hates me, she hates Travis Shepherd more.

"Mr. Shepherd." She gives him an icy nod. No handshake. "I believe I left you a message that Casey is doing fine and already preparing for his race this afternoon."

"You can't blame a father for wanting to see for himself." Shepherd gestures to Tierney's office. "May we speak in private?"

Tierney glances at me, telling me with her eyes to get as far away from the administration building as possible. Is she actually going to let me off the hook? She turns and opens the door to her office, leaving me stunned.

As I turn to get the hell out of there, Travis Shepherd grabs my arm. He leans in close to my ear—so close I can smell cologne and coffee and what I think might be nicotine gum. "Stay away from my family, Anne Dowling," he whispers. "Or it'll be the last thing you do."

CHAPTER
THIRTY-NINE

Anthony warned me to stay out of trouble for a few hours, yet somehow I managed to punch Casey Shepherd in the face, piss off Dean Tierney, and get threatened by Travis Shepherd. I hold this little piece of irony back when I call Anthony, because I don't think he'll appreciate it.

"Did you get ahold of Dennis?" I'm on a bench behind the library. I know no one is listening to me; they're either playing Frisbee on the quad or getting ready to see the Wheatley vs. Downington race this afternoon. I couldn't bring myself to go back to the dorm. All of the evidence related to Matt Weaver—his letters to Cynthia, my notebook, the box key, the crew team photo—are in my bag. Lesson learned from last night: There's no such thing as a safe hiding place at the Wheatley School.

"Yeah. He's still on call for the next few hours, but he says he'll see what he can do," Anthony says. His voice is clipped. Annoyed.

"It sounds like there's something more."

Anthony lets out a stream of air. "He's pissed, Anne. That I didn't tell him what this is really about. If Den got caught pulling records for us, and someone figured out Sonia Russo's connection to the Weaver case . . ."

"And that's my fault?" I ask. "You didn't want to tell Dennis the truth, either, Anthony."

"Did I say it was your fault? Don't give me an attitude 'cause you didn't get your beauty rest."

I breathe out my nose. Let my grip on my phone tighten. Convince myself to let it go. I'm not going to snipe back at him, let this conversation turn into some battle of the egos that leaves us not speaking to each other. That never ended well for us in the weeks after Isabella's murder. And I'm not going to lose him again. Not when it feels like I just got him back.

"I'm sorry," I sigh. "I'm just scared, and I don't know what to do."

"I know," Anthony says. "But we can trust Den. I've known him for most of my life. He's not like those other cops who give themselves to the highest bidder. He's going to get out of Wheatley, someday. At least I hope."

I don't say it, but I hope we all get out of Wheatley.

Remy doesn't answer after my first knock. She does turn off her light and The Fray song playing on her laptop. I roll my eyes.

"I know you're in there," I say. "Please talk to me, Remy. I'm so, so sorry."

The light flicks back on. More silence. I sigh and turn to walk away, when the door creaks open an inch. I push it open and find Remy lying facedown on her bed.

I sit by her feet. "I was such a bitch. It's just, I wasn't mad about you and Brent at first, but the more I thought about it, I convinced myself there was a *reason* you guys didn't tell me. I felt so stupid, like the two people I trusted most were in on some joke I wasn't't."

Remy just lies there. Unresponsive. I put a hand on her back to make sure she's still breathing. She is.

Finally, a muffled sound comes out. She turns on her side and looks at me with red-tinged eyes. "Do you love Brent?"

My insides curl. What does that have to do with anything? "I don't know, Rem. I was really falling for him. But he's not who I thought he was."

Remy wipes her eyes. "None of those stupid guys are. That's the problem. They tell you you're the smartest, prettiest girl in school, and the next day they're back to their girlfriends and you're just a home-wrecking slut."

"Do not call yourself that ever again," I say. "It's just their word to make us hate one another. And we can't."

Remy's voice is far off. She stares at the opposite side of the room, as if she sees something I can't. "Alexis was my best friend growing up, but she was so controlling and manipulative. We had to play at *her* house. I had to be the ugly stepsister when we acted out *Cinderella*. Cole was the only thing she wanted and couldn't get."

I've never heard Remy like this—not bubbly or excitable but monotone, sad. Real.

"You probably think I'm horrible," she says.

"No. I think you're more like me than I realized before."

Remy smiles. "I've never had, like, a real girl best friend. Alexis doesn't count, and Apes and Kelsey are closer to each other. You're the first person I could see, you know, making a toast at my wedding. It sounds dumb."

I lie down on the bed next to her. We stare at the black decal of the Eiffel Tower on the ceiling. How did she get it up there?

"So you don't hate me?" I ask.

Remy links her pinky through mine. "Nope. You really punched Shep for me?"

"And I'd do it again in a heartbeat."

When Anthony said we were meeting Dennis somewhere "discreet," I didn't imagine the back of his police cruiser, pulled up to a scenic overlook. The Wheatley School is visible in the distance. From far away, it looks much less grand. Like a toy village a kid would play with.

Beside us is a sign that reads DANGER! NO TRESPASSING. VIOLATORS WILL BE PROSECUTED UNDER MASSACHUSETTS PENAL CODE.

Anthony was right about Dennis being pissed; he hasn't said a word to us the entire drive up here. He puts the car in park, reaches under the seat, and emerges with a brown paper bag. I half expect him to take a swig out of it, but instead, he hands it back to me.

"What is this?"

"Open it." Dennis's voice is flat.

The bag is heavy. I get a sour taste in my mouth for a minute. *Please don't be a gun.* I reach in the bag and pull out something that looks like a men's facial-hair trimmer.

"It's a Taser," Dennis says. "Put it back until I show you how to use it."

"Whoa." I can barely contain my glee. "I've always wanted one of these!"

Dennis turns around and gives me a look that shuts me up instantly. "Sorry, sorry."

Anthony throws me a dirty look as Dennis gets out of the car. When Anthony and I don't motion to follow, he sticks his head in the door. "C'mon."

We follow Dennis to the railing separating us from plunging two hundred feet to our deaths. Beyond the Wheatley School, I see the shape of a cliff over the river. The quarry.

"Before I give you anything, I need you to tell me everything you know about the Matt Weaver case," Dennis says.

By the time I'm done, Dennis's expression has darkened.

"It's like you guys have a freakin' death wish or something, man." Dennis runs a hand over his buzz cut. "I can't even—do you know how stupid it was to get involved in this? Especially after all the attention you guys brought to yourselves a couple months ago."

I grit my teeth. I don't need a lecture right now. I need to know whether Dennis can find the man who, after the pepper-spray incident, probably wants to find me and cut up my body into little pieces.

Anthony says as much, ad-libbing with a few choice words. Dennis looks like he wants to hit him. He catches himself and leans against the guardrail.

"JR's Electric is a real company. Based out of Southie. A few weeks ago, someone robbed the place. Stole some uniforms and cash," he says. "The cops talked to all the employees, since it looked like the guy knew his way around the alarm system."

"An employee," Anthony says.

Dennis nods. "Tom Petrocelli was one of them. I looked him up. Middle-aged guy. Big scar on the side of his head from a surgery a while back."

"That's not our guy," I say. "He was young, like late twenties."

"What about the other employees?" Anthony asks.

"They all checked out fine," Dennis says. "But according to the police reports, a few of them mentioned a guy that worked there eight months ago. Sketchy kid. Got fired for lying about having a record. Jeff Kowalski. Couple of petty-theft and assault charges. Mostly bar fights."

The ground seems to sway beneath me a little bit. I can't get rid of the image of the guy in my room, trying to crush Anthony's trachea.

"So what happened with him?" Anthony asks, an edge to his voice as if he's picturing the same thing.

"Didn't have enough to hold him, I guess," Dennis says. "The case is still open, but the guys over in Roxbury are stretched too thin to waste time on a small business robbery."

"And this Tom Petrocelli guy," I say, "—he didn't report his ID stolen or anything?"

Dennis shakes his head. "Not according to the report." He reaches into his pocket and pulls out a black-and-white mug shot. "Is this the guy that came after you?"

With his thumb, Dennis covers the name on the mug shot. It's obvious he doesn't want to influence my answer, but it doesn't take a rocket scientist to know the guy standing against the wall is Jeff Kowalski. His blond hair is an inch or two shorter than the fake electrician's, but there's no mistaking the sharp planes of his jaw and the hollow-looking eyes. The eyes of someone who just doesn't care about human life. Someone who would stamp it away like a spider under his boot.

"That's him." I have to look away.

"What are we gonna do to find him?" Anthony is behind me. He puts a hand on my shoulder.

"*You're* not doing shit," Dennis says. "I'll try and track down Kowalski, and you two please, for the love of God, stay away from this. Pretend you never even *heard* the name Matt Weaver. You've already put me in a crappy spot. If they find a body at that house in Brody, I have to act like I didn't know a damn thing about it."

Anthony's eyes flick to the ground. I've only seen the look on his face once before: when I confronted him about stealing money from Isabella. Dennis means more to Anthony than I realized, and because of me, they're both involved in this mess.

"I'm really sorry," I say, to no one in particular.

Dennis turns to me. Takes me in. I do the same. He can't be more than twenty-three, twenty-four. He looks like any one of the marines I used to see outside of the recruiting building on Broadway back home, minus the USMC uniform. I have to believe he chose this life, staying in this shitty town, for a reason.

Dennis sighs but gives me a brotherly pat on the shoulder. "Don't be sorry. C'mon, I better show you how to work that taser so you don't kill anyone."

CHAPTER
FORTY

There are no surprises waiting for me back at Amherst. No angry voice mails from my father to suggest he's heard I punched out a classmate. No security guard to drag me to Goddard's office and expel me. No ex-cons hiding in my room.

It's a quiet night, as well. Wheatley lost this afternoon's race against Downington, so the guys are having a beer-soaked pity party over in Aldridge. Remy, Kelsey, April, and I are in Remy's dorm, piled onto her bed, watching movies on her mini LCD TV. She's pushed Alexis's bed into hers to make a double.

Remy has cracked open the bottle of 2007 Chardonnay she was "saving for a special occasion," for no reason other than that we all need it. Remy is tired of Cole not speaking to her, and people are calling her a skank, and Kelsey is tired of having to choose between Cole and Remy. April . . . well, I guess she wants to get out of April-Land for a little while. It's not that she's completely vapid—she would just rather live there than in Wheatley-Land most of the time.

I really don't blame her.

As for me, I need a little liquid assistance with Dennis's command to forget I ever heard the name Matt Weaver. Especially since I'm now toting around a taser, like I'm in Trenton, New Jersey, and not a small town outside of Cambridge.

The girls are recounting the drama of the race, which includes Cole melting down and screaming at Justin Wyckoff after a disastrous performance in the men's 8.

"You should have seen it," April says. "It was hilarious."

"Well, I doubt I would have been welcome there." I dip a piece of celery into the container of hummus sitting on top of the latest issue of *Marie Claire*. "By the way, how does Casey's face look?"

"His nose is swollen and bruised," Remy says, as if it made her happy to study the damage. "You did a nice job. It was almost as awesome as Mr. Shepherd screaming at Coach Tretter after the race."

I swallow. Try to forget the sound of Travis Shepherd's threat in my ear. "He screamed at him?"

"Yeah," Kelsey jumps in. "You should have seen them nearly going at each other."

"What were they fighting about?" I ask.

"Probably losing the race," Remy says. "Men are such babies about that stuff. Mr. Shepherd kept yelling, 'I told you this would happen!'"

A chill creeps up my spine.

"He's just pissed because the naval academy recruiters were there to watch Casey," she adds. "I heard him shout something about 'that bastard Conroy.' They're blaming Brent for choking at the end of the race."

Kelsey adds her own commentary, but my mind is racing. It's possible Shepherd wasn't yelling about Brent but another Conroy: his father. I swallow away a wave of anxiety, thinking the argument might be related to the box and Jeff Kowalski.

"Speak of the devils," Remy says. She nods to my phone. Murali is calling me, and I hadn't even heard it ring.

Murali?

There's arguing and what sounds like a scuffle on his end. "Hello?" I say.

"Anne," Murali grunts. "You, uh, should come downstairs. I tried to stop him, but he wouldn't listen."

"Who?" I say at the same time as I hear Brent's voice let out a blistering yell.

He's *singing*.

"I am *so* not in the mood for this," I tell Murali. "But I'll be right down."

Murali calls me again when Remy and I get downstairs.

"Outside," he says. "By the back door."

There are a few people hanging in the lamplight outside the dorms, along with a few stragglers on the quad. Remy and I turn the corner to the back of Amherst, where Murali is holding Brent by the sleeve of his shirt. Brent is clawing at the air, trying to break away from him.

"What's wrong with him?" I ask Murali. As soon as I say it, I smell the awful stench: a cross between beer, skunk, and vomit.

"I don't know," Murali says. "He was normal until he got a phone call a little while ago. Then he flipped out and started ranting about how he needs to talk to you."

"I was not *ranting*. Anne." Brent's eyes light up when he sees me. Or maybe it's the fact he is totally, completely, 100 percent *shitfaced*. "I need to talk to you."

There was a time when I might have found this whole situation slightly adorable. Now I want to slap him. "You *need* to get back to your room."

"Please." Brent yanks himself away from Murali and holds his hands up as if he's surrendering.

"Fine," I say. "Five minutes."

"Just you, though." Brent glares at Murali.

Remy looks at me if she's about to protest. "It's okay." I stare Brent down. "I can handle him."

Murali walks Remy around to the front lobby, leaving me with Brent. "You have five minutes," I say. "I'm cold."

"Don't be like that," he slurs. "I came to apologize."

"For what?"

"Isn't it obvious?" He smiles. "For being me."

"I have bigger problems to deal with than your existential crisis, Brent."

"I know. That's why we broke up, right? You think I'm part of the problem." His eyes are glassy. "And you're right. I'm just a fucking monkey in a uniform. That's all I am to everyone. A GODDAMN MONKEY!" He yells the last part to a pack of freshmen guys walking back to Aldridge.

I grab Brent and pull him to me, so it looks to the casual observer as if we're embracing. His face is an inch from mine. I wish I could forget the little details of it. The freckle on his lower lip. The way his hairline comes to a point at his forehead. Suddenly I'm back on the floor of the woods with him, my chest pressed to his as he kisses me for the first time.

"Tell me what you want from me," he pleads. "I'll be whoever you want me to be, because I'm better with you."

I want to believe him. I want to believe him so *badly*, 'cause up until all this Matt Weaver nonsense, I felt the same way. But I'm also furious that the only times he's capable of telling me how he feels are when he's drunk or on the brink of death.

"Funny how you waited 'til you got *obliterated* to tell me this. Come talk to me when you sober up, okay?"

"No, it has to be now." Brent breaks away from me, swaying slightly. "I have to tell you now that you were right. About everything."

"What are you talking about?" I ask at the exact moment he trips over his feet. "Brent!"

He looks up at me with bleary eyes as I kneel beside him. "I don't feel good."

"What do you mean, I was 'right about everything'?" I give him a little slap on the face when he closes his eyes.

Voices sound in the distance. Panicked, I think about calling Murali to come help me get Brent inside. Then I remember what Murali said earlier: Brent freaked out about a phone call before he came over here.

"Brent." I put my face in his. "Who called you earlier? Did they tell you I was right about everything?"

"You . . . are so pretty," he slurs.

Then he passes out.

Five minutes later, Cole is holding Brent beneath the armpits as Murali lifts him by the feet. Brent's face is a shade of gray that makes me sick to my stomach.

"Is he going to be okay?"

Cole ignores me. Murali shrugs, and I want to grab him by the neck and shake him for not having the balls to talk to me while Cole is around.

"Hey," I call as they cart Brent off toward Aldridge. "You need to get him to the infirmary before he chokes on his own puke."

"No. We need to get him to his room, before he gets us expelled," Cole says without looking back at me.

Screw all three of them. I stalk back to Amherst, bypassing Remy's room and making a beeline for mine.

I let the door slam behind me. I yank off my boots and hurl them into the closet. My heel leaves a black scuff mark on the wall. Damn it. I'm trying to rub it away with my thumb when my phone starts ringing.

I don't get to it in time. When Anthony immediately calls me again, I know something is wrong.

"Are you alone?" he asks.

"Yeah. What's going on?"

"Dennis just called. He got something on Kowalski."

I chew the inside of my cheek. "Okay."

"You might want to sit down," Anthony says.

"Just tell me already."

"Okay." Anthony lowers his voice. "Dennis pulled Kowalski's rap sheet. Kowalski beat up a guy a couple years ago, but he had help. From the Grabiecs."

"Who are the Grabiecs?"

"They're a crime family," Anthony says. "Eastern European, I think."

"Great," I say. "The guy who came after us has ties to *the mob*."

"They're not the mob," Anthony huffs. "They're like the Kardashians of organized crime. All for show. They're known for doing sloppy jobs, like the one Kowalski did the other night."

"But Shepherd, Conroy, Westbrook—they all have enough money to get someone who could do a decent job."

Anthony is quiet for a beat. "There's something else. Jeff Kowalski is Bill Grabiec's great-nephew."

"Bill Grabiec. I've heard that name before." I sit up straighter and rack my brain. "Wait. I remember my dad talking about his case. He's the guy that killed all those women at truck stops. Isn't he on death row in Ohio or something?"

"Pennsylvania," Anthony says. "He was sentenced three years ago. Dennis says it caused a lot of chatter on the force, since Grabiec killed his first victim in Boston."

"What does that have to do with any of our guys?" I ask.

"Grabiec tried to get his sentence down to life in prison. He told the DA he'd exchange a plea for information about a hit he carried out in 1995 Said there was a politician involved. The DA rejected it as a last-ditch attempt—Grabiec trying to save his ass from death row."

I tighten my grip on the phone. "1995. That was the year of Cynthia Westbrook's car accident."

"I don't think the senator hired Kowalski to come after you," Anthony says. "Because it looks like Bill Grabiec killed Westbrook's son and wife."

CHAPTER
FORTY-ONE

"What are we going to do?" Anthony and I ask at the same time.

"I don't know," Anthony admits. "This is so much bigger than us, Anne. I think we have to admit that we're out of our league."

"No." My grip on the phone tightens. "I don't care if this is bigger than us. Maybe I should have dropped the Matt Weaver thing weeks ago, but that asshole was in my *room*, Anthony. I know too much. And now you see what happens when you know too much at this school. You go for a car ride in the middle of the night and you never come back."

"Anne. Shh. Calm down." Anthony's gravelly voice is anything but soothing, but it's sweet he's making the effort. "I'm not going to let anything happen to you."

I cough—a big, snot-and-tear-fueled cough. I'll bet Sonia Russo and Cynthia Westbrook heard the same thing, and they're still dead. My heart pounds as the weight of it hits me: I could wind up dead, too.

"I'm going to find out who sent Kowalski," I say. "Whoever it is was stupid enough to hire someone who could tie him to Grabiec—"

I own you, dumbass.

"Anne? You there?"

"Larry Tretter," I say. "It had to be him. Who else would have access to my room number? I bet he even helped Kowalski get past the security gate."

Anthony's response is drowned out by a knock at my door. "I'll call you back," I say.

I pad over to the door and peer through the peephole. Darlene stands with her hands in the pocket of her Harvard hoodie, her expression nervous.

Because Detective Phelan, the officer in charge of Isabella's murder investigation, is standing behind her.

The detective and I sit across from each other at a table in the first-floor lounge. Darlene puts on a pot of coffee for him at the kitchen counter. He didn't ask for it. I think she just wants an excuse to be in the room.

Detective Phelan knits his hands together and watches me over the top of them. I've always liked Phelan. Twenty years ago, he probably looked like Ben Affleck.

He leads off with, "You're not in trouble."

It's probably not in my best interests to admit that being in trouble with the law would be welcome news to me at this point. At least Larry Tretter can't have me killed if I'm in prison. "Okay."

"Campus security called us," Phelan says. "They saw something on last night's security feed that worried them."

The coffee pot gurgles behind us. I give Phelan my best vacant stare. "What does that have to do with me?"

"You signed in right after someone named Thomas Petrocelli. Did you see anything out of the ordinary on the way to your room?"

Out of the corner of my eye, I see Darlene stiffen. She's probably thinking of my "sleepwalking" incident last night. I swallow.

"Um. I don't think so," I say.

Detective Phelan's radio blips. He turns it off. "Are you sure there was no one in the elevator with you?"

"I took the stairs." I study Phelan's face. It's expressionless. I try to picture what he saw on the security tape: me leaving Amherst. Kowalski entering Amherst. Me taking off after him, and Kowalski leaving Amherst again shortly after that. "I was heading to the convenience store, but I forgot my wallet. So I ran back to the dorm to get it. I didn't want to wait for the elevator."

Phelan nods. I can't tell if he's buying it. He must know by now that the fake electrician was Jeff Kowalski. All he had to do was cross-reference JR's Electric and make the connection with the robbery, like Dennis did.

"Actually, I think I did see someone." I grip the edge of the table. "An electrician. A younger guy. I didn't think anything of it until now."

The detective raises an eyebrow at me. "What was he doing?"

"I dunno. Wasn't really paying attention." I feign a yawn, hoping Phelan will take the hint that he's not getting any more out of me.

"Thanks, Anne." He motions to get up. "We think we know who the man is, but we're not sure what he was doing here. We thought you might have some insight."

He holds my gaze. I command myself not to look away. "Is he dangerous?"

Phelan is the one who finally blinks. "Not to you."

It kills me that I can't tell him he's wrong again.

Brent's phone goes straight to voice mail in the morning. I decide to wait until after breakfast to swing by Aldridge to check on him; I need time to figure out what I'm going to say. I don't know what prompted him to tell me I was right about everything, but I have to warn him about Tretter.

I meet Remy, April, and Kelsey downstairs. I know they must

have been discussing Brent's little performance last night, because Remy switches to her *Let's change the subject* voice when she sees me.

"Ugh. Finishing that wine was an awful idea." She slips on a pair of oversize sunglasses as we head outside. "I'm never drinking again."

"You always say that." April yawns and stretches. "Then you forget."

Kelsey grabs a copy of *The Boston Globe* from the dining-hall lobby. Wheatley kids are superneurotic about reading the news. At my old school, the kids *were* the news. When you're the son of the owner of the New York Jets and the daughter of a notorious rapper, it's headline worthy if you get high and try to free the macaques at the Bronx Zoo.

"Did you guys see this?" Kelsey's nose twitches. It's her nervous tic when she's not wearing her glasses. She holds the front page of the paper for us to see.

"Oh my God," Remy says.

I snatch the paper from Kelsey. I almost black out when I read the headline:

HUMAN REMAINS FOUND AT BRODY LAKE HOUSE OWNED BY
LATE MEDIA MOGUL MAXWELL CONROY

CHAPTER
FORTY-TWO

Matt Weaver is the name on everyone's lips Monday morning.

"It has to be him," I hear Dan Crowley whisper to Zach Walton in Matthews's class. "They're saying the remains are *wicked* decomposed."

"Mr. Crowley," Matthews snaps. "If your conversation is so riveting compared with my lesson, please feel free to finish it outside."

An awkward quiet fills the room. Yelling is not Matthews's style. His upper lip quivers as he stares out at us, daring someone to bring up Matt Weaver or the Conroy family again. When he resumes his lecture, I check my phone for a message from Brent that I know isn't there.

I have to know if he's okay. I heard the guys saying this morning that Brent went home yesterday morning. Cole looked right at me as he said it, as if to tell me he knows this is all my fault.

I bite the inside of my cheek, hoping the pain will distract me from the urge to lose it in the middle of class. Brent was right. I didn't care whose lives I ruined. But I never actually believed his father was capable of murder.

A fifteen-year-old girl is buried in the backyard of a house that Brent's dad owns. Matt Weaver knew about it—he might have even helped him put her there. Did Sonia Russo fight back, unlike Vanessa Reardon?

When I'm confident Matthews isn't moving from his spot in front of the blackboard, I pull up the news article on my laptop. I practically have it memorized by now.

Brody, Massachusetts—Human remains were uncovered behind a home on Lake Brody Saturday night. Authorities say they received a "credible" tip about a body buried at the location. Few details are available at this time, but sources say preliminary decomposition estimates posit the remains are at least twenty years old.

Late Saturday night, the *Boston Herald* confirmed that the property on which the remains were uncovered was owned by media mogul Maxwell Conroy from 1959 until his death in 2003. Pierce Conroy, owner of the *Boston Times*, released the following statement this morning:

"The Conroy estate was shocked to learn of the discovery of human remains on a property that has been in our family for decades. In response to initial allegations that my father is somehow connected to the existence of said remains, I feel compelled to point out that hundreds of persons have had access to the lake house and its adjoining property over the years. Lake Brody is located within five miles of a well-known Native American burial site. Conroy Media denies any involvement with this discovery and is cooperating with Brody authorities completely at this time."

Authorities have not commented on early speculation that the remains belong to missing Wheatley School student Matthew Weaver. Weaver disappeared from his dormitory in 1981. His body was never recovered. The Brody Police Department is working with local precincts

to compose a list of active missing-persons cases in light
of Saturday's discovery.

It's only a matter of time before the media hears about the box,
and Sonia's necklace, and the note in Matt Weaver's handwriting. And then where will that leave Brent's family? If Tretter, Shepherd, or any of the other guys in the photo were involved, they'll be
on their private jets to Europe before you can say *subpoena*.

Pat Carroll's words haunt me: *Whatever it is you're looking
for . . . I hope it's not a happy ending.*

I don't know what sort of ending I was looking for, but it
wasn't this one. It wasn't Brent's father being the one who killed
Matt, and Sonia, and God knows who else.

I get up and push my chair in. The sound is so loud Matthews
stops lecturing. But he doesn't try to stop me from packing up
my things and leaving.

I don't know how long I have before someone realizes I'm cutting
all my classes and sends Dean Snaggletooth after me. I don't even
know what the punishment is for cutting at Wheatley: It's kind
of an unwritten rule that when you live at school, you have to
show up for class every day.

I sneak past security and head into Wheatley. Once I reach the
bottom of the hill separating campus from the townie plebs, I
call Anthony. I have to bite back tears when I hear his voice.

"Can I see you?" I ask.

"Now?" He pauses. "I kind of can't leave until tonight."

"It's okay."

"Wait. I'll give you directions to my house. I'm a quick walk
from the T."

The air rushes out of my lungs. Anthony's house. *Isabella's*
house.

Anthony lives in a brown ranch-style house surrounded on all sides by rhododendron bushes. There are four wooden birdhouses on the porch alone. It looks like someone carved them all by hand.

I ring the bell and Anthony calls for me to come in. I don't know what kind of scene I was expecting to see inside, but it wasn't Anthony and his father sitting at the kitchen table eating mini pizza bagels.

Mr. Fernandez is in pajama pants and a Denver Broncos sweatshirt. He's thin, with ghastly white skin. His hair is thick and curly like Isabella's was.

He takes me in and looks over at Anthony. "Is she here to wipe my ass, too?"

I stand in the kitchen archway. Anthony looks at my face and bursts into laughter.

"Apparently you found Dad's sense of humor on your way here," he says.

I take a tentative step toward Anthony's father. He closes the rest of the distance between us by wheeling himself toward me. "It's nice to meet you, Mr. Fernandez," I say.

He surprises me by clasping my hand between his. He doesn't speak. His soft brown eyes probe mine. Does he know who I am? I don't know. It doesn't matter. I squeeze his frail hand as tears slip down his cheek.

I can't bring myself to give Isabella's father the empty condolences I was raised to say when something terrible happens. I can't do anything to change the fact that it should be his daughter holding his hand right now, and I can't drive away the cloud of darkness that will follow him for the rest of his life.

So I hold on to Mr. Fernandez and let him cry, for I don't know how long, before I feel Anthony's hand on the small of my back.

I'm in Anthony's room, sitting on the edge of his bed. He has flannel sheets.

He doesn't say anything as he climbs behind me and brushes my hair away from my neck. I close my eyes, feeling guilty at how much I'm enjoying his lips on the area right below my ear. He hooks a finger in the back of my collar, pulling my sweater down so he can trace kisses along my back.

I turn enough for my mouth to meet his. "What are we doing?"

He ignores my question and kisses me. I put a hand to his chest and push him away, gently. "No. Really."

Anthony stares at me. "What are you talking about?"

"All of this . . . fooling around," I say. "Does it mean anything to you?"

Anthony takes a lock of my hair between his fingers. His eyes flick downward in a way that makes my heart sink. He can't even look at me.

"I like you," he finally says. "And it scares me."

"Am I *that* bad?"

"No." A smile plays in his eyes. "It's just that most things I like aren't good for me."

"I'm going to pretend you *didn't* just compare me to a cheese-burger." I hold his gaze. "There's something you should know."

"Oh, really?" Anthony's voice is playful. He leans in to me, but I put a hand to his shoulder to stop him. His smile lilts.

"When people were accusing you of . . . those awful things, I didn't stop caring about you." I take a breath. "I still do. A lot. But Brent . . ."

Anthony stiffens at his name. I force myself to keep going.

"I care about him, too. Maybe in a different way, I don't know. Everything is so screwed up and confusing, and I shouldn't even be thinking about this right now, but you need to know I care about him," I say. "And if there's any chance his dad isn't in-volved in this, I want to prove it."

Anthony's eyes are on his wall. I knew he wouldn't under-stand, but I can't tell if he's angry. He inhales as if he's going to reply, at the same moment a crackling sounds from his dresser.

"Eighty-nine Glendale Drive . . . officers on the scene."

I look at Anthony. "Is that a police scanner?"

"Yeah. Got it this week to see if I could pick up anything," he grunts.

"Isn't that illegal?"

"Man, you say that like *you* haven't broken three different laws since you woke up today." Anthony goes over to his dresser and picks up the scanner. It looks like a car radio.

"Guy who called us is Dwight Miller . . . isn't he that nasty son of a bitch?"

Another voice on the scanner responds: *"Yep. Usually his wife is the one making the calls. What's his problem?"*

"Dwight Miller," I say. "That name sounds familiar."

"Sonia Russo's foster father," Anthony deadpans.

There's more crackling on the scanner: *"Complained about a disturbance. Woman started banging on his door and screaming at him to come outside so she could kill him. She seems to think the body they found over in Brody is her daughter."*

"She still there?"

"Yeah. Officer Manfrate's talking her down."

"Got a name?"

"Russo," the voice crackles. *"Antonella Russo."*

According to White Pages, there's one Antonella Russo in the Wheatley area. She lives in Harrison, which is about twenty minutes from here. Anthony sets his father up in front of the television and tells him we'll be back within the hour and to call Mrs. Hanley, the neighbor, if he needs anything.

We have to get gas for Anthony's motorcycle, so we don't leave until almost half an hour later. Antonella Russo lives in a federal low-income housing development on the outskirts of Harrison. As soon as we pull into the development, I want to leave.

Antonella's neighbor, a nosy elderly woman, tells us she's not home. "She works afternoons at the salon on Main Street."

We thank her and head back the way we came, getting lost

twice before we wind up on Main Street. There's only one salon—a dumpy little place called Hair Razers. Anthony slips a few quarters into the parking meter as I stake out the salon.

"I don't see what she's gonna be able to tell us," Anthony says. "Dennis said she's been in and out of jail for years."

"She obviously knew Dwight Miller was Sonia's foster parent." My patience with Anthony is wearing thin. "Maybe she had more contact with Sonia than we think. Look."

A sickly-looking woman stubs out a cigarette on the sidewalk outside the salon. She's wearing a black apron, which does little to conceal the sharpness of her limbs. I glimpse her face before she enters the salon.

"I think that's her."

I run across the street and ask the girl at the reception desk if I can speak with Antonella.

The girl narrows her eyes, which are thickly rimmed with liner. "You her probation officer?"

"No. Please tell her I need to speak with her about her daughter."

I wait outside after the girl disappears into the back room. Anthony watches me from across the street, his satisfaction tugging at his mouth as the minutes tick by. Antonella Russo is not coming to talk to me.

I'm about to go back inside the salon when the door swings open. The most frightening woman I've ever seen stares back at me. At one time, she was probably beautiful, like her daughter. Now her cheeks are sunken like something from a Tim Burton movie.

"You askin' for me?" Antonella Russo is missing more than a few teeth. The rest are brown and chipped. I'm speechless.

With trembling hands, Antonella Russo lights another cigarette. Her skin is tissue-paper thin. "Thought you might be the cops, come to tell me they found my baby girl."

"I'm sorry to bother you, Ms. Russo." Across the street, Anthony watches us. "I think I may have some information about your daughter."

Antonella coughs into the crook of her arm. I find the yearbook photo in my bag—the one where Vanessa Reardon and Sonia Russo stand together to the side, talking as if they're both in on a secret.

I hand the photo to Antonella. Her eyes go straight to Sonia. An animal-like cry slips out of her. "Where'd you get this?"

"A yearbook at the Wheatley School."

Antonella grips the picture and speaks as if I'm not even here. "My baby girl. My beautiful baby girl."

I look over at Anthony. His eyebrows knit together and he motions to step off the curb. I shake my head at him.

"How old are you?" Antonella Russo asks, taking me by surprise.

"Seventeen," I say.

She lets out a phlegmy laugh. "I was your age when I had her. My daddy threw me out. Doctors called Sonia my miracle baby. Even with all the poison I put in my body, she was perfect."

Antonella hands me the picture. "They took her from me. I spent the first ten years of her life in an' outta jail. Court said I couldn't see her. She found me, after they sent her to live with that monster."

She must mean Dwight Miller. It occurs to me that Antonella is speaking to herself.

"She was fifteen and so beautiful. She loved to read. Gonna get a job at the library that summer, she told me." Antonella wipes her eyes. "She was seeing a nice boy. One of them Wheatley kids. Bought her a name necklace, real diamonds and everything. Told her he'd marry her when they were old enough. My baby girl was so, so happy."

My throat tightens. "Did she tell you the boy's name?"

Antonella shakes her head. "She was real secretive about it. But she showed me his picture."

My blood pounds in my ears as I shuffle through my bag. I find the picture of the crew team and show Antonella. "Is he in this photo?"

Antonella's eyes sweep over Matt Weaver. Over Pierce Conroy. "That's him," she says, pointing to Travis Shepherd.

CHAPTER
FORTY-THREE

"Do you believe her?" Anthony asks. We're still outside Hair Razers. Antonella Russo is inside, sweeping the floor as if we never spoke.

"She's definitely not playing with a full deck," I say. "But it fits. Most of Matt's letters to Cynthia say he needed to tell her something. He must have known Travis was cheating on her with Sonia. He was going to tell her."

"So Shepherd killed Matt Weaver to stop him?" Anthony's voice is skeptical. "Seems a little extreme."

"He wasn't going to tell her he was cheating," I say. "Think about the box. Sonia's necklace. The note inside."

Realization dawns on Anthony's face. "You think Shepherd killed her? And Matt knew about it?"

I run through the facts in my head, trying to fill in the story's holes. "The woman who witnessed a boy going into the woods the night Matt disappeared . . . maybe she didn't see Matt after all." I show Anthony the picture, pointing to Travis Shepherd. He and Matt are the same height. Around the same weight. Both have brown hair.

"Holy shit," Anthony says. "But what about Jeff Kowalski and Grabiec? If Shepherd was going to pay someone to kill Westbrook's wife, he had the money to do it right. And why would he wait almost fifteen years to get rid of her if she knew something?"

"I don't know," I murmur. "Maybe we were right about Coach Tretter being involved somehow. Shepherd definitely has something on him."

"So how does Conroy fit into all of this then?"

I pull the yearbook photo out of my bag. The one I showed Antonella, where Travis Shepherd is on the couch with Matt Weaver and Cynthia. "Look at the room. It's not anywhere on campus. They could be at Pierce Conroy's lake house."

Anthony leans against the parking meter. "But we can't prove any of this. At least not until they identify Sonia, and the papers are saying it could take months with a body that old."

I curse under my breath. By then, Travis Shepherd will have destroyed any remaining evidence linking him to Sonia Russo and Matt Weaver. I did *not* come this far and risk this much to sit back and let that happen.

"Oh, man," Anthony says. "You have that look on your face. The scary one."

I close my eyes, trying to stay one step ahead of Travis Shepherd. Somehow, he must have figured out it was me who called Thom Ennis and sent him and the others that e-mail. That I would go after Matt's box once I knew it existed.

The photo. The one I stole from Travis's office. I was dumb enough to think he wouldn't notice, or that his wife wouldn't tell him she saw me in there the night of the party.

But the photo of Isabella's dead body . . . someone left it for me before I put the pieces together, before the party and the photo. Someone who knew I was in the crew team office. Someone who saw me hounding Zach Walton about the hazing.

Someone who has been able to watch my movements here.

"Take me back to school," I tell Anthony. *Take me back so I can find Casey Shepherd and end him.*

After sitting in traffic, it's nearly five by the time Anthony drops me off at Wheatley. Sports practice is ending. I hurry past Sebastian, who tries to stop me on the quad to "help" him with his campus-engineering-survey project for physics.

I stop outside the athletic complex, watching people trickle out. Jill, Brooke, and Lizzie, in their track and field uniforms. Lee Andersen, holding what looks like a squash racquet. I avoid his eyes and accidentally meet Cole's. He pretends he doesn't see me and turns to Murali and Phil, jumping in on their conversation.

I run up to him. "Have you seen Casey?"

"Are you serious?" Cole lets out a breathy laugh and shakes his head at me.

"I'm trying to help Brent," I snap. "So if you could stop hating me for like two seconds and tell me where Casey is, I'd really appreciate it."

Cole blinks at me. "What are you talking about?"

"I don't have time to explain. I need you to trust me. You know I wouldn't lie, Cole."

He scratches his shoulder and lets his hand rest there. He opens his mouth, but no sound comes out at first. "I think . . . Casey hung back. Coach wanted to talk to him. He seemed pretty pissed off."

"Is he alone in there with Tretter?"

"I—I think so. Why?"

I take off for the entrance of the athletic complex. There are a few stragglers in the lobby by the trophy cases, but almost everyone has cleared out. I head straight for Tretter's office. It's locked. I press my ear to the door. Nothing.

That's when I hear the shouting come from down the hall. The boys' locker room.

I run for the door, which is also locked. I wind up and give it a kick without thinking. I cry out in frustration, then I search my bag for a bobby pin. When I wedge it in the lock, I hear Casey's voice.

"Get *off* me."

The sound of a body slamming into a locker makes me jump. "Where is it?" Tretter demands.

"It doesn't matter," Casey says. "You're done, dickhole."

Something that sounds sickeningly like a skull crashing into a locker. Casey cries out. The bobby pin nearly slips through my fingers, but the lock clicks and I push my way into the locker room.

I hurry past the bathroom and shower stalls, one hand in my bag. When I get to the rows of lockers, I peer around the corner. Tretter is holding Casey up against a locker, his feet dangling an inch from the ground. Half of Casey's face is covered in blood. I cry out without meaning to.

Tretter's head swivels toward me. Panic fills his eyes as he glances at the back door of the locker room. I can tell at that moment Larry Tretter is not the type of man who would ever hit a girl.

"Stop," I command. Tretter has Casey by the throat, and his skin is turning as blue as the locker behind him.

Tretter freezes. He's going to kill Casey. I pull the taser from my purse and aim the laser at Tretter, like Dennis showed me. Before Tretter can react, the two prongs shoot out and attach to his chest. A horrible, sickening clicking sound meets my ears as Tretter falls to the floor, smacking his head on the bench on the way down. I smell burning flesh and urine. Casey doubles over, gasping for air.

I take a step toward him. "What did he mean by 'Where is it?'"

Casey holds his hands up. "Get away from me, psychobitch."

"Call me that again, and I'll leave you facedown in your own drool and piss like him." I nod to Tretter. My hand shakes around the handle of the taser.

Casey lunges for me but trips over the bench separating us. He's still gasping for air, disoriented.

"Let's try this again," I say. "What was Tretter looking for?"

"Fuck yourself," Casey says.

I point the taser at him. I don't even think I can shoot it again after using the last cartridge on Tretter, but Casey doesn't need to know that. He backs against the locker.

"Start from the beginning," I tell him.

"I knew it was you who followed us to the quarry after I saw you with Walton." Casey's eyes are on the taser.

"How'd you get the picture of Isabella?" I demand.

"Isabella? What are you talking about?"

"The picture of her with her throat slit," I hiss. "The little message you left me to back off."

"I didn't leave you any message. I just wanted to know why you were up the crew team's ass. I told my dad you seemed pretty interested in us. Then I heard him yelling at Coach. Something about Matt Weaver and how someone was 'onto them.' He told Coach to take care of you. When he said no, my dad said he had something in his safe to make him change his mind."

Casey looks at Tretter, lying on the tile floor, unconscious. Casey clutches his chest, and I'm afraid I've given the guy a heart attack.

"I wanted to know what my dad had on Coach, so I checked his safe at the Cape house. There was a tape in there, of Coach admitting to hiring a guy to kill Steve Westbrook."

"The senator?" I ask.

Casey nods. "Coach said the guy was supposed to screw with the brakes. Steve had a meeting in the morning, but his wife took the car before he did."

I'm so shocked that I don't realize Casey has stopped hyperventilating. He leaps across the bench and reaches for my throat. I wind up and elbow him right in the nose. He collapses in pain as I examine the sleeve of my sweater, which is now covered in his blood.

Ugh. I look down at Casey, who is cradling his face in his hands. "I'm sending you the dry-cleaning bill," I say. "Asshole."

I almost forget something before I leave the locker room. I stand over Casey, pointing the taser at him. He cringes. "What's the code to the safe?" I demand.

"Four-three-two-one," he spits.

I kick him in the balls. "The real one. Come on, Casey. You're all done for, anyway. I know where your dad buried Matt Weaver," I lie.

"Oh-nine-one-five," he cries out, rolling onto his stomach. "Crazy *bitch*."

Casey flinches as I reach into his back pocket.

"Relax." I pat around until I find his iPhone.

"You know, Dowling, you could have bought me dinner first," Casey snarls. With one hand, I keep the taser pointed at him. With the other, I swipe a finger across the screen of his iPhone.

"Oh-nine-one-five. That your birthday?"

Casey nods, sweat breaking out on his brow and mixing with the bloody bruise Tretter gave him. I type the numbers into the phone. It doesn't work.

"Try again," I snap. He gives me the finger. I aim the taser at his chest.

"One-oh-two-eight," he cries. "Get that fucking thing away from me."

The 1-0-2-8 code unlocks Casey's phone. "Is this also the code for the safe?"

He nods as I leave him writhing on the floor next to Tretter. When I'm outside the athletic building, I call campus security from his phone and ditch it.

CHAPTER
FORTY-FOUR

Anthony didn't question it when I called him and told him we needed to get to Shepherd's Cape house ASAP. He picks me up in his mom's sedan. I slide into the passenger seat and refill the cartridge on my taser. Anthony watches me, but he doesn't say anything.

The next thing I do is call Alexis Westbrook. I get her voice mail.

"Alexis . . . , it's Anne. I really need to talk to you." I glance out the window, watching the Wheatley School disappear in the side mirror. "You and your dad might be in danger. It's Travis Shepherd. He killed Matt Weaver, and I think he killed your mom and your brother. I'm going to the Shepherds' Cape house. I think he's hiding evidence there. Please . . . , warn your dad."

Anthony is quiet for about five minutes after I hang up, before asking, "Who'd you use the taser on?"

"Larry Tretter. He's the one who hired Grabiec. Casey says there's evidence in his dad's safe."

"Do you think this is a trap?"

"Casey's not that smart." I pull my sweater over my head, not caring that I'm only wearing a camisole underneath. "That's his blood, in case you were wondering."

"Why would Tretter put a hit out on Westbrook if Shepherd is the one who killed Sonia and Matt Weaver, though?" Anthony asks.

"Shepherd blackmailed him," I say. "Maybe Tretter is the one who helped Shepherd get rid of the bodies. He felt like Matt was replacing him, so he could have agreed to do Shepherd's dirty work in order to get on his good side again."

Anthony taps out a nervous beat on the steering wheel as he gets onto the freeway.

"The house doesn't have an alarm system," I say. "At least, I didn't see one when I was there."

"It's because they don't need one." Anthony runs his hand across the stubble on his chin. "It's *Cape Cod*. The neighborhood watch will be on us in seconds. This isn't gonna work."

"It has to," is all I can say. We're quiet for a few minutes. "Drop me off at the house, then drive to the end of the road. Call me the second you see any cars turning onto the road."

"Are you nuts?" Anthony looks over at me. "You think I'm going to leave you alone there?"

"I have this." I gesture to the taser in my lap. "And I know my way around the house already."

"I'll take the Taser and go inside." Anthony's voice says there's no room for negotiation. "You keep watch at the end of the street."

"*I* have the safe combination," I remind him. "Plus, I don't know how to drive."

Anthony lets out a sound of frustration. I call Brent and reach his voice mail for the millionth time.

"It's me," I say. "Look, I *wasn't* right about everything. Not about your dad. And I'm sorry. For everything. I just thought you should know."

I glance over at Anthony, but he's looking out his window. A sign tells us Cape Cod is in thirty miles.

The Shepherds' street is mostly dark when Anthony and I arrive an hour later. He turns his headlights off and creeps along until I spot the familiar two-story colonial.

"I'm pretty sure it's that one." I point to a house on the right. "Drop me off by the driveway so I can make sure no one's home."

Anthony grabs my wrist as I open the door. "Remember, if I call, it means get the hell out of there."

I nod. As an afterthought, I kiss him on the cheek.

The automatic lights on the porch flicker, but I peer into the garage. The Range Rover is gone. I give Anthony a thumbs-up and I run around the back of the house, holding a crowbar from Anthony's trunk.

The windows of the Shepherds' sunroom are as flimsy as I remember. I wedge the crowbar into the windowsill. I push down until I hear a crack. I pause, waiting for an alarm to go off inside. Silence. I swallow and push the window up.

I put one leg through at a time and stumble into the dark sunroom. I know better than to turn a light on. I hold my phone out in front of me so I can see as I pick my way around furniture. When I get to the hall, I grip my other hand around my taser.

The floor creaks beneath my feet. I don't remember the house being this old. I tiptoe up the stairs, looking out the two-story window onto the street. No headlights. So far, so good.

I inch down the hall, trying to remember which door leads to Travis Shepherd's office. I don't remember seeing a safe inside it, but I figure I'll start there. A draft ripples the curtains on the window across the hall. I turn my head, thinking it's weird someone left it open.

Something isn't right. If Shepherd is hiding evidence of multiple murders in this house, why not invest in better security? I swallow down the feeling of foreboding as I rest my hand on the office doorknob.

I open the door and flip on the light. I cry out when I see Travis Shepherd sitting in his office chair, pointing a rifle at me.

"Have a seat, sweetheart," he says, unsmiling. "I've been expecting you."

CHAPTER
FORTY-FIVE

I stand in the doorway, frozen.

"It wasn't a suggestion," Shepherd says. "Sit."

I obey, thinking it's the best chance I have of getting out of here alive.

He gestures for me to hand over my taser. I do.

"Now, I think we can have a civil conversation." Shepherd smiles. My eyes fall to the rifle in his lap.

"An 1887 Snider-Enfield," he explains. "Had my eye on it for a while. I won it at an auction."

"Oh." My voice cracks on the single syllable. Shepherd leans back in his leather chair, as if this situation couldn't please him more.

"I have to hand it to you," he says. "I'm impressed you found Matthew's clues. I've been searching for years, and all you had to do was sweet-talk his parents. I guess I'm not as charming as you.

"You see, Anne," he says, "I don't like when things get away from me. You got away from me, very quickly. I'm going to tell you the story of someone else who got away from me. His name was Matty."

Shepherd leans over his desk, and I flinch. It makes him smile.

"I met Matty at the end of my first year at Wheatley," Shepherd says. "I suggested he try out for rowing. The kid was a bit of a social chameleon. Would have done anything to fit in. Unlike the other guys, who saw a piece of trash trying to be one of us, I saw an opportunity."

Shepherd folds his hands in front of him. "I took Matty under my wing. He worshipped me. I could do no wrong, in his eyes. I'm sure you know what that feels like, Miss Dowling. You and I are alike in that way, I think. I've heard a lot about you. And I think that for all your bravado, you're trying to hide the fact that you're as wicked as I am."

My heart thumps wildly. *He's wrong. So wrong.*

"Matty's ego grew along with his popularity," Shepherd continues. "He needed to be knocked down a few pegs. Almost no one would talk to him after they heard what he'd done to Vanessa. I almost felt responsible, since I'm the one who told him how *badly* she wanted to get him alone." Shepherd's eyes gleam wickedly.

Acid creeps up my throat. I can't stop myself from asking: "Why involve Conroy? He wasn't really there, was he?"

Shepherd smiles. "Sometimes rumors get out of control. Like a fire that spreads too fast to be put out. Innocent people get burned."

All of the blood drains from my head. It finally hits me: Shepherd was manipulating his friends from the get-go. Larry, Pierce, Matt. If he didn't have something on each of them, they were worthless to him.

I watch Shepherd, waiting for him to look away long enough for me to dial Anthony and hang up. He never breaks my gaze, though. *He's going to kill me. He's finally telling me the truth because it won't matter once I'm dead.*

"I would have done anything for Matt," Shepherd says, almost sounding mournful. "And how did the shithead repay me? He tried to take what was mine. I don't like when people try to take things that belong to me."

I follow his gaze to the empty space in the photo frame.

"Cynthia Westbrook," I choke out.

"Durham," Shepherd snaps. "Yes. Matty thought it would be cute to use my slipup to win Cynthia over."

"So Sonia Russo was a slipup? Her mother thinks you would have married her."

"*Impressive.* You tracked the cokehead down." Shepherd's voice is mocking. "Matty never got the chance to tell Cynthia about Sonia. He saw firsthand what would happen."

"Is that why you killed her?" I ask. "She was going to tell Cynthia?"

"She was as arrogant as Matty was. But I never meant to hurt her." He says it in a way that almost makes me believe him. "Sonia liked to run her mouth when she was tweaked. Must have gotten the itch from that cokehead mother of hers. When she showed up at the lake house, threatening to tell Cynthia everything, I grabbed her. She slipped and hit her head. Matty saw the whole thing and panicked, thinking Pierce would think *he'd* killed Sonia. A compelling enough reason to help me bury her body."

Compelling. It's so obviously code for *I threatened to make Pierce Conroy think Matt killed Sonia and get rid of him for good.*

"At the end of the day, I didn't think Matty'd tell anyone," Shepherd continues. "He cared too much about being a 'Wheatley Boy.' About being the first person in his family to go to college. To be able to afford the things his parents couldn't. Then I realized he'd taken Sonia's necklace. The bastard actually *dug it up.* Leverage, I suppose. He was biding his time until he wasn't afraid of me anymore.

"I didn't appreciate that. I told him to meet me at the quarry that night. I made him believe I was ready to confess about Sonia, and that I needed him to testify it was an accident. He was supposed to bring the necklace." Shepherd's eyes are cold, as if Matt's withholding Sonia's necklace is the worst part of this whole story. "If he'd simply brought me the necklace, he might have walked away that night."

"What happened?" I whisper.

"Do you realize how lucky you are? After all these years, *you're* going to get the real story," Shepherd says. "Lawrence followed us to the quarry. The stupid ass never knew when to listen. He saw Matty push me, so he intervened. I don't remember which of us shoved him off the cliff, but does it really matter now?"

I stare at Shepherd, letting his face splinter through the tears in my eyes. "No. I guess it doesn't."

Shepherd reaches over and pats my hand. I jerk it away. "Anne, I'd like the photo you took from me. If you don't hand it over, I'm sure I won't have any trouble finding it later." *After I kill you.*

Whimpering, I fish around in my bag. "I'll give it to you. Please don't hurt me."

"Of course not," Shepherd says, through a smile.

I whip my pepper spray out of my bag. There's just enough left to make Travis Shepherd double over in pain when I release the contents onto his face.

I fly out of the office and down the stairs. A tall figure leaps out of the shadows when I reach the bottom, covering my mouth before I can scream. Travis Shepherd's angry footsteps sound on the stairs.

The man holding me turns me around so I can see his face.

It's Steven Westbrook. He's holding a gun.

He holds his finger to his mouth before he shoves me into a closet.

CHAPTER
FORTY-SIX

"Steven?" Travis Shepherd's voice is surprised. And, I'm happy to note, pained. I pull out my phone and text Anthony. *Call the police.*

I peek out the closet door, which is slightly ajar. Steven Westbrook stands five feet away from Shepherd, a handgun pointed at his chest.

"Oh, how the mighty have fallen," Shepherd laughs. "Going to kill me, Steven?"

"That depends." Westbrook's voice shakes a little. "Was it really you who killed my family?"

"Of course not." Shepherd's face is red and swollen. He squints at Westbrook. "That was Larry."

"Liar," Westbrook roars, spit flying everywhere. "I know Larry doesn't shit without you telling him to. Did you tell him to kill Cynthia?"

Shepherd tries to point his rifle at the senator. Westbrook's gun clicks. "Drop the rifle."

Shepherd lowers it. "I had no reason to kill Cynthia."

"Me," Westbrook says. I realize he's crying. "You were trying to kill *me*. You thought I'd tell that I saw you and Larry sneak into the dorms and throw out your clothes. The night Matt disappeared. I knew—"

Westbrook's free hand curls into a fist. He presses it to his mouth to suppress a sob. "I always knew you would come after them. But I won't put my daughter in danger any longer."

He raises his gun again. It clicks, and I swallow away vomit. Alexis got my voicemail and warned her father about Shepherd. That's why he's here. I've inadvertently put us all in danger.

"What would you have done?" Shepherd holds up his hands. His voice is pleading, trying to talk Westbrook down. "You were a rising star. Typical Wheatley 'Good Old Boy.' Bound for the White House. I knew you'd come clean about what you saw so you could become senator with a clear conscience. What happened to you, Steve?"

Westbrook lets out a wail that brings a lump to my throat. He sobs for his wife. For his son. "How could you, Travis? How *could* you?"

I break out into a cold sweat as Westbrook raises his gun. Shepherd seems to shrink. "Steven. Remember what they say. You take your revenge on me now, you better dig a grave for yourself, too."

"I already have," Westbrook says.

The sound of glass shattering jolts me. Anthony calls my name. I begin to scream as Shepherd lifts his rifle and points it at the front door.

I don't realize the shot came from Westbrook's gun until I see the hole in Travis Shepherd's chest. Blood flowers around it. On the floor. Everywhere.

"Oh my God." I push my way out of the closet and into Anthony's arms. He drops the baseball bat he used to smash the glass pane on the door. Steven Westbrook stares at the gun in his hands. At Travis Shepherd's lifeless eyes.

I know what he's going to do before he raises the gun to his head.

"Don't," I scream. "Alexis. Please don't do this to Alexis!"

Westbrook's eyes meet mine. They're gray, just like his daughter's. He drops the gun and falls to his knees. He tilts his head upward and cries out—a horrible, guttural sound. Anthony holds me closer to him until I can't tell whose heartbeat is whose. Sirens sound in the distance.

Westbrook looks at me. "Get out of here."

"But—"

"You were never here," he says. "*Leave.*"

So we do.

Travis Shepherd is dead. I can't erase the image of him, lying on the floor of his foyer with a gaping hole where his heart used to be.

By the time Anthony gets me back to the Wheatley School, everyone knows Travis Shepherd is dead. It's breaking news, interrupting Monday-night sitcoms. Steven Westbrook confessed to breaking into Travis Shepherd's Cape Cod home and shooting him to death.

There are police cruisers outside the athletic building. I tremble as I watch the officers come out without Larry Tretter. Security guards and RAs usher the gawkers back to their dorms.

"I can't do this," I say. "I need to talk to Detective Phelan. Tell him what we saw."

"Anne." Anthony rests his hands on my shoulders and looks down into my eyes. "We broke into Shepherd's house moments before he was murdered. We cannot tell *anyone* what we saw. Ever."

"But I screamed at Westbrook. What if someone heard me?"

I'm shaking as Anthony puts a hand on my neck and pulls me to his chest. "It's going to be okay. It's over. We're okay."

I'm not going to be okay after what I saw. I don't know if I'll ever stop hearing Steven Westbrook's cries of *How could you, Travis?*

I hear Brent before I see him.

"Anne?"

I pull away from Anthony, wiping at my eyes.

"I got your voice mail." Brent's eyes are on Anthony, even though he's talking to me.

"Brent," I say.

"Thanks." He interrupts me with a wry smile. He's still look-ing at Anthony. "I heard about Sonia Russo's necklace. Coach Tretter just gave a statement to the police that Travis Shepherd bought it for her. I know it was you who found it. So thanks, for clearing my dad."

"Brent. Please look at me."

He does. But I can't find the words to tell him how sorry I am.

"I just need to know if this"—Brent gestures to me and An-thony—"was going on when we were together?"

"What?" I can't breathe. *I can't believe Brent could think that.* I look to Anthony to help me out, but he looks away.

"It wasn't." I don't even know whom to direct my rage at any-more.

"Goodnight, Anne," Brent says. When he's walking away, An-thony tries to wrap an arm around me. I shrug him off.

"Why didn't you back me up?" I demand.

"Why does it matter?" he snaps.

"It does matter." *I will not get hysterical. I will not get hys-terical.* "It's *always* going to matter when it comes to him, An-thony. So take it or leave it."

I'm crying, wishing I felt as sure of myself as I sound, because I know he's going to leave. Again.

But when I open my eyes, he's still there.

CHAPTER
FORTY-SEVEN

Darlene is pounding on my door at 6:00 A.M., telling me to get dressed. Dean Tierney needs to see me in her office.

The secretary barely looks up at me. Her eyes are glued to the TV in the office. A news anchor is reporting live from the edge of the Wheatley School campus. Apparently Larry Tretter turned himself in to the police last night.

"The Wheatley rowing coach alleges he and Travis Shepherd are responsible for missing teen Matt Weaver's death. . . ."

"Good God," the secretary says, oblivious to our presence. Dean Snaggletooth opens her office door and gestures for me to come in. Her hair is frizzing at the crown, and she forgot her makeup.

"Casey Shepherd claims you assaulted him and Coach Tretter," she says, before my ass is even in a chair.

"Casey Shepherd has bigger problems than being beat up by a girl."

"I'm sorry. Is there something funny about your classmate's father being shot to death in his own home?"

I feel as if Tierney has slapped me. I close my eyes, hoping I'll see anything but her face, but all I see is the pool of blood on Travis Shepherd's floor. The shocked look in his eyes as the life left his body.

But worst of all is the sound of Steven Westrook's cry of despair before he killed him.

"No," I manage to choke out. "There is nothing funny at all."

Tierney shuffles the papers on her desk. "Your father is on his way to Massachusetts."

"I had nothing to do with what happened last night," I blurt—forcefully, as if saying it will help me convince myself Anthony and I didn't see the horrible things we saw.

Dean Snaggletooth nods absently. "Anne, I have to let you know that Headmaster Goddard has recommended you for expulsion."

I knew this was coming. But I still feel as if I've been hit in the head. *Recommended for expulsion.*

"He doesn't have the final say?" My throat is dry.

"Your case will go to the board of trustees at the end of the month. Until then, you are temporarily suspended. You will be expected to complete your schoolwork from New York, via online correspondence with your teachers, until your hearing."

"Do I get to defend myself?"

Tierney shakes her head and lists my crimes: "Breaking curfew. Unexcused absences from class. Unauthorized entry into restricted areas on campus. Assaulting a fellow student. Assaulting a faculty member and a fellow student" (again).

I barely hear her over the buzzing in my ears. I can't believe it. I'm going home.

My father is going to be here in four hours. I spend the time packing, since everyone is in class anyway. I don't even know who I have left to say good-bye to.

There is one person. I head to Ms. C's office before lunch.

I know something is wrong the moment I see that her door is closed, the light off.

I rap on the door because I don't know what else to do.

"Excuse me," I ask a teacher across the hall. He looks up from his desk and blinks at me.

"Is Ms. Cross sick today?" I ask.

"She no longer works here," the teacher says.

"What?"

The teacher blinks at me, as if I'm some sort of simpleton. Forget him. There's one person who may know what's going on.

I race-walk all the way to the sciences building and look up Dr. Muller's office number.

His door is closed, a note taped to the outside.

I am currently at Boston Common for a surveying trip with my PHY101 class. I will return at the end of the day.

Panic creeps up my spine. I don't have until the end of the day. I scroll through my phone until I find the number Ms. C gave us for "emergencies only," like being really late to class or our Blackboard app crashing in the middle of a take-home test. I don't think this is what she had in mind, but I call her anyway.

"The number you have dialed is in not service. . . ."

My nightmare has only gotten worse. Ms. C is gone, and I know in my gut it's because she helped me.

My feet carry me all the way back to the administration building. Goddard's secretary does not look pleased to see me.

"I need to see the headmaster."

"He's not in."

"When will he *be* in?" I demand with the force of someone who has nothing left to lose.

"The headmaster won't be back," the secretary snipes at me. "If you have a problem, you'll have to wait until the interim headmaster arrives."

There's a light on in Goddard's office. I run up to the door and shout through it. "Where is she? What did you do with Ms. Cross?"

That's when the secretary calls security to escort me out of the building.

"Don't bother," I tell her. "I'm leaving."

I pull up the news app on my phone as I'm leaving and search for *Benedict Goddard*. The first headline is from an hour ago.

WHEATLEY SCHOOL HEADMASTER STEPS DOWN, CITING
FAILING HEALTH IN THE WAKE OF SHEPHERD SCANDAL

I almost scream. That *bastard*. He made sure expelling me was literally the last thing he did.

I sit on my bed, surveying my empty room. I feel like I should do something, perform some ritual to say good-bye to it for good. I flop onto my back and stare at the ceiling.

This is stupid. I roll on my side, reading more news articles on my phone. The media is going nuts, trying to piece together the details of what lead from an anonymous tip about the body at the Conroy's lake house to Steven Westbrook killing Travis Shepherd. The latest story says Larry Tretter told police Matt Weaver's body is under the driveway at the Shepherds' Cape house.

Matt Weaver is dead. So is Travis Shepherd, and Casey will have to deal with it for the rest of his life. I'm not sure he deserves that pain, even though if I had the chance to punch him in the face again, I'd do it harder. And although he destroyed so many lives, I'm not sure that Travis Shepherd deserved to die.

I'm not sure of anything anymore. Sonia's body being found at the Conroy lake house will probably damage Brent's family's reputation forever, even if his dad has been cleared. I put Anthony in danger by bringing him to the scene of Travis Shepherd's murder. And I sealed my fate as the girl who can't stay out of trouble long enough to graduate from high school.

They say a butterfly flapping its wings can cause a tsunami on the other side of the world. None of this would have happened if I'd never started that fire at St. Bernadette's and been kicked out. Probably the best thing to happen to the Wheatley School now is for me to go back to New York and bring my chaos with me.

A knock at the door startles me. It can't be my dad—it's an hour too early.

Through the peephole, I watch Brent outside my door. He curses under his breath and motions to walk away. Then he stops, ready to knock at the door again. I open it.

"Hi," I say.

"Hi."

He doesn't protest as I hug him. In fact, he rests his head on my shoulder. "This sucks," I whisper in his ear.

Brent pulls away, but he takes my hands in his. "You're really leaving?"

I nod. He pulls me in, and I think he's going to kiss me, but instead he presses his cheek to mine. When we break apart, he looks at me.

"I was wrong. About everything."

"I was wrong about stuff, too," I say.

Brent looks like he's struggling with something. I wish he would say something, anything to make it feel slightly less shitty that this might be the last time we see each other. He sighs and takes in the empty room. "There's always a chance the board won't vote to uphold your expulsion."

I laugh. He does, too. I realize I've missed the sound so much it hurts. In that moment I'd do anything to pick up where we left off, but a feeling of dread streaks through me as I remember the photo of Isabella's body. The way Brent hesitated just now, as if there were something more he wanted to tell me.

Casey said he wasn't the one who left the photo. A few weeks ago, I never would have considered the possibility Brent would do something like that. I squeeze my eyes shut, willing away the scene in Travis Shepherd's foyer.

I'm not the same person I was a few weeks ago. And I'll never doubt the terrible things people are capable of again.

My dad meets me in the lobby of Amherst, where Remy, April, and Kelsey finish their teary good-byes and promises to come see me in New York. I smile at them, even though I know by the expression on my father's face that I'll be lucky if I'm allowed out of our apartment ever again.

He doesn't say a word to me for the first three hours of the drive. This is worse than I thought. I spend the whole time thinking of how I'm going to defend myself, and when we get near the George Washington Bridge, I open my mouth.

"I don't expect you to forgive me or even believe me, but I had a reason for all the things I did. I can't tell you most of them, because it's better if you don't know. You have to trust me that I did the right thing, though. You always told me that that's all that matters. I know it's hard for you to believe that; you always say you hate your job because it's hard to tell the difference between right and wrong sometimes. I understand you now. And I'm sorry I got expelled again, but I promise you that this time it's because I did something right, for once in my life. I found my white rabbit, Daddy, and I didn't let it go."

I think I see the corner of my father's mouth twitch.

"Also, I want to learn how to drive this summer," I say.

"Oh, Jesus," my father mutters.

I smile to myself and look out the window. The sight of the Empire State Building fills me up with a happiness that replaces my regret over everything I've lost.

I didn't find the happy ending, but at least I know it's the right one.

My phone rings as we go down the FDR. Daddy looks at me as if to say *Go ahead and answer it—you'll never own a phone again once we get home.* I glance at the screen. I don't recognize the number, but I answer, thinking it might be Anthony calling from a different line.

"Hello?"

"Is this Anne?" a voice asks. A male voice. With an accent.

"Yes. Who is this?"

"It's Dr. Muller. From the Wheatley School. I heard you were looking for me at my office this morning."

"Ms. Cross," I blurt. "Do you know why she left? I went looking for her this morning—"

"Anne, you won't be able find her." Dr. Muller inhales sharply enough for me to hear, and all I can think is: *He's going to tell me she's dead.*

Please, please, don't let him tell me she's dead, because I can't take anymore.

"Why not?" I keep my voice steady so I don't alarm my dad.

"Because," Dr. Muller says, "Jessica Cross does not exist."

Read on for an excerpt from the next title in the
Prep School Confidential series

DEADLY LITTLE
SINS

A PREP SCHOOL
CONFIDENTIAL
NOVEL

Suspicion is the companion of mean souls

—Thomas Paine, *Common Sense*

CHAPTER
ONE

The first time I looked death in the face, I blinked and it was gone.

They say your life is supposed to flash before your eyes, but all I remember is the moment after. The adrenaline that filled me, knowing I survived. The weightlessness of having dodged a bullet. Literally.

Watching someone else die was different.

The details are the hardest to forget. The smell of cinnamon-and-pine furniture polish. The sound of glass breaking at the front door. And worst of all, the way Travis Shepherd's eyes froze as the life left his body.

It's been more than a month since Anthony and I watched Steven Westbrook shoot Shepherd, his former classmate, in the chest. Since then, I've been unofficially expelled from the Wheatley School, grounded for what's quite possibly the rest of my teenage years, and exiled from my friends.

I know that having my phone, computer, and social life taken away is my parents' way of ensuring I have nothing to do all summer but to think about the things I've done. If only they knew the whole story—the one that starts with a thirty-year-old photo of a missing student and ends with watching his killer die on the floor of his own foyer—they'd understand that I could never *not* think about what I've done.

I would give anything to be able to close my eyes and not picture the blood blossoming around the hole in Travis Shepherd's chest. If I could, I'd stop it from happening in the first place.

Even though he had killed four people, including a five-year-old boy. Even though deep down, I believe that Travis Shepherd deserved to die.

Or maybe that's what I *want* to believe, because if I'd gone to the police instead of to Alexis Westbrook that night, Shepherd would be alive.

It was like a horrible move in a game of checkers—a move where *bam*, all of the kings get captured. Shepherd is dead, Steven Westbrook is in jail, Headmaster Goddard is in hiding, and the only person at Wheatley I thought I could trust—Ms. Cross, my favorite teacher—disappeared without a trace.

And I'm in New York. Right back where I started, but so, so far away from the person I was.

I still don't know where I'm going to school in the fall. My parents said, "We'll cross that bridge when we get there," which obviously means no one wants me. There was a time I would have made that work in my favor. Now, I mostly just stay out of their way and hope I don't end up at a school where everyone either has a baby or a probation officer.

I technically haven't been expelled from Wheatley. Yet. My disciplinary hearing has been postponed until July, because of "internal re-structuring." Which is a fancy euphemism for the fact that Wheatley, formerly Massachusetts's #1 secondary preparatory school, is up Shit's Creek.

The administration of the mighty Wheatley School has fallen and now Jacqueline Tierney, aka Dean Snaggletooth, is the last person standing. Maybe she'll wind up running the place. If you ask me, they could use a womanly touch over there, even though Tierney has all the femininity of a jock strap.

Anyway, none of that matters because the board is almost certain to turn my suspension into an expulsion, which will mark my second expulsion from a school this year.

The official citation in the letter Dean Tierney sent home said I "assaulted another student." I guess they were willing to give me a break for using a Taser on Larry Tretter, the boys' crew team coach and Travis Shepherd's accomplice, since he's currently in jail for conspiracy to commit murder.

The version of the story I gave Tierney and my parents is that I used the Taser on Coach Tretter because he was beating the crap out of Casey, Travis Shepherd's son. Then I took a couple shots of my own at Casey, just for being a Class A prick.

My parents were probably too pissed at me to dig further into what happened. My dad wanted to know why, if I had to kick a boy in the balls, I couldn't wait to do it until we were off-campus. My mom just wanted to know where I got the Taser.

Their reactions probably explain a lot about why I am the way I am.

So my sentence for being not-officially-but-basically expelled was virtual confinement to our apartment until the hearing. At first it wasn't so bad, because I had a ton of schoolwork to finish. Then I turned in my final exams and realized I had no purpose in life. I was a prisoner in my own home. Except I think I'd prefer actually being in jail, because then I wouldn't have to see my parents every day.

I told my dad this, and he didn't think it was very funny. He decided I needed an attitude adjustment in the form of going to work with him.

His plan to further my misery backfired, though, because I love interning in his law office. I get to research cases and read trial transcripts, and my dad's assistant, Leah, lets me tag along when she picks up lunch. If we have time, we browse Sephora or the bookstore and I get to feel like a real human being again.

Today is a particularly glorious day, because my father has to be in court at nine A.M. I've been waiting for this moment for weeks.

"Go *straight* to the office," he says as we cross 51st Street outside our apartment. "I'm calling Leah in ten minutes to make sure you're there."

"Daddy, chill. I already snuck out to meet my meth dealer last night."

He whirls around and gives me the worst look I've ever seen. I half-expect him to put his hands on his hips and say, "I brought you into this world, and I can take you out of it." He did that a lot when I was younger.

"You are not half as funny as you think you are," he says.

Well, that's a little upsetting, because I think I'm hilarious. I lift the hair off the back of my neck and tie it into a loose bun. I'm already planning which layers of clothing I can ditch when I get to the office.

"I mean it, Anne," he says when we're across the street. He lifts his hand up, as if he wants to say something else, but lowers it. "Make sure you're home by five-fifteen."

I give him a captain's salute, even though I know it irritates him. I don't know what's wrong with me. It's like I feel if I keep digging my hole, eventually it'll get deep enough that I can disappear.

I catch Leah by the thermostat when I get to the office. Since my dad will be gone all day, we can crank the central air without him bitching about the bill.

And if I play my cards right, I can check my e-mail for the first time in weeks.

Seconds after I set my bag on the extra desk, Leah drops a stack of collated papers on my desk. "Need you to read up on State of New York versus Helen Peters. I flagged the pages."

Crap. This is going to take me at least until lunch. As I flip through the photocopied pages, I watch Leah at her desk. She rolls away from the computer on her chair and starts thumbing through a stack of legal journals.

"I need to make a couple more copies," she says. "Think you can handle the phone if anyone calls?"

"Sure."

"Remember, no personal calls. Your dad *will* find out."

"I know," I say. "He's got this place under *Homeland* levels of surveillance."

Leah flounces out the door. I'm not stupid—she's going down to the lobby to call her boyfriend. First off, we have a perfectly good copy machine in the backroom. Second, she didn't even take the journal with her.

It makes me feel a little less lousy about using her computer. When I hear the elevator ping, I slide into her chair and log into my e-mail.

I was able to sneak a few e-mails to Brent Conroy—my ex-boyfriend—before my dad figured out I was using my school e-mail for personal business. Disappointment needles me when I see he hasn't replied to my last message. He's in England for the summer, visiting family, so I can only assume he's met a British girl with an adorable gap between her front teeth.

Brent and I broke up under epically bad circumstances. I snooped through his phone so I could follow him and the rest of the crew team into the woods during one of their hazing rituals. And I also may have implied his father was involved in Matt Weaver's murder.

The fact that Anthony, the other guy I was kind-of-sort-of involved with, hasn't responded to any of my e-mails isn't surprising either. The last time I saw him, we'd just made a promise to each other not to tell anyone what we saw in Travis Shepherd's house. Then I had to leave Wheatley without getting the chance to say good-bye. He probably thinks I did it on purpose—almost as if I wanted to leave him, and everything we saw together, behind.

The more I think about it, I don't blame either one of them for wanting nothing to do with me.

I take a deep breath as I scan my inbox; it catches in my throat when I spot a message from *Muller, Rowan.* It's dated two weeks ago.

Dr. Muller is a physics teacher at the Wheatley School. I saw him hanging around campus with Ms. Cross a few times before she disappeared. He was the one who called and told me I shouldn't bother trying to find Ms. C—I had to hang up before he could tell me why.

All he'd said was that Jessica Cross doesn't really exist.

I open the e-mail.

Anne,

I apologize for the delay. I'd preferred not to say what I had to tell you through e-mail as long as I was still employed by Wheatley, but my situation has changed. Is there any chance you could speak in person when I'm in New York at the beginning of August? In the meantime, I think you should check out the following.

Best,

RM

He's pasted two links in the e-mail. I click on the first, which leads to a LinkedIn profile for a Jessica L. Cross from Cliftonville, Georgia. According to the page, she has a double B.A. in English and Classic Languages from the University of North Carolina, Chapel Hill. Her current occupation is *teacher.*

And the woman in the black and white photo is definitely Ms. C.

I don't understand—all of this fits with what Ms. Cross told me about herself. I X out of the page and click the second link. The page takes forever to load—I glance at the door to make sure Leah isn't on her way up, but the hall is quiet.

The page—an article from the *Cliftonville Gazette*—finally loads. I have to blink a few times to process what I'm reading.

An obituary for Jessica Leigh Cross, who died eight years ago.

CHAPTER
TWO

I select *print* from the menu and respond to Dr. Muller's message. Yesterday was the first day of August—he should be in New York by now.

Wajima on 61st, Friday at 1. If you can't make it, call 917-555-9687 and hang up twice. That's my dad's office.

I log out of my e-mail and I delete my tabs from the browser history.

The elevator pings just as the obituary is done printing. I slip it between the journal pages and pretend to be staring out the window aimlessly when Leah comes back inside.

When she's settled back in her desk, I open to the obituary.

Jessica Leigh Cross, beloved daughter, sister, and UNC Chapel Hill graduate, passed away unexpectedly after an illness. She is survived by her parents, Marie and Alan Cross of Cliftonville, and sister, Arianne Cross-Duncan of Canton. Jessica is remembered for her generous and kind nature. In lieu of flowers, donations may be made to The Acworth Home for Women.

Either Muller is messing with me, or something completely fucked is going on here.

For the next couple days, I jump every time the phone rings, waiting to see if it's a hang-up call. On Wednesday, the phone rings at a little past ten.

"Dowling and Associates," Leah says. "How can I help you?"

There's a pause. "He's in court all week," she replies. "What is the best number to call you back?"

She's quiet, listening to the caller. When her gaze lands on me and doesn't move, my blood runs cold.

"One moment." Leah is frowning. "I'll connect you to his cell."

My heart sinks to the pit of my stomach. There are about a million reasons someone would be calling about me, and none of them are good. Fear cracks through me; what if the thing I've so desperately trying to escape has caught up to me? I've been dreading this phone call ever since Steven Westbrook was arrested.

What if he told the police or his lawyers that Anthony and I were there that night? Or what if Casey Shepherd figured out I was involved? What if it's the police calling my father right now?

Leah presses the transfer button on the phone. "Mr. Dowling, I have Jacqueline Tierney on the line for you."

I think that's almost worse than the police.

I knew this moment was coming, but even though I convinced myself I was okay with it, I'm not. Tierney is going to expel my ass without losing a minute's sleep over it, and I'll probably never see most of my friends—April, Kelsey, Cole, Murali—again.

Janelle whispers my name and motions for me to come over to her. She presses a finger to her lips then points to the phone. And hands it to me.

I could kiss her. I have to hold the phone a few inches away from my face, because I'm breathing so hard I'm sure my dad will hear me. Janelle bites her thumbnail.

". . . and Dylan?" my dad asks.

"Away at lacrosse camp," Tierney says. "I never thought I'd miss having a house full of pre-teen boys."

Dad laughs, and my blood boils. Dean Tierney is calling my dad with the fate of my future in her hands, and they're talking about her damn KIDS? I don't realize I'm making a fist with my free hand until Janelle reaches to take the phone away from me, panicked. I spin the desk chair away from her.

"—about the delay, I'm sure you can imagine," Tierney is saying. "We're interviewing headmasters, but no one wants to touch this mess with a ten-foot pole."

"Jackie, I asked how *you're* holding up," my dad says, with uncharacteristic gentleness.

There's silence on Tierney's end for a beat. "Quite frankly, I'm sick over the whole thing and would leave this place tomorrow if I could."

I nearly fall out of Leah's chair. This is the same woman who threatened to expel me for suggesting that the murder of my roommate, Isabella, was anything but an "unforeseen tragedy." The same woman who threw me out of her office when I told her I knew Matthew Weaver assaulted her sister, Vanessa.

"In any case, I'm sorry to keep your family waiting about the hearing," Tierney says.

The hearing. Of course.

Crap.

"We don't make these decisions hastily," she continues. "The last time a student was even expelled from Wheatley was fifteen years ago."

That should make an interesting detail in my college entrance essay. My toes curl in my sandals. I think Tierney has set some sort of record for shutting my father up.

"That's why the board has to vote unanimously to expel a student."

"We understand," my dad says.

And that's how I know there really is no hope left for me. Despite all my dad's huffing and puffing, he knew the fire at

St. Bernadette's was an accident. That's why he fought to get me into Wheatley. Because he still believed in me. Believed that I wouldn't screw up again.

"You should know, then, that in light of evidence, the board deliberated for a while about Anne," Tierney says.

"Evidence?"

"Yes. Quite a few of Anne's friends submitted testimony about her character. They believe that Casey Shepherd antagonized her before she assaulted him."

"Well, that does sound like my daughter."

"Regardless, considering the circumstances, there was a board member who felt uncomfortable expelling Anne."

WHAT?!

My father is speechless in what I can only hope is some sort of new trend.

"You . . . want her back?" he finally stammers.

"She's not expelled," Tierney says firmly. Message received, Tierney. The feeling is mutual.

"I'm going to need to discuss this with my wife," Dad says. "Obviously I would have reservations about putting her back in that environment."

"*You* have reservations?" It spills out of me in a whisper. I clamp my hand over my mouth and meet Leah's horrified expression.

"Excuse me, Jackie." My father's voice is eerily calm. "I'll have to call you back."

Seconds later, the office phone rings. Leah answers it with a meek "Yes?"

I catch *speak to my daughter*. She hands me the phone.

"Are you TRYING to push all of my buttons?" my dad shouts.

"Are you trying to make my life miserable?" I shoot back. "You'd really decide to send me back there without asking me how I feel?"

"Who said I'm sending you back there?"

"That's not the point." My eyes prick, and I don't even know why. "You should at least care how I feel about it. At least ask me."

"Anne," he says, firmly, "We'll discuss this later."

"You mean you'll discuss it with Mom. While I'm locked up in my room." I don't even know why I'm doing this—trying to pick a fight I'll never win. I don't even know why I'm on the verge of tears, or feeling like my lungs are going to collapse.

Maybe it's because the only thing that scares me more than the thought of being kicked out of Wheatley is going back there.

By the time Friday rolls around, there still haven't been any hang-up calls to the office. I know, because I made it a point not to leave my desk at all this week. Not even to pee.

"Are you okay?" Leah asks me around noon. "You seem antsy."

I shrug, not realizing I've been gnawing at my thumbnail until all of the pewter polish on it lifts off. "Just nervous. About school and everything."

It's not a complete lie: My parents still haven't reached an agreement on how to deal with Tierney's invitation to take me back. Every night, they close their bedroom door, and I hear murmuring.

I shoot a glance at the clock, hoping Dr. Muller got my e-mail about meeting today. I can't help but gnaw the rest of the polish off my fingers. I really think my father may consider military school or electro-shock therapy if he catches me sneaking out for lunch with a man twice my age.

And for what? The last time I got involved in something I shouldn't have gotten involved in, I lost my boyfriend, my parent's trust, and a man died. There's absolutely nothing to gain from trying to find out what's going on with Ms. C.

She was my favorite teacher, and I want more than anything to know she's okay, but if Dr. Muller thinks she's in danger, I'm not the person he should be going to. He can't make the same mistakes I did.

But what is he supposed to tell the police? *Hello, I'd like to report a missing person, and by the way, she's sort of been dead for eight years.* I know better than anyone that it would be a lost cause.

I should probably hear Dr. Muller out.

It doesn't take much to convince Leah we should order Japanese. When I say I could go for a red dragon roll, her eyes glaze over. Sushi is her catnip.

"Call in an order to Matsuki in fifteen minutes," she says. "Ask for extra soy sauce."

I trace an invisible circle on the corner of her desk. "Ugh, their eel sauce gave me such a stomachache last time. Can we do Wajima?"

She looks up from her computer. "But they don't deliver."

"I could pick it up." I shrug, as if I could care less either way. "I mean, I finished reading these case studies so I'm just sitting around."

Leah contemplates this. Normally letting me leave the office would be an automatic no, but my father is in court all day. It's just us in the office. And if she gets rid of me for half an hour, she can go buck wild and call her boyfriend or do whatever it is she does when the office is empty.

"Okay." She passes me the company credit card. "Just no side excursions."

Am I that obvious? I salute her, making sure I avoid her eyes.

At ten minutes to one, I'm waiting outside Wajima with our takeout order. I settle in for the wait, but before a minute or two passes, I spot a tall, dark-skinned man at the opposite corner of 52nd and Lexington. I crane my neck to get a better look at him as he waits among a gaggle of tourists to cross the street.

I can count how many times I've seen Dr. Muller on one hand, so I'm not sure it's him. If it is, he buzzed his hair recently. He's wearing khaki shorts and a salmon polo. Not many men can pull off salmon, but Dr. Muller can.

"Anne?" He extends a hand. "I don't believe we've officially met."

I have to swallow away a smattering of butterflies that rises in my stomach. He's totally a perfect specimen, and I don't use that term lightly. "Hi."

His amber eyes move to the bag at my feet.

"I can't stay more than fifteen minutes," I say. "I'm kind of under house arrest."

Dr. Muller massages his chin with his thumb and forefinger. I can't tell if he knows what I did to get suspended. "Alright. Shall we go somewhere a little more private?"

We wind up at the sushi bar. Dr. Muller orders a lunch box special and I get a green tea so I have something to do with my hands.

"So," I say, after a moment of uncomfortable silence punctuated by the sushi chefs shouting over each other. "What the hell is going on here?"

Muller smiles with half his mouth. "I wish I could tell you."

"You were dating her, weren't you?"

"We were . . . friendly."

"So, yes."

"Yes." Dr. Muller allows himself a small smile. "You know, she talked about you often."

This catches me by surprise. "Really?"

"You reminded her of herself, when she was your age. She said you were extremely bright. But unlike her other students, you didn't equate money and brains with the right to be a jerk. Her words." He winks at me.

Stop blushing. Stop blushing. "Oh."

Muller takes a sip from his tea. "I would have told you all this when she left, but I was still employed by Wheatley at the time. I'd hoped they would hire me permanently, but they found a more experienced candidate."

"So you're not going back there in the fall?"

He shakes his head. "I've completed my Ph.D. at MIT, so my visa is expiring soon. I'm staying in Queens with a friend from university for a few weeks until I return home."

I want to curl up and live inside Dr. Muller's South African accent. He even makes Queens sound actually regal.

"The obituary." I swallow. "I don't understand. Did she fake her own death or something?"

Muller blinks at me. "That wasn't her in the obituary. You know that, right?"

I will away my embarrassment. "Yeah, I mean, duh. But the details . . . it seems like it was the same person."

"I think that's the point. Let me back up a bit." Muller sets his tea down and folds his hands together. "We started spending a bit of time together after I started at Wheatley. Both of us were new to the faculty. But we found we had a lot more than that in common, and, well . . .

"Anyway, I noticed that she was fiercely private. She never wanted to socialize with any of the other teachers, and she didn't like to talk about her past. I didn't think anything of it until early May."

"What happened?"

"I'd invited her to sightsee in Boston a bit with me. We ate at an Indian place, and we were supposed to go to the Isabella Stewart Gardner Museum. I thought we were having a great time . . . but when we left the restaurant, she was upset. Said we had to go straight home, and she wouldn't say why."

"After that, I started to pick up on other things that seemed . . . off. She didn't have any photos or personal mementos around her apartment. Never got any mail, or phone calls. I supposed it was because she was new in town, but one night, I noticed she owned a Boston Bruins hockey jersey."

A detail surfaces in my memory: Ms. C had a Bruins pennant hanging in her office.

"She says she's from Georgia, she went to school in North Carolina . . . yet she's a Boston Bruins fan?" I say.

"I thought it strange, too. I asked her about it, and she got very defensive. Said it was a friend's. Then she didn't call me for a few days." Muller traces the rim of his teacup with his fingertip. "I knew something was off with her, then, but I didn't want to make her uncomfortable. We all have things in our past we'd like to hide from." Muller hesitates. "But I'll admit I was curious. I broached the subject with Jess. I didn't accuse her of anything; I simply said I thought it was unusual. She was angry with me for insinuating she was hiding something, and said she needed time apart. Two days later I found out during a faculty meeting that she'd resigned."

I'm quiet as I digest all of this. Muller must have confronted Ms. C around the same time I'd asked her to help me find out what happened to Vanessa Reardon, the girl Matt Weaver assaulted. So Ms. C's disappearance may have had nothing to do with helping me, like I initially thought, and everything to do with Muller figuring out that she was hiding something.

"I did some searching around, and found that there really was a Jessica Cross of Cliftonville," Muller says. "So the woman we knew was an impostor."

"Like identity theft?" I ask. "How did no one figure it out?"

"It's actually quite simple to assume the identity of a deceased person," Muller replies. "It's called *ghosting*. All you need is his or her Social Security number. It's even easier if you can obtain a duplicate of the person's driver's license or birth certificate."

"But Ms. C—why?"

"It's more common than you'd think," Muller says. "There's any number of reasons why someone would want to disappear and become someone else. Abusive ex-lover, massive amounts of debt, criminal charges—"

"That doesn't sound like her." I realize how dumb the words sound as soon as they leave my mouth. "I mean, it doesn't sound like the person she pretended to be. Around us."

"It just goes to show you can never really know a person." There's sadness in Muller's voice. He must really care about Ms. C. My stomach clenches as Anthony's face works its way into my mind. I know what it's like to feel connected to someone, only for them to be gone as quickly as they came—to have that intense, staccato burst of feeling, followed by just . . . nothing.

"Do you think she's okay?" I ask.

"I stopped by her cottage," Dr. Muller says. "Everything looked secure. Nothing suspicious."

I let out a breath. "So she's not in trouble or anything."

"Oh, I absolutely think she's in trouble." Dr. Muller's eyes meet mine. "But in danger? That I don't know."

Frustration gnaws at me. "What are we supposed to do?"

"I don't think there's anything we can do," he says. "They call it ghosting for a reason—how are you supposed to find a person who technically doesn't exist?"

Ghosting. The word sends a chill up my spine.

I glance at Dr. Muller's watch. If I don't get back to the office soon, Leah may send out a SWAT team. I thank Dr. Muller for meeting me, even though I have more questions than I showed up with.

"It seems I have the rest of the day to myself," he tells me as we release our handshake. "Any tips for a newbie in New York?"

"Stay far, far away from the people dressed as Elmo in Times Square." I smile at him and turn to leave.

"Anne." He's holding up my takeout bag. I'd almost forgotten it.

"You know," he says, his face thoughtful as he takes me in. "I've had a lot of time to think about her. Jessica. Sometimes the best we can do is stay in place and hope whatever we're running from doesn't catch up with us. Remember that."

I think of the blood blossoming around the hole in Travis Shepherd's chest. Of the promise Anthony and I made to each other not to tell anyone we were there that night. Of the fear that someone else already knows.

I don't know if Dr. Muller would feel the same way if he knew what I was running from.

PREP SCHOOL CONFIDENTIAL

KARA

"IMPOSSIBLE TO PUT DOWN"

WICKED LITTLE SECRETS

A PREP SCHOOL CONFIDENTIAL NOVEL

TAYLOR

WITH PREPPY OVERTONES
Reviews on Prep School Confidential

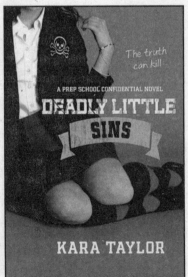

The truth
can kill

A PREP SCHOOL CONFIDENTIAL NOVEL

DEADLY LITTLE SINS

KARA TAYLOR

St. Martin's Griffin

THOMAS DUNNE BOOKS